I0761749

ALIBI BY ACCIDENT

KAYLEIGH SUGGETT

Severn River Publishing
www.SevernRiverBooks.com

ISBN: 978-1-64875-731-0 (Paperback)

ALSO BY KAYLEIGH SUGGETT

The Verona Montero Series

Alibi by Accident

Hot Girls Die First

Burn After Cheating

To find out more about Kayleigh Suggett and her books, visit

severnriverbooks.com

To anyone dealing with the shit life throws at you.
I hope this helps you escape the way countless books have helped me.

PROLOGUE: THE WEDDING SUCKED BALLS

Blair Walker (née Grayson) signed her name on an official form like all brides do on their wedding day.

"Is that your current legal name?" a man asked her as she passed the piece of paper to him.

"Oh, for fuck's sake!" She grabbed the form, scribbled out *Walker*, and wrote *Grayson*. She couldn't be Walker yet, as the wedding hadn't gone off quite as expected. Well, to be honest, it sucked balls. Big, hairy, saggy balls.

She finished fixing her name and, with the paper cussed out, crossed out, and corrected, she handed the form over to the man, who was wearing a police uniform, because they just so happened to be sitting in a police station, because the wedding sucked...well, we've been over that.

Instead of walking down the aisle to applause and bird-exploding rice, her not-yet-husband had been marched down the aisle between two officers to provide a DNA sample in connection with a murder investigation.

He'd been shell-shocked and sheepish. Everyone had looked at her, expecting to see the famous tableau of a bride bursting into tears and running off, but she wasn't that kind of woman. She felt the opposite of weak and sad and delicate and disappointed. She felt intense rage and bloodlust toward the person who had made her the best-dressed woman in the police station that day: a Nancy-fucking-Drew wannabe named Verona Montero.

PART I

BEING THE EVENTS THAT SET THE PROLOGUE IN MOTION

1

THE LIFE OF A PRIVATE DICK

Calgary
One year earlier, Tuesday 1 p.m.

Verona Montero always called herself a private dick. Not a private investigator, not a detective—a private dick. She was adamant about that point for two reasons: one, it meant she got to say the word "dick" a lot, and two, it sounded as if she was living in a movie from the '40s. Big band jazz, smoking, alcohol—those were the good old days.

But even if these weren't the good old days, the profession still had its perks. Sleeping in until 11 a.m. on a Tuesday was one of them. Being paid to be a devious, sneaking, eavesdropping human was another. People tend to get annoyed when you do that kind of thing in your personal life. Of course, like any job, it held its quirky annoyances. This meeting place was one of them.

Verona's idea of a bar was a place with a polished wooden counter, beer on tap, and fish and chips. A place with low lighting, low music, sports on the TV, and old guys in flannel. It was not the thrumming of bass notes heard outside a door blocked by a doorman.

If she'd been invited here for a date, she'd have bailed the moment she saw that the sign for the name of the club, STUL, was fashioned in glitter.

Like some kid making a craft for mommy. But this was her business—something she thrived at.

She approached the pink-and-silver exterior of the club and smiled at the doorman whose name tag read MR. ABBOT. "Hey, Mr. Abbot, how's it hangin'?"

He was the strangest-looking doorman Verona had ever seen, dressed in immaculate white tie, complete with creases in his trousers so crisp you could cut yourself. He looked like he belonged at the Banff Springs Hotel instead of a few blocks down from Calgary's last resort of the homeless, Alpha House.

"Good afternoon, madam. May I help you find your way?" His British accent was as crisp as his creases.

"Yes, you can do your doormanly duty and open the doors."

"You mean to go in, madam?" he asked in his best I-don't-think-that's-advisable voice. He clearly thought her attire of tight jeans, leather jacket, and tank top weren't a match for the club. Good thing he didn't know about the knife in her purse.

"Yes, I do mean to. I have a meeting in there."

"Of course, madam. Might you give me the name of the club member who awaits you? This is members only." He punctuated "members" as if the word might scare her off.

"It's *miss*, actually, if you don't mind." She was only in her thirties, and definitely not ready to be called "madam" like some old spinster who names her cats Ruth, Bader, and Ginsberg.

He was only doing his job, but Verona felt he was taking a bit too much sadistic pleasure in his control over her fate. *Maybe if I make him call me "sir," that'll change his attitude.* "Here." She thrust her phone under his nose to show him the text message inviting her to the club.

Mr. Abbot nodded and gave a smile that was devoid of warmth. "Of course, *miss*. Right this way."

Verona's first impression of the club was that she was walking into Barbie's uterus. The walls were a horrendous shade of bright pink, and the dim rosy lights glinted off irregular-shaped mirrors hanging on the walls and ceiling.

Her path to the bar was riddled with flower arrangements in large brass urns that seemed deliberately placed to create a labyrinth of ostentatious annoyances. When she found her way blocked for the third time, she gave up on decorum, shoved the damn thing out of her way, and marched to the bar. *I'd like a word with the interior decorator*, she thought. *No, I'd like two: Fuck you.*

With the sanctuary of the bar beneath her elbow, she scanned the room for her client. She hadn't seen a sign that said "women only," but perhaps it was an unspoken rule. Other than the bartender, there wasn't a man in sight. She inhaled deeply and was transported back to her childhood, walking through the perfume section of The Bay with her mother—the maze of kiosks as confusing as the mix of scents. She still wondered how anyone chose a perfume out of that mess. She was a deodorant-only kind of gal. Usually one of the more masculine scents.

Along with the annoying urns, the club was dotted by tiny glass cocktail tables with young scantily clad women perched on the edges clutching sparkling cell phones. She had assumed her client would be watching for her when she came in, but all the young women were so engrossed in their phones, not one of them had looked up, not even when she'd manhandled the urn out of her way.

She dug her phone out of her pocket and texted: *I'm by the bar, where are you?*

A few tables away, a young woman tucked her phone into her tiny purse and stood. They locked eyes briefly before the girl shuffled over as best she could in her miniskirt and heels. With her long shapely legs, shiny golden-blond hair, and set of perky, bouncy breasts, the girl looked ready for a photo shoot with *Maxim*.

"Veronica!" She squealed like a sorority sister seeing one of her own after a long summer of giving blow jobs to the football team.

"It's Verona." She extended her hand. She'd had her name mispronounced too many times to be annoyed by the mistake.

"Oh!" The client threw her hands up in surprise and delight. "How profesh!"

She giggled and took Verona's hand with the tips of her fingers, shook it from side to side like a cat toying with a dead mouse, then tried to pull her in for a boob-enveloping hug.

Verona resisted the gesture with a redirect. "Shall we take a seat?" She didn't usually hug clients on a first meeting. In fact, she couldn't remember *ever* hugging a client. It wasn't the sort of business that inspired people to hug her. Usually there was a lot of swearing and crying.

"Oh!" the client repeated, as if every new thing Verona said was impossibly cute and exciting. "Yeah, let's go back to my table. I can, like, get you a drink and stuff, and like, um, yeah."

"I'll take a Dark and Stormy," Verona said over her shoulder to the bartender.

"Oh!" the girl said yet again, and Verona cringed at the lack of conversational acumen. "Like, what's that?"

"A drink," said Verona. She couldn't help herself. Maybe it was the urns, maybe it was the doorman, or maybe it was the heady mixture of strong perfumes from all the women, but she was starting to feel a bit pissy. She reminded herself to check her period app and her tampon stock.

The girl tittered. "Oh yeah, of course—ha ha!" She took her phone back out, clearly unaccustomed to so much eye contact.

They settled themselves at one of the tall glass tables. Verona's drink came in a classy crystal glass on a crisp white napkin while the client's drink arrived in a small margarita pitcher—pink, feathered, glittering, umbrella-laden, and cherry garnished. It looked as if someone had blended a My Little Pony. It looked as if it would *taste* like My Little Pony.

Verona flipped her long dark hair over her shoulder, took a grateful pull of her Dark and Stormy, and let the warmth of the rum run through her and take the edge off the sensory overload. She longed for some old men in tweeds to dull the place down. Or some quantum physicists to lecture. Maybe some nuns with rulers could beat people and demand they don sackcloth and sit in silence for a while. That would be refreshing.

This is why you love this job, remember. If you wanted to spend your days in sterile silence with dull Linda from HR, you could've taken that finance job and made Mom proud. Her skin prickled with goose bumps just imagining it. "So, uh, Miss—?"

"Miss? What did I miss?"

It took all of Verona's effort not to give in to her natural inclination to judge a woman who seemed so impossibly vapid. Verona's Italian mother would have had little patience for such a girl, raising her own girls to be smart, capable, and ambitious. The ingrained attitude of dismissal was hard to shake.

"What is your name?" she asked, coaxing her mind to be friendly instead of sarcastic.

"Oh." The client tittered again. "Miami."

Despite her efforts, she bristled at the name. *Who names their kid Miami? I mean, were they hoping she'd become a stripper? Sure, Verona is the name of a city, but it's a fucking sophisticated city. An old city. One that isn't known for beaches and bros, spring break, and girls gone wild.*

"So, Miami, what did you want to talk about today?" Miami's texts to set up the meeting had been bafflingly full of emojis and bereft of words. The bits Verona pieced together were enough to let her know there was some infidelity involved, but that was it.

"Well..." Miami was only half paying attention to Verona as she tapped at her phone like a woodpecker with OCD. "It's like I said in my texts."

"Uh-huh." Verona looked around for a complimentary bowl of nacho chips or garlic bread, but there was nothing—not so much as a peanut for the less anorexic of the bunch to lick the salt off and discard. She was getting hangry. "But just so we're both on the same page, why don't you walk me through it again."

With a confused lean of her head, Miami looked up from her phone. "What page?" Head instantly back down to the phone. Laughing and tapping and scrolling. So much fucking scrolling. Like she was stroking the phone's clit to get it off.

Must be fucking nice. "Just to make sure I understand the complete pict...problem."

Verona's jacket vibrated against her ribs. Normally she'd ignore any text messages until her meeting was over, but what the hell, it wasn't like Miami would notice. Or care. She probably thought Verona was some strange form of alien to *not* be on her phone. Plus, Verona didn't want Miami's phone to be the only one getting a hand job.

Just thought you'd like to know I managed a huge fucking settlement for Mrs. Albany. Nice work!

A sudden rush of heat flew up her neck when she saw who sent the message. Quentin. She knew it was sad that just seeing his name made her crotch tingle, but there wasn't anything she could do about it. Except numb it. She took a heavy pull from her Dark and Stormy. Maybe it was ovulation instead of PMS? Was that why she was feeling extra randy?

Miami hadn't noticed Verona's lapse in conversation, barely looking up from her mad scroll session to continue the conversation. "So, like, I'm married, right?"

"Who are you married to?"

"Oh!" Miami looked around the room as if other people might be as surprised to hear the question as she was. "Well, like, most people know that! But, like, I'm married to Javier Luis Cavallero."[1] She said it as though it should mean something, but to Verona it was only a name.

"Who's that?"

"Oh! He's, like, the boss of some drug company or something."

"*Some* drug company? Which one?"

Miami shrugged and returned to her phone to distract herself from the fact that she had no idea what she was talking about.

"So, like, he's rich and stuff."

Verona decided to let it go. If Javier was the CEO of a pharmaceutical company, then yes, he was likely rich, and she could look him up later. "Right, er, good for you," she said to keep things moving.

"Thanks," said Miami, with the self-effacing pride of an honors student who'd won a full scholarship.

Once again the conversation died as Miami was distracted by her phone buzzing and chiming. Verona was reminded forcibly of her last date. No matter what they tried to talk about, the conversation slowly dripped away until they were both left staring at their plates thinking, *I wonder if my shoelaces are strong enough to hang myself from the pipes in the washroom.*

These dates were typical for Verona and a great disappointment to her mother, who craved more grandbabies, even though Verona's perfect sister had supplied four already.

---

1. Before you read the whole book pronouncing this wrong (no one likes doing that, and I'm being nice and telling you right away, unlike certain other authors who waited until book four to tell us—ahem!), please recognize the Spanish pronunciation, where *j*'s sound like *h* and double *l*'s sound like a *y*. Thus, Havier Luis Cavayero. You're welcome.

"Miami, I assume you need help with something, because, quite frankly, being married to a super-rich dude doesn't sound like a problem."

"Oh!" said Miami again, as if just realizing Verona was still there. "Um, yeah. So, like, Jav's all rich and stuff, and like, it's super cool 'cause I get to do whatever and stuff, you know? The house is so big, and we've got a pool, and I can have my friends over and we can drink and, like, just chill and stuff."

"Sure," said Verona, more curious than ever. Perhaps she had underestimated this trophy-wife gig.

"Jav's totally jelly and stuff, right? Before we got married, I was supposed to sign this, like, paper thing 'cause he's been married a lot before, right? So, like, if he divorces me, I might not get very much money. And I like being rich."

"Don't we all?"

"Right? So you should make it happen so that, like, I don't lose the money."

"Miami, what you signed is called a prenuptial agreement. It is a legally binding document that gives certain rights in the event of a divorce. If you signed it, there's nothing I can do." She tapped her index finger on the table, some of her impatience returning.

This, surprisingly, didn't fall on the same empty head as everything before. Miami was, after all, a creature conditioned by millions of years for survival. So although she couldn't be bothered to know certain things—say, if the sun rose in the east, or what her kidneys were for—she did pay closer attention to anything that might stand between her and the wads of cash that would keep her in bikinis and alcohol.

For the first time, she put her phone down. "Okay, but, like, that paper thing says that I don't get anything if I cheat on him. I know he's trying to prove I am because he's bored of me. There's this new skank he's spending all his time with. Calling her his 'niece' and driving around with her in his limo. And we used to do it all the time. Like, he'd come home and we'd be at it. And now...it's, like, maybe once a week. So he's bored of me, but I knew he would be. His last wife didn't even last this long. But, like, I'm bored of him too. He's so angry and pushy and, like, he doesn't ever wanna party with me anymore. He used to buy me stuff all the time and, like, he never does now." A small pout here, for effect. "So, like, I'm cool with a divorce, but I don't wanna lose everything."

It was typical enough, and it even made sense. Of course anyone would want to keep as much money as possible without having to stay married to a boring older dude. It was, however, a job for a lawyer, not Verona.

"Okay, Miami, what you need to do is get a lawyer. They can review your prenup for you and see what they can do. Perhaps most importantly, before you pay for a lawyer, have you cheated on Javier?"

Miami lowered her voice. "I'm not stupid. I knew that, like, if I slept with a guy, I'd be done. I get bored, so like, sometimes I get hot guys to come over so I can play with them, but, like, I never do it with them."

Verona was a little impressed. If—and it was a big if—Miami was telling the truth, she had managed to do the one thing that might save her. And if Javier was already screwing his next piece of ass—and there was a good chance he was—a competent lawyer could use that as leverage. As far as young decorative wives went, Miami had played this right.

"So, like, I need a lawyer?"

"Yes." Verona rose from her tiny uncomfortable stool.

"Can, like, you get me one?"

Verona rubbed her hand over the rough plastic case of her phone, as if she could caress the memory of Quentin's last text. She'd not known when the next opportunity to call him would come, and here Miami was, just dropping it into her lap?

Good thing you didn't turn around when you saw the glitter, Montero.

"Yes, I can find you one." She held her hand out to shake goodbye.

"Oh!" Miami looked shocked and extended her hand as well. "Cool!" She handed Verona $200.

"What's this?"

"Your tip."

Verona pocketed the money. "I'll be in touch"—she turned to go, then stopped—"but I'm curious."

Miami was already tapping at her phone and sipping her pink drink. "Oh?"

If not My Little Pony, Verona thought, *it must taste like bubble bath*. "How did you hear about me?"

Most of her clients came to her via word of mouth or internet searches that read "I think my skeevy whore of a spouse is messing around on me." She couldn't imagine any of her previous clients rubbing elbows with Miami, and she figured Miami didn't use the internet for information so much as for entertainment. She might not even be aware there *was* information on the internet.

"Oh, one of the guys I invited over to watch me take a bath told me about you," she said, as if everyone, from time to time when they're bored, invites a cute guy over to watch them take a bath.

Back on the street, a welcoming wall of fresh air blew away the funk of the club from Verona's mind. "It's a weird business, ain't it, Abbot?" she said to the doorman.

"Yes, miss." He frowned. "And what I wouldn't give for a nice cup of tea."

Well, thought Verona, *that's dedication.*

2

NOT THE HOT GUY, PLEASE!

Calgary
Tuesday 3 p.m.

Despite having a legitimate reason to do so, Verona felt like a stupid kid whenever she called Quentin, as if she was making up an excuse to hear his voice. It was too bad, because he was a damn good lawyer, and that made it worse.

He was the kryptonite to her strong, independent, I-don't-need-a-man sense of self. He was tall, broad shouldered, with firm biceps and pecs and a jawline you could crack your skull open on if you weren't careful during sex—and you knew you wouldn't be.

He was always professional with her, but with a hint of playfulness. It only made her want him more and reminded her how much she wished she didn't. She liked the part of herself that didn't fall head over heels for men. Quentin ruined all of that with his fucking chiselled features and voice that reverberated off her ribs like the primal echo of a drum beating across a cavern.

She swivelled in her office chair to look out the window, which faced busy Seventeenth Avenue, took a deep breath, and made the call. He had given her his cell phone number instead of his office line, and although she'd tried not to read into it, a small part of her went ahead and read into it anyhow. She didn't like that part of herself and gave it a stern telling off.

Quentin answered after two rings. "Verona."

"Afternoon," Verona said, trying to sound breezy, but she thought it came out more gassy. Wrong kind of air.

"What can I do you for?" Quentin asked, chipper and carefree as usual, and unaware he was giving Verona the shakes.

You can do me for free, frequently and fiercely, she thought. "How's the caseload? Got room for one more?"

She heard the subtle sounds of someone settling in and imagined he had been walking around the office but was now seated in his chair. "Well, that always depends. However, you *are* my favorite private investigator, so I'll hear you out."

The pathetic part of Verona grasped at the word "favorite" like a lifeline. She told that part of her to cool it and act like a respectable woman. "Private dick," she corrected.

"I am *not* calling you that. What have you got?"

"Well, in some ways, I'd say this is an easy one, but in others, I'd say less so." She put her feet on the windowsill.

"Hmm, cryptic. But remember, *you* like to solve puzzles. I prefer to grandstand. Make long speeches. Say things like 'Ladies and gentlemen of the jury' and 'Objection.' I go in for clever in a whole other way than you do. So maybe you want to be more descriptive?" Verona could hear the smile in his voice and knew he was having fun teasing her.

"Right, sorry," she said, though she wasn't. "Part one is the easy part: client is in a marriage that will likely be ending, but isn't sure what the prenup guarantees her. She wants a lawyer to make sure that when she's sent packing, she gets her just deserts."

"Check," said Quentin.

"Okay, part two is the hard part: your client is named Miami—"

"Is she a stripper?"

"No, but fair question. Do you want to hear the rest, or are you done?" Half of her wanted him to say he was done so that he'd never lay eyes on Miami. The other half desperately wanted him to be all in so she'd have an excuse to see him.

"No, I'm not done. I'm intrigued. A person named Miami who is *not* a stripper. Are you sure? Was she once a stripper? Does she secretly want to be a stripper? Does she at least take those fitness classes that teach you how to be a stripper?"

"Did you want to hire me to look into that for you?" A crowd of pigeons clustered around the window. Verona tapped the glass to get them to move along, but all she got in response was a chorus of excited cooing.

"Do you want me to start billing you for these little chats we have?"

"Fine. But no, as far as I know, she is not, nor has she ever been, a stripper. I can't speak for her future. That might depend on whether you agree to help or not." Her stomach flipped like a dolphin being promised a herring. She knew she was teetering on the edge of the chance to spend a lot more time with Quentin.

"But if I step in and help and she doesn't become a stripper, I might be preventing her from fulfilling her destiny. That'd be really bad karma."

"I thought you were Episcopalian?" She kicked off her shoes and sat cross-legged in her chair. Being her own boss meant she never had to worry about an executive storming in and seeing her sitting "unprofessionally."

"Everyone believes in karma, Verona."

"Anyhow, beyond her name, she's young and stupid."

"How young are we talking? I thought you said a divorce? Can't be that young."

"Nineteen. Been married a year, maybe? It wasn't a marriage for love—we'll put it that way." Verona left the window to the pigeons and swivelled back to her IKEA desk. She rented a modern office-sharing space that featured smooth gray and black surfaces everywhere. She hadn't put much money into her furniture or decor beyond a few Rothko prints and an office plant that only lasted one week before it died of neglect.

"Okay, so rich older dude controls the finances, then?"

"That sums it up. She knows infidelity on her part would null and void any provisions in the prenup for her, so she claims she's never *technically* cheated on him."

"*Technically?*" Quentin asked.

"Yeah, I knew the lawyer would latch on to that word. I also know you can work with it. I think it's kind of like when religiously repressed teenagers aren't allowed to have sex, so they do everything but intercourse to satisfy their horny little selves."

"Ah. Yeah, I can work with that."

"I'm sure you can," said Verona.

"What does that mean?"

"Nothing. Just that you're a very competent lawyer, and technicalities won't hang you up."

She picked up a pen and started doodling random lines and swirls in her notebook. They often turned phallic in nature, and she wasn't sure she wanted to know what that said about her psyche.

"Sure..."

"There's a lot of money to be made, and although she's not the sharpest tool in the shed, I don't think she deserves to be tossed out on her round, bouncy tushy with nothing. Neither of them married for love, so if Javier's getting what he wants by sleeping around with some new little piece of tail, why shouldn't Miami get a nice cash settlement?" She was surprised by how much she wanted to stand up for Miami when she had originally thought the girl was a waste of space. Or maybe it was just her distaste for Javier. That was more likely.

"Whoa, whoa, talk about burying the lead. You say he's being unfaithful? And she's got a bouncy tushy?"

"According to *her*. The adultery, not the tushy. *I* can attest to the tushy."

"Well, that's our case, then. I was wondering why you were saying this would be easy. Prenups are notoriously hard to do anything about after the fact, but if there's proof he's unfaithful...we can work with that. Provided there *is* proof. Tell me there's proof."

Verona's silence was the answer he needed.

"Oh boy." He sighed. "You said this was a half-easy case. This isn't sounding half easy at all. So we've got a young woman who feels divorce is imminent, locked in with a prenup she doesn't understand, and she claims she's been faithful but her husband hasn't, none of which can be substantiated?"

"Yeah, like I said, *sort* of easy." She knew she had him. If he really didn't want the case, he'd have told her by now. The little flip in her stomach turned into a full-out triple-twisting dive.

"Okay, how much money are we talking here?"

"You know the pharmaceutical company Xeylon?"

"Yeah."

"The husband is the CEO."

Quentin whistled.

"Yup."

They were both silent for a while, giving the vast pile of money the respect it deserved. Then Quentin broke the silence. "Say, Verona?"

"Yeah?"

"Do you think if Miami's new lawyer suggested to her that it would be prudent for her to hire an investigator to get proof of Javier's dirty deeds, you'd have time to take that job on?"

Verona had the time. For Quentin, there was always time. "Why else would I be calling you?"

The pigeons by the window had redoubled their cooing. Verona craned her neck to look, only to find some seriously freaky pigeon lovemaking happening. There were disadvantages to windows in the office that her Realtors had neglected to mention.

Quentin said, "Glad we got that settled. Now tell me more about this tushy."

"Bye, Quentin."

After Verona hung up, she was happy for a few blissful seconds, thinking of working on a case with Quentin. Then she became a little unhappy when she realized most of her time wouldn't be spent anywhere near him. And then she became extremely unhappy when she remembered that Quentin liked to meet all of his clients in person, and as dumb as Miami was, she was hot. Quentin was a professional, but he was also a man.

Well, good, she thought. *If he proves to be the kind of guy who only wants to screw a hot piece of ass, then I can stop having this stupid crush on him.* She knew as she thought it that it wasn't true. She'd take those sloppy seconds in a heartbeat, and she hated herself for it.

3

THE PRICHARD RULE

Calgary
Wednesday 1 p.m.

Quentin refused to meet first-time clients anywhere but his office. He called it "the Prichard Rule" after the woman who had necessitated its existence. He had only told the story to one person, and they had laughed pitilessly at him until they were crying and gasping for breath. Never made that mistake again. If anyone questioned what he meant by the Prichard Rule, he said it had to do with an obscure bit of case law. That was enough to shut most people up.

And that was why his new client, Miami, was going to meet him in his office instead of him driving down to STUL to meet her. She seemed bewildered at his insistence on meeting at the office, as if nobody had ever declined the offer to have a drink with her before. And they likely hadn't.

His appointment with Miami was for one o'clock, but it wasn't until 1:23 that his paralegal, Nora, knocked on his door. Nora was plain, dependable, professional, and one of the most blasé people Quentin had ever met. If she had a personal life, she never spoke of it. It reminded Quentin of being a kid in school, when you assume the teachers are a part of the institution and you don't spare a thought wondering what they go home to. You don't even think of them going home. He knew Nora must go home because he'd seen her leave the office, but if she faded into the walls for the night, it wouldn't surprise him.

"Come," he said, opening a blank page on his electronic notepad.

When Nora opened the door, it was with an expression Quentin had never seen on the woman's face before. If he had to describe it, he'd say it was a mixture of shock, amusement, disbelief, and starstruck. "Miami Cavallero to see you," she said in a voice that was trying to stay professional despite having the wind knocked out of it.

That alone was enough to make Quentin take notice, but once Nora stood aside, it faded from his brain to make room for the spectacle that was his new client.

She wore a tight gold minidress, the neckline exposing not only her back but a deep canyon of cleavage. Her breasts defied gravity and stood at attention like well-trained infantry.

Quentin's jaw dropped. It wouldn't be obvious to the casual observer, but he felt it. He promptly closed it, smiled warmly, stood, and extended his hand to her. "Good afternoon."

Miami took his hand lightly, as if waiting for him to kiss her hand in an old-fashioned way, like a knight. "Oh, um, hi," she said in a cutesy, girlish voice.

"Won't you take a seat?" Quentin asked, reseating himself.

She took her clutch purse from her thigh, slid it up her body, then bent toward the desk to put it down. The bend was perfect—just far enough to give anyone from any angle a look at her curves, but not so far as to be exaggerated. Using soft swishing movements, she swept her hair away from her neck. She sat down slowly and leaned forward onto Quentin's desk, using her elbows to press her breasts together, which was gratuitous, as they were already plenty cozy.

"It's a pleasure to meet you," he said, using his best "I'm a lawyer, I'm a professional, I'm here to help" voice to cover the buzz of desire that had started at the base of his skull and was radiating throughout his body.

Miami didn't respond. He supposed she was used to men drooling over her and being pleased to meet her. Perhaps she wasn't as used to a man keeping the interests of his brain and his penis separate. He had to admit, it wasn't coming as easily to him as it usually did.

Out of respect and curiosity, he gave her a few moments of silence. Some clients entered and couldn't wait to start blabbing. Some took time to settle in and collect their thoughts and needed silence to make that happen. Some needed to chat for a while about mundane things before they could open up. Some required direct questions.

Quentin felt his jaw drop, for the second time, as she took her phone out of her purse and began tapping at it. Miami, it seemed, didn't realize, or didn't care, that Quentin's hourly rate was $400. If almost any other person on the planet had done this, he'd have thought it was a power move, but in Miami's case, it had to be cluelessness.

He liked the idea that he could still be surprised after ten years on the job. He considered putting his feet on his desk and waiting for Miami to clue in that she was paying for his time but decided he couldn't do it. Morals and all that.

And also...something more: as he looked over at her, he saw her beauty, yes, who wouldn't see that? He saw the effort she had put into being undeniably sexy. But as she smiled at something on her phone, he saw beneath the makeup and the clothes that she was young. He saw her naïveté about the world as she sat there texting or doing whatever she was doing on her phone. He saw someone who was very good at getting men's attention but had no idea about anything else. He wondered what he was getting himself into.

"Would you like something to drink?" he asked.

"Well, you should've, like, met me at STUL." She gave him a playful smile. "Then we could have as many drinks as we wanted." She walked her fingers across his desk as she spoke and punctuated the words "many," "drinks," and "wanted" with little taps on the wood.

Quentin smiled back. So this was his way in. He never flirted with clients, but it seemed to be the only language Miami understood when conversing with men. "True," he admitted, "but I like to meet people on my home turf. Gives me a chance to check them out."

Miami giggled inordinately. It hadn't been that funny, but she was obviously practiced at making men feel they were funny and interesting even if they were complete dullards.

"Nora brings me tea at this time," Quentin said. "Would you like one? Or coffee? Soda? Sparkling water?"

Miami leaned in closer. "And, like, if we were at the bar...*Nora* wouldn't be interrupting us."

Quentin conceded her point with outstretched palms and buzzed Nora and asked her to bring in sparkling water and tea.

Quentin waited for Nora to leave before he spoke again. "So, Miami, you want my help getting you a settlement in a divorce?"

"Yeah, well, like, I know he's seeing someone else 'cause, like, a few weeks back, he had to get treated for syphilis, and I'm clean."

"Well, I don't think I can use the syphilis, but then again, who can?"

The joke flew over Miami's head, so she continued as if she didn't hear it, a tactic he thought she probably employed often. "And we've been married almost a year now, and like, that's the longest he's ever been married. So I know he's gonna divorce me soon." She readjusted her position to provide maximum boob heft.

Quentin tried not to stare, but the damn things were like homing beacons. Half of his brain wondered what they felt like, while the other half told him to focus on the job. "Right, so your concern is there will be a divorce soon, and you want to make sure you're looked after."

"Worried about me?" She placed a hand behind her neck and gave him a sideways glance.

Nether regions began stirring. He considered spilling his hot tea in his crotch to keep himself in check. "And you're pretty sure you signed a prenup?"

"Well, I had to sign this, like, paper that said I wouldn't sleep with anyone else or I wouldn't, like, get anything."

"Infidelity clauses are standard in prenups. Did Javier sign a similar statement?"

"I didn't, like, read it all. I just wanted to get married."

Quentin normally had no patience for a client who'd agreed to sign something without reading it and knowing what they were getting into, but he had also never represented such a young and vapid client. The paycheck he knew he'd bring home made her ignorance a lot easier to overlook.

"So have you violated the agreement?"

Miami's eyes widened. "Oh, um, what?"

Quentin searched his brain for a delicate way to ask the question that didn't involve euphemisms that might further complicate things. In the end he couldn't find any, so he had to be direct. "Have you slept with anyone else since you married Javier?"

Miami clearly took this as some kind of a pickup line because she reached out and tapped Quentin on the nose twice. "I've, like, had offers..." A coy, leading remark, said with inviting eyes.

Had anyone, ever, tapped him on the nose? Maybe his nana? Did that really turn other men on? Did he like it? Normally, he'd say no, but there was something about her that had him wondering. Maybe if she tapped it again...

"Right. Of course you've had offers."

"You're sweet."

"But have you acted on the offers?" He kept his voice soft, playing along with her little game.

Miami pouted. "No. And some of them, like you, have been so hot!"

Quentin nodded. He wasn't sure if he believed her or not. But he also didn't underestimate what a girl would do for money. If she was willing to marry a man thirty-five years her senior, she was probably willing to forgo a lot of things to keep that money.

"Okay, Miami, here's what we're going to do. I'm going to get a copy of your prenup so we can see what it says. Whether or not it precludes Javier from infidelity, we can generally count on the law to be on the side of the faithful partner. And to be safe, I think you should hire Verona to find proof of Javier's infidelity. That will help our case a lot."

Miami wiggled even closer to the edge of her chair. "You're sure excited to get me divorced..."

"Well, in a way, yes. I think, under the circumstances, it might be better for *you* to file for divorce before he gets the chance. But of course a lot of that will depend on Verona's luck."

"You keep talking about, like, Veronica." She spoke in sad baby-talk tones. "Trying to make me jealous?"

Quentin gave Miami his best charming-fellow-with-a-heart-of-gold smile. "Who *wouldn't* be looking to make you jealous?" He had to remind himself he was just acting.

"When will I see you again?"

Quentin held her gaze. "Hopefully soon, when I have some good news."

"I hope so too..."

A soft knock came, and Nora entered. "Sorry, Quentin—" She stopped at the tableau in front of her: Miami leaning so far over Quentin's desk that her breasts were practically in his lap, and Quentin staring into her eyes.

Miami looked over her shoulder at Nora and gave her a knowing smile. She scooted back on her chair, one toned cheek at a time, making it obvious she didn't mind being caught doing something naughty.

Quentin tried to maintain some dignity by refusing to lean back in his chair. He stayed perched on the edge, pretending he always sat that way. Good for posture and core strength.

"Nora?" Quentin asked.

"Uh..." she said uncertainly. "Right. Sorry to interrupt, but your two fifteen is here."

Quentin nodded, putting on his best airline-pilot monotone. "Quite all right. Miami and I were finishing up anyhow." Miami gave him a wink, which he pretended he didn't see. "Nora, can you please arrange with Miami how she'd like to pay her bill?"

Nora nodded.

"Thanks. You can show Miami out now."

Nora gave him the look you give your dog when it's eaten the hot dog you dropped on the floor. You know the dog couldn't help it but feel like it should know by now it's just going to get sick on the rug later. And then eat the vomit.

"Of course, Mr. Ellsworth." She held the door for Miami.

Quentin placed his chin in his palm in thought. Nora had never indicated any interest in or had any reaction to any client before. Just one more first in a day of firsts. Perhaps she didn't fade into the walls after all.

4

F*CK IT

Calgary
The next week, Friday 2 p.m.

Javier Luis Cavallero was a smart man—smart in all senses of the word. His dress? Smart: tailored suits of various colors and fabrics, always on palette and season specific. His brains? Smart: he was the CEO of a multibillion-dollar company. His private life? Smart: he had an obvious penchant for easy young women but had somehow avoided public scrutiny in the modern #MeToo era.

Finding pictures and even office locations of billionaires on the internet is easy. Catching a glimpse of them in the flesh is a lot harder. Men like Javier tended to have assistants to do everything for them, from driving their limos to picking up their coffees. They lived in houses with long, gated laneways and worked in buildings with underground parking garages.

Verona didn't see the Mexican-Canadian man until he made an unexpected foray from his office along Fifth Avenue into the street, deciding he wanted to purchase his own smoothie instead of having one of his minions collect it for him.

He wore a Fresco suit in light gray, with a crisp light blue shirt and navy tie. In his mid-fifties, he was tall and well built with strong shoulders and no gut. His dark hair was streaked with gray around the temples, and his dark eyes were framed by well-defined eyebrows.

Verona sat up in her seat and thanked her lucky stars she didn't have daddy issues. Because as far as rich older guys went, this one was a looker.

Day one of the stakeout was predictably dull. Javier was the kind of man who rarely deviated from schedule, like most type A people and psychopaths.

- 7:00 a.m., depart from his house in his limo
- 7:30 a.m., arrive at work
- 1:00 p.m., head to smoothie shop across the street
- 1:10 p.m., back at work
- 3:00 p.m., leave work to go to an apartment building (obviously where he's screwing his mistress)
- 4:30 p.m., leave apartment building to go back to work
- 7:00 p.m., limo arrives at office
- 7:30 p.m., back home

Verona waited at the house until 10:00 p.m., when Miami texted her: *he's asleep*

Days two and three followed the same pattern. A man so dedicated to his schedule and discretion was unlikely to suddenly throw his mistress onto the hood of his limo in a fit of passion. Still, Verona decided she'd give it one more day before reevaluating her tactics.

On the final day of her stakeout, Verona walked to Javier's smoothie shop for a break. After three days of sitting in the car, she wasn't at her best, appearance-wise. Her sweats had wrinkles, her top was stained with coffee, and her hair needed a wash. She dug a finger into her ear to relieve an annoying itch and squinted with concentration and relief.

"Verona?" said a familiar voice.

Usually when her name was said in that tone, by that voice, she felt inexplicably happy. Today she wished she could melt into the frozen yogurt and be blended away. But she was a professional. She hitched a smile on her face, remembered to remove her finger from her ear, and turned to face Quentin in all of his splendiferous glory.

"Hey." She tried to sound nonchalant, as if her basic car-vagrant appearance was how she wanted to be seen. She was grateful for her olive complexion and dark brown eyes on days like today. Her dark eyes always stood out even without makeup, and her complexion evened out the dark circles under her eyes.

"You look well," said Quentin. "What is it, the spirulina they put in the smoothies? You've got a glow!" He was well turned out in an immaculate steel-blue suit, white shirt, and no tie. His hair was coiffed to perfection, he was clean-shaven, and he smelled like fresh tobacco and ginger. It made Verona's breath catch and her heart palpitate every time she got a whiff.

"Fuck you—I'm working." Maybe her complexion didn't make up for as much as she thought it did.

Quentin gave her a once-over, then pulled the collar of his shirt as if it was making him itch. "Man, I chose the wrong profession."

"You did. However, your salary can pay for that suit you're wearing, and mine can't, so there is that. You come here often?" she asked, unintentionally using the world's worst pickup line.

"My office is a few blocks over, so I drop in here now and then."

"Right." She'd been so focused on the case, she forgot how close they were to his building.

He put his hands in his pockets, enhancing his air of casual perfection. "I like the Erratic Energy Emerger. It's tangy."

She was confused until he nodded at the menu board on the wall. Instead of having ordinary names like "Banana Pineapple Kiwi," the smoothies were all given incomprehensible adjective-laden names.

"Or you could try the Different Dramatic Dissent. It's more berry based."

"Why on earth do you come here? You can't tell what the fuck is going on."

"That's kind of the fun of it." He stepped up to the counter and addressed the peppy-looking kid behind it. "I'll take the Comprehensive Consistent Consciousness, please."

She had no idea what to order and tried to ask him for his recommendation, but the worker had started the blender, and her words were lost in the violent whirring of fruit and yogurt.

“What?” Quentin asked loudly.

“Never mind!” she shouted back.

“No, they don’t make those here!”

“I don’t want tomatoes in my smoothie!”

“Let’s wait until the blender’s done.” He gestured at the madly whirling machinery.

“Oh, fuck it!” Verona said, and predictably, that was when the kid shut off the blender, allowing the hard *k* sound to ricochet off the walls.

Not quite so predictably, the clerk said, “Good choice!”

“What?” Verona looked at Quentin, perplexed.

Quentin pointed at the menu. At the very bottom was a choice called F*ck It.

“Have you had it?”

“Nope.” Quentin took a sip of his newly delivered beverage. “I’ve always been able to make a choice.”

The blender started up again.

A few minutes later, smoothies in hand, Verona and Quentin strolled down the street.

“You know what?” Verona said, after tasting hers. “F*ck It is really good. Sort of tropical, sort of nutty.” She felt some butterflies in her stomach when she realized this was the first time she’d been out with Quentin. Even if it was an accidental meeting for something as simple as a smoothie.

“So you’re working?” Quentin asked.

“Yup. On *our* case.”

“It’s not *our* case. You’re working on *my* case.” He sidestepped a splotch of half-congealed liquid on the sidewalk. His shoes probably cost as much as her phone.

“You wouldn’t have a case without me. In fact, you won’t have a case if I don’t do my job.” She did a little hop over the offending splatter.

“Fine, it can be our case.”

“That’s more like it.” She hoisted her smoothie in cheers.

They turned down Eighth Avenue, a street set aside specifically for pedestrian traffic. The buildings were a mix of early 1900s sandstone brick with plenty of arches and character, and gleaming modern giants plastered with glass. Small trees with green foliage were planted every few meters, with flower baskets in vibrant reds and purples in between. Bustling businesspeople walked among slow, lumbering homeless people with carts full of bundles of God only knew what.

"What's with the sweats?" he asked.

"Stakeout! Trust me, you do *not* want to do a stakeout in anything tighter than sweatpants. You start out fresh and debonair and end up with creases in places that weren't meant to crease."

"Ouch." He took a sip of his drink. "But you're not in your car now. You're out in the open, in sweats, walking next to a guy in a fancy suit. That's going to draw the eye. People are going to think I'm your social worker or something. Or that you're harassing me."

"Maybe people will think *you* owe me alimony and that's why I look like this. Maybe they'll be judging you."

"Doubtful. People don't like to judge men if there's a woman around they can judge instead."

Verona glared.

"I don't make the rules!"

"Fine. They're judging me. But they're making a big mistake."

"I'll bet they are. That still doesn't answer the question of why your stakeout now involves walking me to my office, which I appreciate, by the way. I don't always feel safe walking alone downtown." He gave a mock shudder as they stopped for a red light.

"You're welcome. I'm on a break. Javier won't be out of his office for two hours, and I got hungry. And then I ran into you and thought I should be chivalrous and walk you back to your office."

"Well, as I said, I appreciate it. I mean, no one's gonna mug me when they see me with you."

"Because I am so obviously trained in the ways of the ninja?" Verona asked as they crossed the street to the gleaming black building Quentin worked in.

"No, because you're so obviously homeless and/or deranged and/or drunk."

"Whatever works." She waved him into the revolving doors of his building.

Despite acting cool and unfazed at being seen in total frump mode,

Verona was pissed off at whoever the fuck was running the universe. She wasn't so vain that she needed to be seen in a good light at all times. *But it would be nice*, she thought, *if when, for the first time in months I see one of the most gorgeous men on the planet, I had at least showered. Or that he'd just had a bad haircut. Or an unfortunate diarrhea incident.*

"Fuck it," she said, and took a hearty sip of her smoothie.

Friday 10 p.m.

Verona was looking forward to going home and crashing, knowing she wouldn't be following Javier for a fifth day, even if that meant that she'd need to come up with a new plan to catch him at it. So at 10 p.m. when she was expecting the customary "He's asleep" text from Miami and instead saw Javier's limo headed toward the mistress's apartment, she was equally disappointed that things were dragging out longer and excited that something might finally break in the case.

It was Friday night, after all. Even men like Javier must feel the pull of unfettered freedom of Friday.

Any diversion from a pattern was a chance to catch someone off guard. Routines were protection. Deviations were risks where mistakes could creep in. Where you didn't have the shielding of familiarity but were forced to improvise.

After Javier picked up the mistress, Verona expected the limo to head somewhere swanky, some upscale restaurant or VIP club, so when it turned off toward the SE industrial area, she wondered if she was about to witness something much more thrilling than a man with his pants down. What could a man like Javier want in the warehouse district? Was he about to watch his goons beat the crap out of a competitor? But he wouldn't bring the girl along for that, would he? Unless she liked that kind of thing.

More likely he just fancied a fuck in a field somewhere, and it was unlikely he'd get spotted out here. It was a pleasant evening for an outdoor fuck. If you were into that kind of thing. Verona preferred to only bare her skin with four walls around her.

The sky was darkening quickly, making the concrete rectangular warehouses look even more drab and lifeless than they did during the day. Not even the green grass and evening birdsong carrying on the breeze through her open windows made up for the utilitarian feel the entire area had. Here was a section of the city built to make things, store things, and ship things. Verona had never enjoyed passing through.

There were few cars in the area at this time of night, just those in the parking lots belonging to the night shift workers, so Verona ensured she pulled back her tail on the limo. As confident as she was that most people were too distracted or clueless to notice a tail on the main city streets, this was a place where her constant headlights in the rearview mirror might draw attention.

The limo pulled into a building tucked into the far south of the area, set apart with green space around it, the only neighbor the landfill several kilometers away. Verona pulled up along the side of the road a block back and cut her lights as the limo turned into the parking lot.

The building was similar to others in the area, concrete, single story, with fading beige paint. There was no sign that Verona could see that identified it as a business, and other than the lights from the limo, it was dark.

Were they just going to screw in the back of the limo in the dark parking lot? Surely they could do that anywhere, what with the tinted windows. No, they had to have come here for something more, and she'd never know what that was trying to see through the darkness in her car.

There wasn't a lot of dense vegetation amidst the buildings, but even in this part of the city they had planted poplar and pine trees, and with the darkness, she figured she'd be able to sneak closer without being seen.

She exited the car and closed her door as softly as she could. The night was still pleasantly warm even with the light breeze, but she put on her leather jacket to hide the brightness of her T-shirt. Thankfully, her sweats were black, and the moon was barely a sliver in the sky.

The lights on the limo went out, and she heard the tires grinding along the pavement slowly.

She hugged close to the tree trunks, reminding herself of playing capture the flag with her cousins as a kid. She'd always been good at sneaking, even back then, and the exhilaration of capturing the prize without being caught hadn't changed much since then. Her heart beat faster as she drew nearer to the parking lot, squatting low behind a bush with tiny pink flowers giving off a honey-sweet scent.

With her eyes fully adjusted to the dark, she saw the limo pull around to the back of the building, and followed in a low crouch from tree to tree until she climbed under the low hanging branches of a pine where she could easily see out. The dead pine needles crunched under her feet, but she knew the sound wouldn't carry far enough for anyone in the limo to hear.

The back of the building was similarly nondescript but held a single feature that was extremely unusual for this part of the city—a ramp leading to a parking garage with a keypad. The limo edged forward slowly. A hand emerged from the window and punched in a code, and the door slid open to admit the car.

The shutting of the door behind the car might be the signal of defeat for some, but for Verona, there was only the surge of possibility in her stomach.

So, you want to be a sneaky bastard, do you? Clearly you've never played capture the flag against me, motherfucker!

5

MCFLY IS THE ANSWER

Calgary
Saturday 1 p.m.

The adage "absence makes the heart grow fonder" is meant to apply to some person you apparently love. But you can't love them that much, because if you did, you wouldn't need to get away from them to start to care for them. It's a shit adage when it comes to love.

But for other things? Oh-so spot-on. Some things feel amazingly better after you've taken a break from them: Sex. Sugar. Deep-fried food. Sleep. Laughing.

And hot showers.

Glorious, steamy, hour-long hot showers. Not much felt better after several fifteen-hour days stuck sitting in a car. The way Verona sighed in the shower, you'd think she was in one of those tacky Herbal Essences commercials from the '90s.

In a post-shower glow, she sat on her west-facing balcony, the cloudless blue sky giving the illusion that the Rocky Mountains were resting on the edge of the horizon, so close she could reach them if she could fly off her balcony.

"Javier is, by far, the trickiest man I've ever tried to catch with his dick out." She was wrapped in an airy cotton robe, enjoying the way the breeze blew the summer heat into her body, like an outdoor sauna.

Runi Soon sat to her side, a bottle of wine and a plate of cheese and crackers on the table between them. Her soft laugh preceded her response. "In my business, I tend to have the opposite problem." No bathrobe for Runi—she was always immaculately done up, showing off her beautiful Korean features to their full extent. Never a hair out of place, never a no-makeup day, never a chip in her fingernail polish, and never wearing flats.

Verona spread some cranberry goat cheese on a cracker. It was Saturday, and she had slept late, so even though it was technically the afternoon, this counted as breakfast. She could get used to wine and cheese for breakfast. If only she could find herself a nice Frenchman to marry. "Yes, yes, I know. I still think you should reconsider my idea for your business tag line: *Nix your dix pix!*"

"And what did I say?"

"You said it was too gendered. To which I replied, you could always add "*Remove your boobs from the 'Tube!*"

"And I said?"

"That it was way too long of a catchphrase, and that no one calls videos on the internet 'the 'Tube.'"

Runi sipped her wine slowly, a show of dignity in the face of Verona's childishness. "My clients are CEOs, doctors, lawyers...professionals. They don't want fucking ridiculous catchphrases."

"Oh, come on, my clients love mine. *The go-to lady for catching wandering willies or eager beavers.* They read it and they don't forget it. Or me."

Runi waved her hand to whisk that particular conversational thread away as if it was a spider web. "Anyway, why is Javier so hard to catch with his dick out?"

Verona settled back into her Adirondack chair, her mouth thick with cracker mush. "Followed him for the past four days, and other than a quick trip to the smoothie shop, the man never shows his face. And what's worse, he's got some secret underground lair. Like a fucking James Bond villain."

"Underground lair?"

"See for yourself." She sent Runi the map pin for the warehouse. "The building has no name, Google Maps doesn't even have a good street view of it, and I can't find any information on a business at that address. So, the only explanation is that it's his underground lair. He took his new screw toy there with him, but who knows what other depraved acts go on down there?"

Runi was silent for a few moments while she consulted her phone. "Hang on, I think I remember this place."

"You *remember* it? Damn, Runi, I knew you were kind of a badass, but I never pegged you for being in league with Blofeld."[1]

"No, you idiot, from a client." One of the benefits of being a social media scrubber was that Runi often acquired knowledge of those parts of the internet Google searches couldn't touch.

"Please tell me it's not the one who liked to do things...with the apples."

"No, this is too classy for vagina apples." Runi threw this nickname out as if the story, involving Granny Smith apples, a snorkel, a pink plush monkey, and a granulated cylinder hadn't been one of the grossest stories Verona had ever heard. And that was saying something, considering Verona spied on people having sex for a living.

"This place is called Coronis. It's a super-top-secret fight club for fucking. Entry is by rotating password, and it is so hard to break into the elite scene to get that password that people will do almost anything to avoid breaking the rules. Rules which include a zero-tolerance policy for social media posts."

"Which your client needed you to erase before they were excommunicated?" Verona made a sandwich with a cracker, sausage, olive, and blue cheese and took a messy bite.

"Excommunicated is right. Once you're on the blacklist, you don't get off it. Ever."

"Any chance you can hook me up with the password? From your client?" She inadvertently spat cracker crumbs as she spoke the *f* of "from."

Runi brushed Verona's spit crumbs off her lap "Not a chance in hell. If word ever got back that they gave a PI the password...fuck, Verona, this is literally a sanctuary from people like you."

Verona nodded, watching as tiny gray-and-black chickadees darted

1. Kind of like a serious Dr. Evil. With a cat and everything.

from tree to tree, calling and responding their melodic songs back and forth. "I guess that means I'm going to have to think laterally."[2]

"Whatever the fuck that means. Listen, I don't have all fucking day. My eomma is coming to visit soon, and I have to seriously clean up all the smut around the house. And I have art class in a few hours. I didn't come here to talk about Javier's dick."

"Speaking of smut," Verona said under her breath.

Runi glared at her, in what Verona believed was a decent impression of what her eomma's look would be when she saw the slightly pornographic art Runi had made and hung. It was a relatively new hobby for her, but she was surprisingly good at the details. Much better than Verona's phallic doodles in her notebooks.

"Let's talk about a different dick. What did Quentin say when you told him about Javier?"

"Haven't talked to him." Verona kept her face as straight as possible. The truth was, she had considered inviting him over to her balcony instead of Runi but had dismissed it quickly when she imagined the conversation: "Oh, hi, Quentin. Yes, I invited you here to update you. There are no updates." Idiotic.

"Why don't you jump his bones already?" Runi said, as if the suggestion was as commonplace as conversation about how the flowers were blooming late this year.

"Jump...did you just say jump his bones? Does anyone say that anymore? Did they ever? In real life, I mean?"

"Well, I just said it. And I meant it. Why not?"

"Easy for you to say, Mrs. Happily Married to a guy hot enough to be Chris Hemsworth's stunt double and likeable enough to be Tom Hanks."

"I know what deflection is too, Verona. Just answer the damn question." Runi savagely spiked a cube of cheddar with a toothpick and tossed it in her mouth.

"Why don't I jump his bones? Because I do have a *little* self-respect. I

---

2. *Midsomer Murders* will tell you all you need to know about this phrase. Give it a try after you finish that Christopher Moore novel you just ordered.

don't go around throwing myself at guys." Verona threw a slice of Havarti on a muesli cracker.

"Could be fun, though."

"Yeah...or mortifying."

"Probably a bit of both, to be honest. But seriously, how long are you going to aimlessly flirt with this guy?"

"Forever. It doesn't seem like he's interested in making any moves, and I *do not* have the balls to ask him out. He's got hot guy powers. I'm like George McFly[3] on this one—I just don't think I could handle that kind of rejection." At least if she kept it casual, she could lie to herself that there was a chance and not have to face the truth of him not wanting her.

Runi swirled the wine in her glass. "But he might say yes."

Verona didn't bother arguing the point, partly because she'd rather tell her mother every single detail of her last sexual encounter than even consider asking Quentin out. But mostly because of George McFly.

Fucking George McFly. That's the answer! Well, Marty really, but let's not split hairs.

~

Saturday 3 p.m.

This is why they always do a fucking scouting mission on TV shows, Verona thought as she swatted a mosquito off the back of her neck for the tenth time and shifted from one foot to the other, attempting to avoid the ant nest she'd inadvertently squatted over.

She'd not bothered with one, of course, thinking she was familiar enough with the area to not need one. She'd selected the building of one of her clients that she knew had an underground parking garage. She'd driven around and found the ideal hiding spot behind some bushes—done! She'd

3. *Back to the Future*. You should see it, by the way. It's iconic and fun, and the future in the movie is now the past, and if that's the case, I want my flying car, self-lacing shoes, and auto-dry jacket, dammit!

never considered ants, but then again, who does, other than picnickers? Those damn overprepared freaks!

It wasn't just the ants—it was the sun, which was blazing down directly overhead. It was also the lack of a breeze, which caused sweat to pool in uncomfortable areas, and the ants to stick to her as if she were covered in honey.

All of this in service of her grand plan: The McFly Maneuver.

If the password to Coronis was impossible to get, then she wouldn't bother trying to get it. No, she was going in lo-fi.

At last, like the hazy mirage of an oasis in the desert, a blue sedan steered into the driveway and approached the garage. Verona took a few calming breaths as the driver's window rolled down and a thick finger reached out to punch in a code. Now that it was time to go, a light rush of adrenaline and excitement made Verona forget her discomfort. She executed a low run to the back of the sedan and rested a hand on the bumper as she followed it into the garage.

Just like Marty McFly. Minus the skateboard.

As soon as she was clear of the door, she peeled off to the right and hid behind a parked red Audi. She waited for the sedan to park and the driver to get out before straightening up and following him into the elevator lobby.

He pressed the call button and gave her a friendly smile, which turned slightly to surprise, but he hid it quickly. She smiled back as they entered the elevator. This was fine. Normal. She was just another resident returning home after a day out. He was just surprised because he'd never seen her around before.

She pushed the button for the main floor, and she caught her reflection in the mirrored sides of the elevator. Her face was beet red, sweat was running down her temples, and her hands were coated in dirt, which was turning to mud as it mixed with her sweat.

No wonder this dude had given her the odd eye. She looked like she'd returned from a marathon gardening session. Or burying a body. She thought of making an excuse, but figured anything she said would make her seem *more* conspicuous, not less.

She gave him a little wave as she exited the elevator, and after the doors closed, she headed straight out the front doors back to the street. Well, if she could pull this off in broad daylight looking like a sunburnt zombie, she could sure as hell pull it off in the cover of darkness.

There was just one problem—she needed a partner.

But who would she want to take to a secret fight club for fucking? One name materialized in her mind, quickly drifting down to get tingly like things always did when she thought of him.

Quentin.

6

WILL YOU BE MY... SECRET SEX CLUB LOVER?

Calgary
Saturday 6 p.m.

There was no way Verona could just ask Quentin to be her partner in sex club infiltration. There were rules about these kinds of things, and the rules definitely had to state that she could not ask a sexy colleague to pretend to be her lover. Especially to a secret sex club. Especially when all she could think of was the way his skin would feel brushed up against hers—warm and enveloping. Like the way the summer sun cradled her skin as if she were lounging in a hot bath.

But there were ways around these things. Making it seem like *his* idea was top of that list.

After a quick cleanup at home, she'd decided to get started on a new case she'd taken just before Miami. Clarence and Abbie. It was a bit of a strange one, because as much as Clarence seemed certain Abbie was bonking the guy from the pizza cafe on the bottom floor of their building, he didn't seem bothered by it.

Another one of these guys that likes to watch, she thought. It was fine, she didn't judge, but she also wasn't in the pornography business. They could take their own damn photos, fucking creeps. Okay, maybe she did judge just a little bit.

Abbie was easy to spot, sitting on the patio two tables down from Verona. Mid-forties, with blond hair and a figure just slightly losing its shape, dressed in a low-cut sundress. She stood up as a man in a black tracksuit exited the restaurant and joined her. Definitely *not* Clarence. The way she grabbed his bicep before they sat down told Verona everything she needed to know.

This was not a couple who was going to hide their affair. They were either too dumb or too arrogant to think no one would notice them sitting on the side of a street in broad daylight. Honestly, cases like this made Verona wonder why the spouse hired her. All Clarence had to do was set up shop nearby, and he'd see all he needed to know what his wife was up to. Unless Verona was right about him wanting the photos for *private time*.

She didn't mind the easy case, though, it was still money in her pocket, and it meant she could call Quentin while she worked. Especially since Abbie was already scooting her chair closer to Tracksuit. They'd have their tongues down each other's throats before Verona's pizza made it out of the oven.

"Verona, I'm kind of busy," he answered.

"Sorry, Quentin, but if you're so busy, then why'd you answer?" Okay, so that wasn't the warm reception she was hoping for, but she could work with it.

"Because we're working on a case together, remember? So I wanted to answer in case it was important, but I also wanted to be quick to tell you I was kind of busy so if it wasn't important, you'd hang up and call me back. I was going for concise. But now I've already said about fifty words, so what's the point?"

Verona heard a muffled voice in the background. Sounded female. Had she disturbed him on a date? Her stomach lurched with curiosity and jealousy.

"Okay, well, it's not super important, but it does relate to the case."

"Are you intentionally trying to take up more time than is necessary?" Quentin sounded annoyed.

"No, sorry. Why don't you call me back at a better time." Annoyed

Quentin was not what she wanted. She needed playful Quentin. The kind of Quentin that might decide breaking into a club would be fun.

Tracksuit put his hand on Abbie's leg beneath the table, and Verona double-checked that her phone was on silent. If she was going to snap a few photos, she didn't need the shutter sound giving her away.

On the other end of the phone she heard clinking noises and other voices and guessed he was at a restaurant. She heard him cover the mouthpiece of his phone and say, "No, sorry, I'll just be a few minutes. You go ahead."

The ambient noise turned into cars and wind as Quentin stepped out of the restaurant and onto the sidewalk.

"Did I interrupt you on a date?" Verona blurted out before she could stop herself. Her face flushed from the boldness of her question. She'd never prodded into his personal life before.

"Yes, actually, you did. She's waiting inside for me now, so if we can make this quick?" He still sounded terse, but his tone had relaxed since he no longer had a date staring at him.

"What kind of a jerk answers his phone on a first date?" She needed to cover for her momentary slip into the personal. If she cast a few negative connotations on his dating experience while she was at it, then so be it. *Don't be a bitch about this.*

"Who says it's a first date?" A teasing tone came back into his voice.

"Never heard you talk about a girlfriend before. Private dick hunch." She hoped it was. Imagining Quentin with another woman was near the bottom of her list of things to think about, right next to a pap smear.

Tracksuit reached a hand up to tuck a loose piece of hair behind Abbie's ear as the waiter came out to deliver their Neapolitan-style pizza. Verona wondered what it would feel like to have Quentin's fingers brushing against her cheek like that. So soft, a mere tease to the intensity that lay within. She sucked in the air and shook her head. Now was not the time for fantasies.

"So, what do you need?" He sounded fully relaxed now. Maybe the date wasn't going so well and that's why he'd been so uptight?

I'm betting you have the goods to fill every need I have. "A partner. For a sex club." *Damn, that didn't come out nearly as suave as I needed it to. Bury the lead a bit, Montero!*

"You must have me confused with a dating service. They have these apps now, Verona. You swipe left or right. Pretty simple."

The sarcasm was a good sign. "Yes, thank you, I've done my fair share of swiping left. This is much more important. For the case. To catch Javier. I've been following him for days, and this sex club he goes to on Friday nights is literally the only time I'm liable to catch him outside of his limo." She'd had Miami confirm that Javier went out each Friday night. It would have been good intel to have from the outset, but strategic planning didn't seem to be Miami's strong suit.

The waiter deposited Verona's margherita pizza, and she was pleased to find the crust suitably thin and bubbly around the edges. The earthy smell of fresh basil made her miss her mother's herb garden. She could grow her own, but who had the time?

"So, why call me, then?" He didn't sound annoyed, just curious.

She'd hoped he wouldn't ask that question, that he'd just put the pieces together on his own. Answering it would put her in an awkward position. Best to avoid it. "Well, they sure as hell aren't going to let me in on my own. I need someone to come with me or they'll likely kick me out."

The waiter returned with fresh pepper and parmesan. She covered the mouthpiece and said, "Lamaze class. They won't let you do it alone. Did you know that? I sure as hell didn't. And now this asshole is trying to get out of going with me." He nodded sympathetically and left the table in a hurry. It was so easy to fuck with people.

Well, most people.

Quentin's silence stretched out longer than usual. Was he going to agree to come? Was he wondering if she was really asking him that? But perhaps most importantly, was he going to fuck his date tonight?

The faint wail of a siren filtered through the phone, and she heard him exhale. "Look, my date has been waiting for me for five minutes now, so I have to go. I'll think about it tomorrow and let you know, okay?"

"You mean you'll think about it when you get home tonight?"

"Hopefully not." He hung up.

Hopefully not, thought Verona. *That could mean a lot of things. Hopefully not because it's not something he cares to think about on his time off, or hopefully not because he hopes he'll be getting laid?*

All of the joy she'd felt imagining going undercover (and maybe under the covers?) with Quentin evaporated like cat piss off hot cement. *That son of a bitch is going to get laid.*

Not even capturing a burst shot of Abbie and Tracksuit giving sloppy kisses over their greasy pizza was enough to lift her up from that depressing knowledge.

~

Sunday 2 p.m.

Verona checked her phone for the dozenth time with shaking hands and blood pulsing in her neck. She didn't usually get so nervous when meeting people, not even with clients she knew would blow up when faced with the glossy photographic truth of their partner's misdeeds. As usual, it was Quentin who had this special ability to upend every part of her, from her independence to her stability.

His message was simple: *Meet me at Denizens this afternoon. I've got a plan*, but it had sent a cascade of what-ifs through Verona. The most pleasing of the what-ifs ended in the back seat of a car, but she'd had to shut that particular fantasy down when she realized her face was starting to flush.

She'd arrived fifteen minutes early, like a deranged fangirl, but she needed the time to calm down and act like the put-together, calm, and badass private dick she needed Quentin to think she was. The strong, sweet coffee helped.

Denizens was a quaint, cozy coffee shop a few blocks from Quentin's apartment. The bulky furniture, made up of random salvaged pieces, was haphazardly positioned around low tables. The walls were covered in antique wallpaper ranging from damask, to leafy greens, to minimalistic geometry. Plants, including macramé-wrapped hanging pots, littered what little space wasn't taken up by chairs and tables. It was as though five different grandmothers had thrown their collective living rooms together, but the effect somehow made young hipsters flock to the place in droves of scarves, hats, glasses, and ankle pants.

Each time the bell above the door jangled, Verona forced herself to shift her eyes to the door slowly and casually. She didn't want to look like a hummingbird who forgot to take their Ativan when Quentin arrived.

When she was halfway through her drink, he finally walked through, the sun framing his body, dressed down in jeans and a fitted T-shirt.

She waved him over, and he made a detour to the counter to order his drink before joining her.

She was distracted by his casual look, which was somehow more alluring than his expensive suits. It was the reverse of how men who rarely dress up look like a movie star when they put on a suit. Quentin's lack of suit was tantalizing because it was different, yes, but also because it turned him from a movie star into the cute boy next door. Someone you could rely on to help you fix a flat tire and share a soda with after a game of catch.

He joined her with a simple black coffee. "So, a secret sex club, eh?"

She swirled her drink around, encouraging the last of the whipped cream to mix in. "Yeah. I should've guessed it would be something like this. I mean, Javier does everything better than the rest of us. It only makes sense that he would be involved with a super exclusive cheater's club."

"But you've got a way in?" His face needed a shave, a change from the usual fresh look. She'd always imagined running her finger along his jaw, smooth like the edge of a knife.

She ran her finger on the handle of her coffee cup, mimicking the motion. "I do." She could tell him, but where was the fun in that? Better to show him.[1] The idea of running behind a car with him, the two of them breathless with adrenaline and excitement—

"Well, good thing I've found your perfect partner, then."

A wave of heat settled into her chest in sudden disappointment. *Found* the partner? Not him? "That's why I called you." No way she'd let him see this wasn't what she'd expected. That this wasn't what she'd assumed he'd do all along.

"Yeah, should be here any minute now." He looked over his shoulder as the door bell jangled again, then stood with a smile on his face. "Owen! Grab some drinks and join us."

---

1. As the craft books like to say, "Show, don't tell!"

Two men went to the counter to order their drinks. The younger of the two was around Quentin's age, tall, with coily black hair cut short and neat and brown eyes. The older man looked to be about fifty and had kept himself fit, with a long, narrow face and close-cropped blond hair.

Verona remembered Quentin talking about Owen in passing over the years, but she had no idea who the older man might be. When they returned to the table, Quentin gave Owen a hug, and they all sat down again.

Owen placed a hand on the older man's shoulder. "This is my buddy, Henry. The best damn drag queen I've ever met."

This statement was met with silence from Verona and Quentin. It wasn't that she cared he was a drag queen, it was that she'd never been introduced to someone in that precise manner. She was just recovering herself with a polite hello when Henry cut her off.

"I know, I know, you can't stop picturing me in a dress. Don't worry about it—I do it to everyone I meet for the first time too."

Quentin laughed and gave Henry a playful nudge on his shoulder. "I think that will be my new thing from now on: picturing everyone I meet in a dress. Thanks for agreeing to take on this slightly unorthodox project."

"I rather enjoy the unorthodox," Henry said. "I did drag before it was fashionable, you know. Before RuPaul made it cool. Before there was internet. It wasn't all fun and games back in the eighties when I'd walk into a women's department store looking for accessories." He leaned into his green wingback chair, cupping his coffee with both hands. "And my wife, then my girlfriend, was rather possessive of her wardrobe, so there was no sneaking pieces from her."

Wait, am I supposed to be going into a sex club with...a drag queen? Did Quentin understand her assignment? Sure, as Henry alluded to, the world was much more accepting of all types of relationships, but the idea was to be inconspicuous. Waltzing into a sex club with a drag queen on her arm definitely would draw some attention.

Henry must've noticed her confused expression, because he leaned forward and whispered, "I look amazing in a suit as well."

Owen put his foot on the edge of the table. "Henry is one of the best actors I know. You get that way doing shows five nights a week. Heckling from the audience, from the other queens, witty repartee? You need a partner who's quick on their feet? Henry's your man."

How Quentin got from "I need a partner" to "Here's a drag queen!" she'd never know, but if she had to go in with a stranger, then someone with some acting skills was probably a good idea.

"What's your drag name?" she asked. If she was going to be pretending to be this man's lover, she'd better start getting to know him a bit.

"Alexis Cumming." Henry pulled a few flyers from his pocket and deposited them on the table. "Info for my shows, if anyone's interested."

The flyer was full of vibrant neon colors, with Alexis Cumming front and center, striking a pose to compete with Beyoncé. It promised music, humor, sass, lights, glitter, food, and drinks, with a tag line that read "PG show until eight, and then things get grown-up!"

Verona looked up from the flyer. "People bring their kids to drag shows?"

Henry nodded. "Oh yes—it's no longer a dirty little secret. It's very mainstream. We read books to kids in libraries now. If the religious zealots don't scare them away first."

"And Quentin told you what we're doing here, right?" She had to assume he wouldn't have shown up if he wasn't interested, but assuming and asses and all that.

Henry crossed his legs and placed his cup on his knee. "You mean to catch a truly despicable man in the act of exploiting a young woman for the purposes of sex?"

"Yes," said Verona and Quentin together.

"In a secret sex club," Verona added.

Henry gave a sideways smile. "I'm no stranger to secret clubs."

The charged image of ending up in the back seat of a car with Quentin was quickly being replaced with the kind of asexual numbing the makers of breakfast cereal[2] envisioned. But at least she had a way forward for her case.

Henry and Owen stayed until their coffees were done, Henry giving

---

2. Look it up. Those dry, crunchy flakes that are supposed to be part of a balanced breakfast were invented to keep you flaccid.

Verona his number so they could connect before their undercover operation, and Owen bugging Quentin to go out for beers in the near future.

Quentin and Verona lingered in the soft, amiable aura that good company creates.

"So." Verona leaned on the table, cupping her second mug of coffee, letting the warmth cascade through her and coax her body into contented relaxation. The fluttering of earlier was gone now that she knew her chance with Quentin wouldn't come. "Have you not been to a drag show, then?"

Music played in the background, a mishmash of your grandmother's favorites: Elvis, Paul Anka, Pérez Prado, Sinatra, and Clooney.

"No," Quentin admitted. "But don't give me that smug look. The way you were staring at Henry, I bet you haven't either."

"You got me. No, I haven't. Haven't even seen *RuPaul's Drag Race*."

"Is it because you're a bigot?"

"Absolutely," Verona said. "I prefer to hate, judge, and keep separate from me everyone who leads a lifestyle that is different from mine in any way. What's your excuse?"

"Never had the chance to, I guess."

"But you're going to go now, right?"

"I guess maybe if Owen goes, I could tag along. It'd be kind of weird to show up to a drag show alone, wouldn't it?"

"Well, as you know, I'm the consummate expert on drag show etiquette, so yes, that would be weird."

"Is it possible to get a straight answer from you, ever?" Quentin tapped his fingers on the table in time with "Fly Me to the Moon" playing softly in the background.

He'd never pushed her on that before. They'd always been content to jab at each other, or at least she assumed they had been. She certainly preferred it. Anything more was too risky, too *close*.

"Okay, fine. I don't think it'd be too weird to go to a drag show alone, but I do think it'd be more fun to go with someone. Want to go with me?"

The last sentence escaped her before she could tell herself not to say it. Her stomach dropped at once, and all the warmth left her fingers as she awaited his answer. *Well, I guess if I can't answer questions, I might as well ask them. If I can't have him in a secret sex club, I guess a drag show will have to do.*

Quentin looked as shocked as Verona felt. "What about Owen?"

"What *about* Owen? He's been before. We haven't."

Quentin looked at her as if he was deciding if he'd like to rent a particular movie. "Yeah, I guess that could be okay."

It was hardly an enthusiastic yes, but her stomach started to float back up from the pit of mortal terror it had sunk into. Then it flopped around in anticipation and anxiety as she realized she had a date with Quentin.

Well, she thought, *at least I'll have something more to report to Mom when she calls and reminds me of Isabella's four children, architect husband, and giant mansion*. Verona didn't care to have the mansion or the four kids hanging off her fun bags, but maybe the husband would be nice.

7

THE SHOW WAS A DRAG

Calgary
Thursday night. Date night. No pressure.

The theater was small, seating around a hundred people, and set up with small round tables in a scattered pattern so everyone had a decent view of the raised stage. The stage had classic red velvet curtains and a polished wood floor. The lighting was low and atmospheric, with candles on the tables. The decor was tasteful but opulent, with red tablecloths, golden accents in the form of draped fabrics along the walls, and clusters of red and white roses.

Verona hesitated in the entryway and peeked in at the patrons. Quentin was already seated with a drink in front of him. Why was it that the tiniest thing, from his smile, to his smell, to the way he put his hands in his pockets, was enough to make her loins contract and beg for mercy? She wasn't sure what it was about him; no one else had ever affected her that way, and she couldn't decide if it spelled destiny or disaster. The two are so often related, intertwined, and one tiny moment away from each other.

For a moment she considered running back to her car and inventing a sickness to get out of the date, but she forced herself to stay. *This is what you wanted*, she reminded herself, *so get the fuck in there.*

She squared her shoulders, walked to the table, and sat across from him. "Starting without me?"

"Couldn't help it—look at the drink list!" He seemed relaxed and happy, a good sign.

Verona picked up the menu and saw for herself what he was talking about. All of the cocktail names were plays on standard drink names: Shirley Temptress, Marge Ariba, Cause My Pole to Sin, Wise Guy Sour Puss, Manhandler, Mimi Osa, Primp Cups, and Jack Queer Eye.

She looked up. "Right. I forgot you've got a thing for wacky names. Like that smoothie place."

"I like the creativity. I ordered the Cause My Pole to Sin. Sounded like a good idea." He lifted the pink drink in the air before taking a sip.

"But a cosmo is a girl drink," Verona said. It was, and yet in his hands it didn't look overly feminine. Hell, he could hold a frilly fuchsia purse and still look manlier than the Old Spice Guy.[1]

Quentin swished his drink around in blatant disregard. "How very sexist of you."

"Drinking, darling?" a waitress asked Verona in a light, husky voice.

Her name tag read MINDI SKIRT, and it was an appropriate moniker. Her long legs were barely concealed in a turquoise minidress with a sequined bodice like an Indian sari.

"You bet!" Verona said. "My usual drink is a Dark and Stormy, but I don't see it on the menu."

"The bartender can make it, but none of us could come up with a name for it, so it's not on the menu. Want to try?"

Verona thought for a moment. "Uh, Dirk N. Store Guy?" She shook her head. "Yeah, not great."

"You'd think with the word 'dark,' it'd be easy. I can bring you one if you like." She wrapped her hands around her hips, golden nails catching the light and glinting.

"No, no," said Verona. "I'll try something else—I want to embrace the atmosphere."

---

1. I assume you've seen these commercials, but if not, it's worth a look. So much manly manness. Brilliant advertising.

"That's the best way, darling. So what'll it be? I have other adoring guests who want a piece of me, you know." She indicated the room with a wave of her hand, sending a row of gold bangles cascading up and down her forearm in chiming waves.

"Right. Sorry. I'll take the Manhandler, please."

"You look like you can do that just fine on your own, gorgeous!" Mindi gave Quentin a meaningful look, and he blushed. She spun on the spot and sashayed away to the next table.

Quentin sipped at his drink until the red cleared from his face. Mindi returned and deposited Verona's drink on a custom coaster decorated with a vibrantly colorful painting of a penis. Verona picked up the program for the evening from the table. "Did you already look at this?"

"Yeah, it looks like we're in for a good show."

The program gave a basic overview, along with a list of those involved. Verona saw their waitress's name, Mindi Skirt, along with a host of others. Hanna Jobb, Trish Kits, Mya Humps, Bonita Fajita, George Cloney, Minty Jewels, and Luke Midyck.

Verona smiled at the childish genital humor. "I kind of want to do drag just so I can come up with my own name!"

Quentin leaned in closer, and Verona breathed in the heady mix of tobacco and ginger. "I thought the same thing, but then I thought, I can still have fun coming up with the names without all the work of wigs and makeup!"

They smiled at each other, enjoying themselves in this new element. The low lighting, the slight inhibition from the drinks, the way they had to lean in to hear each other over the rising noise level.

A ball of warmth settled in Verona's pelvis, expectation and desire stoking her inner stove. His jaw was close enough she could reach out and finally find out what it felt like to caress it. Her hand on the table was a few inches from his. Did she imagine it, or did his hand twitch, as if he thought of touching her? Her mind was a blur of ideas and images. His hands on her collar bone, teasing until they moved lower, the way he would taste, the squeeze of her legs around his waist. A magic bubble descended upon them, giving them a moment to discover if there truly was something more between them.

A hand on Quentin's shoulder popped the bubble like the messy splash of explosive diarrhea. "Quentin!" said a cheery voice.

Verona and Quentin looked up to see Owen. They both fell back into their chairs, like kids whose teacher has returned from the lavatory. Verona felt the heat in her face start to dissipate, and the dull ache of unfulfilled promises in her abdomen.

"I didn't know you were coming tonight!" Owen said. "This is awesome. You can join me and Felix!"

Quentin stood up and hugged Owen. There was nothing to do but be polite and accept the offer. What could he say? "No, sorry, I was hoping for some alone time with Verona"?

"Yeah, sounds great!" He beamed at Owen.

Verona had to follow suit. What could she say? "No, sorry, this is my one night to try to make something happen with Quentin, and you've ruined everything, you asshole"?

"Of course." She grabbed her Manhandler and stood up. *Pretty sure I'm not going to handle any men tonight*, she thought.

They walked a few tables over to join Owen and a young man with a fair complexion, deep red beard, long red hair in a ponytail, and barrel chest.

"My partner, Felix," Owen said. "Felix, you know Quentin, and this is Verona."

Felix stood up to shake hands, his muscled forearms rippling in the low light.

"Felix is interested in trying drag," Owen said.

Verona looked at the burly, Viking-like Felix and couldn't wrap her head around it. His appearance was so masculine, it was a surprise he was into drag.

"Really?" she asked in what she hoped was a kind, interested voice, and not one of incredulity.

"Oh yeah," Felix said in a deep bass voice. "I'm fascinated by the idea of mixing masculinity with femininity. I saw this one drag queen with a beard and colorful makeup, and I thought, 'I could do that.'"

"It would certainly be a unique take," Quentin said. "However, I'm not an expert, as this is my first show."

Mindi was passing by and stopped dead in her tracks. "Do we have a drag virgin here tonight?" she asked loudly.

Cheers and hoots came from the audience, and then a smattering of raucous applause.

Quentin blushed but nodded. "Yeah, you got me!"

Mindi put a light hand on his shoulder. "Don't you worry, darling—you'll be well tended to tonight." She hollered to the room, "All right, girls, we've got ourselves a virgin. What do we do with virgins?"

The queens yelled back, "Always get consent!"

Mindi clapped once. "And?"

"Don't skip the foreplay!"

Mindi clapped twice. "And lastly?"

"Do it so well, they'll never get us out of their heads!"

Three claps. The audience laughed, and the room went back to its buzz.

Quentin looked like a deer caught in the headlights. "What have I just signed up for?"

"The night of your life," Owen said.

Quentin pointed at Verona. "She's new too!"

Felix slapped his palm on the table. "It's too late now. You bring that up and they'll think you're trying to get out of it. They've chosen you. Just go with it."

All thoughts of any kind of intimate moment with Quentin vanished as Verona pictured him being marched on stage and toyed with by various drag queens and kings. It would be amusing, but she was hoping for spice, not lighthearted fun.

She waved her hand to order another drink to drown her sorrows in. A stunningly handsome waiter in a black tux came over. He had coiffed dark hair and a five o'clock shadow along a strong jawline. His name tag identified him as George Cloney, and he did look surprisingly like Mr. Clooney.

"Yes, doll?" he asked in a gravelly whisky voice.

"Can I get a Wise Guy Sour Puss, please?"

"Sounds like something the two of us could make together, toots."

Another hand appeared from nowhere, this time on Owen's shoulder. "Owen! Felix! I had no idea you'd be here tonight!" said a young woman with the kind of natural good looks that meant she would always be the most attractive woman in the room, even if she showed up in sweatpants and a baggy T-shirt. "I'm here with some friends. We should make a big table, especially if your friend's the virgin. It'll be way more fun that way."

Two tables were put together, and in the shuffle, the seating got rearranged so that Verona and Quentin were nearly on opposite sides, with Quentin seated next to the young hottie.

Verona watched bitterly as Quentin laughed and the woman rested her hand on his arm. She didn't move it when he stopped laughing. *Well, fuck,* she thought, *I might as well go home, put on the sweats, and eat all the cheese in my fridge*.

The curtain finally rose, and they were met with the glittering spectral vision of Alexis Cumming, resplendent in a floor-length gown in the style and color of Jessica Rabbit's. Gorgeous red hair, pouty lips, toned legs, pushed-up breasts, and a smooth voice to sing the sultry song "Why Don't You Do Right?"

Verona looked over at Quentin and the woman, sitting cozy and gazing with rapt attention at the stage.

She hadn't been done right at all.

8

HIGH-HEEL HELL

Calgary
Friday 10 p.m.

The club throbbed with heavy bass, the kind of low reverberation that shakes rib cages and makes conversation impossible. In the immense darkness, strobe lights flashed on and off in time to the music, turning each scene into a stop-motion pantomime. Bodies danced, swayed, laughed, and grabbed at each other as if no one else could see them, and in effect, no one could, because when you frequented Coronis,[1] your privacy was guaranteed.

Verona danced close to the bar, Henry's arms slung around her waist as she held a pink cosmo aloft, not caring that it was sloshing over the edges as they danced. A Dark and Stormy wasn't a party-girl drink, and the cosmo was top of the mind after her disastrous date the previous evening. She took another sip of the tart vodka drink, wanting to down the whole thing to numb her from her disappointment.

They'd arrived earlier than Javier, knowing it would be easier to spot

1. I'll save you flipping back through the book to find this name—it's the top-secret fuck club.

him coming in and keep tabs on him than risk losing him falling behind in the chaos of the entryway. If Javier followed his usual pattern, and there was no reason to believe he wouldn't, he should be arriving within the next half hour.

The McFly Maneuver had gone off without a hitch. Henry had loved the excitement of running in behind the car, and it had been strangely satisfying to waltz into a password-only exclusive club knowing they'd hacked the system in such a simple way.

Henry's body was warm and solid behind her, and she was surprised by how much she enjoyed the nearness of him. It wasn't a sexual attraction—she knew he was happily married, and though he was attractive enough, he was too old for her—but her body relaxed into him, knowing he'd take care of her. The realization of how much she could lean into that filled her with an ache. How long had it been since she'd had a man she felt that secure with?

But it was something she needed as she tottered around in her high heels, miniskirt, and tube top combo she'd borrowed from Runi's closet. Runi still owned every piece of clothing she'd ever bought, so she was able to dig up some clothes from her college days for Verona to use. She hoped there wasn't a stampede for the fire exit, because she would be one of the ones that got trampled.

Henry looked dapper in a navy-blue suit, red tie, and gold cufflinks. His hair was swept back in a politician-crisp look, and he made a show of throwing hundred-dollar bills around. She turned around and wrapped her arms around his neck so they could talk above the music. He rested his hands near the top of her ass in a gesture that felt so natural she envied his wife for a moment.

Practiced hands, lucky bitch!

"Let's dance around a bit. I want to see if there might be a good place to grab some photos without drawing attention."

Henry nodded and spun her around with such ease, she felt like she was floating instead of stumbling in her heels. She was *not* used to high heels. The last time she'd worn a pair was probably five years ago for a cousin's wedding, but as Henry pulled her in, his shoulders firm and his back straight, she felt like she could dance a tango.

"Henry, you're a fucking amazing dancer, but remember, we're undercover. Let's go for more drunken swaying than *Dancing with the Stars*."

"Right," he said, dropping his posture and wrapping an arm clumsily around her midriff. "Better?"

"No." She immediately felt her stability go. "So yes. Nice work."

They circled around the dance floor, the people around them lit up in flashes of purple, blue, red, and white. The floor was polished and almost reflective, the bar was glass-topped, and the liquor displayed was all top-shelf. This was not a club for college kids to fuck in the washroom. This was high class.

But it did beg the question, if not in the washroom stalls, where was the fucking happening? People certainly weren't shy with their PDA, but it wasn't as if it were a giant orgy where you could just get at it with everyone watching.

She leaned into Henry's ear, putting what she hoped was a lustful look on her face so she could whisper in his ear without it looking odd. "Where do you suppose all the legendary fucking is happening?"

Henry spun her around, one hand on each of her hip bones. If Quentin's hands had done that...*focus up, Montero!*

He whispered in her ear, and she smelled his aftershave, tart and fresh. "In my day, well, in anyone's day, if you want to find the best action, get away from the flashing lights and doorway."

Lining the far wall of the club were rooms partitioned off with heavy velvet curtains. A bouncer in a black suit stood guard outside of each one. As they danced, a couple exited the room on the far left, clothes and hair rumpled in the universal signal of "we just fucked."

She spun back around so she could see over Henry's shoulder to the doorway of the club. "I guess we know where Javi will be going, then. And, speak of the devil."

Javier had entered the club, a young woman in a glittering navy minidress on his arm. Henry turned to look, his hands on Verona's shoulders. "Hmm, if he waxed that face up, I think his eyes would be gorgeous with the right liner."

Verona nudged him playfully in the ribs. "Shh! We're not here to picture men in dresses."

"Speak for yourself," he muttered.

Javier took his young thing to the bar and ordered her some kind of bright blue drink with an orange slice but, strangely, didn't order anything for himself.

"Stay here and fucking behave," he said, grabbing her wrist before she could take a sip of her drink. "I'll keep the tab open, *if* you can be good."

The girl's brown eyes registered a moment of hurt, but it was quickly covered by a smile of her bright red lips. "Sure, baby, anything for you."

He released her wrist and walked with purpose to the far end of the club.

"Is it just me, or was that strangely close to a parental relationship?" Henry asked as they danced their way after Javier.

"They don't call it 'sugar daddy' for no reason," she said to keep herself calm. When Javier had grabbed the woman's wrist, a wave of anger had rushed over Verona's body, but that wasn't helpful at the moment. The helpful thing was to do her job.

Why was he going to the booths *without* his mistress? Was it possible he was meeting yet another woman in the club while the mistress waited outside for her turn? Was he that insatiable?

They watched as he went into the booth second from the right. She'd expected some complicated procedure to gain entry, but all he'd done was whisper in the bouncer's ear, and he'd been nodded behind the thick velvet curtains.

"Does he have another woman waiting for him in there?" Henry asked as they hovered on the edge of the dance floor.

"I don't know. Honestly, I wouldn't put it past him."

"What do you want to do?"

She shook her head and looked down, grimacing as the straps of her shoes dug into her skin. She was going to have blisters for sure. How did women do this?

"You need to put more of your weight onto your heels," Henry said.

She almost snapped back with "How would you know?" before she realized he probably spent more hours in heels in a single week than she had in her entire life. "Thanks. I say we dance around and see if anyone else joins him. If no one does, we can assume she's already in there, and we're giving them time to get nice and indecent."

He pulled her in closer, taking some of the weight off her feet. It felt heavenly.

"Yes, but how are we going to get a picture *inside* the booth?" he asked.

"Well, I don't know about you, but I'm extremely drunk. And feeling very unsteady on my feet." She winked.

They waited ten minutes, but no one else showed up outside the booth. Verona had no way of knowing if Javier was the kind of man who preferred a quick fuck bent over a table, or if he'd luxuriate in the moment. In either case, in her experience, ten minutes was usually an adequate amount of time.

"Let's do it," she said.

Henry nodded, and they danced toward Javier's booth. Verona took out her phone and started recording, leaving it hanging loosely at her side. They gave each other a meaningful glance, and he spun her wildly out. She stumbled on her high heels, and they pretended to lose hold of each other. Verona helped the momentum along with a few extra fake drunken stumbles and spun off-balance toward the booth.

The burly bouncer saw it happening a second too late. She crashed right through the curtain, bracing herself on the table. She held her phone up as she pushed herself up off the table. Behind the table was another set of velvet curtains, held hanging open to reveal a bed.

Verona had seen a lot of things in her private dick career, but she hadn't been expecting what greeted her behind those curtains.

"Oh my God, I'm, like, so sorry." She put a hand to her mouth to hold in a fake retch.

Two beefy arms reached into the curtain and grabbed her by her waist. The bouncer yanked her out unceremoniously and placed her on the dance floor on wobbly legs. Henry was waiting to collect her.

The bouncer looked grim and spoke to Henry as if Verona was an annoying dog at an off-leash park. "Sir, if you can't keep control of her, please don't bring her. Or neither of you will be welcome back."

Henry apologized profusely, passed over a few bills to pay for the next hour for the patrons in the booth, and assured the bouncer he was taking her home right away.

When they got to the sanctuary of Henry's car, he asked, "Did you get it?"

Verona guzzled a bottle of water, confusion and disappointment making her feel unreasonably angry. "No. I got fucking nothing." She reached down and pulled the shoes off her feet, exhaling in pain as some of the inflamed skin tore as the straps dragged off. "Ow! Motherfucker!"

Henry reached into his back seat and came back with a pair of white tennis shoes. "They'll be a bit big, but even a diva needs a pair of comfies once in a while." He smiled. "But if you tell anyone, I'll disown you."

Verona took the shoes between her fingers and thumb and rested them on her lap as she threw her head back into the headrest. "All of this. For nothing."

Henry put the car in gear to begin driving her home. "What was he doing in there?"

She put the shoes on, her feet sliding into the pillowy soles with palpable relief. "He was with another man."

Henry raised an eyebrow. "Well, I don't know much about these things, but I'd say infidelity is infidelity, no matter the sex of the partner."

She shook her head, yanking at her skirt in a futile battle to bring it down far enough that she could sit without her thighs glued together. "No, not *with* another man. Just with another man. Sitting having whiskies. There wasn't even a skank in the back waiting to be shared. Just two guys in suits with whiskies."

Henry hummed in thought.

"I'm sorry, Henry. I'm not usually such an inconsolable bitch. This is just fucking frustrating. This was my one chance to catch him. Now what am I going to do?"

"Well, a better question might be, why did he feel the need to meet with this man in the secrecy of a sex club?"

Verona was suddenly still in her body and mind. "Fuck, Henry, you're good. I may need to hire you again sometime."

He smiled. "It was fun. But how often can one use an undercover drag queen?" He mimed pushing long locks off his shoulder, beauty-queen style.

"Well, you may have to be willing to work in your suit and tie again instead of a dress. But you never know, times are changing. A guy in a dress might be necessary now and then."

Henry cocked an eyebrow. "Honey, a guy in a dress is *always* necessary."

9

BIGGEST DICK IN TOWN

Calgary
Saturday 8 a.m.

Verona slept the wretched sleep of the discontented. Between a failed undercover operation and a failed date with Quentin the night before that, there were a lot of negative emotions and unfulfilled desires fighting for elbow room in her mind.

She didn't kid herself that she'd have another chance with Quentin anytime soon. He was the kind of guy who didn't have to wait around to see if things would pan out. You got your one chance, and if that didn't work, he was on to the next thing.

Must be nice, you fucker!

At some point, she became aware of a chiming intruding on her unconsciousness. Her head pounded, and sweat plastered her hair to her forehead. She rolled over and saw the illuminated screen of her phone. Her eyes were bleary with sleep, so it took a few moments for her to focus.

First, she made out the giant time display: 8:00 a.m. Then as she looked muzzily at the screen, she saw the name of the caller: Quentin.

"Hello?" Her morning voice cracked with dryness. Her neck was so stiff, she couldn't move it properly and had to ease herself into a seated position.

"Rough night?" Quentin sounded as chipper as usual.

Verona cleared her throat. "You could say that."

There was another reason why Verona had slept so poorly—adrenaline. As Henry had driven her home, she'd become aware of headlights behind them. There weren't a lot of cars on the street at that time of night, and those headlights stuck with them all the way into her parking lot.

Henry didn't seem to notice, and she didn't want to worry him, but she was glad that he'd dropped her right at her door and watched to make sure she got in safely before driving away. The black SUV remained parked in the lot for five minutes before driving away.

They had been following her. And they were either very bad at it, or they wanted her to know it. She guessed the latter. The question was, were they Javier's men or the other guy's? She put Quentin on speakerphone so she could text the video she took to Runi. If anyone could find out who a guy was just from video footage, it was Runi. Well, also the FBI, but as she didn't have them in her contact list, Runi would have to do.

"I was expecting you might send me an update when you were done last night," he said with a smile in his voice.

He had no way of knowing how much that statement would irk her. Rubbing her failure in her face while going back to acting like they were just friends. Like nothing had happened between them. Even though nothing *had* happened, the almost was a shadow between them he was choosing to ignore.

"Well, I would've if I had something to share." Her tone was unenthused, and she did nothing to hide it.

Quentin seemed surprised she didn't have any witty riposte. "Uh, right. That sucks. What happened?"

Verona's head throbbed with every heartbeat, and her tongue stuck to the roof of her mouth. She was tired of flirting and being charming to a man who wasn't into her. "I got nothing."

Silence. Then, "Everything okay?"

"Other than my failure? Sure, you just woke me up."

"Right. Sorry. Well, I'd still take the story if you want to tell it. I've been dying to know how your night with Henry went." His teasing tone took on a hint of hesitation due to her frosty responses. He went tender on her. "Who knows, maybe I can help? I did get you a partner for this secret sex club thing after all."

The tenderness was like the fizzing sting of the hydrogen peroxide the school nurse insisted went on every damn cut she ever got. She wanted it more than anything, her reaction to Henry last night was proof of it, but she didn't want it from a *friend*.

She swung her feet over the side of the bed, thinking about putting on a pot of coffee to help clear the fuzz and pettiness from her brain. She relished the feeling of the cool floor on her feet; it was like a balm to her flushed skin.

Her apartment was small and basic but bright and new. Pale gray laminate flooring ran throughout, with clean white walls. The kitchen had beech cabinets, deep gray countertops, and white tile with gray marbling. The main perks of the apartment were the walk-out balcony, the windows on three sides, and the ten-minute walk to the office.

She put on the coffeepot and took down her favorite red mug, the words on it facing out to the world. It read BIGGEST DICK IN TOWN and was a gift from Runi. She tried to soften her manner. It wasn't anyone's fault things hadn't worked out at the drag show. She didn't need to punish him for that.

She walked him through the infiltration, the entrance of Javier, and his strange choice to leave the mistress at the bar instead of taking her with him to the booth. The coffeepot made its last strangled noises of birth, and she poured a cup, inhaling the steam as she added milk and sugar.

"Wait, so he was meeting *another* woman there? How is this a bad thing? It's a twofer! Double cheating."

"It would be, except it was a man." She took her coffee to the balcony. At least during the summer, she could enjoy the sun and fresh air after being woken up too early. In the winter, she'd just cocoon and languish in bed.

Silence on the other end. As angry as she was about everything, it was fun to make Quentin imagine Javier in the throes of passion with another man. "So, he was...?"

"No, sorry I can't indulge that fantasy." *Fuck, there I go, sliding right back into the friend zone where he wants me.* "It was some kind of business meeting."

"In a sex club? The guy's a billionaire. One of his likely over-the-top boardrooms wouldn't suffice?"

She sipped her coffee, the warmth of the cup in her hands mimicking the warmth of the morning air on her skin.

"Must be something off-books."

Her phone buzzed with a text from Runi: *Don't mess with this guy. Black market pharmaceuticals. Tell you more later.*

A spike of adrenaline burst up her spine. Could the tail have been from Mr. Black Market instead of Javier? If she kept investigating, would she find a tie between the two? Or would she end up with a bullet in her skull? It should scare her, but deep as she searched, she couldn't find the fear. Perhaps it was all too hypothetical for now.

"Why would Javier be involved in something off-books? See previous statement about being a billionaire."

"Well, maybe not. All I know is there was another man and no hanky-panky." She decided on a whim not to fill Quentin in on the full details. If he knew the truth, he'd probably have a message similar to Runi's: Back off. But she didn't want to back off. This was still her case, and drug lord or no drug lord, she was going to close it.

Maybe to Quentin it seemed insane that Javier would be involved in illegal business, but to Verona it made complete sense. It was all tied in with the kind of man he was. It was the same reason he decided to get married and cheat on his wives. He didn't have to have a wife. He could easily remain single and sleep around like the horn dog he was. But he *liked* the idea of cheating on a wife. Of trying to get away with it. Of *knowing* he'd get away with it. He felt invincible. Money tends to do that to people, and the men at the top rarely go down.

And if this guy was into pharmaceuticals? So many countries had tight regulations on bringing in narcotics and amphetamines. She'd learned that when Runi's husband, Ash, had to go on a different ADHD medication to accompany her to Korea. The illegal trade of those drugs was big in many of the countries, but often with tainted supply. With Javier's clean supply and this other guy's distribution? They'd be rolling in the tax-free dollars. She could almost hear the waves on the beach of their offshore bank accounts.

She heard a muffled voice in the background on Quentin's end, and she heard him open and close a sliding door. Likely he'd gone to his balcony as well. But who was the mystery person? Had he been fucking that hottie from the drag show while she was busting her ass in blister-inducing high heels? This day was just getting better and better.

"So, you're saying the case is still open, then?"

A bit of her frost came back as she imagined the gorgeous woman waiting to have breakfast with Quentin inside his apartment. "Yeah. Don't worry, I won't be licking my wounds for long. I'm already working on a new plan to catch him."

It was a lie. She had no idea what her next move would be, but if he had some hot little thing there, she needed him to imagine her on top of her game, not cowering in the corner.

"Well, that might prove a bit tricky."

"Of course it'll be tricky. That's why Miami hired me to begin with."

"No, I mean, because Javier isn't here anymore. He's left the country."

"What?" She sat up straighter and was rewarded with a sharp pain from her neck to her shoulders. She massaged the spot to calm the spasm.

"Yup, apparently he's gone to Greece for at least a few weeks. Maybe longer. I assumed it was because you caught him with his woman and he needed time to make a plan."

She had caught him, not with a woman, but with a drug lord. Was that the reason he left? Was he afraid she was an undercover agent? Was that why she was followed?

"But good news!"

"What's good news?"

"I got Miami to hold you on a retainer. You know, like a lawyer."

"You did?"

"Of course. I'm looking out for you. So when he gets back, you'll have plenty of time to put your new plan in action."

"Thanks." Verona was grateful to Quentin, but he was talking to her now as if she were an employee he'd arranged a bonus for instead of a devastatingly interesting woman he wanted to ravish.

"Verona?" he asked, his voice tinged with significance.

"Yeah?"

"About the other night—"

"Forget it," she said. She was in no mood for the soft letdown, the "let's not mess up what we have" speech, or the "I hope we can still be friends" bullshit. Everyone said that stuff like it would soften the blow, but it never did. The message was clear: "I'm not interested." Might as well just say it.

He paused. "Right, yeah. Forget it. That's what I was going to say."

Had he been about to say something else? She'd never know. The moment was gone.

"Well"—she went back inside to the kitchen—"thanks again for getting me the extra money. I think I'm going to try to get a bit more sleep." For the first time she could remember, she was lying to get him off the phone instead of trying to prolong their chat.

"Sure. Sorry to wake you."

She hung up the phone and rested her head against the wall. Friend zone confirmed.

PART II

WHAT HAPPENS IN GREECE...

10

REMEMBER THE COUPLE FROM THE PROLOGUE?

Mykonos, Greece
Monday 7:30 p.m.

Blair Grayson sat on the patio of the Mykonos Muse Hotel, a raised gray stone balcony dotted with white tables with bright blue umbrellas facing the sea. Behind her, the rest of the hotel perched up into the rocky hills, its white plaster with blue trim traditional and iconic for the area.

A waiter deposited a refreshing pink lemonade by her elbow, and she took a small sip. The drink was the perfect mixture of tart and sweet, and the condensation on the glass sparkled and glistened in the setting sun. A college English major could write a whole poem about the beauty of the way the light refracted the orange and red of the sunset and mingled with the pink liquid.

She lifted the glass, took a sip, then shook the condensation off her hand, spoiling the lovely poem and striking deep regret into the heart of the poet but leaving her feeling rather satisfied and content.

Only an idiot college kid[1] stares at the condensation on the glass when

1. I apologize if you are an idiot college kid...sorry, a college kid. Remember, these are the thoughts of the character and in no way represent the views of the author. Extra apologies if

they could be enjoying the drink and staring at the actual sunset. The sun, being a blazing ball of red fire, was sending out rays and ripples of colors bleeding from red to orange to yellow and vibrant pink in the vivid blue sky.

From her view on the patio, the light of the sun somehow appeared more golden than anywhere else in the world, the intense blue of the Aegean Sea bluer than any other sea in the world.

Blair was in The Perfect Moment, suspended from time itself, a little bubble of unreality and harmony. She tried not to think of the perfection of the moment, aware the tiniest disruption would cause her to lose it forever.

"Pardon me?" said a soft British voice.

Blair cringed at the disruption. Time got off its lazy ass and started marching along once more. The serenity and certainty that all was well with the world evaporated like the end of an intense morphine high. There was no point trying to recapture the moment by pretending she hadn't heard the man; she knew from experience that once it was gone, there was no way of getting it back.

She didn't bother to answer him but swivelled around to grant him her attention. She was pleased to find he was handsome: he stood about five foot ten, had a lean build, well-groomed sandy blond hair, and greenish-brown eyes. He was fair with a light tan moving to freckles here and there. He wore a blue chambray shirt and gray linen pants that fit in a casual yet sleek way.

"Sorry," he said, "but would you mind terribly if I joined you for, oh, say, ten minutes or so? Or until you finish your drink? Whichever comes first?"

Blair considered this. She wanted to enjoy the sunset alone, was relishing the time relaxing with nobody's company but her own. She was, after all, very good company. Then again, an unexpected, charming distraction wasn't something to dismiss too quickly.

"Are you trying to do a speed dating thing here?" She wasn't about to make this easy for the poor sap.

"Dear God, no. Those ghastly timers and prearranged questions? They

---

you are an English major. But you'll probably work your feelings out in some very deep and brooding poem, so you'll be fine.

can be terribly awkward...or so I hear." He let the full weight of his charming smile fall upon her.

Or was the smile merely charming because of the accent? It was hard to tell. That was the problem with accents; he could say, "I just murdered a baby and ate its intestines raw," give a little wink and a wide Ewan McGregor smile, and everyone would chuckle and think, "How absolutely charming."

The thing with guys with accents was you had to reserve judgement. Likely why speed dating hadn't worked out for him.

He dropped his overt charm and went for sincerity. "Look, have you ever felt the need to sit with another human being...if only just for a few minutes?"

"No, actually. Sitting with humans is not something I usually crave."

"An introvert? Cheers! Me too. That's why I'm trying to leave all of the power on your side of the table, as it were."

Blair raised an eyebrow that said, "Convince me."

"Ten minutes or until you finish your drink. I mean, if I'm not a terrible lout, you could *sip* your drink. And if I am the most annoying arse you've ever met, you could, er, chug. And then I'd be forced to leave or else expose myself as a bald-faced liar."

It wasn't the worst proposition Blair had ever received. If he was trolling for sex, it was a very soft approach, so perhaps he had something else in mind. She inclined her head to an empty seat as if to say, "Permission granted. Don't fuck with me."

"Cheers," he said, taking a seat. "I'm Zane."

"Oh." Blair took a hefty gulp of her languishing lemonade. "Just don't fucking tell me that's spelled with a *y*." She held her drink up in a threatening manner.

"Actually," said Zane, very matter-of-fact-Discovery-Channel-narrator-this-is-how-they-mate-it-isn't-horrifying-it's-quite-normal, "it is spelled with two *y*'s and a silent *h*: Z-a-y-y-n-h-e." He had the kind of straight-faced, dry wit only a Brit knows how to deliver to its full and glorious extent.

A passing waiter stopped, and Zane ordered a pint.

"You're fucking with me." Blair lowered her glass.

"Yes, of course I'm fucking with you. 'Zane' is pretentious enough without mucking it about further, isn't it? I mean, who names their kid Zane? Well, my parents did, but what the fuck were they thinking? I've asked them, but they claim it's a simple Hebrew name, much like Benjamin or Jacob. Yeah, sure—that's why I remember coloring pictures of Zane on a fishing boat with Peter and Andrew in Sunday school."

Blair tried to hide her amusement by tucking a stray piece of hair behind her ear. The wind immediately blew it back out, tickling her cheek. "Well, I've got the name of the mean but pretty blond girl in everyone's high school. You know, she's either a cheerleader or the captain of the field hockey team. Perhaps both." She made rah-rah pompom-wielding hand motions, then feigned throwing up.

The waiter deposited Zane's drink, and he took a grateful pull before responding. "Hmm, okay." He took a moment to think. "So your name is something like Ashley or Amber or Taylor."

"All good guesses, but no, my parents were also a bit more original: Blair."

Zane nodded as if the pieces were falling into place. "That *is* a mean-girl name. And every school has one. I had one in my boarding school too. Except, of course, it was an all-boys school, so the mean girl was a gay boy by the name of Sebastian. And come to think of it, he *was* captain of the field hockey team."

"Really?"

Zane's eyes sparkled with mirth like a kid who just discovered knock-knock jokes. "No. No, I'm taking the piss again, but that never gets old!"

She didn't mind him taking a swing at teasing her. She could give as good as she got. "Am I missing something here?" She waved the waiter down for another drink.

Zane rested his chin on his palm. "It's just that if you say certain things with a British accent, people just accept it. I reckon most people in the world believe *all* Brits attend boarding school."

"Well, that's not fair. I don't know you. How am I supposed to know if you went to boarding school or not? I mean, plenty of people do go to boarding school."

"You reckon? You don't think people are just ignorant of British culture and believe that I eat scones and tea every day, play cricket, and attended boarding school?"

"Well, now that you mention it," said Blair, "I was thinking you looked like a cricket player."

"You see?" Zane pointed to her as if she proved every theorem ever. "And it's 'cricketer.'"

"Fascinating," Blair said. "Do you charm all the ladies this way?"

"It's not my fault you said it wrong."

She liked that he didn't back down when she insulted him. He'd be a hard deck of cards to collapse, and there was nothing sexier to her. "But if we're going to keep chatting, I think it's important to note at this juncture, that although I have a mean-girl name, I was not, and am not, a mean girl. Or a cheerleader." Blair held her hand over her old drink to prevent the waiter from taking it away when he deposited the new one.

"But I did actually have a mean girl at my school," said Zane in a distant voice. "She was popular and unforgivably mean. Her name was Miranda, and last I heard, she was still maddeningly delicious. And rich. She likely clubs baby seals in her spare time. But I'm not bitter and resentful that she told the whole school I had trouble performing sexually."

"She did that?" Blair laughed. It was the kind of thing she might've done. But only to someone who deserved it. Hence, not a mean girl.

"Yes." Zane sighed. "Which is not true," he added quickly, in case that was in question. "But she was very upset that the prime alpha jock turned her down because he wanted little ol' *moi*." Zane fluttered his eyelashes like a beauty contestant making up for a shortage of breasts.

"And you're proud of that?" Everything he said made her want to smile or laugh. He was doing well, but he didn't need to know that yet.

Zane leaned back and looked off into the distance, remembering. "He was the most popular boy at school: six-pack, tan, pecs like soup bowls. Tall. Alpha male. *Anybody* would be flattered they were his number one pick."

Blair shook her head.

"Come on—it's flattering when the beautiful people want you, even when you're not playing for their team."

"Okay, so here's the big question, then—"

"Not gay. Me 'n' Seb were just friends!"

"You said Sebastian wasn't real!"

"Right!" Zane threw his hands up in defeat. "This is why they say, when you're making up stories, stick close to the truth."

"It's good advice for people like *you* who are fucking terrible at it, yes. But the real question is"—Blair leaned in conspiratorially—"what was the name of the alpha jock who thought you were so cute, he wanted to hold you all night long and brush your hair and whisper in your ear that you were his precious unicorn?"

"Brock," said Zane flatly. "But when you say all that stuff about hair and unicorns, it makes it sound weird."

"Riiiiight." Blair traced the arc of the word in the air with her eyes. "Because it was normal before."

The setting sun illuminated his freckles, making him seem extra boyishly rogue. She tried not to stare, but found herself being drawn back to his gaze. It was refreshing to talk to someone who had a quick and dry wit like Zane.

"I guess your pretty girl wasn't as hot as Brock was," Zane said.

"If you're going to keep talking about Brock and his dick, you can leave." It was a threat she hoped he didn't take. It was a rare man that had her wanting him to stay longer.

"I don't think I mentioned his dick. Never saw it. Probably miniscule."

The last rays of the sun glittered off the sea as its fiery orb rested on the horizon. Soft lights along the walls lit up the patio, casting a pleasing and gentle glow. Blair's second drink was half empty, and Zane had finished his pint. It was the time when saying goodnight would be easy.

Zane seemed to sense this and made his move. "You wanna get out of here? Go someplace new?" His voice was low, husky, inviting, and he stared right into her eyes, inviting her in.

Blair did, very much. But that would mean she'd probably end up fucking him, and as good as that would be for the travel article she was writing, she wasn't in the mood for a one-night stand. She'd left enough of those littered in her early days at the magazine in her twenties.

She looked at his forearms, his shoulders, his chest and could almost feel what it would be like to have his body pressed against her. Tight and fierce, banging against a wall, or soft and secure, delicately cradling her into a bed.

"I've been all over this island. And my drink's gone." She gave him a soft smile to let him down a bit easier.

"I know one place you've never been," he said, resting his fingers gently on her wrist.

Goose bumps flared up her arm, and she suppressed a sigh of pleasure. *No. Not tonight.* Being responsible fucking sucked. She moved her hand away gently and left the table without another word. She didn't trust herself to speak, or she might change her mind and straddle him right there on the patio.

11

A TRAGEDY AND STUFF

Calgary
Monday 11 a.m.

"This is a crucial time for us," Quentin said from behind the protective barrier of his desk.

Not that he usually thought of the desk as protection, but today it was serving that purpose against Miami's overt and inviting sexuality. She perched on the edge of her seat, leaning so far forward onto the desk that he wondered how she didn't fall off. Her breathtaking cleavage was on full display, and greater men than Quentin had tried and failed to resist its tractor beam–like pull.

He wondered, briefly, if he should institute some kind of new rule, the Miami Rule, for insanely sexy clients. He had no idea what the rule would entail, but for now it involved some kind of mandatory choir gown all clients must wear upon entering. He knew it was insane, and fucking sexist, but you could cut the sexual tension in his office with a knife. It would have to be sharp enough to cleave a head off with one stroke, though. Maybe a katana.

"You didn't return my text the other night," she pouted.

"Javier has gone out of town," he said as if she hadn't spoken. "I'm not sure if it's just a business trip, or if he's trying to clear out to catch you cheating, but you have to be careful."

"I waited all night. In the hot tub. Thinking of you." She got up from her chair and walked around his desk, dragging a finger along the surface until she was on the same side as him.

So much for that protective barrier.

She sat down on top of his desk, her smooth, tanned thighs inches from his left hand, the toe of her high-heeled foot searching for purchase on the arm of his chair. He moved to let her find her footrest instead of insisting she get off and go back to her seat. She gazed into his eyes unabashedly, the pout gone, replaced with the kind of soft smile he associated with an invitation to kiss.

A weaker man would cave. A stronger man would shut it down. Since he found himself somewhere in the middle, he had no choice but to press on like an idiot. "If I were Javier's lawyer, I'd advise him to get out of town and make plenty of room for you to screw up. Then I'd hire someone to keep an eye on you and get the evidence. If I can think of it, you can bet they have."

"Will *you* be keeping an eye on me, then?" She leaned to her left, resting her palm on the desk right in front of him.

His mind knew this script. This was when he could throw everything off his desk and find himself pressed between her thighs, the two of them so eager to give into their passion that they'd find themself climaxing before they'd even fully undressed.

She moved her foot from his armrest to the edge of his seat. He could run his hand up her leg to her thigh, right up under her skirt—

His right hand twitched toward his intercom. He could buzz Nora, tell her to take the afternoon off, cancel his appointments. There was no ambiguity here, Miami wanted him, and as much as he tried to tell himself no, the image of her splayed across his desk would not leave him. He reached for the button.

But she's still a client.

Some great lawyer he'd be if *he* were the one to screw up her infidelity clause. Sure, no one would know, but *he* would know.

Now, how the fuck do I get myself out of this one?

He reached to the right, away from Miami, and opened a drawer of his filing cabinet. He didn't need anything in the cabinet, but he needed the drawer. He opened it, put a few of his fingers inside, and slammed it.

The pain was instant and sharp, then throbbing with each heartbeat. It hurt like hell. It was perfect.

Miami barely reacted to his accident but did say, "Put some ice on that or you're gonna swell up."

"Uh, thanks," he said. He wasn't expecting first aid advice from her. True, it was basic, but it was the first time she'd offered him anything other than seduction. He got up under the guise of needing to shake his hand out a bit and walked around to the other side of the desk.

She slid off the edge of his desk, and he was worried she was going to follow him, but instead she sat down in his chair.

"So, I guess I'll go ask Nora for some ice." He shrugged his shoulder toward his door. *Why am I asking for permission to leave my own damn office?*

Miami sighed as she stood. "It seems like something's always getting in the way of our love story. Like Bella and Edward."

He was too relieved that he'd dug himself out of certain career-jeopardizing trouble to care that she was expecting him, a man in his thirties, to know the intricacies of *The Twilight Saga*. "Or Romeo and Juliet," he laughed.

But Miami stopped him before they got to the door. "Romeo and Juliet is not a love story. It's, like, a tragedy and stuff." She swept past him to the lobby.

He watched her go, his concept of reality feeling more and more like his throbbing fingers. *Did I just get corrected on Shakespeare by a woman who doesn't even know what a prenup is?*

Mykonos
Tuesday 12 p.m.

Zane's flight had been delayed by several hours, and he found himself standing aimlessly outside the hotel, wondering how to fill the time. He'd seen all the tourist locations he was interested in, had basked on the beach, and gotten drunk with the locals. Now he was in a no-man's-land of empty time, made worse because there *was* something he wanted to do, but he had no way of making it happen: seeing Blair again.

The delayed flight was a gift on a platter from whoever ran life, the universe, and everything.[1] Someone was saying, "See what we've done for you, you nutsack? Get after it, you knob. You were supposed to be gone, no chance to see her again, yet here you are, so do something about it, you fucktard. Man, this guy is as useless as tits on a bull!"

He wasn't sure why the power in charge was so rude about it, but he supposed he deserved it since he was standing there drawing little spirals in the sand with his toes instead of doing anything proactive.

But as rude as they were, whoever was out there had his back, because as he was considering going back to his room, a firm voice called out, "Zane."

He raised his head to see Blair waving to him, and even he, useless as he was, couldn't ignore that kind of push. He walked over to her, grinning.

She was every bit as gorgeous as she had been the night before. All long, tanned limbs, dazzling blue eyes, and understated sex appeal. She wore a flared white dress with red flower designs that exposed a hint of cleavage. Her dark hair was pinned up under a straw sun hat.

"What are you doing out here, looking all guilty and bashful?" she asked.

"Was I?" Hope unfurled in his stomach, and his fingers slipped against the sweat on his palms. He'd got his second chance, now all he had to do was not mess it up. She'd turned his offer of more down the night before, but here she was, seeking him out.

"You were."

"Hmm, well, did I look so pathetically adorable that you took pity on me?" He gave her a pathetically adorable smile.

She crossed her arms. "No, I don't go in for pathetic. You looked, well, like I said, guilty. Bashful."

---

1. We don't know exactly who runs it, but we do know that the answer to the question is forty-two. If that makes no sense, you've got some reading to do.

He switched his smile to what he hoped was less pathetic and more bashful. "Ah, well, I was raised in a religious home. And that generally means there is always something to be feeling guilty about. Easy default, I'm afraid."

"Sure," said Blair. "That's fucked up."

"Maybe. I was supposed to be flying out this morning, but my flight was delayed. So I've got some extra time and no plans." He spread his hands out, palms skyward.

She shrugged her right shoulder. "Well, that's easy. You're coming to lunch with me."

"I am?" Zane felt like a small hook was trying to tug his stomach into his chest cavity. For some sick and twisted reason, he liked it.

"Yes, you are. Aboard the *Kalloni*."

Hope fell from his stomach as if he were a boy who has been promised candy and puppies, only to realize that he will have to climb into a dark van with a bearded guy to get them. "Erm, uh..." The *Kalloni* had a very amazing, very unique, and very *expensive* gourmet restaurant on board.

"My treat!"

"Cheers," Zane said, recovering his joviality and wondering what kind of jackpot he had hit to find a beautiful, crass, and wealthy woman who didn't have any hang-ups about paying for dates.

The boat was only a short walk away, and as they passed through the lazy streets, Zane checked the mental notes his dad had given him on impressing a lady. They all seemed to hinge on what side of the sidewalk you took to keep her feet dry. Useless.

"Love the hat," he said. "Very old Hollywood. Like Hepburn or Loren."

"Every traveler needs a good sun hat. Where's yours?"

He gave an inward fist pump. He'd managed to say something to her that she didn't immediately throw back at him. He loved that about her, but if he was going to actually get somewhere with her, he needed to break through a bit. Sun hats were a good start. "I'm afraid we don't have much use for them in London."

"But you're not in London, you're in Greece. You don't pack for where you were, you pack for where you want to be."

"Well, maybe if I looked as devastating as you do in yours, I'd remember to pack it."

She had no answer to that, but he thought he saw a smile under the brim of her hat.

The *Kalloni* docked at the end of a pier, and it was watched over by a maître d' in traditional Greek attire including a baggy white tunic, a red sash, and a skirt. With his deep olive complexion, black hair, and friendly light brown eyes, he looked as though he belonged on the cover of an erotic novel called *The Greek Position*, except then he'd most certainly be sans shirt.

The maître d' and Blair exchanged a few sentences in Greek, and Zane could see that the man was impressed by her use of the language. Zane was impressed too. Was there no end to Blair's allure?

Was he wrong, or was the maître d' giving Blair a slightly flirty glance? Zane was glad the bronzed statue of a man would not be coming along to compete with his freckled English skin and comparatively tiny, tiny, tiny pecs. *I mean*, he thought, *what does a man need pecs like that for, anyhow? Bloody useless.* He stared back at the man a few times on the way to the boat to make sure he and his pecs stayed put.

When they were out of earshot, Zane asked, "You speak Greek?"

"Conversational. I'm not fluent," she said, as if everyone could pick up a second language in a few days if they only applied themselves.

He wasn't about to let a chance to flatter her slip by. "Still, it's—"

She stopped. "Do not make an 'it's all Greek to me' joke, or I'll tie bricks to your shoes and throw you the fuck overboard."

"Is that something people say?" He feigned naïveté. "I was going to say that it doesn't seem like it'd be an easy language to pick up." Okay, they were back to threats of physical violence. At least she wanted to be physical with him. All he had to do was change that violence to passion.

"Unlike you, who I have had absolutely *no* trouble picking up." Blair turned away as she stepped onto the boat.

He gave a shocked laugh at her overt chat-up line, took a deep breath, and followed. Maybe that switch wouldn't be as hard to flip as he thought.

The boat was done up to look like a trireme, but with modern upgrades negating the need for hundreds of slaves to propel it. It had billowing blue-

and-white sails, and the sun gleamed off the polished wood. The tables were spaced generously to allow for intimacy, but in a way that facilitated the fullness of the scenery and sunlight to be appreciated.

Zane and Blair were seated by a young man, also in traditional dress but just reaching the ability to shave, and thus less of a hindrance to Zane's romantic prospects than the maître d'.

Wine was brought over, as well as a plate full of colorful and aromatic meze and steaming herbed bread. Zane had no idea what anything was, but it didn't matter because it tasted so good, he couldn't believe it. It was voodoo-witchcraft-deal-with-the-devil kind of good.

Their waiter, a middle-aged man named Evangelos, never brought them menus, but Zane hardly noticed. The restaurant prided itself on tailoring meals to the individual, which meant their waiter deftly and unobtrusively discerned their wants and communicated them to the chef. It was the most effortless dining experience around, which meant lots of time for basking in the Mediterranean glow, or romancing your date.

Blair chose to bask in the glow, and Zane opted to attempt romance. Composing a sonnet would be too much for a first date, and his only experience with poetry was in the dirty limerick category: "There was a fine lady whose name was Blair, she liked to wear crotchless underwear..." No, that wouldn't do.

"So," said Blair, the glow of the sun making her skin shine with little iridescent patches, "what brought you to Greece?"

Thank God, thought Zane, *she didn't ask me what I do for a living*. That was the most banal and predictable conversational thread, and her avoiding it felt like a good omen. "I'd like to say I came here for some enlightened reason. But the truth is, I came here because, well, it's fucking Greece, ain't it?"

"All right, then." She raised her glass. "To fucking Greece!"

They clinked glasses, drank, and sat for a minute smiling at each other like little kids sharing a joke with the punchline "booger."

There was a tightness in Zane's groin that made him glad he was seated as he looked at the stunning woman sitting across from him. But he also wanted to hear her life story and hold her hand while the sun set. Nothing more, just hold her hand.

"And you?" Zane managed to ask. "What brings you to Greece?"

Blair took a few bites of the meze, in no rush to answer the question. Greece wasn't about rushing through pleasures; nor was it about being overly polite or courteous. It was more about letting each moment have its place.

"I'm a travel writer," she said. "I was hoping to keep that one under my hat for a while so you'd think I was hot shit to take you out to lunch on the *Kalloni*. But there it is. I work for *Tieri* magazine."

"So you get to travel for a living? I didn't think that was a real job anymore. I reckoned it'd be more freelance, or the travel agencies would have all the business."

"Well, sure, the basic traveler will look to an agency for their details, but this magazine is tailored to high-class travel. They want to know where the best places are. They want insider tips. Hence the *Kalloni*."

He stared wide-eyed at Blair. "I'm so fucking jealous." He hoped she wouldn't take it the wrong way, but figured even if she did, the worst he'd be in for would be one of her creative threats. And he kind of liked those.

She laughed softly. "Yes, most people are. They don't usually say it. I like that you said it." She paused and stared at him as if he were a fly caught in her web and she was considering if he was juicy enough to eat. It wasn't an altogether unpleasant look.

She said, "But I worked fucking hard to get this job. Not just in journalism either. I can speak seven languages."

"Seven?"

"Yeah, well, I'm only fluent in five, but I'm getting there with the last two. English, Spanish, French, Italian, and German are all fluent. I'm working on my Portuguese, and I've got a pretty good handle on Greek too, even though they're not in the same family."

"You're amazing." This got a little smile from her again.

She lazily moved some of the food on her plate around with her fork. "Apparently, some people have an aptitude for languages. I'm one of them."

"So I guess that's why you've got the dream job, then."

"Partly, but you also have to enjoy traveling alone. Which I do. Apparently you do too? Unless you just happened to come here to kill your wife overseas so the evidence can't follow you home?"

The waiter delivered the main course, and there was a slight conversational lull while Blair and Zane tasted their first bites. The flavors melded together into a perfect taste that hit Zane's palate with such an explosion of sapidity he had to close his eyes to appreciate it. Blair did the same.

"Oh, fuck me!" she said.

"Dear seventy virgins waiting in heaven!" Zane added.

"What?" She opened one eye, appraising him.

"You've never heard that one?" he asked, giving her one eye back.

"Never mind." She closed her eyes again. "This food is too good for you to be fucking with me right now."

"But you just said, 'Fuck me.' You didn't mean it?" If he didn't have any talents to impress her, he could at least keep her interested with his cheek.

"Shut up and eat."

They both shut up and ate, enjoying the silence, the sun, the wine, and the food.

"So, then," said Zane when only a few bites remained, "you want to know the real reason I'm traveling alone? Like am I so repulsive, I have no friends who want to travel with me? Or do I even have friends? Or am I one of those traveling perverts who does their dirty deeds away from home?"

The waiter dropped by in time to catch the bit about the dirty pervert. He lifted a single eyebrow as he deposited the desserts.

"Something like that, yes," she said. "Or you could have, you know, a normal reason for traveling alone. Like I do." She put down her fork and looked him in the eyes. Really looked for the first time, without appraisal, without her vicious tongue waiting to unleash on him.

"Ohhhh, one of those!" he said as if the thought had never occurred to him. *Okay, don't fuck this up.* "I guess I just thought there is so much beauty in this world, I have to start seeing it. On my deathbed, I don't want to regret the places I didn't go." He rested his hand on hers briefly. "Or the people I didn't meet."

He expected she might have a retort to that, another deflection to keep him from getting too close.

Instead she turned her hand over, so they were palm to palm. He caressed the small divot between the tendons of her wrist, enjoying how she seemed to relax into the gesture, like it was something they'd done hundreds of times.

"That's some sweet bullshit right there."

They pulled their hands apart so they could get to the dessert, but she rested her leg against his under the table.

The dessert, like every other part of the meal, was full of flavor combinations and textures that Zane had never experienced. Smooth mousse with sharp vanilla, deep chocolate, and some kind of spiciness that shouldn't belong but somehow worked.

"You know," she said after a few bites, "before this, I never understood it when people compared food to sex, but..."

"Oh, I know," he said. "I could be left alone with this dessert." *More like take the dessert to go so we can be alone together with it.*

"I don't need to be left alone with it," Blair said dreamily. "I don't care who watches."

Zane almost choked.

12

FOLLOWING ME FOLLOWING YOU

Calgary
Tuesday 10 a.m.

Verona cringed when she saw Quentin was calling her. After their little chat where she had been relegated to the friend zone, she imagined every conversation between them would now be overtly pleasant. And the fun of Quentin wasn't overt pleasantness. It was the thrill of the *maybe.*

But they were still working on the same case, so she had no choice but to answer. "Hi, Quentin," she said, trying to keep her tone the same as usual. Since she had wrapped up the case on Abbie and Clarence (it turned out Clarence *did* enjoy looking at the photos of his wife with another man), and she had the retainer from Miami, her workload wasn't as full as she was used to. She had one last case to tidy up before she could clear her schedule and focus on a new plan to catch Javier.

That case was Julia and Robin. Robin being the gal of interest in this one, suspected of nailing her yoga teacher. It sounded like a cliché, but Verona's experience had taught her that these clichés existed because they happened. A lot.

"I know you're probably still working the Javier angle, but I think we need you to pivot on this case a bit." He sounded like he was talking to a boardroom. Especially with the word "pivot."

"Yeah, just need him to come back so I can put my new plan in action." He'd just left for Greece; he'd likely be gone for at least a week. That was time enough to come up with a new plan. She hoped.

Thankfully, catching Robin with the petite redheaded yoga teacher didn't require Verona to actually take any yoga classes. There was a smoothie shop in the same building, which looked directly through the wall of windows into the studio.

She sipped on the sweet mixture of strawberries and bananas (no fucked-up names at this place), wishing for a drop of rum to put in it. If she had to endure a friendly chat with Quentin, she deserved it.

"Pivot to what? Javier's in Greece. Until he gets back, I'm coasting on that retainer." The air conditioning in the smoothie shop blasted against the back of her neck, making goose bumps flow over her skin like pimply waves. She pulled her hoodie up over her bare shoulders as Robin moved her mat to the front of the yoga class to be in prime place to see the teacher's ass when she did all those bendy poses.

"Yeah, it's precisely because Javier is in Greece that I need you."

In the past, she would've grabbed onto the line "I need you" as some idiotic double meaning, but even her pathetic fantasies had been ruined with the friend zone. The sun slanted through the windows of the studio, lighting up the hair of all the participants, making them all look like anime characters ready to unleash their special powers.

"Need me for what?" She didn't have the energy to play games with him. She just wanted to focus on the brain freeze, the way Robin exchanged a knowing smile with the teacher, the six-pack of the guy doing yoga without a shirt, and the black SUV waiting for her in the parking lot.

"Miami. I think Javier got out of town to tempt her into cheating. And I'm afraid she might end up doing it. I try to remind her of the money, and she usually perks up at that—"

—She seems plenty perky to me—

—"but my guess is he's hired his own people to watch her. Maybe even someone to encourage her to stray, make her believe that since he's gone, she can't be caught."

"So, what, you want me to babysit Miami? She's the one paying us, right? Won't she protest paying us to watch her?"

"I doubt she's looking at her invoices in that much detail. Or any detail." This little foray into the less professional was refreshing. Perhaps there was a way back for them after all. Even if it was just going back to banter. She could handle that.

Her hand was icy cold and slightly wet from holding the smoothie cup, and she brushed it off on her jean shorts. If she needed to start snapping pictures, she didn't want her touch ID to get in the way. "I don't care how much she pays me, I can't hang out with her. My brain will melt."

"No, don't worry. I don't mean you should hang out with her, just, I don't know. Keep an eye out. Maybe see if you can find out who's watching her. That way we could at least make sure she knows who to watch out for."

Well, if he was open to becoming playful again, there was one way to know for sure. Go right for the jugular. "You want me to double-dick this?"

Quentin sighed heavily. "What?"

"One private dick detecting another private dick? It's a double dick."

"Yeah, I'm pretty sure that's not what that means. Are you in?"

"I thought men hated that question." She smiled at her own joke, giving it enough pause for him to realize what she said. "What if there isn't another private dick out there?"

"Well, then we'll know that too."

Okay, so it wasn't completely the old them, but it had gone a hell of a lot better than she expected. She just wished she could say the same for her current cases.

Robin may or may not be fucking the yoga teacher, but Verona had watched the class five times now and not seen the two of them leave together. She'd followed Robin after class, and Robin had gone either to work or somewhere innocent, like a park. She'd have to start following her on non-class days as well. She'd assumed if Robin was getting it on with the teacher, they'd take advantage of being together at class to make that happen, but perhaps this was just an extended foreplay to a different conclusion on a different day.

As she returned to her car to tail Robin, she gave a moment's thought to the black SUV at the far end of the parking lot. Out of anyone, whoever was in that SUV probably understood her frustration.

After all, they'd been following her around since she'd come home with Henry, and the most interesting thing she'd done was trip over a curb. She should be concerned after what Runi told her about Kent Choi, the ruthless international drug supplier whom Javier was meeting with, but she still wasn't sure they were even Choi's men.

Even if they were, despite what Runi said, she didn't think she had anything to fear from them. Eventually they'd realize she was a nobody and move on. There had to be only so many times they could follow her following Robin from yoga to Bowness Park before they lost all semblance of sanity.

But she hadn't told Runi about the tail, because Runi would insist she drop the Javier case, and she was not going to do that.

No one bested Verona Montero. She was going to catch that man with his pants down or die trying.

Perhaps literally in the back of a black SUV. But hey, that's the life of a private dick.

Mykonos
Two days later

Tasoula Kyrkos began her shift as a housekeeper at the Mykonos Muse Hotel with a work ethic you only get from life experience. She was fifty-eight years old, mother of four children (one girl and three boys), and grandmother of ten so far. She'd been widowed at twenty-five, remarried at thirty, miscarried three times, bandaged up cuts, held together broken limbs, caught vomit in her hands, stayed up all night sitting by the toilet, brushed thousands of knots out of glossy, thick black hair, threatened girlfriends, scared off boyfriends, and worked her way to head manager of a prestigious bank. She had taken the job at the hotel for a little extra money after retiring from the bank. It was a low-key job that didn't involve copious interaction with the public, and they let her use the hotel's pool and beach with her grandkids.

Room 345 had displayed a Do not disturb sign for three days in a row. But today was checkout day, so she ignored the sign, knocked on the door, said, "Housekeeping," and walked boldly into the room to begin top-to-bottom cleaning. In her months at the hotel, she'd seen all manner of disgusting things left behind by hotel guests, but she wasn't fazed by any of them. Not the used condoms stuck to the bathroom ceiling, not the shocking splash of blood left in a tub, not the urine sprayed everywhere but in the toilet, not the shit-stained underwear left lying around, and not the odd-smelling, indecipherable blob of something left in the microwave. She waved her hand when the younger maids' gag reflexes set in and went to work.

So when she was greeted with the intense stench from the bloated dead body of Javier Luis Cavallero lying near the door, her only reaction was an exasperated but wholly resigned "Shit." She left the room, being sure not to touch anything, let the door fall shut, and called the police, all with the same calmness she'd use to order a pizza for dinner.

When the news of the body in room 345 made it to the rest of the staff, Lyra Xenakis felt a little bad for switching sections with Tasoula, but mostly she felt a great wave of relief. She hadn't found the body. She didn't have to deal with the police, with the mess, with the smells. She'd heard that there aren't many smells worse than a dead body, and she imagined the heat and humidity would only add to the bouquet.

For her part, Tasoula felt relieved she had switched routes with Lyra because she'd worked with the younger woman for a few months already and knew that the girl didn't have the constitution to handle it. There was something fragile about the younger maid, and Tasoula's mothering instincts led her to stretch out her protective wings to the girl and tell her, "Don't worry, my girl."

But Lyra wasn't worried. Not anymore. Still, it was kind of Tasoula, so she thanked her and accepted Tasoula's dinner invitation for that night with the entire family, grandkids and all. Tasoula made sure to tell Lyra that her son would be there, and that they were around the same age and probably would get on well.

Didn't all that sound lovely? Oh, except for the man in room 345. But he was dead, and life goes on for the living.

13

IT'S A DOUBLE DICK

Calgary
Thursday 8 a.m.

"I think I've got him," Verona said, her voice croaky with disuse.

She sat in her car down the laneway from the Cavallero residence. The lawn was strewn with bottles and lost jackets, and the help was out in force tidying things up. The sun had been up for several hours and lit up the sculpted topiaries to a brilliant, shining green. Birds took turns flying from tree to tree, with the crows claiming ultimate dominance over the robins, sparrows, and chickadees.

"You sure?" Quentin asked from the other end of the phone.

"Well, no, I'm not sure. That's why I said 'I think.'" Verona turned up her air conditioning against the blazing heat of the sun, which had turned her car into a greenhouse. Sweat stuck her shirt to her back and pooled between her breasts and in the crease of her stomach.

"Okay, so what good does that do me?"

"Not a lot, I guess, but I figured you'd want to know."

"Right. Why?"

Verona sighed. This kind of thing was to be expected. She had been sitting around in her car for the past two days waiting for *something* to happen. All the waiting around doing nothing naturally heightened her excitement at a possible success. Someone like Quentin, who had got on with life, wouldn't feel the same elation.

"Never mind, then." She tried to take her bug-eyed intensity down a notch for him. "Say I'm right—what's the play?"

"Hang on, aren't you going to fill me in at all?" Throwing her a bone.

"Well, someone like Miami doesn't exactly have friends, from what I can gather. Just people attracted to her money and all the booze in that house. And we were right to be concerned about her acting out now that Javier is away. She's thrown a raging party two nights in a row."

"Damn it!" Quentin exhaled. "I told her she needed to be careful."

"Yeah, well, I assume she thinks that means just no hanky-panky." Verona held her fingers in front of an air vent, the icy air following the line of her arm up to her damp armpits. "Anyhow, most of the partygoers were what you'd expect: young, loud, and brash upon entering, drunk, stumbling, and incoherent upon exiting. With so many coming and going, it was hard to see if the same people were at both parties, but there was one guy who stood out."

"Because he was the party clown?"

"Yes, actually. How did you guess?" She switched arms on the air vent, allowing her other side to get dry and cool.

"Seriously?"

"No. You fuck with me, I fuck with you." So here they were, back to the lighthearted jabs and talking about work. As far as friend zones went, this wasn't the worst. If any friend zone could be considered a hospitable place to remain.

She dug around in her stakeout bag for a drink to help clear the funk from her throat. The only thing left was a lukewarm bottle of water. Years of stakeout duty had rid her of any insistence on ideal beverage temperatures, so she unscrewed the cap and chugged.

Quentin said, "Okay, okay. Why did he stand out?"

"Well, first, he was fucking hot. Ridges and angles and bulges in all the right places."

"Sure. But not every hot guy is a private detective." He paused for effect. "Some of us are lawyers."

Was this him giving her permission to flirt a bit again? She wasn't sure if she was ready to go back down that road. So much effort for absolutely no gain. She chose to ignore it for now. "And second, he arrived to both parties early and left late. Sober. Almost the first guest to arrive and nearly the last to leave."

"Ah, you're thinking the kind of behavior of someone who's trying to hang around to witness something."

"Exactly. And third, dude dresses like a private dick."

"And how does one dress like a private detective?" His voice held a hint of a chuckle.

"Well, sort of like you'd imagine. Dress slacks, trench coat, fedora."

"Fedora? You're fucking with me again."

"Nope."

"Wow. That's...I don't even know what to do with that."

"Exactly. So what do you think?" Her stomach growled. She considered eating her last granola bar for breakfast, but after two days of stakeout food, she couldn't bring herself to do it. Besides, she'd spotted the other private dick, she deserved a proper breakfast. Maybe she should invite the guys from the SUV, they had to be just as hungry as she was. At least their car was still in the shade under a tree, unlike hers.

"I think you should make sure you're right, then snap his picture and send it to Miami. Tell her to not let him back on the property."

"Oh, I think I'll do more than that." Verona's voice was full of playful plotting. All of the time being cooped up had given her restless energy that she needed an outlet for.

"Why?"

"Fuck with him a bit. Let him know we're onto the scam."

"I guess so." Quentin didn't sound sure. "How are you going to confirm it's him?"

"Follow him when he leaves."

"And if you're wrong?"

"Then I suppose you'll need to have a chat with Miami about these parties, won't you?"

"In that case, Godspeed."

Verona felt a slight lift in her stomach. At least Quentin wasn't taking any excuse he could get to see Miami again.

Friday 5 a.m.

Verona felt like a teen emerging from the basement after a twenty-four-hour video game marathon. Five a.m. always felt that way; five a.m. was not meant for the living. It was made even worse because she had been up most of the night waiting for the private dick to leave the house.

She'd allowed herself a short nap during the early hours of the party, but somehow that had left her feeling even more tired. Naps were jerks like that, always taking more than they gave.

People began to spill out onto the lawn in a disjointed, ugly parade of drunkenness and dishevelment. Verona kept her eyes peeled for the man and got lucky almost at once. He was easy to spot because he didn't carry the same haziness from staying up all night that the other guests did, and he walked with the smooth stride of the sober.

A young woman with a diamond pendant sandwiched between her cleavage left the mansion a few steps behind him. She too was sober, her face tired and annoyed, but Verona had eyes only for the man.

He got into a gray Subaru Outback and pulled out. Verona followed him at a slight distance, not worrying she would get caught. As she had experienced many times in her career, she knew most people are too occupied with their radio, their phone, or with thinking about what they'll do once they get home to pay close attention to who's behind them.

She peeked in her own rearview mirror and saw her own tail following close behind. At this point, they had to know she knew she was being followed, so what was their end goal? To scare her off? It would take a lot more than that.

They arrived in an upscale neighborhood that had formerly been a Canadian Armed Forces barracks, and the dick pulled up in front of a row of modern townhouses, constructed in blocks of cement and gleaming glass. Verona whistled; this man was at a different level of PI work than she was, probably raking in the money since he was attached to whatever expensive lawyers Javier employed.

She watched him go into his house, waited a few minutes for him to get settled in, then approached the front door and gave it a light knock. He opened the door wearing nothing but sweatpants, and Verona inhaled sharply at the image he presented. Abs with so many ridges, her eyes got lost for a while, well-formed shoulders, biceps, and chest. A five o'clock shadow and shiny, thick auburn hair.

"Hello?" he said in a soft voice.

"Hi," she said, finding it hard to stand, speak, or think for a moment. She made her gaze leave his abs to find his eyes, but they were dark, sparkling, and entrancing, so it didn't help.

"Sorry to bother you so early," she said, "but I was given your information by a friend, and, well, you know how these things go...I didn't want to come when I could be seen. I'm interested in your services."

He seemed to take her comments in stride. "Of course, of course. Not to worry—I keep odd hours anyhow." His voice was gruff but lyrical. You'd want him to say almost anything to you; even hearing him reading junk mail would be titillating.

"That's what my friend said." Verona's voice caught in her throat. She was too tired to resist this kind of charm in a dignified manner.

"Though I must say, a house call is a little unusual. Surely a phone call would've worked?" He leaned against the doorframe, his body language comfortable even if he found her showing up on his doorstep puzzling.

She had an urge to tumble against him as he leaned over. *Pull it together, Montero!* "Yeah, I'm really sorry, but I also didn't want the call logs to show up. I can leave if this is way out of line." She held her hands out in apology.

"Not at all. Just unusual, like I said. But I understand the need for discretion."

"Thank you."

"How about I give you my card?" He reached for a table behind him to retrieve a card, leaving the door ajar. The inside of his home gleamed with smooth surfaces and cleanliness. "I'm used to speaking in secret, so you'll see I have a few options for you to be in touch in ways that can't be traced. We can talk about it all then. Sound good?"

"That would be perfect."

The man handed her his card and leaned in to squeeze her shoulder. "I look forward to talking with you," he breathed, tantalizingly close to her ear. Then he pulled back as if nothing more intimate than a handshake had taken place.

The skin at the base of her neck tingled, and blood rushed across her whole body. If he could inspire that kind of reaction in her with nothing more than a brush of his lips, she wanted more of it.

He smiled as he backed into his home. "Bye for now."

"Bye," she breathed. She could hardly believe this intensely flirty interaction with a smoke show had fallen into her lap, and she rode the wave of elation all the way back to her car.

It wasn't until she inspected the man's business card that her smile faded into a scowl.

14

A SPICY GYRO

London, England
Friday 1 p.m.

Zane sat in his flat with a freshly brewed cuppa by his side. He took it black and strong, with a dab of honey and tons of cream. He joked about British stereotypes, but there were a few he just couldn't escape, and his cup of tea was one of them. There was nothing quite like a nice cup of tea. He also enjoyed clog slippers and a thick Irish wool sweater.

He lived in a renovated Victorian conversion, an upper flat with natural light, radiator heating, oak floors, a fireplace, and laundry in the kitchen. He had room for a modest double bed and antique armchairs facing the window. It was small but comfortable, the best he could afford in the city on his salary working as a nurse in a hospice. But he'd not give his job up for anything, not even a flat with reliable heating.

Today, like most days, the view was gray and rainy, but he smiled as he sipped at his strong, sweet tea. He had made himself wait several days before texting Blair (no need to appear too desperate), and she had texted him back. Within minutes.

Zane: *I've been thinking about our lunch every day since I got back.*

Blair: *Well, English cuisine would do that to anyone. Why must everything be cooked so much it can be mashed?*

He gripped his mug with his left hand, the heat spreading through his skin nothing compared to the way Blair's teasing lit him up inside. It was her challenge to him, to see if he could get past it. Well, he'd done it a few times already, and he was up for it again.

Zane: *Yes, but I am in London, we do have options beyond mashed everything. Although, I think even mashed everything would be my favorite meal if I could eat it on that boat with you again.*

He watched the three little dots that told him she was composing a message with a smile hitched so far up his face, the people in the street below might fear he was The Joker. Would it work?

Blair: *There's your sweet bullshit again.*

Zane: *It's my own special brand, I guess.*

He had to assume she liked it, because when she said it, it was never followed with one of her teasing comments. Must be her code for "keep going, it's working."

Zane: *Speaking of the sun, the boat, and the orgasmic dessert, how is your feature coming?*

He wished more than the dessert had been orgasmic, but he'd had to leave her after lunch to catch his flight. There was no chance to invite her anywhere else, to see where it might lead them. One kiss. That's all he'd managed. He'd made it count, slow and soft, with a promise of all the desire he was holding back. He hoped she could sense it, and judging by the way she was reluctant to untangle their bodies, she did.

Blair: *Ripping through it. I'm padding it with a story about meeting a handsome, exotic stranger. People eat that shit up. You know—'Travel opens you up to new experiences and gives you the chance to meet interesting people.' It gives them hope that they might bone a hot guy on vacation too.*

Zane: *So this handsome and exotic man...What was his name? Gyro?*

He wanted to believe she was talking about him; why else would she bring it up? As rough around the edges as she was, he didn't think she'd go so far as to throw another man in his face. Even if Zane was not exotic, and he had not boned Blair.

Blair: *Gyro?*

Zane: *Yeah, you met some hot and exotic Greek man on vacation, like you said.*

Blair: *And you think his name is Gyro?*

Zane: *I don't know. It's Greek, isn't it?*

Blair: *For sandwich.*

Zane: *What?*

Blair: *Gyros are Greek sandwiches. That'd be like me guessing your name was Scone.*

Zane: *My parents did say if I'd had a brother, they'd call him Scone.*

Blair: *Well, the only Gyro I had in Greece was a delicious sandwich.*

He had to go with her tangents now and then. It was fun, pushing back at her, and he knew his sweet bullshit would hit harder if he allowed her to think he was just content to tease.

Zane: *Right. So the name must've been something manlier? Xander? No, Maximus?*

Blair: *Say his name was Maximus. Say I met him on vacation. You'd be okay with me texting you while Maximus was still in the picture?*

Of course he wasn't okay with that. But he was almost certain she was messing him about, and he was willing to play along. If Maximus was still in the picture, Zane would have to hope that his wits were stronger than Max's pecs. *I'm fucked.*

Zane: *Nah, I don't need to worry about a guy like Maximus. They don't stick around. Too hot and exotic. He has his pick of cute women on holiday who have read fancy travel magazines that promise them if they travel to Greece, they will bone some hot and exotic guy named Maximus.*

Blair: *But you're not factoring in how mind-blowing I am. Maximus would never get me out of his head.*

Just like Zane hadn't been able to get her out of his head. He wasn't interested in her blowing his mind, though of course that would be brilliant. No, he knew he'd need to blow *her* mind. He was up for it.

Zane: *I doubt any man could get you out of their head. I know I haven't.*

There, she wasn't expecting that out of the blue, was she? It would be more effective if he could see her react, but he didn't want to push for a video call on their first contact since they left each other. She took longer to respond than usual, so that had to be a good sign. Or a very bad one.

Blair: *Is that so? Well then, how about you call me tomorrow? See if we can make that a wee bit worse for you. I do like to cause problems more than solve them.*

Zane: *Pretty sure I might have the answer to a lot of them.*

It was bold, but Blair wasn't a woman he was willing to play it safe with. She was already across an ocean.

Blair: *Call me tomorrow.*

Zane: *Okay, but before you go, can I suggest an edit for your story?*

Blair: *What?*

Zane: *I don't think anyone has ever called an Englishman exotic.*

She'd not yet admitted he was the man in the story, but he was going to make her do it, damn it. Perhaps that's what she wanted from him all along.

Blair: *Then I can be the first. Αντίο.*

Zane stared into his empty mug with energy buzzing around his head. He wasn't the most practiced at seducing gorgeous women, but he was rather proud of himself for how he handled that. It was as if for every barb she had, he had the plating to absorb and soften it. She seemed to like that about him, perhaps because not a lot of other men had managed to cut through the thorns to her soft spots.

But he saw it like sex. He'd be patient and slow and with the right touch, he knew he could make her melt right into him.

Calgary
Friday 10 a.m.

"He's a what?" Quentin giggled into his phone.

"A male escort," Verona said dully. She read his card. "*Rocky Laird, Escort for Hire. Indulging your most passionate fantasies.*" She was back at her apartment and staring at her bed with longing. It was 10:00 a.m. If she went to bed now, she'd fuck up her sleep schedule even more than it already was.

She heard uproarious laughter. Quentin took a full two minutes to compose himself. "And...he...thinks...thought...you wanted to hire him?"

Verona laughed along. It was always more fun to laugh at herself than bother to be embarrassed. "Hey, who's to say I *won't* hire him? He was smoking. Plus, it's hard to find a man to indulge my most passionate fantasies the way *I* want them indulged."

Quentin adopted his best Verona voice. "I'm not going to sit here and objectify men with you, Verona!"

"Yeah, yeah." She left her bed behind with one last longing glance and went to the kitchen to start a pot of coffee.

"So still no idea who the real private investigator is, then?"

"Not a clue. Obviously, the escort was hired to tempt Miami to stray, though. No idea if he's been successful or not. I suppose if he keeps going back to her house, that's good news." She sat down at her kitchen table, closed her eyes, and leaned her forehead against the cool surface, the small rest a promise her body wanted her to deliver on.

"Hmm, but do you think Javier's PI knows about the escort? Or were they hired separately, each without the other's knowledge?"

"Well, I suppose it depends on the morals and business standards of the PI and the escort. Personally, I wouldn't touch a case like that with a forty-foot pole, because I don't think hiring someone to seduce your partner so you can catch them at it is really in the spirit of things." The coffee machine started to gurgle and emit the enticing aroma that meant her brain would soon be clearer.

"And the male escort? What was his name? Rocky Road?"

"Rocky Laird. I know nothing about the escort business." Her forehead had warmed the table so that it no longer gave her any relief. She sat up her elbows, propping her chin up.

"Did you ask him what his rates were?"

"No. But maybe I will. He did give me at least three different ways to get in touch discreetly." The machine stopped gurgling, and Verona got up to get her BIGGEST DICK IN TOWN mug and filled it with coffee, sugar, and milk. The first sip hit her brain like a bullet train made out of pure caffeine. It was heaven.

"You do that. I'm curious."

"Being a lawyer doesn't pay well enough for you?" Him teasing and needling her about another man was more fun than she remembered. Maybe things weren't as over as she had assumed? He couldn't be completely turned off of the idea if he was back in suggestive flirting mode. This idea added a new kind of jolt to her energy that had nothing to do with the caffeine.

"It's nice to have options," Quentin said, the smile ringing in his voice.

She went to the living room and nestled into her burnt-orange recliner couch. She was looking forward to a low-key day of coffee and TV, and maybe later a run to encourage her body to reclaim daytime living.

Her phone beeped with a text. "Oh, hang on just a sec, Quentin." She put him on speakerphone to check it.

The text read *OMFG they think i did it* 😡😲 *i need ur help* ☂️ *meet now* 🙀 *its Miami* 👙 *btw.*

"Quentin?"

"Yeah?"

"I'm sorry—I've got to go. Miami just sent me a very cryptic message, but it doesn't sound good."

"Hang on," Quentin said. "I just got one too." Silence while he read it. "'They think I did it'?"

"That can't be good. She wants me to meet her."

"You go. Get her to call me once you're done."

15

THAT DOES SOUND HARD

Calgary
Friday 12 p.m.

The doorman outside STUL had changed since the last time Verona paid a visit. Verona guessed that unlike the barman, who got exorbitant tips, the doorman got little more than a few bucks here and there and the vague thrill of copping a feel when drunk girls needed help getting into their limos.

The new doorman wasn't pretending to be British like "Mr. Abbot" had; he had gone in a different direction, likely due to his appearance. A handsome young Persian man with dark hair, brown skin, and striking light brown eyes, he was wrapped in gorgeous white silks with intricate red-and-gold embroidery. He was beautiful. Verona imagined *this* doorman might have some luck with the bored young wives of fifty-somethings.

Young, young, young, she repeated in her head as a mantra to keep from making a fool of herself in front of him.

The hot doorman's name tag read FARRIN, and as she approached, he gave her a grandiose bow and an emphatic "*Salam.*"

Verona wanted to reply with some cute quip, but the only thing that came to mind was "Salami," so she wisely gave that a pass. "Where's Abbot?" she asked.

Farrin shook his head. "I don't know, miss, but I welcome you to the heavenly oasis of STUL." He had a thick accent, or he pretended to—she wasn't sure which.

Well, thought Verona, *at least this doorman doesn't think I'm too old to go in.* "Heavenly oasis?"

"Indeed, miss. A veritable sanctuary in the desert of life."

"Wow," she said, "that's fucking dedication." *How on earth does a shitty place like STUL attract these men who are so willing to put their heart and soul into being crappy stereotypes?*

A young blond thing wiggled by in a minidress, its tight little tushy bouncing pertly.

Right, that's how.

"Listen, Farrin," said Verona, determined to find the humanity in him before she left, "I'm not one of these women. I don't belong here. I would've thought that was obvious based on the fact that I'm thirty-two and haven't showered in three days."

"Miss smells as radiant as a spring shower," said Farrin, bowing again.

"No, miss does not," said Verona. "But good answer."

"I live only to serve."

"Really?" asked Verona before she could stop herself. "I mean...uh, Farrin, what time do you get off tonight?" A man who lived only to serve sounded pretty perfect right then.

"Off, miss?" Farrin asked, looking confused—the first genuine expression she'd seen.

"Yes, as in, off duty. No more work."

"Ah, miss, I do but live to serve. I am a humble servant of this establishment, and thus am never off duty."

"Holy fuck."

"Indeed, miss." Farrin gave a reverent nod.

"I take it that means you never go out for drinks?"

Farrin, bless him, so young and naive, shook his head.

"Right. Well, I guess, just let me in the doors, then." She proffered her phone with the invite.

Farrin obliged with a bow and a "May you be richly enveloped in rapturous joy."

Verona mouthed the words "rapturous joy" while shaking her head as she entered the perfumed, pink, and throbbing interior of STUL. She found Miami at one of the tiny tables, with her signature My Little Pony drink all a-sparkle and a-feather. She was wearing what looked like a bikini trying to be a dress—or a dress trying to be a bikini—gold high heels, and, strangely, a black veil.

Miami pointed to the veil and said, "I'm, like, mourning and stuff."

"In mourning?" asked Verona. As far as she knew, Javier being out of town was a good thing.

"Javier's dead!" Miami screeched, drawing the eyes of the other patrons briefly before they all lowered their heads back to their phones, deciding Miami's emotions were not their concern.

Of all the things Verona had expected, this wasn't one of them. "I'm sorry for your loss." She wondered why this was bad news. Surely Javier's death meant all the money would go to Miami?

"Thanks." Miami tapped at her phone, barely looking up at Verona as she spoke. "It, like, really sucks, because Javier is finally gone, so I should be able to do what I want, but now the police are being all mean to me and stuff, and I didn't even do anything!"

"Yes, that does sound hard." It didn't sound hard, but it was easier to go along with her. Especially when she was running on zero sleep and two interactions with attractive men that hadn't panned out. "So you texted me because"—Verona dug out her phone—"they think you did it? Is that what you're talking about?"

Miami threw the veil off her face. "They haven't, like, said it, but they were asking a lot of weird questions about the divorce and the money. But he wasn't, like, even in the country."

"Right." Verona was starting to put together a picture she didn't like. "He died while he was in Greece? Did they say how he died?"

"I didn't, like, ask, because they were so mean to me. I was just trying to get some sleep after my party. And they told me Javi died, and then they asked me if I knew anyone that would, like, wanna hurt him and stuff."

That didn't sound good; if they were asking those questions, it was looking like Javier had met a suspicious end. "Miami, you should be talking to a lawyer about this before you answer any more of the police's questions."

Miami pouted because the type of men she attracted thought it was cute and it got her whatever she wanted. To Verona it was annoying and made her want to put Miami in a time-out.

"I thought you'd, like, wanna help."

Verona barely held her exasperation in check. Maybe the bartender could make her an espresso instead of booze. She doubted it. "Miami," she said, "I'm a private detective. I don't just *help* people. I get paid to investigate things."

"So, like, investigate, then! Since you were watching Javi before he died, you'll be, like, up to...um, steed or whatever."

Verona clenched her jaw at the effort required to not correct Miami's turn of phrase. She was sure the girl was overreacting. If Javier had died in Greece, there was no way the police would think her a viable suspect for very long. Still, she was reluctant to give a flat-out no. Javier wasn't going to best her just by dying. This was still her case, and if she couldn't catch him with his pants down, she'd make damn sure her client was still satisfied.

Miami pouted again as she waited for an answer, trying to look desperately sad and sexy at the same time. It was an odd expression, but to her credit, she nailed it.

"Tell you what," said Verona. "Why don't you talk to Quentin and get him to call me?" Quentin wasn't a criminal defense lawyer, but as Verona didn't know any of those, he was the best they could do on short notice.

Miami smiled and used her arms to hoist her immense breasts even higher. "Cool!"

"Yes," said Verona in stolid calmness, her mind already working on the problem. "Cool."

The sunlight outside the club was an unwelcome spectre to Verona's tired eyes, so she kept her head down as she walked back to her car. Parking downtown was always a nightmare, so she had several blocks to go. Over her shoulder, she noticed her old friend, the black SUV idling slowly behind her.

If they were going to tail her this obviously, the least they could do was give her a lift. She shouldn't do it, but...she was fucking tired.

She stopped and waved at the SUV. They put on a burst of speed and pulled up to the curb right next to her with a rush of hot wind and the smell of engine oil. She stumbled back with the sudden arrival. She knew she was being cheeky, but she didn't expect them to actually react.

The passenger door flew open, and a pair of hands reached out to grab her. Some beefy guy in a black suit and sunglasses. She took a few steps back from him, taking herself out of reach, but he was already climbing out after her.

All the fear she claimed she didn't have caught up with her like she'd fallen off a cliff and the ground was coming no matter what she did. Her stomach dropped, her skin turned icy, and she could hear the blood rushing past her ears.

The rest of the world faded, there was only this big guy with a really pissed-off look on his face. She should scream. She should fucking gouge his eyes out. She should try to implement any number of moves she'd learned in her weekly martial arts classes, but for all her bravado, she was frozen.

She'd never frozen in her life before this. But as the man drew closer to her, her body refused to obey her.

Friday 12:30 p.m.

Strictly speaking, the magazine didn't need another story about the British Isles. The type of high-end traveler *Tier1* catered to wasn't interested in a basic sightseeing tour of Buckingham Palace, Edinburgh Castle, or Stonehenge. They were well aware of London's West End and had likely flown into Heathrow more times than they had cleaned their own home.

"Think about it." Blair paced in front of her editor's desk. "Who were the original elite of the world? The Brits, that's who. They created high-class living, and you know our readers will want a piece of that lifestyle if it's presented right."

The editor, Tory Hathaway, wore an exquisite deep coral shift dress with a tailored white linen blazer that set off her brown skin and black hair tied back in long, thick twists. At fifty-three, Tory had been in the business a long time and could easily spot a story pitch based on personal desire rather than the magazine's profit. Still, Blair was undoubtedly her best travel writer, so she was willing to hear her out. But Blair knew she wouldn't fold easily.

Tory leaned back in her chair and removed her reading glasses. "The British Isles aren't exotic enough. Our readers want to go to places that would be prohibitive for other travelers. That's not the British Isles."

Blair hadn't expected Tory to go for the pitch right away and was unconcerned about her dismissal. She liked to be up against the challenge, to flex her powers of persuasion. "Sure, in the typical sense, in the way that every other travel magazine and agency presents them. But I'm not talking Big Ben and Westminster Abbey here. I'm not even talking Oxford and Cambridge. I'm not talking history for history's sake. I'm talking luxury, romance, and prestige. I'm talking royalty and seclusion."

Tory shifted in her chair with interest—maybe not so much in the story, but in Blair. Blair had never been so desperate to sell an idea before. All of her other articles had been born out of a passion for travel, or a desire for the edge on an up-and-coming destination. But this? This was something else. And she could see Tory knew it.

"So, what's his name?" Tory asked.

Blair dropped her guard and sank into the chair opposite Tory's desk. She'd been standing for the pitch because it conveyed more authority and energy, but the time for posturing was over. The chair in Tory's office was the same as everything else in it: luxe, expensive, and comfortable. Leather with a full back, it was mustard yellow, Tory's chosen accent color.

"It's Zane," Blair said, "and I'm going to England either way, but I'd rather do it on the magazine's dime."

"Of course you would. We all would. How did you end up head over heels for a man in England? Please tell me this isn't some mail-order bride thing."

"I'd be the one mail-ordering a husband." Blair let her gaze drift as she imagined the man she'd choose from a catalog. "Tall, gorgeous, muscular, excellent cook, a generous lover, funny."

"The man you're describing wouldn't need to put himself on a mail-order service. He's taken." Tory looked at her. "They're all taken by the time they're your age."

"Gee, thanks. I'm only thirty-three, you know."

"I'm speaking from experience. Now me? I'm fifty-three. That means all the good ones who were taken are starting to become available again. I'm finally starting to meet some handsome, smart, and decent guys. Sure, some of them are a little damaged from years with a passive-aggressive bitch, but I'll take that over pathological liars, cheaters, addicts, self-absorbed narcissists, and guys who still live at home with their mom." Tory paused as if letting the memory of decades of bad dates sink in. "That's the stage *you're* in."

"Thanks. You should have been a dark comedy writer instead of a travel editor."

"But writing is more work for less pay. So, about this man, then?"

Blair thought about Zane, his wide smile and easygoing aura that made her feel calm and free to be herself. A lot of people seemed to get a high after almost every first date, but the number of times it had happened to her was...once. *This time.* She was still shocked she was doing all of this just to go and see him. But there it was. "I met him in Greece."

Tory cradled her chin in her palm and shook her head. "Ohhhhh, so *he's* the exotic stranger you wrote about in your article? I thought that was made-up fluff to hook the readers."

"Well, it wasn't strictly based on fact. I mean, I only met him the night before he was leaving, and we didn't fuck on the beach. But I know what people want to read, and it isn't the truth."

"You've got that right," Tory said. "Still, you met him once, and that's enough for you to want the magazine to put out a substantial fee for you to go and see him?"

"Twice, actually. And we've been talking since then."

"Still, seems a bit out of character for you."

"Well, we all do things that are a bit out of character when we're falling in love." *Completely out of character*, she thought. Yet she was still doing things her way. This meeting was proof of that.

Tory put her palm down on her desk and sat up straight, doubt curling her mouth down. "You're in love? After two meetings?"

"No, I'm not in love. That's why I said *falling*. As in heading that way. As in infatuation, interest, chemistry, fancy, the possibility that it could be love if given the chance."

"Good," Tory said. "But I still can't approve this story."

"You didn't let me finish my pitch." Blair shifted in her chair.

"If it's for a man, that's all I need to hear. Go on your own dime." She put her reading glasses on and rested a hand on the lid of her laptop—a signal the meeting was over.

Blair stood back up, her pitch mode reactivated. She leaned over the desk, both palms down. "Tory, haven't I been your best writer for the past five years? Aren't my articles constantly top rated by our readers? Have I ever not delivered the best in secret locations, exclusive perks, and hidden gems? Don't I always find a way to sneak in the human story that hooks the reader and helps them imagine themselves wherever I go?"

Tory held her hands up. "Okay, okay, yes. Finish the pitch."

Blair removed her hands from the desk and paced slowly. Nothing distracting, just enough to show she felt certain.

"As you and our readers know, the British Isles contain some of the oldest and most revered castles and private estates in the world. But if you were to go there, how would you know which ones to stay at? How would you know which would make you feel like royalty and which would make you feel like you're staying in a musty old farmhouse in the middle of nowhere? Which are just secret enough that you'll be treated like royalty and rub shoulders with the elite? Which are remote and romantic for that extra-special getaway? Which immerse you in flawless luxury? Which are owned by actual dukes or earls? At which ones might you have the chance to meet a member of the royal family?"

Tory still looked unconvinced. "Has any other magazine run a story like this?"

Blair knew if Tory was asking that question, she was starting to come around. "As you'd expect, there are a few internet lists with the top ten

British castles and a few booking sites, but from my research, no magazine has done an extensive cover story on them."

"Working title?" Tory asked. This was often her way of seeing if her writers had a concrete idea or if they'd wing it.

"'Royalty and Romance: Hidden Castles.'"

"It has a ring to it."

"And some great keywords."

"So we're talking about more than England here?"

Blair stopped pacing. "Definitely. I'd like to feature at least two castles in each country in the British Isles. One for romance, one for royalty. Maybe a third that could combine the two."

"And we're looking at top budget for these castles, right?"

"Of course. The castles that are accessible to the general public will already have their ratings on TripAdvisor. Our readers want to know about the ones no one reviews because the rich don't bother with that sort of thing."

Tory was nodding along now and staring up to the left in concentration. "And you're going to want to stay at least three to four days in each castle to ensure you've got a proper feel for it. This is becoming more than an article —it's becoming a feature issue. High-gloss photos, extra-special edition. At least twice the price of a regular issue. To make this feasible, we'll need substantial discounts for our exclusive insights from these places. And you're going to need to be there for at least a month."

Blair didn't bother to hide her grin now that she realized Tory was going to approve the feature. "Yes, and for the romance portion—"

Tory looked at Blair over the top of her reading glasses in a way that showed she knew she'd been played, but was not unhappy about it. "Yes, you'll want the booking for two. I'm not an idiot. I see what you've done here."

"But the thing is, it's an excellent idea."

"Yes, it damn well *is* a good idea. And I sort of hate you for it. On principle, I want to deny your request because it's a blatant attempt to use magazine funds to further your love life." She took her reading glasses off, and a resigned grin played across her face.

"But you're not going to."

Tory dismissed Blair with a wave of her hand. "Go. Get planning. I'm going to work on budget approval, and get our marketing department working on promoting the issue and the requests for discount stays for you."

Blair left Tory's office in a conquering spirit. This would be one of the features of a lifetime, and that always felt good. But she had also played the system for personal gain, and that felt even better. It made running off to see a man feel a lot less flighty and girlish and a lot more badass and sly, and that's what she wanted to be.

16

KGB MEET-CUTE

Calgary
Friday 12:45 p.m.

The dark bulk of the man was coming for her, like the tunnel of light after death. If she was going to do anything, it had to be *now*.

Just breathe, damn it. Come on, Montero, breathe!

She took a deep breath, and that broke her body free. She didn't have the time or the finesse to retrieve the pocketknife from her purse, and she figured that might end poorly for her anyhow. This guy was so strong he would likely take the knife from her, and then he'd have a weapon plus his size.

Instead, as he reached out a hand for her upper arm, she pulled her cell phone from her back pocket and brought the edge of it down on his knuckles in one swift, hard motion. He pulled his hand back and shook it out, gasping from the pain. But when he looked at her again, the impassive grimace he'd worn was replaced with a scowl of anger.

She stepped back from him again, judging how much space she'd need between them before she could run without him grabbing her. He had a long reach, so she'd need to create a lot more space.

She brandished her phone at the man, wondering when he might lunge to grab her wrist and disarm her and planning her countermove—a nice shot to the balls when he was distracted by her phone—when his buddy tapped him on the shoulder and shook his head, his own phone held up to display a message she couldn't read. He said, "Dead guys don't pay."

The man relaxed his body posture, but she kept her phone at the ready. "Want some advice?"

No, she didn't, but this wasn't a time to break the bad news. "What's that?"

"If you're ever followed again, don't fucking wave."

He turned and got back in the SUV, slamming the door behind him. She stood back on the sidewalk and watched them pull away slowly. The passenger window opened, and a hand with some light swelling popped out, the middle finger flying in a salute. She itched to wave back, but she didn't think he'd find that as cute as she did.

A man jogging by detoured to her side. "You okay?" he asked. He was handsome, with dark shiny hair, brown eyes, and a sharp jawline. She had a thing for jawlines. He smelled like sweat and sunscreen.

Her hands and knees felt shaky. Adrenaline did that to a person. "Yeah," she said. "Thanks for checking."

"Should I call the police?" He scrunched his brow, clearly concerned, but also uncertain about what he'd just witnessed. "Do you know those guys?"

She smiled. Oh, how she wished this was just another meet-cute. But this wasn't a story she wanted to tell anyone, no matter how handsome this guy was. "Sort of. Let's just say it's not the first time I've had to turn down KGB recruiting agents."

Sunday 1 p.m.

Given the unprecedented fact that both Quentin and Verona had a client who was a suspect in a murder investigation, they skipped the usual phone conversation and decided to meet face-to-face. Quentin chose the pretentious smoothie shop, mostly, she assumed, to annoy her, but also because it was close to a park where they could sit at a picnic table and discuss the case while enjoying the pristine summer day.

She felt lighter than she had in weeks, partly because cloudless blue skies and the scent of cut grass always relaxed her, but also because she'd not seen the black SUV since they'd flipped her the bird. If she was a good private dick, which she damn well was, she'd take all the evidence and conclude it was because Javier had died. "Dead men don't pay," the guy had said.

Even if they hadn't been Javier's men, she doubted Drug Lord Kent Choi would bother following her after Javier was out of the picture. She had clearly been following him, and after he left, her only interest had been Miami. Well, Miami and yoga teacher screwing Robin. Not exactly the résumé of an undercover cop looking for a drug bust.

Verona gripped her F*ck It smoothie and sucked heartily at the straw. She hadn't bothered trying to read the list of ridiculous names and just went with what she knew. It was also pleasing to have the words "F*ck It" on her cup instead of a jumble of nonsense words.

Quentin tried a new flavor, the Immediate Icy Ironic. He said it was coconutty and icy, and that he wasn't sure what made it ironic. He wore jeans and a white linen button-front shirt, his rolled-up sleeves the only sign the weather was a tad on the warm side.

"So are you continuing on, then?" Verona asked between slurps, wondering how he always looked so damn perfect. Sweat was pooling in the crease of her stomach, and she sat up straight to get rid of the uncomfortable sensation.

"In terms of Javier's will, that should be handled by *his* lawyers. However, I can be relied upon to ensure she's given her fair share."

"For a fair share of your own?"

"Naturally. No one works for free."

"And the murder?"

Quentin took his time sipping his smoothie. "I'm not a criminal lawyer—I play in the divorce sandbox. That being said, I doubt any of the suspicions around Miami will last long. Whenever someone's killed, their spouse is always going to be a suspect. But come on—he was out of the country at the time. She was throwing all those parties. We had her under surveillance. Javier's lawyers had her under surveillance. When was she supposed to have committed the crime?"

"I suppose they think she hired someone to do it?"

"If we've thought of it, they have. But Miami isn't nearly smart enough to pull that off. She wouldn't even know where to look for a hit man. And she'd have left a trail a mile long."

Verona nodded. She didn't think Miami was capable of that kind of crime, but what if this wasn't about her at all? Could it be that Javier had gotten himself killed because of his dealings with Mr. Choi? Had he already done something to cross his new business partner?

She hadn't shared anything about the SUV with Quentin. Even now that the tail was gone, she didn't want to endure his lecture about how stupid she'd been to ignore it for so long. How she should've backed off the case. How she should've at least told someone, or had someone watching her back. And that meant keeping her ideas about drug-trade killings to herself. For now.

As long as they could protect Miami from bearing the blame, she didn't much care who had killed Javier. If it was the drug lord, perhaps even better. Bad people taking out their own.

"So, what does that mean for our case?" Verona found herself staring at the divot between Quentin's collarbones and quickly looked away before he noticed. Her finger would fit in that divot perfectly. Instead she watched as a magpie scared a squirrel away from a particularly juicy bit of moldy hamburger on the grass a few meters away.

"Well, I'm staying on because she asked me to, until this whole thing is wrapped up and she's got some of Javier's billions in her hands. She hasn't been charged with anything yet, so it's premature to pass her case on to a criminal lawyer. I'm going to consult with a few on her behalf. Javier's lawyers are trying to file motions to keep her from the money until the murder is cleared up. They're arguing that Miami, as a possible suspect, shouldn't have access. I'm arguing that this is complete shit, as she hasn't been formally charged."

"How utterly selfless of you to stay in her service and continue collecting that hourly fee." The magpie called to the heavens with jubilant squawks over its battle spoils, shredding the hamburger with its beak.

"Hey, I don't hear you screaming to be cut loose from your generous retainer either."

She returned her gaze to Quentin, imagining once again what it would be like to trace her finger along his jawline. "No, I'm not. But I don't really see how else I can help." She punctuated this with a loud slurp.

"Well, I hate to disappoint you, but Miami wants to keep you on retainer a bit longer."

"That's not disappointing. I like cash." She stirred the last annoying slushy bits of her smoothie around to make slurping them up easier. "What does she want me to do? I can't retroactively prove Javier was cheating, but him dying sort of solved that problem for all of us, didn't it?"

"True, but until your client is completely satisfied, you can't close the case, can you?" Quentin remained dignified concerning his smoothie, simply letting the dregs lie instead of annihilating them like a wild beast.

She focused her energy on flirting with him instead of torturing herself thinking of all the places she wanted to touch him. "I don't know, do you ever leave a client unsatisfied?" She sucked on her smoothie and was rewarded with a few splashes of taste and a whole lot of echoing slurping noises.

He rolled his eyes but smiled. Her childish innuendos still amused him, it seemed. "Of course not."

"Why *does* she want to keep me on, though? Really? I mean, I understand you, you can help her with the will and shit. But me? What can I do?"

"I think she thinks you're way cooler than you are."

"But I am cool," Verona said, removing the lid of her smoothie and tipping the last bits directly into her mouth.

"Sure you are. But you're not solving-a-murder cool."

"Of course I'm not *that* cool."

"Right. But Miami thinks you might be that cool."

"What?"

"She believes that if she's charged with murder, you'll be able to find out who really did it and get her off."

Verona went for a three-point shot with her smoothie cup, aiming at the nearest trash can. "I hope you told her that's ridiculous!" The cup hit the rim and bounced off. "It'd be like you offering to represent her as a criminal defense lawyer when you're just a divorce lawyer. The police investigate murders. Private dicks do not." Not real ones, anyhow. She'd never imagined she'd be like Poirot or Sherlock when she started her career, and she was fine with that. Her real job was plenty fun.

Quentin got up to throw his cup away and picked up Verona's. "I take issue with that 'just a divorce lawyer' remark. I chose to do divorce law, and I'm damn good at it."

Verona waved this away. "Yes, I'm sure. And if you wanted to be a criminal lawyer, you could, blah, blah, blah...but let's get back to the part where you told Miami I could investigate a murder."

As he sat down, Quentin made downward motions with his hands to calm Verona. "Okay, yes, I did tell her the odds were long. But she still wants you. Thinks long odds are better than no odds. But I don't think she understands odds."

"Will you shut up about odds?" *Could* she actually investigate a murder? She'd not say no to trying, as unrealistic as that was. She still felt like Javier had bested her, and if she was able to solve his murder, she'd feel like she won.

"Sure." Quentin gave a one-shouldered shrug as if she was the one being silly, not him. Odds are cool, after all.

"Okay, so, best-case scenario: no investigation necessary, and I just get paid to keep a clear schedule?"

"Right."

"Worst-case scenario: I'm expected to interfere with an ongoing police investigation and find evidence to exonerate our client?"

"Well, I didn't think you would interfere with the investigation. But poke around the fringes."

"At that point, wouldn't Miami be working with a criminal defense lawyer, though? I mean if it's serious enough that it warrants investigation? And wouldn't they have their own investigator?"

"You've been watching too much TV. But any smart lawyer is going to want to keep you involved because you're so familiar with the case."

What he had done for her started to sink in, and her voice came out a bit thick. Or maybe that was the phlegm from the smoothie. "So you..."

"Convinced Miami to keep you on so you'd have the chance to possibly work on a high-profile murder case? Yes, I did." He graced her with a big "I'm-a-nice-guy" smile.

"Wow." The wow was as much for the smile as for the gesture.

"You're welcome." Quentin leaned his elbows on the table. "Oh, and Verona?"

"Yeah?" She leaned in too. She was close enough to see the faint laugh lines around his eyes, and like everything else about him, she found them sexy. *Well,* she thought, *that's a first. Being turned on by age lines.*

"When did you become so sexist?"

"What?" She sat back up a bit.

"Well, it's just that you assumed the private investigator trying to catch Miami cheating on Javier was a man. Hence your debacle with the male escort."

"So?" Maybe she should give Rocky a call after all. She clearly had some pent-up horniness to get rid of if she was drooling over age lines.

"So that was very sexist of you. And surprising, since you're both a woman and a PI." He rapped his knuckles on the table.

"Will you just get to the point?" His hands were so close she could grab them. She folded her fingers together to control herself.

He gave a self-satisfied grin, knowing he had her on the hook. "If you hadn't assumed the PI was a male, you might have spotted the gorgeous woman hired to watch Miami. I found out today, when I was discussing the will proceedings with Javier's lawyers. Looks like you've got competition in the pretty-lady-private-dick sector."

Verona got up from the table and walked away, in part to hide her smile because Quentin had called her pretty, and in part because he was being an ass.

"What?" Quentin called after her. "It's not my fault you're sexist!" He shouted it louder than was necessary so everyone else in the park could hear and judge her.

17

BUT IF I CAN GO FOR FREE...

London
Sunday 11 p.m.

It was late, and Zane had to be up early the next morning, but he didn't care. He was waiting patiently for Blair's after-work video call while sipping yet another cup of tea. Decaf this time so it wouldn't interrupt his sleep. Actually, it was a proprietary blend of herbs meant to calm and prepare you for sleep, but it made him feel like an old man to admit he drank it, so he called it decaf. He was already in bed but sitting up to keep himself awake. Even so, he started to nod off before his phone chimed and startled him back to wakefulness.

He accepted the video call, and Blair's face filled his screen. All of the texting they'd done had kept her image fresh in his brain, but seeing her again made him realize he'd forgotten too much already. The exact shade of her eyes, the way her dark hair framed her face. Her smile, rare but all the more beautiful because of that. But she was starting with a smile, so he fancied his chances on this call.

"Feature approved! I'm getting a whole month in the British Isles." She was sitting outside somewhere, perhaps the balcony of her flat. He could hear the birds and traffic in the distance.

"A whole month? Good thing I've been saving my holidays." He'd take every last day he could. Personal days, mental health days. All the days. If he didn't get to do a single other thing for the rest of the year, he didn't care. She was worth it.

"Rather presumptuous of you to assume you're invited the entire time, isn't it?" She cocked her head in a gesture he was quickly learning was her challenge mode.

"You're the one that booked a whole feature just to be with me." He'd never felt like a commodity before, and now here he was, with this beautiful, unique woman arranging her life to see him. He had to play that up. "Don't worry, I'll make it worth your while." Amazing how he'd gone from nodding off to wide awake. The images of what he'd like to do to make it worth her while might have something to do with that.

Her head tilt disappeared, and her mouth parted slightly in surprise. "Someone's feeling cocky these days."

"I don't hear you saying no." *Fuck, that was a good one.*

"What woman would?" She changed her grin to one of sly seduction. If he could, he'd prove it to her right then, but phone sex wasn't his strong suit. Especially not for their first time.

They were silent for a few beats, the rain cascading outside his window in direct juxtaposition to the sunlight shining on her dark hair.

She cleared her throat, perhaps a sign he was making her feel the same craving he was. "What is it you do for work, anyhow? I realized today I never asked you that."

Ah, changing the subject to safer topics? He'd take that kind of deflection. "I know. I took it as a good omen. It's always the worst—you show up at a party where you don't know anyone, and the first question everyone asks is 'What do you do?' Like that sums up the entirety of your being. And then you get stuck talking about work when there are so many other interesting things to talk about. Like how I'm going to be spending my holiday." He gave his eyebrows a little wiggle. Why not?

She laughed. "Okay, tiger, easy does it. You still didn't answer my question."

He shifted his position, pulling his dark navy blanket up and lying down. He had finished his tea, and if they were going to get out of the exciting territory and into the basics, he might as well relax. At least for now. He wasn't going to leave her without something more to think about, though.

But he'd have some fun with her first. She seemed to like that. "What d'you reckon I do? If you had to guess. Based on what you know about me."

She lifted a glass of wine to her lips and sipped. White wine, he noticed. He'd remember that. "I have no idea! Your personality doesn't dictate what job you do. You could be a lion tamer. You could be a sewage worker. You could be a museum curator. You could be almost anything."

Lions and tigers? All I need is a bear and I've got the complete set. "A lion tamer? Cheers! If only I'd known that was an option when I picked my uni."

"A man who avoids answering 'What do you do for a living' is probably hiding something. So what is it? Serial killer? Live with your mom? Selling black market dick pills?"

He laughed, partly because it was outrageous, and partly because he bet she wouldn't mind if that were the case. "I'll give you a hint: I see a lot of dead people in my line of work. But I don't kill them."

She thought for only a minute before going rapid-fire on him. "A mortician? A cop? A paramedic? A gravedigger? A doctor?"

"None of those. Another hint: although they're dying, I don't try to save them."

She flipped her hair behind her, revealing her bare shoulders. What he would give to be able to run a finger along the top of them. Soft and steady.

She said, "So you deal with the dead and dying? Are you Death? Because I have a few people you could take care of for me..."

Zane thought, *Oh, hello, Mr. Death!*[1] But he couldn't say that to her, she'd likely be utterly confused, and that wasn't what he wanted. "I'm much cheerier than that guy. I don't like being grim. Plus I already said I *don't* kill them."

She took another sip of wine and considered for a long moment. His body was starting to feel heavy, relaxing into the bed, and he wanted to close his eyes. But he couldn't, not with Blair waiting.

1. *Monty Python and the Meaning of Life*. Yes, they did more than just *Monty Python and the Holy Grail*, and it's all gold. GOLD!

At last she said, "Nurse. Hospice worker."

"Brilliant! So now you can see why I'm averse to discussing my profession at parties. Sort of a downer, isn't it, to say, 'Well, I keep people as comfortable as possible while they die.' But people will insist on asking."

"Well, you're certainly cheery for a guy who spends every day with death."

"Death just makes life that much more precious. It's a lot easier to focus on the good, the joy, the small moments, when you're constantly reminded that it could all be over in an instant. Plus, the people I deal with, for the most part, teach me so much in their last days. And their families do too. It's something that is very sacred to me in a way. Hard to explain."

He'd never really tried to explain it to anyone before. No one had bothered to ask. Most people were so uncomfortable around death that once they heard what he did, they changed the subject.

She smiled, not the kind meant to appease or whitewash, but one where he felt like her guard was down. "That's quite beautiful. Not sure I've ever heard anyone talk about death like that before." She was soft with him, present. Gone were her jabs and pokes. She was *with* him. He felt seen, even though she was across the ocean.

He could lie there and soak up that feeling until he fell asleep, but he sensed she had something more she wanted to talk about.

Sure enough, she changed the subject again. "Did you hear that some rich guy got murdered in the hotel we were staying at in Greece?"

Zane was stunned. It was one of those weird pieces of information that has you thinking a lot of things all at once. An "It could have been me" sensation. And he wondered if it was...but no, there had to be plenty of rich dudes in Greece. A tingle of anxiety wound its way up his spine. He'd check the news later to be sure.

"That's a bit unnerving," he said. This wasn't how he imagined ending his conversation with Blair. Hopefully there would be time to turn it around. "After we left, or what?"

"No, that's why I'm telling you. Apparently it happened while we were there." She picked up her wineglass to take a sip, realized it was empty, and put it back down.

"But we never heard about it." He sat back up in bed again, all the lazy happiness sinking away.

"They didn't discover it right away. They're saying he was killed with a nail gun."

Zane tried not to imagine the carnage a nail gun could do to a person. He'd stepped on a nail once as a kid; that was bad enough. "A nail gun? You're saying we were staying at the same hotel as a nail gun murderer?"

"I'm not sure this is like an ax murderer type of killing spree. They only killed the one guy, after all."

"I guess you're right. Still, you never know. Maybe they planned a nail gun shooting spree but something distracted them. Like the gelato bar." He had to get them out of this dark territory back to some place he could feel good about saying goodnight from. As much as he wanted to, he couldn't stay up much longer without seriously damaging his capacity to do his job. His patients deserved more from him.

"Well, thank God for gelato, then." She laughed.

"It's good for a lot of things. Incredibly refreshing after physical activity. Better call ahead and make sure we can get it for room service."

"You think we'll need it?" She put a hand behind her neck, unconsciously, he thought, but that made it better.

"I *promise* you will."

"Just me?"

"That's my priority. If there's some left for me, I'll take it. But I'd rather make sure you get all the...gelato you need."

He couldn't be sure, but he thought she blushed. Well, plenty more where that came from.

Calgary
One month later, Monday 11 a.m.

"I think you need to go to Greece." Quentin sounded serious, and he looked serious, but there was no way he could be.

He'd invited Verona to meet him at his office, which was a first. They conducted most of their business over the phone, and she wasn't sure what to think of the change in pattern. This was the second time he'd invited her to meet since their failed date attempt. Was this him being more comfortable with her since they were in the friend zone, or was it him feeling things out to see if there could be something more again?

"Sure, and you need to go to Cabo."

"I mean it," Quentin said. "Miami keeps trying to flirt with the cops, and she's inadvertently saying incriminating things. We need something to change their focus."

Verona squeezed her lips together to try to keep from smiling. Of course Miami was trying to flirt her way out of this one. It was her one move. "And how would going to Greece change their focus?"

"Easy. We can make a statement to the press that Miami, far from being glad that Javier is dead, is broken up with grief and has, at great personal expense, sent her own private investigator to get to the bottom of what happened."

Verona was still excited at the possibility of working on a murder case, more so now that a whole month had gone by without a single SUV sighting. If there was a drug angle to Javier's death, she wasn't in the picture for it. She could go to Greece and poke around in safety. She hoped. This time, if she saw anyone following her, she would have to back off. There were only so many times she could count on someone dying to save her from abduction.

"And the police, upon hearing this, are supposed to open the doors to their investigation in Greece and allow an amateur like me to review their findings?"

"Of course not. They're not going to let you anywhere near the official case."

She wondered if the police had any idea about Javier's connection to Mr. Choi. Were they looking into that as a possible angle, or had he successfully kept that a secret? She'd fill them in on it herself if she had any real evidence. But a shaky video of two men in a booth didn't prove anything. Plus, as a PI, they'd probably assume she was trying to punch above her weight and dismiss her. No, until she had hard evidence that

Javier had been killed because he'd screwed over a drug lord, she'd have to keep it to herself.

She said, "So what are you expecting me to accomplish?" Even without access to the official case, could she dig up some real evidence? Well, she'd stumbled upon Javier's drug connection on her own, so maybe she could. But it was important to control the expectations of others. It was always going to be a long shot.

"You've got to understand that we're all swayed by the media. And that's what this is about."

Oh, so that was his game? She could work with low expectations and a free vacation. "But if you're trying to spin the media, aren't some of them going to say she really did do it, but she wants someone to drum up false proof to get her off the hook? Or she's just doing it to look innocent?"

"Of course they'll write some reports that way, and that's fine," he said. "Right now the *only* spin is that the police suspect Miami. What we need is some spin that says she may be innocent. A handsome lawyer on TV"—Quentin indicated himself and gave a big, beaming, handsome-guy smile—"assuring the public that his client is innocent, and that he's dedicated to finding justice."

Verona mimed throwing up. Even if his smile was the best part of her entire day, the idea he presented was shady. "You know this is why people don't trust lawyers, right?"

"Oh, come on, Verona—we both know she didn't do it." He leaned back in his chair with annoyance. "It's not as if I'm going out there professing her innocence when deep down I know she's guilty. If our system of law could sustain real justice, I wouldn't need to do this. But the truth is, no system will do that because all systems are made up of humans. And humans are fucking biased, emotional, and irrational. So I do what I have to do to get as close as I can to justice. In this case, giving Miami a chance to be seen as innocent."

Verona held her hands up in a calming manner. "Okay, okay, keep your panties on." *Even if I'd like to take mine off... Focus up, woman!*

He continued. "Anyhow, of course you're not going to be able to get into the official investigation. The investigation in Greece is being handled a hundred percent by the Greek authorities. They've only asked for our police to help because it's cheaper than sending their own members here. From what I've been able to glean, so far the relationship is amicable. Neither department would thank us for screwing that up."

"So the point of my going to Greece is so you can stand up, smile, and say, 'Look, Miami does care'?" She was ninety percent sure she would go. Maybe she'd run into an exotic stranger who would make her forget all about Quentin.

"Well, in theory, yes. But in practice, no," Quentin said, giving her a cheeky grin.

Yeah, like you could ever forget that grin attached to that jawline.

"Well, that clears it up, thanks." Verona leaned back in her chair to emphasize her heavy sarcasm.

"I'm hoping you'll poke around a bit—"

She opened her mouth to interrupt, but Quentin put up a hand to forestall her. "Before you get all uppity again, let me finish."

"Uppity?" Verona laughed. "Really? Been taking tea with my gran, have you?"

"Yes, and you're a great disappointment to her," he said without missing a beat. "I'm not asking you to bother the Greek police. I know you won't get access to shit from them, and that makes perfect sense. But what you can do is stay at the hotel and chat up the staff. People are morbid and love intrigue, and most of all, they like to play up any connection they have to it and brag about it to strangers. You've worked with people about as long as I have, you know I'm right."

This vacation was getting better and better—she'd be getting paid to gossip. "And if I come back with nothing?"

"We can simply say that despite Miami's best efforts, her private investigator is hitting the same roadblocks as the police, and reiterate that means that neither of you have a viable suspect and the case may go unsolved."

"And we're talking all expenses paid here?"

"Yeah, I knew you'd like that. Javier's executors are still doing their best to block funds, but when it comes to putting money into investigating his murder, they can't argue against that."

"Sounds like a pretty cushy assignment. I'll take it."

"I do expect you to actually try, you know. There is an outside chance, even if it's small, that you might find a real murderer and bring them to justice."

Verona was surprised Quentin was so vehement about justice without considering whether the person deserved it. "You think he deserves that?"

"You think we get to decide who deserves justice?" He raised his eyebrows, as if her lack of moral fortitude surprised him.

"A conversation for another time." Verona stood.

She had little desire to match wits with a lawyer on the concept of justice. She'd rather join a philosophy class and discuss the morality and implications of going back in time to kill Hitler. *Fuck the time paradox, that evil bastard is going down!* Still, the look Quentin gave her as she left wasn't one she hoped to provoke again anytime soon: as if he had seen a new part of her and he didn't like it.

18

WHEN IN ROME. OR ENGLAND. OR GREECE

England
Two weeks later, Monday 9 p.m.

The rain thrashing outside the mullioned windows was the perfect soundtrack to the fire flickering against the stone walls in Blair's tower room. It evoked the feeling of ages past, when mead and giant legs of mutton would be on the great tables, the dimness of the light encouraging the revelry that thrives when the brightness of day and electric bulbs are absent. As humanity has civilized itself, electricity has kept us in the light much longer, hiding our baser selves with the inherent fear of the dark, and the excitement it brings along with it.

Here, in a medieval castle, primitive emotions were let loose. It wasn't exactly the type of high-class ambience *Tier1* readers were used to, but if Blair put the right spin on it, it would sit right with those who liked to rub elbows with the elite and let their hair down. Especially if she wrote about what she hoped would happen next.

Her casual flirting and teasing with Zane was fun, but it did little to satisfy her memory of her physical desire for him. The beating rain meant there would be no talk of innocent strolls, or dinners on patios, or anything that would take them from the shelter of their room. While some might find the idea oppressive, she relished it, as if nature itself was conspiring to keep her and Zane no more than ten feet from the bed.

She'd arrived first and took the opportunity to shower the rain, mud, and travel creases away, order a bottle of whisky, take the phone off the hook, and instruct the staff to steer clear. She wore only a silky rose kimono over her bare skin, ignoring the slight shiver she felt as she passed the drafty castle walls. She poured two glasses of whisky, neat, brought one to the fire and sipped it slowly, waiting.

Ten minutes later, Zane entered the room with a rush of English mutterings. She wondered if it was possible for an Englishman to ever enter a dwelling without describing the weather. "Bloody rain was falling *up*, I swear—" He stopped dead, dropping his duffel bag on the floor, the raindrops on his bright green jacket glistening in the firelight like little orange fireflies.

The door fell closed, and Blair rose to meet him, removing her kimono as she did.

"Bloody hell," he said, his eyes drinking her in with surprise and captivation tampered with tenderness.

His reticence made her flush with yearning. A man that had control over his lust was not something she usually sought, preferring men with brash courage in their sexual desires. But the way he looked at her, as if he could stare at her all night and be satisfied, intrigued her.

She retrieved the other whisky tumbler and sauntered over to him, daring him to look away.

He stood like an idiot in his rain slicker, took the tumbler, locked eyes with her, and said, "Cheers."

She laughed. "That's all I get?" She sipped her whisky, enjoying the warmth coursing through her body, a precursor to how she imagined she'd feel when he finally touched her. Her flesh prickled with the cold and anticipation.

He threw back his whisky in one swig, then carefully removed and hung his jacket as she watched on, astonished at his restraint. He took her glass from her and placed it next to his and then slowly wrapped his arms around her, the warmth of him igniting a spasm of lust in her as she ran her hands up his arms beneath his sleeves. She inhaled the earthy scent of the rain on his skin, a slight undertone of juniper spiking her ache for him.

She didn't want to wait any longer, but perhaps he knew that. He was, after all, a great tease. She lifted a leg and harnessed it around his waist, daring him to take any longer.

He drank her eyes in with his and kissed her, tenderly at first, then deeply as he grabbed her other leg and brought her to the bed. Explosions of pleasure radiated through her as she rushed to remove his clothes while he patiently and tenderly found the places that made her gasp.

She'd never known lovemaking like this. Slow, tender, intent. She'd expected a frenzy of passion, an uncontrollable urge to fuck after so long just talking, his desire to have her outweighing anything else. But this? Not once.

But there was no time to weigh the pros and cons of passion versus tenderness, because the pros were presently engulfing her being with intense insistence.

Mykonos
Wednesday 3 p.m.

Anyone who has ever taken a transatlantic flight can tell you the vacation does *not* start on the plane, unless, of course, you're one of the smug bastards in a first-class pod. Although Miami was paying for everything, Verona still wasn't fortunate enough to call a pod home. She was unceremoniously thrust into a cloud of screaming babies, cramped knees, snoring neighbors, and that guy that can't figure out how to share the armrest and thinks he's entitled to both of them, even when one of them has the entertainment system controls.

"Excuse me," Verona poked the man's shoulder, "but your arm is on my volume control." This was the fourth time she'd asked. *You asshole*, she thought.

"Huh? Oh." He shuffled his arm off with great reluctance.

Next time, thought Verona, *I'll smack him on the wrist like a nun whose only pleasure left in life comes from inflicting pain on others.*

Verona was accustomed to spending long hours sitting in her car on various stakeouts and had wrongly assumed a long flight wouldn't be much different. What she didn't account for was the seats in her car reclined past the ten degrees allowed on the flight, and she could put her feet up on the dash in the car. Oh, and there weren't two hundred people jammed into the car with her.

When her final flight landed in Mykonos, Verona emerged with sweat stains under her arms, her hair flattened in the back from the headrest, and her clothes twisted from turning in her seat to find a comfortable position, which, she discovered after hours of experimenting, didn't exist. She rolled her carry-on bag down the tunnel to the airport and longed desperately for food, a shower, and most importantly, a bed covered in bleached-white hotel sheets.

Her hotel was only fifteen minutes away, and a shuttle bus would be taking her there. She found the waiting area and joined the other dishevelled, smelly, and harassed-looking people waiting for the shuttle. Then she spotted one peppy-looking, immaculately turned-out, well-rested-looking bitch. She, Verona decided, was one of the pod people.

She felt as most travelers did at this point, wondering, *Why the fuck did I come here?* Twenty hours of being trapped in flying tin cans with strangers would do that to anyone. Not to mention the sleep deprivation from the time change and inability to get comfortable enough to rest. *Perhaps modern torture techniques come from cross-the-globe air travel*, she thought.

When her shuttle was announced, she got heavily to her feet, wearily dreading what new hell awaited, and finally stepped out into the splendour that was Greece. The sun warmed and cradled her skin and dazzled the skies into a deeper blue than she was accustomed to. She took a heady breath of the humid air and inhaled something floral and spicy. After the recycled air of the airplanes and the air-conditioned airports, a breath of fresh air was particularly invigorating.

She heard birds chirping around her and felt a light breeze play across her skin. In the distance, the sun glinted off the Aegean. The feeling of long years of history lingered in the stones of the streets, in the architecture around her. There was something alive in the atmosphere, as if the air was richer with the multitudes of lives that had lived and walked in this exact spot.

Oh, she thought, *this is why people travel.*

The bus ride was exponentially more enjoyable than her flights had been. It lasted only the promised fifteen minutes, there was room for her to stretch her legs out, and nobody took the seat directly next to her. Plus, there was scenery on the bus.

Verona took a window seat and watched with renewed energy as the countryside whisked by—low dry stone walls, lush splashes of greenery, and white buildings contrasting spectacularly with the brilliant blue of the sky. As they crested a small hill, the sea came into view along with shadows of nearby islands. The hillsides were rocky and full of brambles, and along the sides of the road, plant life snarled and tangled into itself without the threat of winter to bother it.

The vehicles were mostly compact cars and scooters or motorcycles. Though the street was narrow, it was still used for two-way traffic, and the bus missed locals by inches, but it didn't faze any of them. As the bus drew nearer to the sea, the land became more open, and there were uninterrupted views of the hilly countryside, dotted with white houses.

It wasn't all perfection. A few vacant lots full of rubble were sprinkled in, along with some homes that looked abandoned. Garbage bins littered the sides of the road, and graffiti was splashed here and there on buildings and billboards. But the overall sensation was of solitude and simplicity, and Verona was more relaxed than she'd ever been. After spending a mere ten minutes on the island, she was in love with it.

The driveway to the hotel appeared suddenly at the side of the road, only a small triangle of pavement indicating its beginning. The bus turned in and took the weaving driveway down to the front of a tiered building made of brown-and-gray stone with arches over the doors and windows. The taller tiers were of the classic white plaster with blue accents on the shutters and balconies.

Verona disembarked and was promptly shown to her room by a concierge. She was enveloped by the clean whiteness of the space, softened by wood furniture and a large blue accent wall. Daylight spilled in from her open balcony doors, and she felt content, as if nothing in the world could ever go wrong again.

I wonder if Javier felt the same way before someone popped him off. Not a bad way to go, she mused as she plopped down on her bed.

"Yup," she said, "someone could murder me with a nail gun right now, and I'd not be too fussed about it." She closed her eyes.

Her balcony door swung in with a creak, and a shadow advanced into her room, but she was already nodding off and couldn't convince her jet-lagged self to wake up and investigate.

England
Wednesday 6 p.m.

Zane brushed his hand over the back of Blair's hair as they embraced. It was a tender motion, steeped in gentle care, and it took Blair by surprise that she enjoyed it. Perhaps it was because it had none of the cloying, clinging nuances she associated with such gestures. It was unforced and lacking any need to be reciprocated. It gave her a thrill of remembrance of their first night together. She slowly pulled back from him and returned his smile.

"See you in a fortnight, then?" he asked. His bag, a navy-blue duffel, was lying packed at his feet, and a cab was on its way to take him to the train station. They stood at the end of the winding drive that led to Cariswel Castle, the turrets of which were just visible above the large oaks and brilliantly sculpted topiary.

Blair rested her hands on his chest. "You know you will, you idiot." She would be heading to Scotland while Zane returned to work. She'd never missed a man before, but she was looking forward to the idea of Zane's return when they reunited in Wales. Was that the same thing?

"Can't take anything for granted with you, can I?" His tone was teasing but playful, lacking any plea for reassurance, which Blair adored.

"Bloody well right!" she said, using the English expression because it seemed fitting. She pulled him back in for a last kiss, wrapping a hand behind his neck and resting the other on his jawline, which was freshly shaved. He held her loosely around her waist, allowing her to control how long the kiss would last, and perhaps because of this, it lasted quite some time. Blair had half a mind to drag him back to the room with her to see where that kiss could lead.

When they finally pulled apart, Zane wore a cheeky grin.

"What?"

"Nothing."

"What the actual fuck?" Blair persisted.

"Don't you have work to do? You gonna stand here all day?"

"Fine," said Blair. "I was going to be nice and wait for the cab with you, but I'll just go, shall I?"

Zane looked uninterested. "Do what you want."

Damn it, Blair thought as she left him to wait by himself and marched back to the castle to work on her feature. *Damn it all to hell, I think I love him.*

She smiled ruefully. *And why the hell not?*

19

THE NEXT GAG

Mykonos
Wednesday 6 p.m.

Verona dreamed she was locked in an underwater tank. It was the reverse of being in an aquarium; the water was all around the tank, and she was encased in glass. She heard strange whispering sounds all around her. In the way that you know things in a dream, she knew the sounds were a code, and she had to crack it to get out of the glass case. She even had a handy pad of paper and a pencil to help her solve it. But, because dreams always want to fuck with you, she couldn't use the paper and pencil because her hands were tied behind her back.

As she struggled to free them, she drifted back to consciousness, and returning to the real world, she realized that her hands somehow *had* become bound as she slept. The whispering was probably the sound of the ocean waves drifting in through her open patio. But what was the deal with her hands?

She finally opened her eyes and looked around her. The door to the patio had swung open wide as she slept, and two seagulls had made themselves at home on the foot of her bed. She kicked to shoo them away. They squawked loudly in protest and made a half-hearted flutter to the floor.

She sat up awkwardly, her hands and arms stuck behind her, constrained in an uncomfortable knot of fabric. After a few moments of confusion, she realized it was only her shirt, which she had gotten halfway through taking off before she passed out from exhaustion. She extricated herself fully, put on a fresh one, and decided the thing to do was to get some fresh air.

"Move on, you little fuckers." She made swooping motions at the seagulls.

Hopping slowly to the door, they gave her haughty looks, like teenagers being told to turn off the video games and play outside for a while. She bolted the door behind them, grabbed her bag, and headed out.

The air was hotter than she'd expected, but there were plenty of storefronts on the main street where she could duck in and escape the sun. Plus, it would serve her purpose for being there: figuring out where Javier had gone, and what state of mind he had been in.

On the plane ride over, she'd reviewed the information Runi had found for her about Kent Choi. It turned out that Mr. Choi was known for his rather unusual methods of murder. If you crossed Choi, you didn't get a bullet in the head. That could too easily be attributed to someone else. No, he liked an unorthodox death. Rigging a garage door to fall. Replacing mouthwash with acid. Using jumper cables on ski poles.

Javier had been killed with a nail gun, so it was possible that this was Choi's doing. Perhaps Javier had come to Greece to see if he could handle distribution himself, and Choi had found out? Of course it was just as likely that some jealous lover had taken care of him.

Not that she thought Choi could have any inkling that she was the PI investigating the case, but she'd kept her eyes open for any kind of a tail from the time she went to the airport until she reached her hotel. No one. She'd keep checking, but she felt fairly confident this investigation wasn't putting her in any danger.

The first shop she stopped in didn't look like the kind of place Javier would frequent, but they did sell sun hats and beach bags. She bought one of each, intending to spend just as much time at the beach as she did investigating.

She skipped the trinket stores and the very tourist-friendly shops and only stopped when she came to a place that was selling highly priced leather goods. This was the kind of place a man like Javier might decide to visit.

The shopkeeper was a middle-aged man in a dark green suit. As she entered, he smiled and said hello in Greek.

"Hello," she said back.

"You want purse?" he asked, waving his hand to a wall of handbags in various sizes and colors.

She walked over and picked up one of the small ones. Perhaps Miami wouldn't mind reimbursing her for a few expenses? The leather was buttery soft and dyed a deep purple. It would probably last forever. She flipped the paper tag over to see the price: €500.

She slung it over her shoulder to hide her surprise. If this guy figured out she wasn't a serious shopper, he'd lose interest real fast, and she'd lose her chance to talk about Javier. "What do you think? Too small?"

The shopkeeper just smiled at her. Unlike a lot of other places she'd traveled where English seemed to have seeped into the locals, her experience so far had shown her many of the Greek people did not know much English at all. Not that she thought they should—she didn't know Greek after all—it was just a surprise.

She took out her phone and opened her translation app, asking her question again.

"Ah!" He laughed. He spoke animatedly in Greek and pulled down a larger bag from the top shelf. This one a deep red, and big enough for her to fit several bowling balls in.

"Hmm." She took the bag and twirled around with it. She took her phone out again. "My godfather." She showed the man a picture of Javier, then returned to her translation app. "He told me about your shop. He was here about a month ago. Sent me here to get myself a birthday present."

The man's brow furrowed momentarily, then he brightened. "*Naí, naí,*" he said, which she'd learned was the Greek word for "yes."

She put her phone under his mouth, indicating he should speak into the phone. A string of Greek came out of his mouth, and when he was done, she pulled her phone back to read.

The translation was never going to be perfect, but it was clear that the man *had* seen Javier and had sold him a belt and a pair of dress shoes. He'd been looking for something to match his new summer suit to wear around town.

Verona smiled, pretending to have fond thoughts of her godfather on his vacation. She had to tread carefully for her next question, but it was an important one. It might tell her if he was here to unwind and leave time for Miami to cheat on him, or if he was looking to make his own drug connections.

"My godfather, I worry about him," she said, putting the big purse back and grabbing a simple brown bag with long narrow handles. "Sometimes he works too hard. Even on vacation."

The man read her phrases and smiled. "You're a good goddaughter. The young should always ask after the old. In this case, no need to worry. He told me he had a date with a lovely lady. No business, just pleasure."

She nodded her head in feigned relief, taking down a black bag that looked like it would be suitable in a boardroom. So he was going on a date and seemed relaxed. Perhaps he wasn't here to step on Choi's toes. Or perhaps he was just humoring an old shopkeeper. But that didn't seem like Javier. He didn't do things for the benefit of others. It was all about him. If he said he had a date, if he seemed relaxed, he likely was.

"*Óchi*," the man said, taking the boardroom purse from her. "Your godfather is not buying you a business bag. No business on vacation for him, no business on vacation for you. This one."

He selected a small bag in a soft yellow with a long cross-body strap. It would have room for her keys, phone, and a few cards. Literally the perfect bag for someone like her. He was good at his job.

She went to look at the price tag, but the shopkeeper whisked it away from her. "*Óchi!* Godfather is buying you a birthday present. It doesn't matter what it costs." He brought it to the cash register and rang it up.

She'd been planning to leave, saying she hadn't brought the money with her and would be back, but she didn't think that would work anymore. She smiled and handed over her credit card, really hoping Miami wouldn't flinch at the €350 expense bill she was going to send her.

~

Wednesday 8 p.m.

Accosting the maids was next on her list of things to do. Well, ideally, she'd infiltrate the underground drug scene and ask any of them if a new wise guy was trying to hedge in on the territory, or whatever the real non-Hollywood lingo was. Somehow she didn't think a simple McFly Maneuver and a drag queen partner would get her as far as it had back in Calgary. And where would she find a drag queen on Mykonos, anyhow?

She'd returned to the hotel after visiting a few more shops on the main road, eager to deposit her fancy new bag in her room safe. No one else had been as forthcoming as the leather shop man had been, despite her pulling her "godfather" act with all of them. Perhaps he had his own goddaughter, which made him more inclined to talk.

Or maybe she needed a new routine. As one of her favorite sayings went, "You don't run the same gag twice. You do the next gag."[1]

The maids might've seen someone sneaking around the hotel, but what was she supposed to do, use her translation app to say, "Did you notice any assassins sneaking about?" The police had likely run all the usual questions, and if she showed up as another authority figure, she was sure they'd give her the same thing they'd given the police: nada.

It would be too late to find any maids wandering about tonight anyhow; she'd have to wait until tomorrow to talk to them. For now, after the seemingly endless day she'd had, what she needed was the bar.

The bar was on the main level, and the doors to the patio were open, allowing for a view of the sun setting over the sea. After the cramped, sweaty airplane rides and the heat of the street, the cool evening breeze filtering in through the doors was a soothing relief. The heat in her skin seemed to radiate out into the night air, and she thought longingly of a cool shower. If the night air was this refreshing, the shower would be downright pleasurable.

She took a seat on one of the red leather barstools and waited for the bartender to finish up with his other customers. He was in no rush, happily chatting with a few and offering a commiserating smile to others.

---

1. *Ocean's Thirteen*, Basher. Brilliant quote.

What was it about bartenders that make a person want to immediately open up and share their deepest secrets? It was one of the oldest and most-used clichés, yet it held true. Something about the welcome of a drink, the loosening effect of alcohol, the knowledge that the total stranger behind the counter couldn't possibly tell your secrets to your friends. Better than a confessional or a psychologist, because there was no pressure to repent or answer annoying "Why do you think that is?" questions.

It was why the first stop for any fictional detective was always the bar the victim had frequented. It was surely one of the first places the Greek police had gone. Drilling the bartender for information about the night Javier died was a logical first step, but it also seemed the least likely one to yield any real results.

A good bartender knows to keep his job he has to hold his tongue. Patrons get drunk and spill the goods, and if the hotel wants to maintain its business, it needs staff who keep those secrets so more people will be willing to come and do the same.

He certainly wouldn't be fooled by her "godfather" spiel, so she decided to just order a drink and see if inspiration struck.

"A Dark and Stormy," she said when the bartender stopped in front of her.

He was a man in his forties with dark hair still untouched by gray, dark brown eyes, a strong jaw, and a crisp white shirt, and he gave her a courteous smile and got to work at once. It was obvious he was a practiced professional, with hands that could pour a shot while his gaze never left his customer.

The drink was in front of her in a matter of seconds, placed neatly on a napkin and garnished with lime and fig. She took a sip and closed her eyes; it was the best Dark and Stormy she had ever had.

The bartender smiled warmly, his dark eyes crinkling. "Looks like you needed that. First day here?"

Oh, thank God he speaks English.

It was then, with the pleasing warmth of the drink cascading through her and the kind invitation to spill her weary soul, that inspiration struck. People generally respond best when you speak to them in their language—

and she didn't mean Greek. No, bartenders were used to being *told* things, not asked.

"What gave it away?" she said. "The overt redness of my skin, or how very obviously I needed this drink? Fig." She indicated the garnish. "Amazing touch." She took a moment to read the man's name tag: ANATOLE.

Anatole tilted his head in humble acknowledgment of the compliment. "You are...let me see...Canadian?"

"Very good! Most of the time when I'm overseas, the first guess is American. Makes sense, I guess, since there are more Americans than Canadians in the world."

"A classic problem of quantity versus quality," he said. "The trick is to recognize the quality."

Verona held her glass up in a toast to Anatole. "I'm sure you have some line for the Americans that disparages Canadians?"

"I could never share that with a Canadian citizen."

"What if I have dual citizenship?"

"You were much too happy to be recognized as Canadian for that."

"Okay, you've got me there. I am Canadian."

The evening rush hadn't yet begun and the bar was blissfully slow, so Anatole lingered. "Just traveler's woes that make you need that drink?" he asked, performing his confessor duties admirably.

"Well, that's a big part of it, yes. But it's also because this is a working vacation for me. A lovely working vacation, but still working."

"If time and money allow, I encourage you to come back some day when you don't need to work. The experience is heightened considerably. What is it that you do?"

Verona allowed a short pause and savored her drink. "I'm a private investigator," she said, deciding on the fly that now was not the time to enjoy the humor of "private dick."

Anatole's eyebrows rose a fraction, the only chip in his professional facade. It was obvious a private investigator nosing around wasn't welcome. "And what are you investigating?" he asked, his voice still friendly but with a hint of suspicion.

Verona understood his reaction and was glad she had decided to be up front. If she tried to bullshit him, he would see through it and she'd never get anything. With a murder occurring so recently at the hotel, why else would she be there? Was he to believe she was there coincidentally investigating some adulterer? No, it would be a weak lie, and the only lies worth telling were those stronger than the truth.

"I think it's obvious what I'm investigating, but it's not because I care about the man who died. Rather that his widow isn't falsely punished for his death. I'm not interested in getting you to tell me what happened that night. Instead, I'm here to make a few assumptions. If I'm on the right track, you can just let me keep on talking."

She could see him relax slightly, but he was still on guard in case she was trying to trick him. His lack of response seemed to be an invitation for her to continue, so she did.

"I'm assuming that he was here drinking that night, because it's a classy place, and he's not a frat boy looking to dance the night away at a club."

Nothing from Anatole. A good sign.

"Also, knowing what I know about him, he wasn't drinking alone." *Thank you, Mr. Shopkeeper, for that little tidbit!* "Now, this is where the assumptions end and the hopes begin. I'm hoping his drinking companion was a local, and in that case, I'm also hoping I might run into her as I explore this lovely island."

Anatole eyed her carefully, like a jeweler deciding if a gem is the genuine article or not. Finally, he said, "You should really visit our market by the port. Local farmers and fishers sell fresh food. You could even get a lovely bouquet of fresh flowers for your room. I recommend hyacinths. Leave them on the windowsill, and the breeze will bring in the scent. Another drink?"

Verona downed the last of her drink. "Thank you, no. I'm looking forward to the market. I always love participating in the local economy when I can." She rose from her stool and gave him a nod of thanks.

Anatole deftly swept her empty glass away and gave her a warm Greek goodbye. "Αντίο."

20

AN AVERAGE-LOOKING ENGLISH GUY

Mykonos
Thursday 9 a.m.

Old Port, where the market was held each morning, was a misnomer. Verona had imagined a run-down bit of rubble jutting out into the sea with a few locals selling handicrafts they couldn't afford a shopfront for. Instead she found the port full of activity, with shops lining the streets until they met the seawall, and cruise ships ferrying people in.

It was warm, breezy, and, most of all, laid-back.

She'd walked quickly from the hotel, worrying she'd left it too late and the market would already be overrun with customers, but she slowed her brisk pace when she realized everyone was just getting started. Vans and trucks pulled up, and after the vendors unloaded milk crates full of their goods, they sat on the tailgates. They hoisted umbrellas to provide shade and set out lawn chairs. Shopkeepers set up next to each other, sat together, and drank cups of thick coffee, catching up or shooting the shit—Verona couldn't tell which.

Here was a place where you were expected to dawdle, drink coffee, stare at the sea, and talk to your neighbors.

Produce, fish on ice, handicrafts, and homemade sauces were all on display. Smiles and nods came her way from the shopkeepers and shoppers. She wound her way through the various vendors until a light floral scent carried on the sea breeze signalled the end of her search.

A young woman of no more than twenty presided over a table covered with blooms ranging in color from deep violet to white. Verona leaned in to smell a bouquet and closed her eyes, the light lilac scent evoking memories of long summer days spent lying in the grass.

The girl gave Verona a friendly smile and said in English, "Good morning!" She had an oval face, large, almond-shaped light brown eyes, thick lashes, arched brows, and a mouth permanently curved into a gentle smile. Her innocence and youth, combined with her natural beauty, would definitely attract a man like Javier.

"Good morning. How're you?" Verona needed to test the extent of the girl's English before she attempted any form of questioning.

"I'm very well, thank you. How are you?" Her English was precise and crisp, with only the hint of an accent.

"I'm great." Verona's shoulders relaxed in relief knowing she'd not have to use the dreaded translation app. "When I heard the word 'market,' I was picturing a busy bazaar where I might lose my shoes but leave with a goat. Instead I've been offered half a dozen cups of coffee and pet about twenty kittens."

"Yes, we prefer to remain calm. If it sells, it sells. If not—" She shrugged as if sure that the universe would look out for her either way. Or maybe it wasn't the universe at all but the people. Verona couldn't imagine any of these vendors letting their friends go hungry.

"I like that. Wonder if I can bring it back to Canada with me?"

The girl gave a light exhale of a laugh. "I think it is much harder to do in large countries. Greece is small. We know each other here."

Verona liked the girl; she was engaging and cheerful. It didn't make sense that she would end up on a date with Javier. If Miami was anything to go by, his usual type didn't have brains or conversational acumen. Still, Anatole must've been sure of his tip. He wouldn't send her to harass the girl for no reason. "Look, I'm not really here to buy flowers," she said. "I mean, I'll buy some, but that's not why I came."

The girl widened her eyes. That was it. Cool customer.

"I'm here investigating a death. A murder."

The girl busied herself with rearranging the blooms. The type of activity you do to hide your nerves or to avoid making eye contact. "At the hotel, yes. But I fail to see how you could be investigating. The police are in charge, as far as I've heard."

"Yes, they are, and I'm sure they're doing all they can. But I'm doing my own investigation for his widow back home." Verona picked up a delicate vase that held a single sprig of mauve hyacinth.

"Why would you want to find out who killed that man? He was awful."

"Yes, he was," Verona said. "I'm not interested in justice for him. It's his widow I'm concerned about. She's suspected of his murder, but I don't believe she was involved in any way. She's very young, not unlike you." She let the statement hang between them like a wriggling worm on a hook.

The girl shook her head and placed a sign, BACK IN 15 MINUTES, on the table. "Let's not talk here. This is not the kind of conversation I want overheard."

She led the way to the seawall, and the two of them sat in a secluded section, facing out.

"I'm Verona, by the way." Verona held her hand out to shake.

"Aster." She returned the gesture. "I'd like to help if I can, but I think you'd better explain how you found me."

"Sure, I'll explain. But you're a smart girl. How did you end up on a date with a man like Javier?" The sea was rough this morning, the salt mixing in the air a strange sensation for Verona, who was used to clear mountain air.

Aster waved her hand in annoyance. "Even smart girls make mistakes now and then. When he stopped by my table, he was charming. Kind, even. He was way too old for me, but I am not above accepting a free meal from a charming foreigner. I took precautions for my safety." She paused and gave Verona an annoyed stare. "But now I'm answering your question, and you haven't answered mine."

Verona laughed. She really did like this girl. "Fair enough. Anatole at the bar pointed me in your direction."

"Wait," Aster said. "Anatole told you about me and Javier? I never would have thought it of him..."

"Oh no, he didn't tell me anything. His loyalty to his hotel is admirable. I just inferred a few things, and he didn't deny them. And then he suggested I buy some flowers for my room, and, well, here we are."

Aster nodded, relaxing again. "Once I was out with Javier, he lost his charm. Right off the top, he made comments about my body and offered a little too forcefully to get me a drink. When I said I'd like to order my own, he barely hid his anger. I knew Anatole would look out for me because he knows my family well. Anyhow, I was already plotting my getaway when the perfect distraction happened, and I was out of there."

"Distraction?" asked Verona. The news hadn't reported any of Javier's last moments, and it was always these little details that mattered. Was it a drug lackey? There to warn him off?

Aster waved a hand as if this happened all the time and was hardly worth mentioning. "Some English guy came over and picked a fight—threw a drink at Javier. It was sweet, really—something to do with the dignity of women, but he was horribly out of his league. A man like Javier is used to dealing with a challenge. This English guy was like a little kitten attacking a pelican."

Human dignity? Definitely not a drug lackey. But she'd always known this murder might be about Javier's sexual exploits. She pushed back the excitement bubbling in her stomach so Aster wouldn't see it. If a man picked a fight with Javier on the night he died, that made him a suspect. "Tell me more about this English guy."

"I don't know much more than that. As soon as Javier stood up to grab him, I left."

"No, I don't mean what happened during the fight—I mean the English guy in particular. What do you remember about him?" It was odd that Anatole hadn't mentioned him at all, but perhaps he had wanted to let Aster decide how involved she wanted to be before divulging too much information. Perhaps he had also been nervous about saying too much while still on duty.

"Average," Aster said. Then, at the look of annoyance on Verona's face, she added, "I'm sorry, but he was. Average height, average build, blond."

"Attractive? Ugly?"

"How will that help you? Attraction is so personal."

"Your impression? Please?" She knew she was grasping for any information, but she liked to collect as much as she could.

"Attractive, I suppose, yes. I wasn't really in the frame of mind to be noticing men—I just wanted to get out of there. But attractive in an ordinary way, you know? Nothing special about him. Just a regular guy."

Verona nodded. It wasn't going to be easy to find an average-looking English guy, but still, it was something. "And to be clear, do you mean English, like American, or English like British?"

"From England."

"You said he was talking about the dignity of women? What else did he say?"

"I don't remember—it was more my impression."

"Your impression is good enough for me." More tidbits.

"It seemed like it was personal. He never said who he was or who he was talking about, but he mentioned something about knowing how Javier treats women. I guess I assumed he was mad about a girlfriend or something."

Verona had known jealous boyfriends to do all manner of things, but they didn't rattle on about the dignity of women. No, that sounded protective—like a father protecting a daughter. "How old was the English guy?"

"Oh, I don't know. Your age? What are you, thirty-five?"

"Thirty-two."

"Sure, seems about right."

Verona considered that even a thirty-five-year-old who'd had kids quite young wouldn't have a daughter old enough, even by Javier's standards. So not a father and daughter but perhaps...a brother and sister? "Do you know if the English guy was staying at the hotel?"

"I can't be sure, but I'd say more than likely. It isn't the kind of bar that attracts tourists from the street. Most of the patrons are staying at the hotel."

"Anything else you remember?"

Aster didn't answer right away, which Verona appreciated. She was accustomed to people answering that question immediately without consideration. Finally, Aster said, "I don't have a basis for saying this, but I don't think the English guy would've killed Javier."

Verona had seen too much of life to put much stock in first impressions or gut instincts. Serial killers make good, quiet neighbors, and people are wrongfully convicted by a jury of twelve. Still, she was curious to hear why Aster felt that way. "No basis, yet you said it. Why?"

Aster shook her head. "I don't know. The English guy seemed really out of his element with confrontation."

"Ah, but confrontation and murder are different beasts. I would argue murder is the best way to avoid confrontation."

"I'm just telling you what I think."

"And I appreciate it."

Aster left to tend her flower stall, and Verona stayed at the seawall to think over what she had found out. So the drug angle was likely out. She couldn't be sure, but based on the little bits she'd picked up, it seemed like Javier was just in Greece to get some sun and some ass. And that ass got him killed. Perhaps by an average-looking English guy.

Move over, Mr. Choi. Hello, Mr. Bond.

She did a search for the male population of England just to see what she was up against. Even if she cut out the uggos and hotties, that would still leave about twenty-five million to sort through.

Thursday 11 a.m.

The task of finding a regular-looking English guy wasn't one that had an immediate answer, so Verona decided to ignore that little problem and focus on something new. Perhaps the answer would come to her as it had when she was trying to get information from Anatole. Perhaps she just needed him to make her another of his fantastic Dark and Stormy drinks.

Eleven in the morning was the perfect time to catch a few maids doing their rounds after checkout. She didn't hold out a lot of hope that she'd run into the maid that discovered Javier's body, and even if she did, she knew directly asking about it would get her nowhere. In fact, talking about Javier at all was probably the best way to get them to clam up and claim they couldn't understand her translation app.

She knew her godfather routine had run its course and didn't think pretending to have a wealthy benefactor would likely connect with women who cleaned up after rich bastards for what she assumed was poor pay.

She sat in one of the armchairs by the elevator and waited for a maid's cart to go by. When she heard the muted rolling of wheels on carpet, she got up and pretended she had just gotten off the elevator and was returning to her room.

The maid was young, perhaps in her early twenties, and had her dark hair tied up in a bun. She pushed the cart like she meant business. No time to stop for a chat, just time to dig through whatever filth had been left behind for her to deal with.

Verona waited for the maid to stop in front of a room and then approached with an apologetic smile. She'd prepared her translation app with what she wanted to say, and after saying a quick Greek hello, hit the play button to let the app do the talking for her.

The maid, whose name tag read LYRA, listened but then shook her head in confusion, answering back in Greek before Verona had a chance to cue the app to listen.

Damn these translation apps! Clearly something was...well, lost in translation.

She was in the middle of signalling the maid to wait so she could get the translation going again, when Lyra waved her words away. "You. Wait," she said. She left her cart and walked down the hallway to where a different maid's cart was sitting outside the door.

After a few moments of muffled Greek conversation, Lyra came back down the hallway with another, older maid. This one's name tag read TASOULA. Lyra said, "She speak English," then hurried into the room, leaving Verona alone with Tasoula.

"Lyra says you had an issue with a relative?" Tasoula spoke in heavily accented English, but there was no stuttering or searching for words.

Based on her time in Mykonos so far, Verona had not expected any of the maids to speak English at all. It seemed the only people who did were in positions which directly interacted with tourists on a daily basis. She knew now was not the time to comment on it.

"Yes, my father. He's in the beginning stages of dementia. We didn't know that before he came on this vacation, though." She wrung her hands together in false nervous energy and focused on putting all the worry she could into her eyes.

Tasoula nodded with downcast eyes in a show of sympathy. “I am sorry to hear that.”

“Thank you.”

Tasoula looked at her for a reason for the conversation. Clearly she was used to keeping her peace, as Verona had expected. These kinds of hotels were basically gangs. You didn’t tell anybody anything.

Unless. “Yes, it has been horrible for us. And for him. Anyhow, he’s been saying some very strange things about his stay here, and we’re just trying to figure out if it’s part of his illness or if it is something we need to worry about. We don’t want to assume, you see. It wouldn’t be fair.”

Tasoula nodded again. “A good daughter.”

Verona felt bad about using the obvious respect these folks had for their elders to manipulate them, but that was the job. “Thank you.”

“But, what kinds of strange things? Why would you think we would know?”

Verona shrugged to indicate how hopeless the situation was. “I know it’s silly, and probably a long shot, but I had to try. It would’ve been about six weeks ago.”

Tasoula gave an almost imperceptible flinch. So she remembered when the murder had happened. That was good.

“And my father, he is always up early. Kind of like me.” She smiled wistfully, as if remembering fond mornings with her fake dad. “And he said one morning he saw someone wandering around the halls trying to get into the rooms.”

Javier’s time of death had been given as the early morning, and thanks to all of the attention the press was giving the death, this was common knowledge.

Tasoula’s brow furrowed in concern. “Sneaking around? No. I don’t remember anyone sneaking.”

Verona sighed. “Yes, well, that’s why I thought I’d ask you. You see, I’m worried he just saw the maids and was confused. But then he seemed to speak about the maids separately. I understand how desperate this must sound, but we just need to make sure.” She swallowed hard, as if the emotion of everything was overwhelming. "You're sure there was nobody unusual around? Maybe not sneaking in rooms, just someone walking around the halls?"

This time Tasoula's eyes brightened. "*Naí, naí!* A manager. I remember seeing them walking around. I assumed from the head office. They come now and then to check up on us."

Verona let out a sigh of relief, which worked to mask her disappointment. A manager wouldn't murder Javier. This was a dead end. Or was it?

"This manager, you've seen them before?"

Tasoula shook her head. "No. They're always different."

If she were going to go to someone's room to murder them and wanted to blend in, pretending to be a corporate mucky-muck would work extremely well. The maids wouldn't question it, and with the right excuse, she imagined Javier would open the door to let them in. The question was, was this one of Choi's hired assassins, or did it have anything to do with the regular-looking English guy who interrupted the date?

If he had wanted to go back later to finish the job, it would be an ideal cover.

"This manager, what did he look like?" She sincerely hoped Tasoula was better at describing people than Aster had been. But if she confirmed an average-looking English guy had been there, it would at least mean she had yet another eyewitness.

Tasoula shook her head. "No, not he. She."

21

I'M NOT SYDNEY-FUCKING-BRISTOW

Mykonos
Thursday 11:30 a.m.

The thing to do was to find out if this lady manager was really from corporate headquarters or not. When she'd thought it might be the English guy in disguise, it made sense, but now that she knew it was a woman, she wasn't so sure.

Of course it could still be an assassin sent by Choi, but she doubted if the underground criminal world was so progressive that they were worried about diversity numbers in hiring their killers. Sure, a woman *could* be a killer, but she didn't find it all that likely that a woman would be the go-to for a hit like this.

The front desk of the hotel was set back from the doors far enough that the sunlight didn't shine directly in the staff's eyes, but it glittered on the smooth stone floor all around them. The lobby smelled like chlorine from the pool and the laundry along with the last hints of coffee from breakfast.

The woman behind the desk was petite, with dark hair tied half up, round cheeks, and lips painted deep red. Her name tag read SOFIA, and she smiled in the gracious way all people who are paid to smile do.

"May I help you?" she asked. She had an accent like Tasoula's, except hers was smoothed out, as if she had spent more time trying to capture the correct pronunciations of every word.

Verona leaned forward on the desk, talking in a soft voice. “Oh yes. I’m here to do a little survey on employee wellness. I’m from HR at the head office, and we’re just doing a few of these little impromptu interviews to make sure everyone has recovered after...well, you know.” She smiled reassuringly. “You were working then, weren’t you?”

Sofia nodded. “But I didn’t see anything. It was worse for the maids.”

Verona nodded knowingly. “Yes, I know. I’ll be speaking to them later with my translator. But I figured I could just have a wee chat with you now, since your English is so good.”

Sofia nodded again. Clearly speaking to someone from head office meant you shut up until you were made to talk. Less chance to say the wrong thing, perhaps.

“So, you’re settling back in okay, then?”

More nodding from Sofia, this time a bit more vigorously. “Oh yes. Everyone has been very good.”

So she didn’t want to throw her boss under the bus either. Interesting.

“I’m so glad to hear it. Anything more we could be doing? You can tell me. I know these little visits from head office can be a bit unsettling, but we really are just trying to help.”

“No. It’s all fine. Great.”

Verona gave her impression of a soulless corporate pawn who wants to ingratiate themselves so they can feel like they’ve done a good job rather than out of genuine care for the employee. The key to any good con was leaning into expectations. “But of course this is the second visit in two months you’ve had from the head office. The first one may have left you with a bad taste in your mouth. I know some of our managers can really bring out the nerves in people.”

This time Sofia shook her head. “Manager? There was no manager.”

Verona paused for a moment. It seemed unrealistic that a maid would notice a manager walking around but the front desk wouldn’t. Whoever this manager was, she had walked around obviously enough for Tasoula to notice. And she would undoubtedly be staying at the hotel while she did her inspection or whatever it was. “You’re sure? A woman? Looks sort of like me?" Tasoula had provided a description almost as useless as Aster's had been.

"Young. Dark hair. Like you," she'd said.

Sofia shook her head again. "No, no managers. I would know. I always book their rooms, no one else, because I can move guests around to ensure the managers get the best suites."

Verona feigned innocent surprise. "Oh, my mistake! It must've been one of our other properties. Well, if you do think of anything you want to report, you let me know. Otherwise, let's keep this little chat between us. I want everyone to know I'll maintain your privacy."

Sofia went back to nodding. "Yes, of course."

Verona left through the sunbathed front doors and walked aimlessly until she reached the beach. All roads on an island eventually lead to the beach, after all.

So if there was no manager, who was the mystery lady? Was Tasoula just mistaken? Perhaps a guest got lost on their way to the conference room. Hence the business attire. And how the hell was she going to find the average-looking English guy that picked a fight with Javier?

Calgary
Thursday 3 a.m.

Experts insist that alcohol interferes with sleep and suggest you avoid it before bed. The same experts also warn you to avoid caffeine, even if you're ass-dragging tired. Eat a variety of vegetables and fruit, but make sure they're organic and local, even in the dead of winter when nothing is in season. Basically, the experts want you to do a lot of impossible stuff, and they dangle the carrot of longevity in front of you while sniggering sinisterly, thinking of the next ridiculous and pain-inducing recommendation they can pass off on the unsuspecting population in the name of health.

Quentin didn't care much for carrots, and he enjoyed a nightcap, so he ignored the evil experts. Strangely enough, he found a nightcap helped him sleep. Especially on nights like tonight when he'd woken up at 3 a.m. after falling asleep at 10 p.m. If he wanted a few more hours of rest before he had to be at the office, a nightcap was in order.

Tonight he drank a rum flip: thick, rich, filling, warming, calming, spiced, and just what the doctor would *not* order. The drink sat at his right in a deep crystal glass on the heavy ebony table beside his burgundy leather couch. He had the radio playing with the volume low but the dialogue still audible, the fuzzy chatter giving him comfort in a strange way, sort of like when he used to lie awake at night and listen to his family talking in the living room down the hall. He had the lights low, the dark gray curtains pulled snugly against the windows, creating a perfect cocoon from the world.

In the stillness and quiet his phone rang, and he jumped like a cat being pranked with a cucumber. The ringer was set to low, but he wasn't expecting anyone to be calling at this hour. Then he saw the caller ID, and it all fell into place.

"Verona."

"Quentin," she said, sounding surprised to catch him awake. "I'm surprised to catch you awake."

"I could hang up if that would be better." Sometimes the later he stayed up, the cheekier he felt. He formed a mental picture of her giving him an over-the-top eye roll. Why was it so fun to get her all riled up?

"Very funny. What time is it there?"

"I'm sorry—did you call for the time and weather in Calgary? You can look that up, you know. There's this amazing new thing called the internet."

"You're spry for"—she paused, likely to check the internet—"three a.m."

Maybe it was the alcohol that was making him cheeky. It didn't matter. "So now that we've ascertained that I am, in fact, awake, and I did, in fact, answer the phone, and it is, in fact, three a.m. here, are there any other trivial bits of information I can get for you?"

"Bastard." She hung up.

Quentin smiled in satisfaction. He waited two minutes and called back. "So what time is it there?" he said, blasé as fuck.

"Very funny. You do the math."

"Is that math?" he asked.

"Very simple math. Addition or subtraction. Probably too tricky for you."

"Is it my turn to hang up on you? Only my drink is almost done, and I'm getting pretty tired." He could do this all night. Probably. He was getting tired, but something about Verona energized him. He didn't know what to do with it, and he guessed she didn't either, since they both kept up this constant stream of flirty fighting. Any time he tried to edge closer, to see if something might be there, she put up a wall. Maybe that was best.

"Stop fucking around. I've got news."

"Oh!" Quentin injected as much sarcasm as he could, which was a lot, into his next words. "Oh, you have news! I never would have guessed."

"Shut the fuck up and listen!"

If she was pissed off and wanted to get down to business, that meant he had won. "Okay, I'm listening."

Five minutes later, Quentin was pacing his living room, his bare feet sinking into the thick gray rug, all thoughts of going to bed gone. "Wait—you're saying you've got an actual suspect?"

"No. That's the problem."

"But you just said Javier got into a fight with a guy the night he was killed. That's at least enough to paint a picture that someone else wanted him dead. Maybe went back to finish the job."

"For that to work, you've got to be able to point to an actual person. Tell the story of why this guy wanted him dead."

"So?"

"So, if you'd been listening, you'd have heard me say it was just some guy. An average-looking English guy. That's all we've got."

Quentin waved this aside with an impatient hand. "That's all we've got *for now*. You've got to find out more about him. He was staying at the hotel, right?"

"Maybe. Probably. But I mean, how many English dudes were staying there at the same time? And what am I supposed to do? Ask to see the list of English guests, including contact details? I've already burnt my con at the front desk finding out about the manager. They think I'm HR, but they aren't going to just give me access to their guest lists without some proof or authorization. And I don't have access to a wig shop and face prosthetics to run a new approach. I'm not Sydney-fucking-Bristow[1] here."

Quentin sat back down on the couch, his enthusiasm draining as the alcohol made his limbs feel fuzzy. It had seemed exciting for a few moments to realize there was someone they could point to in order to help Miami's case. Not that he wanted to make someone who was innocent look guilty, but in a murder trial, that's not the point. The point is doubt, the possibility someone else *might* be guilty.

Without some official power behind her, Verona was never going to get a look at that guest list, but there *were* eyewitnesses. If they could find him, the witnesses could prove he was there, and that would be enough for the police to take over.

"Okay, okay," Quentin said, urging his tired and alcohol-enveloped brain to think. "Sure, a lot of Brits likely do go to Greece. But we're not talking Greece. We're talking Mykonos, and a specific hotel during a specific time. That can't be a whole lot of people, can it?"

"Even if it's only five or ten, how am I supposed to find him without a name to go on?"

A new thought struck Quentin. "Maybe I can help. There may have been a lot of Brits staying at the hotel, but why was the guy so pissed off at Javier?"

"Apparently, he never said. Aster got the impression it was jealousy, but she also said that he went off about human dignity, which doesn't sound like a jealous boyfriend to me."

Quentin couldn't imagine himself picking a fight with another man over that topic when it came to a girlfriend. Punch his lights out? Maybe. But a lecture? Never. "Human dignity? Really? No, definitely not a jealous lover. That's always way more about feeling jilted and angry and emasculated than it is about protecting your partner."

"Speaking from experience?"

"Yes. Divorce lawyer, remember?"

"Right. Yes. Anyhow, to me that sounds way more like something another woman would say. In my experience, men haven't been too vocal

---

1. From *Alias.*

about other men taking advantage of women. They just sort of keep their nose out, you know?"

"Thanks," Quentin said acidly. But she wasn't wrong. "So what are you saying?"

"I'm saying it sounds more like the kind of thing a father would say. But being that the guy was about thirty—"

"A brother." He finished her thought.

"Yes, perhaps. How does this help you help me?"

"Well, thanks to this whole shit show of a murder charge hanging over Miami, I have access to Javier's business records. How many young British women have worked for him here in Calgary? There can't be that many."

"Runi," Verona said, her voice implying they were both idiots.

"Pardon?"

"Runi, my friend. I've talked about her before. You know, the social media scrubber?"

"The one who drives that really sweet Bentley?" It was a flashy choice, but one Quentin admired.

"Yup."

"She's good at her job, then." Perhaps he should get himself a showy car so his clients would assume the same of him.

"Obviously."

"And your idea is...?" This was a new level of energy from Verona, and a deviation from their usual pattern. Working *together*. Solving a problem. Forgetting to tease and rankle. As much as he loved the teasing, this felt better. Like they were actually together instead of dancing around each other like two heavyweights.

"Runi is used to digging up crap on her clients so she can erase it. Which means she knows where to look. Either through the sister posting shit about her boss, or the guy posting about his vacation—or a combination of both—she may be able to find them if you give her a starting point with some employee names from Javier's company." The excitement in her voice had returned. He'd always known she liked her job and was good at it, but seeing it in action was impressive. Attractive.

"Oh, well, that's me sitting pretty and letting other people do the work. Lawyer, remember? My paralegal can sort through the files."

"Yeah, when you call Runi, make sure you don't tell her that."

"When *I* call?"

"Sure, it'll be easier for you to do that. Same time zone and all that. Is that a problem?"

"No, it's just she's *your* friend." He knew he was acting like a kid afraid to call an adult that wasn't his parents, but he really didn't want to have to call Runi.

"Uh-huh. But she's also a professional. Don't think she's going to do this for free because she knows me. You'll have to let Miami know one more person is going on the payroll."

"But you'll tell Runi to expect my call, right?"

"Why are you being so weird about calling her? Don't you talk to strangers on the phone all the time?"

Quentin shifted in his seat, trying to put words to his inexplicable discomfort. "I don't know—just the way you describe her, she sounds...frightening."

"She *is* frightening. Anyhow, it's late there—I should let you go."

Quentin had no move but to save face. "Sure," he said as nonchalantly as he could. They hung up, and he sat motionless for a few minutes, rethinking the phone call. They hadn't even said goodbye with a parting jab. She'd just been real with him, flexed her expertise, and invited him to call her best friend. He found it sexy as hell.

Who was this Verona Montero, and why had she taken so long to show up?

22

ABOUT AS USEFUL AS A PAPERWEIGHT

Mykonos
Six weeks earlier

It was Zane's last night of Grecian paradise, and he didn't want it to end. His flight was the next morning, and he considered staying up all night to bask in every last drop of clear skies and warm air before returning to dreary, rainy England. Sure, it wasn't always rainy in England, just usually. Often. Frequently. He didn't miss it.

He wandered into the bar, looking forward to a refreshing cocktail before a stroll through the town. That's when he saw *him*.

Javier Luis Cavallero. The son of a bitch had been his sister Flora's boss briefly when she had moved to Canada at age twenty. Made inappropriate advances, threatened not only her job but also her visa status if she made a fuss. Rumors went around the staff about girls Javier liked and the cost of saying no to him: you wouldn't work in the city again. There was no question of reporting him—he had HR wrapped around his little finger with large payoffs.

Finally, the stress and fear got too much for Flora, and she moved back home. Took her months to admit why, and even then she made Zane swear not to tell their parents. He tried to tell her she had nothing to be ashamed of, but she said that didn't change the way she felt. As if she'd let herself down. Let womankind down.

Zane had never started a fight in his life. Never even been near a fight. He wasn't one of those bawdy, rough-around-the-edges, pub-fighting Brits. He was even-tempered and preferred to talk it out or walk away. He'd never been the jealous sort, and though protective of his sister, had never seen reason to throw his weight around or intimidate her boyfriends. Flora was smart and capable and could pick her own boyfriends without him breathing down her neck.

But that night he saw Javier at the table, laughing lecherously with a young woman, something snapped in him. He remembered all the terrible things Flora had told him Javier had said to her. Remembered how gutted she'd been to return home to England when she was so excited to spend time in a new country. Remembered how, every day, she'd felt afraid something was going to happen to her. How the bottom had dropped out of her stomach on the one occasion she was left alone with Javier.

In a cloud of memories and anger, Zane marched over to Javier with heavy steps.

"Oi!" he shouted. "Dickhead!"

He grabbed a drink from the table and threw it, then just stood there. The rage and adrenaline were still coursing through his veins, but this was as far as they would take him. His brain scanned any information it had on these types of confrontations and found only highly dramatized scenes from the cinema, where the guy picking the fight was secretly a Green Beret, had a black belt, or was a champion boxer with some fast-flying moves. Zane had zero moves.

Javier stood up. He didn't tower over Zane, but he was used to intimidating people. He pulled his broad shoulders back and stuck his chest out like an aggressive silverback gorilla. "What," he asked in a quiet, menacing tone, "the fuck do you think you're doing? Do you know how much this suit costs?"

"Not as much as human dignity!" Zane regretted it the moment he said it. He felt like a door-to-door missionary. Sure, he had conviction, but conviction was useless against ignorance.

Javier's nose wrinkled as he pulled his lips back in a sneer. "Human dignity? This suit costs more than your mother makes whoring for a whole year. How's that for dignity?"

Zane wished he hadn't come over. Flora would be horrified to hear he'd done it. But then again, this man had terrorized countless women over his lifetime, and it was rare someone could stand up to him with little fear of serious repercussions. Except a broken nose, maybe. Perhaps some cracked ribs. A black eye for sure.

"I know the kinds of things you do to women, and I'm not going to stand for it." He looked at Javier's young date, and she started to stand up.

"Sit your ass down!" Javier shouted at her.

She sat, her narrowed eyes slits of contempt.

Heat rushed from Zane's chest to his temples, then radiated through his whole body, making his skin pulse with anger. "Yeah, that's right, intimidate her, like you do all of them. Tell me, have you ever had sex with someone you didn't buy or coerce? Think that makes you a man? 'Cause it doesn't. It makes you the exact fucking opposite."

Javier's chest ballooned as if he were concentrating all of his strength before he let loose on Zane. The patrons in the bar were staring. His date was slowly moving her chair away from the table while he was distracted. "You better shut the fuck up, or you'll never talk again." His jaw tightened.

"Is that why you always try to get them young? Easier to scare?" All of Zane's restraint left him in a reckless idea that since he hadn't been assaulted yet, he probably wouldn't be. He was wrong.

Javier lunged at Zane with both hands. Zane stepped backwards to take some of the momentum out of the attack, but Javier still managed to grab his shirt. Zane grasped Javier's hands and tried to pry them off.

The bartender, who had been watching the scene, hurried over and took the standard referee pose, pushing each man away with outstretched arms.

"Gentlemen," he said in a quiet but strong voice, "I suggest you go your separate ways, or I will need to call the police. I think we can all agree that would be unfortunate. May I suggest that sir"—he indicated Zane—"goes out on the balcony? It is a lovely, warm evening. And sir"—he indicated Javier—"remains at his table?"

Zane's pulsing heart and radiating skin didn't want him to give in, but there was nothing more he could do. What were his options? Throw a half-hearted punch through the bartender's arms and get kicked out of the bar? Pointless.

"Fine." He headed toward the balcony.

As he walked into the humid warmth of the night, the aftereffects of the surge of adrenaline hit him hard. Even though he had little hope of winning a fight with Javier, the adrenaline had protected him from any real fear. He had felt excitement, power, and a daring he'd never known before. Now all that was left was a sense of deflation, of powerlessness, of defeat, and all he wanted was something to make it stop.

Which was why, when he would normally never dream of doing such a thing, he approached the stunningly gorgeous woman sitting alone at a table, basking in the setting sun.

Mykonos
Present Monday, 10 a.m.

Talking to the police in real life wasn't anything like it was in the movies. There was no dark little room with a stark table and a single overhead light. There was just a busy desk in the middle of a cramped utilitarian office with tidy piles of files, pens scattered around, and a desktop computer.

Detective Constantinides was dressed simply in black slacks and a white golf shirt. Her phone, lying face up on the desk, rang once every five minutes, but she seemed unconcerned about its annoying jingle. As other detectives and officers passed by in frenzied activity, she remained focused, as if she were in a still and silent building. Her voice was a calming alto, kept at an even pace and a volume loud enough to be heard clearly but never approaching a shout. She asked a question in Greek.

Verona, who had no idea what the detective had asked, resumed studying the ceiling tiles. She was surprised at how many pencil holes were up there, and even spotted a few pencils still clinging on. She thought it strange that a group of professionals whose job it was to hunt down miscreants would behave like bored schoolchildren.

Aster, who sat to her right in a molded orange chair, answered the question in Greek.

Anatole, on Verona's left, nodded along.

When the interview began, Aster had translated everything for Verona, but as the conversation progressed and she realized the detective had almost no questions for Verona, she stopped. Now the three chatted rapidly to each other, and Verona resigned herself to serving the same purpose as a lamp. No, that wasn't right either. The lamp at least gave off light. She was more like a paperweight. Yes, she felt fairly certain she could hold some papers down if called upon to do so.

As boring as it was to sit on the outskirts of the conversation, it was still somewhat of a relief to her. She was *working* again. The past four days had left her with little to do in the investigation except wait to see if Runi and Quentin managed to dig up a name. She'd had to actually attempt a vacation, which she discovered she was quite horrible at. How long was she expected to sit on the beach doing *nothing*? It seemed other folks were content to spend an entire day lounging there, but Verona gave up after an hour.

She'd half-heartedly considered continuing to investigate the possibility of Javier's death being related to drugs, but the motivation to investigate just wasn't there while the more likely possibility of an angry, vengeful brother existed. If that turned out to be a dead end, she'd get back to it. This was her best lead, well, her only lead. In truth, if this hadn't panned out, she didn't know what other direction to take the investigation.

"She wants to know how you found this man," Aster said, startling Verona out of her interior world.

"What?" Having to pay attention again after zoning out for so long reminded Verona of watching a ten-kilometer race. After twenty-five minutes of dozing off, your heart rate skyrockets for the last few laps.

"She wants to know how you found this man when you weren't here when the fight occurred."

Verona told the story slowly, thinking through each step before she spoke. She had to deliver it as factually as possible. From the detective's perspective, this was important; acting on information gleaned from illegal sources could prove disastrous, potentially tainting her investigation and any hope of prosecution.

She was careful when describing her interviews with Aster and Anatole to minimize any chance of their being in trouble for not coming forward sooner. She didn't blame them for not saying anything initially—no one wanted to get involved in a messy murder investigation, especially not for a man like Javier.

She assured the detective that the information about the suspect had been gotten through appropriate channels: Runi's social media scrubbing business was a legal, registered company, and she was audited to ensure she didn't access any areas of the internet she shouldn't be. Quentin's part was easiest of all, him being a lawyer and being granted access to employee files.

The detective seemed satisfied with Verona's explanations, because she only asked for clarification on a few items before dismissing them from the station.

As they walked down the sidewalk back to the hotel, Verona said, "I did tell you they'd be too happy with the information to care that you didn't come forward earlier."

Aster smiled, but Anatole was unimpressed. "A detective whose job it is to build a case will overlook this," he said. "A defense lawyer will not."

The smile vanished from Aster's face, but Verona said, "A defense lawyer would find some way to make you less credible no matter what. At least now you know what they'll go after. The prosecution lawyer will prepare you for that anyhow. You'll be in good hands."

This did little to cheer Anatole or Aster, so Verona said, "Remember why you did this. You've helped to open the eyes of the police to other possibilities. I'm not saying this guy killed Javier, but now they're seeing that there's a wider net they can be casting."

They parted with little enthusiasm. Even Verona found it hard to be overly excited, despite handing a name and photo over to the police. It was more than she could've hoped for, but something about it felt hollow. Maybe it was the knowledge that she wouldn't be able to continue the investigation; it was up to the police to dig into the evidence. She was used to being the one to hand over the final, unequivocal proof of dirty deeds, and she didn't like that someone else was going to have that moment when she'd put so much work in.

Instead, all she had to look forward to was a long flight home. *Maybe I can trade my fucking expensive handbag for a comfort-plus seat.*

PART III

MURDERS ARE NOT GOOD WEDDING GIFTS

23

NOT THE HAPPIEST DAY

Calgary
Ten months later,[1] Saturday 3 p.m.

Summer was on the way again, a welcome relief from the months of bitter cold and whitewashed snow. The warmth of the sun radiated on Verona's face and bare arms, and she inhaled the scent of late-spring blooms still hanging on to the trees.

She stood outside the police station waiting for her chance to talk to the bride. The building was unencumbered by the press because the news hadn't leaked yet, but Verona knew it would only be a matter of time before they came looking to suck the lifeblood from the living. Her official involvement in the case was nonexistent, since the police had laid charges, but something about it kept pulling her back, even without the lure of Miami's generous paychecks.

Here comes the bride, she thought as Blair emerged from the station.

"Blair?" Verona said.

"Nope," was Blair's response.

---

1. From when the prologue began. Look how far you've come.

"Well, I know you're Blair," said Verona, like she was responding to a kid who had uninvited her to their birthday party.

"So why'd you ask, then? My answer is still nope. I don't want to talk to you, I don't want to answer a few questions, so you can fuck off before I put my heel through your eye socket." Blair pushed by like a movie star desperate to escape their stalker.

Verona hadn't expected a warm greeting and wasn't about to give up because of a little threat. "Sure, I understand. You probably want to get home and get changed. I can give you a lift if you like."

Blair stopped and turned. "Yeah, I do want to get home and change. I also want to go on my honeymoon, but I don't see that happening—do you? A ride home would be great, but not from you. I think I'd rather blow Jim Jones and Ted Bundy until they achieved mutual climax than get in a car with you."

"What about your mother-in-law?"

"My what?" asked Blair, her eyes darting behind Verona as if afraid her mother-in-law might be waiting to jump out from a secret hiding spot.

"Yup. I heard she's on the way to get you now. Wants to help you through this tough time. Get you settled."

It was complete bullshit, but Verona *had* seen an older woman in the parking lot with a ridiculous feathered fascinator in her hair. She spoke loudly in a British accent about who was to blame for what happened to her son. It wasn't too much of a stretch to assume she was Zane's mother. Every mother knows bad things never happened to their darling sons until there was "a woman" in the picture.

"She's technically not my mother-in-law yet," Blair said in much the same tone that a five-year-old says "I don't believe in monsters" while watching their closet with wide eyes.

Verona started to walk away. "Suit yourself, then. I was trying to offer you a nicer way out." She indicated her vehicle, parked in the loading zone for a quick getaway.

Blair rolled her eyes to the sky, as if cursing whoever put her at the mercy of two different bitches she hated. "Fine," she said at last, moving toward the car, "but don't ask me any questions on the drive."

Verona held up her hands in innocence. "I'm just offering a ride here."

Blair snorted.

To let things settle between them, Verona honored her agreement to not ask questions except for Blair's address. Despite everything, she felt a bit sorry for Blair and Zane. It was unfortunate the warrant had been issued on their wedding day; a day earlier or later would have been much better. She couldn't help wondering how it must feel to find yourself engaged to a murder suspect. And did Blair think he did it? Would she delude herself into thinking he was innocent even if the evidence said he wasn't?

Blair suddenly burst out, "Don't you fucking pity me!"

"I wasn't!" said Verona, too quickly to be believable.

Blair glared out the front window. "Yes, you were. You were over there thinking, oh, that poor woman, marrying a murderer. I'll bet she goes home and cries herself to sleep after a long shower, fingering herself to reruns of *ER*, and a fucking Bacardi's cooler."

The corners of Verona's mouth curled up. She couldn't help but like Blair, with her feistiness and crass humor. And the cussing. "Okay. What *are* you going to do, then?"

"Well, you'd be right about the shower. I'm fucking melting away in this dress and makeup. But everything else is complete bullshit."

"Okay, so good—you're not ready for a breakdown."

"Fuck no!" said Blair. "You're dealing with the avenging fucking angel over here. I'm going to call a lawyer. Multiple lawyers. And then I will go to bed and get ready to interview them tomorrow. You know, something helpful."

They drew up in front of Blair's building, and Verona decided to risk one tiny question. They seemed to be approaching a fun territory of being enemies who respected each other's cunning and badass-ness, so maybe Blair would let it slide.

As Blair opened her door, Verona said, "So you don't think he did it, then?"

Blair looked at Verona as if sizing her up to see how much marinade she'd need before putting her on the BBQ. "I *know* he didn't fucking do it." She stormed away, dress hitched up and feet navigating the pavement as if she were wearing runners instead of high heels.

Saturday 4 p.m.

Zane had been given express directions from his blushing bride to "not say a fucking thing." To be fair, the blushing had nothing to do with sweet, womanly emotion and everything to do with being extremely pissed off.

The thing about being arrested in connection with a murder was that it wasn't like on the telly at all. On the telly, the guy gets hauled off to the station in handcuffs, and he's immediately put in one of those little question-asking rooms, where he ends up confessing and everyone's shaking hands, then *poof*, he's magically in jail.

Zane had been cautioned and advised of his right to a solicitor, to which he said, "Yes, please!" Therefore he wasn't being questioned, because —surprise!—he'd asked for a solicitor! He had no idea how he was going to find one, as that bit was often skirted over on the telly. A solicitor always mysteriously showed up. Did everyone have one? Was that part of being an adult that he had missed? Was he supposed to have one on retainer or something? Was "retainer" the right word? He had a feeling that was a mouth appliance.

He was also fairly sure his definition of "can't afford a solicitor" was different from what might officially count as "can't afford." Could he, technically, afford his own legal counsel? Yes. Would it likely eat up all his savings and leave him with nothing? Quite possibly. That was, of course, if he was found not guilty.

His stomach tightened, and not from hunger. *Murder.* As much as he told himself, *They can't find me guilty*, he had a great fear they might. And it wasn't just any old murder charge either. Nope—they were going for first degree.

Zane really wanted to talk to someone, and this, he supposed, was how they got you. When you're in an impossibly stressful situation, the urge to talk it out with someone—anyone—is very strong. And when you're in a holding cell, waiting for a lawyer you haven't hired yet, the only people to talk to are police officers. They can seem so damn sympathetic. Certainly the officers who had booked him in had been very courteous. There was none of the delousing and jeering he'd seen on the telly. He was starting to suspect the telly made up a lot of police procedure for good drama.

If he didn't have Blair's fierce face in his mind, her words running through his head—"Don't say a fucking thing!"—he might've cracked.

Even in this state, a wistful thought crossed his mind: he was so lucky to have found her. He wished he could get more information from her. "Oi!" he shouted to the room in general. "Don't I get a phone call or something?"

No one answered, because no one was in the room. This was another way his telly education about the justice system was letting him down. On the telly, there was always a guy sitting right outside, ready to make wisecracks and fall asleep with the key ring dangling tantalizingly out of reach.

Zane sighed and hugged himself. He'd had to give up his jacket and his waistcoat, so he was only in his shirt and trousers. He had been hot during the wedding preparations, but now that the sweat was starting to evaporate, he was getting chilly. Of all the ways he had imagined spending his wedding night, cold wasn't one of them. He longed for a shower. He longed for a cuppa, damn it! And he longed for Blair.

And that's when the real chill stole over him, the chill that had nothing to do with the temperature. If they found him guilty, this would be his life. Well, not this exactly—no, it'd be worse. He'd be some guy named Buck's little bitch.

Saturday 6 p.m.

Business was booming for Verona, as it always did in the summer. There was something in the air, some sort of memory of the euphoria of the last day of school and a summer full of freedom from responsibility that really cranked up the dial on infidelity. Everyone was eager to relive the camp romances of their youth. Or the camp romances they wished they'd had in their youth. Or maybe all of it was bunk and it was a leftover prehistoric survival instinct urging everyone to breed before the snow started flying.

The reasons were of little concern to Verona as she sat at a table in a coffee shop, discreetly snapping pictures of a couple making ooey-gooey faces to each other while holding hands. This was going to be another one of those easy cases; she'd have it wrapped up before the whipped cream in her coffee melted.

You need a few easy cases like this after the Javier case, she tried to tell herself.

But that was bullshit. The Javier case hadn't exhausted her; it had energized her and awoken an ambition she hadn't known existed. She had enjoyed the total involvement in that case. She'd flown to Greece to do her job, for fuck's sake. She'd conned the entire island to get the lead that led to the arrest.

And you had an excuse to talk to Quentin all the time, the pathetic part of her thought.

She half-heartedly took a burst photo as the couple finally moved beyond "innocent" hand-holding and shared an overdone kiss. Sheila was going to get the proof she needed that Drew was indeed boinking the cute girl from the pet-grooming place. She couldn't blame him really, Sheila was a loud, obnoxious piece of work, and pet-grooming girl was mild mannered, fresh-faced, and happy about life. If only he'd had the balls to break up with Sheila first, he wouldn't be facing the nasty end of the divorce stick.

In other cases, she'd allow herself a moment of satisfaction in knowing she'd clinched the proof, but this time she found it hard to care. She put down her phone and inspected her coffee. Yup, whipped cream still intact.

This was partly why she kept tabs on the Javier case. She was constantly trying to get that high back, hoping something else might come up, waiting for a chance to solve some new problem, yearning for a reason to text Quentin. Or for him to text her. Was it really the case she missed, or him? She had thought she was moving on from her silly crush, but these days it seemed like the opposite was true.

Well, fuck, she thought as she took out her phone to text him.

24

SYMPATHY SHAG

Calgary
Saturday 9 p.m.

Murder charges are hell on your personal life. Since the news broke that Zane had been arrested, people started coming out of the woodwork with phone calls, texts, and emails. As much as Blair wanted to insulate herself and ignore everyone for as long as she could, she recognized this would ultimately backfire, so she dutifully called the people she knew deserved it. Not that she had much to say.

"If you've seen the news, you know about as much as I do" was the party line. This always spurred a volley of questions, a plethora of platitudes, and an annoying amount of "How could this happen?" The thing about people is that all but the most intentional tend to say the same thing when presented with uncomfortable situations. It was tiring.

And all this was before people started showing up at her apartment.

The first person to appear was a stranger with the distinctly well-groomed look of the press. She looked up Blair and Zane's apartment number and buzzed it. And buzzed it. And buzzed it.

Blair was tempted to tell her to fuck off through the speaker but reasoned that admitting she was home would be far worse than enduring the buzzing. She was glad she did, because ten minutes later, a news van pulled up, and she watched as they recorded a segment by the sign of her building. They clearly didn't know if she was home or staying somewhere else, and she was happy to keep it that way.

She called the landlord and asked for her name to be removed from the tenant listing and suggested that her whole damn buzzer be disabled until future notice. The landlord agreed readily, not wanting to deal with a media circus in the parking lot either.

Between fending off all the callers, she'd spent the entire day interviewing lawyers and having all of her worst suspicions about them confirmed. Her brain felt like the sad little shrivelled-up sponge you find hiding under the sink and wonder, "Maybe if I leave it there, it will eventually implode like a black hole and take care of itself and all the other gross crap down there."

She was annoyed and defeated, and slightly panicky that she would have to pick a subpar lawyer so Zane would have *someone* to represent him. The judge had already agreed to delay the bail hearing beyond the usual twenty-four hours until Zane had a lawyer in place, but they wouldn't wait forever. Nor did Blair want him to wait any longer than necessary.

It was late, and all she wanted was a shower and an evening of mindless television, but as she threw some leftovers in the oven to heat, her phone rang. She considered not even checking to see who it was, but something compelled her to have a peek. Hope, perhaps? Hope that the person she needed would magically show up? She didn't know who she needed to show up—only that when they did, she'd feel better.

It was one of Zane's groomsmen, Evan. Both of his groomsmen had been friends with him since they were kids back in England and presumably would be the most likely to believe he hadn't done it. Blair didn't know this one, Evan, as well as the other friend, Dagon, but they had both seemed like good guys. "Decent blokes," Zane would say. Besides, it would be nice to hear someone else—anyone else—say, "I know he didn't do it!"

"Come on up." She turned off the TV. If nothing else, it would be good to tell Zane one of his mates had visited.

There was a soft knock at the door, and Blair opened it and stepped back to let Evan in. He stood about eye level with Blair, had short brown hair, gray-blue eyes, and the kind of pale complexion that revealed his ancestors were from a place with a lot of rain and not much sun. With a deference born of generations of polite and stiff-upper-lipped Englishmen, Evan stepped in. He tipped his head, then held up a small bottle of whisky.

Blair said, "Have a seat," and went to the kitchen for a couple of glasses.

She put them out on the coffee table, and Evan poured, raised his glass, and waited for Blair to follow suit. It seemed an odd time for a toast, but she raised her glass anyhow.

"To Zane," said Evan softly. "May the sorry bastard know his friends toast him, even now."

Evan tossed his whisky back in one go, but Blair took a sip of hers and set it down. Someone like Evan might have the luxury of being able to get stupid drunk and sleep it off, but she didn't.

"Can't hold your liquor?" Evan asked.

"No, I can," said Blair, "but I really need to keep my head. Crucial times."

"Of course. You know he didn't do it."

"Yes, of course I do." Warmth rushed through her body that had nothing to do with the liquor.

"Nah, Zaney could never do that. Not his style, is it? He couldn't even put a tack on the teacher's chair in school. Chickened out at the last minute, didn't he? Made up some excuse to get the teacher away from the chair and took it away." Evan poured another glass and threw it back, grinning at the memory.

Blair sank into her sofa and soaked in the presence of another human who trusted Zane's good nature. He wasn't a wild man, wasn't a troublemaker. He was kind and smart, and liked to help people instead of hurt them. It was part of what she liked about him. She'd never sought out the bad boys, much preferring the good ones. They had heart and a truer kind of bravery.

"That sounds about right," she said.

"Not like me." Evan poured another drink, saluted the air with it, and downed it. "I was the troublemaker. I would've killed that bloke if I knew he'd been at my sister. Hang the consequences."

Or be hung by them, thought Blair. "I suppose that's why you made such good friends. You each gave each other some balance. You kept Zane from being a complete ninny, and he kept you from turning into a...oh, I don't know you well enough, but we'll say delinquent, shall we?"

"Delinquent, yeah." Evan toyed with his glass as if contemplating another shot.

Blair saw the warning signs, and as much as she enjoyed his reassurance, she was in no state to have a drunk friend bunk on her couch for the night. "Look," she said, smiling but getting up to initiate a departure, "I appreciate your dropping by. It's good to know Zane has people on his side. But I've got an early morning tomorrow, and I need to get to bed."

Evan got up too, raising his hands in apology. "Right, right."

They walked to the door, and Evan turned suddenly to embrace Blair, placing his lips on her neck. She wedged a hand under his chin to push his head into the door while pushing her other elbow into his solar plexus.

"Whoa!" She made as much space between them as she could while he still had his arms around her.

"Come on, then, love," Evan said, slurring. "How about a little sympathy shag, then? We're both downhearted, ain't we? Both miss Zaney? A little commiseration for us both?" He caressed her arm as if this might be the secret password that would make her melt in his arms.

His lack of violence allowed her to not feel afraid. In fact, she felt calm, as if she could see the situation from the outside rather than from within it. It gave her an edge of detachment she welcomed. He was a man unafraid to push a bit past where he should. Used to ignoring a no, used to his presence and aggression being enough to win him sex. Coercive and forceful rather than physically violent. If she played this right, she would be okay.

"No," she said. "You can get your sympathy shags elsewhere."

When he didn't move to let go of her, she dug her elbow more firmly into his solar plexus and increased the pressure under his chin, digging her thumb into the soft spot beneath the jawbone. Like almost every woman in the twenty-first century, she'd attended her fair share of self-defense seminars. Him being three whiskies in helped a bit.

He groaned in pain and let her go, and she took several steps back from him.

"Look," she said, holding her hands up, "you're upset. It's a weird situation." She didn't agree with her words at all, but it wasn't about that at that moment. It was about getting him out, and she would give him every excuse to leave. "People react to grief in different ways." She nodded as if understanding.

Evan eyed her, undecided, then turned and opened the door. "Zaney wouldn't have minded," he said. "Would like to know someone's takin' care of you."

Blair bit back her retort, because whatever he wanted to tell himself was fine by her so long as he was leaving. She kept her distance until the door shut, then rushed forward and threw the bolt home. She watched him down the hallway through the peephole, then checked on the door camera to make sure he exited the building.

Her heart was hammering and her adrenaline pumping, but not out of fear. No, she felt amped up because she had been ready. In those few moments when Evan had held her, she'd planned exactly what she'd do to him if he didn't let go, right up to where she'd dump the body.

She took a few deep breaths to calm herself and sat outside on her deck, allowing the fresh air to help soothe her piqued instincts.

What a fucked-up day.

With nothing good coming from the outside world, Blair decided she wouldn't answer her phone anymore. The thought made her happy because she'd no longer have to worry about annoying men who got sad and horny or clueless women. It made her less happy when she imagined the sheer lengths to which her mother-in-law was likely to go to get news. But you can't win them all.

25

A WORM ON LSD

Calgary
Saturday 10 p.m.

In selecting the location for her date with Quentin, Verona tried to go with something obscure rather than familiar. She didn't want to risk running into a crowd of people they knew and being stuck having an evening out with friends again.

"Bit of a hike to get here, wasn't it?" Quentin took his seat opposite her.

Well, she was calling it a date in her mind, but she hadn't asked him out. Not really. She'd texted him to invite him out for beers to celebrate the arrest in the Javier case. He didn't know it was beers with an ulterior motive she hoped to finally make good on.

"I like trying out new places now and then." As extra insurance, she had chosen a neighborhood she felt confident none of her friends lived in. It had been a half-hour drive from her apartment.

They chose the patio and sat at a table with a glass fireplace burning softly to one side. The sun had already set, but the sky still held the last reflections of light, and the night air was warm and scented with sweet pollen.

Their wicker seats were comfortable with soft gray plush cushions, a step up from the usual metal chairs provided for outdoor eating. The low tables were made of dark wood, and partial separation was created by low brick walls. Heaters ran along the pergola overhead, and soft world music flitted around gently, creating a calm and exotic feel.

Now that she had him here, on this romantic patio, she didn't know where to begin. Runi had tried to coach her by telling her to ask him something "real," but her mind was blank. Her usual moves with Quentin were to talk about work or, failing that, make fun of him.

The server stopped by to take their order, saving her momentarily. She ordered her usual Dark and Stormy, and Quentin asked for a cosmopolitan, which still surprised her. She imagined a classy guy like him would order something like an old-fashioned, or a Godfather, or a Tom Collins, but he always went for the pink cosmo.

They ordered appetizers: all the best fried food a bar can offer, from dry ribs, to calamari, to jalapeño poppers, to chicken nuggets, to fries.

"What kind of vacations do you like?" Quentin asked as their drinks arrived.

"What?" Verona looked up from her drink, startled out of her struggle to come up with an opener.

"Vacations," said Quentin. "It seems like forever since I've been on one. I need some ideas. Where do you like to go? I mean, other than Greece, which you must've enjoyed because you came back very tanned."

Quentin's first-date arsenal of questions was a lot better than Verona's. She had been toying with some form of "Any siblings?" despite Runi's advice to *not* ask that very question.

"Oh." Verona felt dazed. "Um, let's see." He had commented on her tan. That was a good thing, right? Talking about her appearance in a positive way? *Fuck, I'm lame.* She gulped her drink for liquid courage. Why could she interview a man in Greek with her translation app, sneak into a sex club, and escape an abduction, but she couldn't talk to Quentin like a normal human woman?

"I mean, if a client isn't paying your way, where do you go?" Quentin said, sipping his drink.

The booze helped loosen Verona's tongue. "Vacations are not my forte. I thought I'd die of boredom in Greece waiting for you and Runi to turn up the goods." *Oh great, talking about work again. Way to go, Montero.*

Quentin saved her again. "Well, not all vacations require lounging on a beach. My last vacation to Mexico I went spelunking and ziplining. You could go to one of those places you need to hike to get in and out of."

She could imagine him cascading down a jungle hill, shirt off, sweat glistening off those abs. *That* was a vacation she could get behind. "Just hiking? That sounds almost as dull as resting on a beach."

The server arrived and deposited their platter of steaming, fatty, salty food, and she grabbed a jalapeño popper and threw it in her mouth, her eyes watering as the hot, gooey cheese burned her tongue.

Quentin noticed, but instead of commenting on it, he just smiled. This was usually where he'd have some sort of smart comment, and she'd throw it back at him. Maybe he was trying to change that? All she had to do was go along with it.

"Well, it isn't *just* hiking. You get to see things you can't see otherwise. Ruins, temples, animals." He extricated a fry, dipped it in ketchup, and took a bite.

It seemed like this particular conversational thread was dying like a worm on the sidewalk. All she had to do was pick a different topic, but all that came to mind was work-related. Asking what he thought of the arrest, asking if he thought they'd be subpoenaed, reviewing the details of how he dug up Zane's info. If he'd met the acerbic Blair. If Miami was still in the picture.

In her panic, she grasped onto the dying worm and tried to throw some water on it. "In terms of places not everyone goes, Afghanistan or Somalia are always options."

Fuck! That was more like LSD than water. Things were about to get weird, and not in a good way. She'd steered them right back to ridiculous joking territory.

"Yes," said Quentin, "I've been meaning to see if I can get taken hostage. And dressed like this, you might say I'd be asking for it."

"It certainly wouldn't help your case."

Quentin leaned back into the cushy seat, looking happy and comfortable. He took a bite of a spicy jalapeño popper and made no further attempt to ask about vacation spots.

She desperately wanted to get them back on some other track, but her mind and mouth were already talking about hostage negotiations and beheadings, and she knew there would be no coming back from that.

Sunday 8 a.m.

The beeping of Blair's alarm jabbed her brain at 8:00 a.m., giving her visions of smashing the damn thing while Eminem said vulgar, angry things in the background. She already had a decent amount of Eminem music, so she made a mental note to buy a sledgehammer and complete the smashing-shit set.

She felt like a sack of groggy, soggy crap. She longed for Zane so she could prod him into the kitchen to put the coffee on, then maybe do a little something while they waited for the pot to brew. The sensation was so powerful, she could almost smell coffee. She breathed in deeply, then sat bolt upright with a surge of adrenaline, realizing this was no psychological trick her mind was playing. She *did* smell coffee, and that meant there was someone inside her apartment.

She got up, threw on some clothes, grabbed one of Zane's multitool pocketknives, and ventured out, her desire for a sledgehammer doubling as she walked quietly out of the room. A knife was fine if you could get close enough and knew where to stab, but a sledgehammer required little in the way of finesse or accuracy. But the knife was what she had, so she held it ready in her hand, hidden behind her forearm in a reverse grip. She rounded the corner of her kitchen, muscles taut, nerves tingling.

"Morning," said a casual voice. The owner of the voice set a cup of freshly poured coffee on the stone counter.

The tension in Blair's body dissolved with a palpable slow release, like a balloon letting out air through a pinhole. "Tea,"[1] she said with a sigh. She

1. Pronounced "tay-ah," not like the beverage, since it's already been established that coffee

threw the knife on the kitchen island, climbed onto a burnt-orange barstool, and took a satisfying pull of the hot, perfectly sweetened, creamy coffee. Tea was the person she had been waiting for, the person who would magically know what to do to fucking help her.

Eighteen years old, with long black hair in a loose ponytail, dark blue eyes, and a porcelain complexion, Tea Lindell was the current intern at *Tier1*. An absolute powerhouse of a human being, she was sharp, worldly, practical, ambitious, and a hard worker. She was willowy and six foot three, but chose to wear high heels anyhow, meaning she towered over most men, which she enjoyed. "Let the fuckers see how they like being looked down on," she'd say with a snarl. She was ruthless in business but human with her subjects and her coworkers. For an eighteen-year-old, she was terrifyingly put together, miles ahead of most thirty-year-olds, and exactly whom Blair needed.

As Blair sipped her coffee, Tea consulted her phone, allowing the silence to linger while Blair got caffeinated. Like other people her age, Tea's phone was an extension of her body; you almost never saw her without it. Unlike a lot of young people, however, it wasn't there for her to obsess over social media. To her it was a tool, and she wielded it with as much skill, power, and authority as Thor with Mjölnir.[2]

"How did you get in here?" Blair asked after Tea poured her a second cup of coffee. The morning sunlight lit up the white-and-gray kitchen through the floor-to-ceiling windows, which revealed a view of the city's skyline, and in the distance, the mountains. All the surfaces gleamed—the cupboards were glossy white, the floor polished oak, the stone counters coated with blue marbling and silver shimmers.

"I know a locksmith."

Tea's answer to things was often that she "knew somebody," as if she were a crime lord who "had a guy" for everything. It was mind-boggling that she had so many connections at her age, but they always came through, and it was part of why she was such a superior intern.

---

is the drink on offer.

2. Or Dumbledore with his wand. Or Obi-Wan with his lightsaber. Or Aragorn with his sword. Or...Picard with his flute? I've got you covered, nerds!

Blair had given up trying to get details of Tea's connections—they were as convoluted as Confucius's family tree.[3] It was easier to nod and smile. At this point, Blair wouldn't care if Tea said, "I had my connections in the Irish mafia break in." It didn't matter—all that mattered was she was here.

"So," Tea said, brandishing her Samsung, "I've got your schedule all sorted. You've got ten more minutes to sit here, and then it's shower, dress, and we're off to the lawyers."

"How did you know I have an appointment today?"

"You gave me access to your calendar at work, and it's connected to your personal calendar—whether by mistake or design, I don't know. But you're old, so I'll forgive you for sucking at technology. In any case, I've fixed your color-coding system and removed the reminders to TiVo *Breaking Bad*.

"Also, damage control. You haven't spoken to the press yet, which is probably a good thing, considering. But if you wait too much longer, your silence will be spun in the way to sell the most stories, and we both know the story that sells is the one where Zane is guilty.

"I'm going to release a statement that's very clear and concise: you support Zane, believe in his innocence, and have faith that the justice system will expose the truth. It's complete bullshit, of course, but using words like 'faith,' 'the justice system,' and 'truth' will put people in your corner. They can't tear you apart too much over that. They'll try, of course, but your statement will make it easy to direct everything to the legal process from here on out and away from your personal relationship and feelings.

"On that note, I've taken over all your social media platforms and shut that shit down hard." She held up a hand when she saw Blair about to question how she got access. "I used 'Forgot your password?' and reset it. Your security questions were a fucking joke, Blair. Everyone had a cat named Mittens, okay? Anyhow, I'm only posting scheduled statements that have been carefully worded. We're only using Twitter, because your other platforms are way too personal, and I've temporarily suspended the other accounts so we don't have to deal with creepers.

"I'm also going to be managing my own news blog that will give the

---

3. Go on, look it up.

exclusive inside story of this whole thing, which is how you will thank me for getting you through this. But don't worry—I'll represent you fairly and only release the facts that need releasing. It'll serve the dual purpose of keeping your friends and family informed without your needing to call them, which I figured you'd like.

"Oh yeah," she said after a brief pause. "I got you a new phone." She passed over a cheap smartphone. "It's not fancy, but I'm a student and had to buy it straight up if I didn't want a contract, which I don't. It's pay-as-you-go, and you can give *this* number to your lawyers and anyone else you want to get ahold of you. You'll give me your other phone, and I'll monitor the texts and calls and let you know if anything needs your attention.

"Also, Tory wants you off work for at least a month while the dust settles. *Tier1* can't afford bad publicity on this."

Blair could only smile and say, "It was a lucky fucking day for me when you walked into our office."

Tea nodded and returned to her phone, pushing buttons that, for all Blair knew, ran the world.

~

Sunday 9 a.m.

"I'm feeling uncertain that Zane is our guy," Verona said to Runi through a mouthful of fresh *bungeo-ppang*. The sweet red bean paste melted in her mouth, and the crisp exterior reminded her of a waffle.

They sat on Runi's massive back deck being served the fish-shaped pastry by Runi's mother. The grease was still sizzling when she brought them out. They were a winter treat in Korea, but Runi's mother made them whenever she came from Toronto because everyone loved them so much.

Runi's salary meant she and her husband, Ash, lived in a modern home in a posh neighborhood west of downtown Calgary. The backyard featured mature trees, their spring blooms spent, leaving lush green leaves creating soft shade over the manicured lawn. A garden featuring plants most adapted to Alberta's climate flourished due to Ash's care and attention.

"Who cares if he did it or not?" Runi asked, licking her fingers one by one, her bright red nails catching the sunlight.

"Me! I thought that was obvious."

"But why? You did your job. Let everyone else do theirs."

"Because I can't let Javier win this one. I didn't catch that son of a bitch with his pants down, and I'll be damned if he bests me by having the wrong guy go to jail for his murder." She helped herself to another piece of *bungeoppang* as Runi's mother came out with a fresh plate.

She smiled at Mrs. Soon and was surprised to receive a scowl back. She'd always gotten along just fine with Mrs. Soon, despite the language barrier. As she turned to go back to the kitchen, Verona heard her mutter something like "You should be praying to the Jesus more."

Verona cocked her eyebrows at Runi, and Runi hid a snicker behind her hand. "Pray to the Jesus?" Verona asked.

"Okay, you remember last time Eomma visited and I stored some of my art at your house?"

"Yeah, and that penis one was a bit much. Even for a certified dick doodler like me."

Runi waved this away. "Whatever. Well, this time I missed a few."

"You *missed* a few? How could you miss a few?"

"It's a big house, and I forgot I'd done a whole series of miniature nipples. Very cute. All only about two-by-two inches. But I had them in a cluster in the downstairs bathroom, and I completely forgot. Eomma found them, of course."

"And this makes her hate *me* why?"

"I told her they were yours. You already investigate adultery, it seemed like an easy extension."

Verona consoled herself with another fish pastry before answering. "So, from now on, your mom will just hate me?"

Runi stretched her legs out from under the shade to get some sun on them. "Better you than us. We have to live with her for several weeks a year."

Verona gave her a petulant glare.

"Relax, okay? I'll just tell her you converted to Christianity and you're not into sexy pictures anymore. She'll love it. Think her prayers have been answered. You may just have to pretend to 'pray to the Jesus' now and again. It's easy. Even Ash can do it."

"Fine. I'll work on it after I solve this case." It wasn't that she was sure Zane was innocent, it was that she wasn't sure he was guilty, and she didn't like that. She'd never tell a client she was "pretty sure" their wife was cheating on them. Then there was Blair's certainty that he hadn't done it. She didn't seem like the kind of woman who would delude herself that way just to hang onto a guy, but then again, Verona didn't really know her.

Runi rolled her eyes. "That's why courts exist. They'll sort it out. Don't they have DNA they're matching to him? That sounds pretty conclusive to me."

She could let the courts sort it out. At this point, she pretty much had to, but that didn't mean she was happy about it. Her avenues to investigate were narrower than they had been before she'd gone to Greece, and unlike then, she didn't have a decent alternate idea. Mr. Choi had disappeared, and, frankly, he was a job for INTERPOL, or whoever handled that kind of thing. She was out of people to watch, out of people to question.

Except for...Blair. But would she ever agree to talk to Verona again? And would it even be helpful when she was so insistent on Zane's innocence?

The breeze brushed her hair across her neck, giving her a shiver. The condensation of her glass was running down her fingers, she'd been gripping it so hard as she thought. She shook the drips off and considered going for one last *bungeo-ppang*.

"Besides," Runi said, leaning back and closing her eyes, "I keep telling you I don't want to talk about all these other dudes you care about. Especially when you haven't said one word about your date with Quentin, and I've been pretty fucking patient."

"That's because I don't want to talk about it." Her throat constricted with the memory of last night.

Runi sat up and looked her in the eyes. "What happened?"

"What happened is, it's never happening." It sounded dramatic, but all she felt was dullness in the place where excitement used to live. That's how she knew it was true.

"You can't know that."

Verona groaned. "I started talking about hostage situations." She covered her eyes.

The unflappable Runi flapped, her voice going a few decibels louder than usual. "You talked about *what*?"

Verona peeked between her fingers, her words muffled by her palms. "Hostage situations. And not the fun ones either."

"What would a *fun* hostage situation be?" Runi asked, back to her serene self.

Verona threw her hands down in disgust. "Oh, you know, *Die Hard*, *The Negotiator, Horrible Bosses* 2. That kind of thing."

"So, fake ones."

"Yes. Point is, I didn't talk about fake ones. I went real. And dark. I'm talking Somalia, *Captain Phillips*, Afghanistan, Amanda Lindhout. Beheadings."

Runi closed her eyes and took a breath. "I know I told you to talk about something real, but I didn't think you'd go that real."

Verona took another *bungeo-ppang* in commiseration. "That's just it. It *wasn't* real. He asked me about vacations. You know, a real conversation starter about real shit, and I somehow ended up talking about journalists being beheaded on video."

"But eventually you got around to talking about vacations?"

"No." Verona slapped her palm on the armrest of her chair, the stinging sensation a welcome distraction from her annoyance. "Not at all. All I had to do was tell him about my time in fucking Greece, and I'd have had a chance. He even brought it up. Mentioned my tan."

"He mentioned your tan, and you talk about hostages?"

Verona moaned and put her forehead in her hands on her lap. "It's never happening."

Runi gave her head a consoling pat. "Maybe all is not lost. What did he say at the end of the night?"

"'We'll talk soon.'"

"Oh yeah, you're fucked."

26

SPRINKLED BADASS

Calgary
Sunday 9 a.m.

"You're running out of time," Tea said to Blair as she drove them to their first meeting of the day. "If you want a lawyer for the bail hearing, you've kind of gotta bite the bullet."

Green poplars sped past as Blair looked out the window. "I know. I just...hate lawyers, I guess. They think they're so smart. Smug bastards."

"But the thing is, the prosecution will have a team of smug, smart bastards all putting their think-they're-so-smart heads together to ensure that your man doesn't taste freedom ever again. So I think it'd be wise for you to have at least one on your side. Besides, I think you'll like the one I found for you."

Blair's head snapped to the side. "Excuse me? The lawyer *you* found?"

Tea waved a dismissive hand as she pulled into the drive-through of Tim Horton's. "You want anything?" she asked, insouciant as hell.

"Lemon filled. I already had a meeting scheduled this morning."

"Oh, I canceled that, of course." Tea placed their order: two sweetened coffees, the lemon-filled doughnut for Blair, and a sprinkled for herself. "Your choices so far have been absolute shit, I had no reason to believe the latest one would be any different. You're still using Google to search. I found this one via some more trusted but obscure sources."

"Like, how obscure? They are licensed, right? Experienced? Not an agricultural lawyer or something?" Tea had never led her astray before, but the stakes had also never been higher.

"You know my research is always accurate, on topic, and deeper than anyone else's." They pulled up to the window to retrieve their order, and Tea handed the lemon-filled doughnut over.

"I still can't believe you eat sprinkled doughnuts." Blair took a bite into the soft, sugary, lemon-filled creation in her hands.

"What's wrong with sprinkles?" Tea expertly handled doughnut eating and car manuevering, dropping only a few sprinkles onto her expensive-looking black dress slacks.

"Nothing, I guess. It's just you're so, well, to be honest, ferocious in almost every other way, but you order sprinkles on your doughnuts. You should order...oh, I don't know, a bear claw or something."

"Only a true badass can order a sprinkled doughnut and not give a fuck."

"True. Still I can't picture The Rock with a sprinkled doughnut, can you?"

"Yes, I can. He's almost as badass as me, after all."

They were silent for a few minutes as they consumed their gooey, sticky treats. Tea finished first and meticulously licked her thumb, index, and middle finger—the only fingers she had allowed to touch the doughnut.

"Plus," said Tea as they pulled into the parking lot of a two-story red-brick building surrounded by blooming lilacs, "of all the lawyers you've considered, this is the only one waaay out of your budget."

"So why the fuck are we here, then?"

"Because you want an amazing lawyer. And those"—Tea got out of the car and forced Blair to keep up if she wanted to hear the rest of her sentence—"don't come cheap."

"I do want an amazing lawyer. But I don't want to end up whoring to pay my bills."

Tea walked toward the building. "We'll get you some loans. You can't put a price on Zane's freedom. Or you shouldn't. I dare say, even if it comes to whoring a bit, it'll be worth it. But perhaps if we get him out, *he* can do the whoring."

Blair stood indecisively for only a few seconds before hurrying to catch up with Tea. "Okay, okay, won't hurt to do the interview. What's the name of the lawyer?"

Tea stopped and pointed at the first name on the shiny metal plate beside the door that read SCURLOCK, GIROUX, & SUNDRY.

"A partner?" Blair was breathless as dollar signs circled in her brain.

"The *senior* partner, yes, and I managed to get you an interview with less than a day's notice. So be nice."

Feeling slightly faint at the idea of being in debt for the rest of her life, Blair was nonetheless impressed. And excited. "How—" she began, then decided not to ask. She followed Tea into the office.

The front waiting room integrated a mix of classic and modern touches. The dark hardwood floors were covered in rugs with bright, cheery colors in geometric patterns. The furniture was sleek dark brown leather with throw pillows covered in fabrics matching the rugs' colors. A huge ornate fireplace stood clean and unlit, with a bundle of wood nearby and fire starters on the mantel, suggesting its frequent use in the cooler months. Large windows let in natural light, and black-and-white art hung on walls still covered in foliate wallpaper from the 1920s.

They were greeted by a young white man behind a curved desk to the right of the door. "Good morning, and welcome! Please make yourselves right at home. Can I grab you anything to drink?" He wore square black-framed glasses, a navy button-up shirt with subtle white dots, and dark blue jeans. He spoke with impeccable articulation, but his voice also held genuine warmth.

"Two waters," Tea said for both of them. "We have an appointment."

He smiled and busied himself with pouring the water from a pitcher on the small counter behind him. "Lemon?" he asked.

Tea raised her eyebrows at Blair, who nodded.

"Yes, for both."

He turned around and handed them each a glass of water, complete with a tile coaster under each. "Yes," he said as if there had been no interruption, "Ms. Lindell and Ms. Grayson, right? I've already notified Ms. Scurlock you've arrived."

Arden Scurlock wore a timeless Max Mara suit combo in basil green with a cream silk camisole underneath. She kept her accessories simple but elegant with nude suede heels, diamond stud earrings, and a herringbone gold chain. Her wrist was decorated with a Tiffany watch and her right ring finger with a sapphire-and-diamond ring. She had steel-blue eyes, copper hair tied up in a French roll, and ivory skin.

At forty-three, she was a no-nonsense woman who had developed a lot of interesting ways of dealing with her clients over the years. The first steps, however, were always the same. No matter how early or late they arrived for their appointment, they were left to wait for precisely five minutes. Long enough to let them settle in, relax, and prepare their thoughts. If Arden was running behind on appointments, they were rescheduled; she didn't think anyone should suffer the annoyance of waiting. After the obligatory five minutes, they would be shown to the office. And that's when it happened: the crucial bit.

Today the pattern was the same, and as Blair and Tea entered her office, Arden gave them each a friendly greeting and invited them to sit. Then just as their knees began to bend, just when they weren't expecting anything, Arden said abruptly and with a hint of steel, "Did he do it?"

Before Blair's ass even touched the polished wood of the chair, she shot back, "No, he fucking didn't." She sat down haughtily and glared at the lawyer.

"Good." Arden extended her hand across the desk to shake. "Arden Scurlock."

It was a technique meant to unsettle, to reveal, and it had only failed her twice in her long career. Most people weren't very good at lying when caught unexpectedly in the vulnerable moment of sitting down. Some, Arden knew, were. She didn't trust the technique implicitly, but it was a damn good start.

Arden took some time to appraise the two women sitting across from her. Blair was young, but not as young as Tea, who looked like a teenager but carried herself in an assured manner. Neither seemed the type to be overly emotional. If they were, it wouldn't be a problem, because Arden could deal with that—but it was always easier if she didn't have to.

"All right," said Arden, not wanting to waste any of her valuable time, "lay it on me. Ms. Lindell here informed me this concerns the murder of Javier Luis Cavallero, but I'm afraid I have very few details." She glanced to her left to ensure her assistant, Jules, was ready to take notes. He gave her a nod.

Blair told the story, ending with, "Of course, I had no idea about his sister working for Javier or the fight when we first met on the balcony. Well, it's not something you share with someone you've just met, is it? I only found out about it months later."

Arden frowned. "Keeping that a secret doesn't look good. Yet you're still sure he's innocent?"

Blair waved her hand, tossing Arden's comment away like a soiled tissue. "He didn't keep it a fucking secret. It never came up. I guess I'll add 'Have you ever started a fight with a billionaire who sexually intimidated your sister?' to my list of questions for every person I meet, shall I?" She did nothing to hide her virulent tone.

Arden was unperturbed by the tone and the words; rather, she was glad to hear them. Blair wasn't a shrinking violet, and while it was too soon to tell, it might bode well for putting her on the stand if they needed to. Except for all the profanity. "A prosecutor will say it was intentionally kept a secret. They'll say a lot of things, and our job is to anticipate them so we know how to respond." She shot a sideways glance at Jules, who nodded to indicate he'd noted this little tidbit.

"Still," she said, "plenty of people have fights in bars. And plenty of people's sisters have been sexually exploited. Point is, that's not proof of, nor even a suggestion of, murder."

"Well, you'd think that, except they've ordered a DNA test, so I'm assuming they think they've got something more," Blair said.

"DNA? What are they checking it against?"

"We don't know. Zane has declined to speak with the police until he has a lawyer, which means they aren't sharing anything with us."

"DNA can make things a bit trickier, depending on what it is. But you say they fought earlier that night. Depending on what they found at the scene, it could be explained by that altercation. Or any number of other reasonable causes. Still, it isn't to be balked at." Arden paused. "Even knowing they have DNA evidence, you are certain he didn't do it?"

Blair was starting to get annoyed. "Look, I understand what you're trying to do, but it's going to be fucking exhausting if I have to answer that question every five minutes I'm working with you. I've answered it once—I'm not answering it again."

Arden tilted her head like a dog sizing up its owner's unusual habit of brushing their teeth. "I will not be asking it again. However, that's a lot of certainty in the face of a potential DNA match and a circumstantial story of motivation and opportunity. I don't like blind faith in a loved one just as much as I don't like defending the guilty."

"My faith is far from blind. I'm not saying he didn't do it because I love him. I'm saying it because I know he's not capable of that type of murder. I'm not saying he could *never* kill—I think we can all murder in the right circumstance. But *this* murder? No."

The shadow of a smile brushed the left corner of Arden's mouth. "Good," she said, leaning in again. "Have you left anything else out?"

"I'm not sure. Maybe. Likely. It's hard to know what you think is important."

"And you say that Zane isn't an aggressive or violent person. I won't find out differently when I interview friends and family, will I?"

"No."

"You're sure? I don't want to waste my time. Or yours. Because I'm not going to cover up the truth. If I ask people and they say he's flying off the handle all the time, we won't have much of a case."

"Definitely sure. He's a hospice worker. His natural state is compassion and care, not aggression."

Arden raised an eyebrow but didn't say anything. She made a mental note to ask her assistant to ensure there were no suspicious deaths at Zane's work. Presumably, with hospice care, there isn't much shortening of life to be done, but even the hint of a "compassionate" death could look very bleak in court. It would prove he had the constitution to take a life.

She slid a stack of papers across the desk. "This is a contract for my services. I've gone as far as I can go unofficially. If you like what you see here, we need to finalize this. Then I can meet Zane."

Blair took the contract and barely stifled a gasp when she saw the fee. "His bail hearing is this afternoon."

Arden stood up to indicate the meeting was over. "I can fit that into my schedule. What do you say?"

Tea kicked Blair under the table.

"Yes," said Blair. "Please."

"Good." Arden stood and buzzed an assistant at the same time. "Because in that case, we need to go. Now."

Sunday 11 a.m.

When Zane learned he was going to meet with his solicitor, he imagined the meeting would take place in one of those rooms with the glass partitions and the phones. But he was brought to a plain white room with green plastic chairs and a table in the middle. Contrary to his movie education, he was neither handcuffed nor shackled at the ankles, and the officer left him there with a middle-aged woman and young man.

The woman stood up as he entered and extended her hand. "Hello, Mr. Walker, I'm Arden Scurlock. This is my assistant, Jules."

"Hi, Ms. Scurlock, Jules. Please call me Zane." He should feel nervous about the meeting, but the whole murder charge had taken the sting out of anything else that would normally rattle him.

Arden nodded. "And do call me Arden." She paused briefly while they all sat, said, "Your fiancée has gone through most of the process of hiring me, but I wanted to meet you in person to make sure before we proceed."

"Sure, makes sense. I'll be honest with you, if Blair reckons you're the right person, I doubt I'll think differently."

Arden gave a small sideways smile. "That's good, but I'm afraid I need to make sure for myself as well. I don't represent everyone. So if you don't mind, I do have a few questions."

Zane held a hand out to indicate Arden had the floor.

"Good. Number one: How did you know Javier?"

"I didn't. He was my sister's boss back when she worked here. So I knew of him, but I didn't know him."

"Had you ever met him before you ran into him at the bar in Greece?"

"No, it was quite a shock to see him there."

"Okay. We'll discuss that confrontation later. How did you know it was him if you'd never met him before?"

"He's a rich guy. His gob's everywhere. Like Elon, Bezos, Buffett, and Gates."

"Do you have an alibi for the evening before he died, or that morning?"

Zane sighed. "Not really, no. I met Blair after I confronted Javier, and we spent the better part of two hours together. I was supposed to fly out early the next morning, but my flight got canceled. I ended up running into Blair again at about noon, and we had lunch."

"You didn't spend the night with Blair, then?"

Remembering that night, Zane felt a lift in his stomach. "No, I didn't. Didn't have the nerve to ask her. Guess I should've, eh? Could've been my alibi—quite by accident, of course."

"Or she could've said no. Or, as the prosecution will say, you didn't ask her because you were already planning to kill Javier."

"Well, it's bloody likely she would've said no. And then maybe she'd never have invited me to lunch."

"But what this means is you have no alibi for the time when Javier was killed."

"I went to my room, giddy like a teenager in love, and eventually fell asleep to reruns of *MasterChef*."

"You didn't go out to find Javier again? Have another word with him in his room?"

"No, I didn't know his room number. I assume he was staying in the luxury suites. I was in the peasant part of the building."

Arden looked at him as if she were a headmistress trying to get him to admit he had been the one to put syrup on all the toilet seats in the teachers' washroom. "It's important that you don't lie to me about any of this. I *will* find out the truth, either way, and so will the prosecution. So if you went drunkenly wandering the halls to find his room, you need to tell me now."

Zane placed both hands on the table. "I'm telling the truth. I don't know what got into me that night. I'm not the kind of person who confronts people like that. But the fact that he was sitting there drinking and having a good time when I knew what hell he'd inflicted on my sister, I was just...so *angry* at him." He flushed at the memory of his rage. Javier being dead hadn't taken any of his anger away, which he found strange. He thought the man being dead would give him some peace.

"That kind of anger can lead people to kill. People have killed for a lot less."

Zane held up his hands in protest. "Look, I admit I was angry. I admit I confronted him, stupidly and awkwardly. But as soon as it was over, I was disgusted with myself. I knew it wouldn't accomplish anything, and I knew my sister would be furious to learn I'd done it. She'd always wanted to move on, pretend the guy didn't exist anymore. I guess I just never expected to have to do that when he was in the same room as me. It caught me off guard."

"That doesn't sound good."

"No?"

"No. Pretending the guy didn't exist? Why not *make* him not exist? And people feeling off-balance have been known to do things very out of character. Like murder."

"Look, if I had been the type to kill while 'off-balance,' as you put it, I would've snapped then and there, but I didn't." Heat prickled at the base of his skull. "Are you on my side or not?"

"I'm on the side of the truth, Zane. I'll do my best to defend you, but to do that, I need to be armed with the truth."

"You actually *care* what happened to that bloody dickhead?" He knew it wouldn't help his case to be so openly glad Javier was dead, but he didn't care.

"I don't know very much about the man, but yes, in my line of work, I find it very satisfying to ensure the right person is held accountable for the right crime."

"Okay. So are you my solicitor, then?"

Arden held her hand out. "Yes, Zane, I will represent you."

"Thank God."

"Your bail hearing is this afternoon. In the meantime, I have a lot of catch-up work to do."

"Thank you."

Arden nodded and stood. Her assistant followed. Then they both left the room, and Zane was alone until an officer informed him he had a phone call.

27

DIFFERENT, MORE, BETTER

Calgary
Monday 11:08 a.m.

Miami sauntered into Quentin's office with her usual *Baywatch* attention to movement. She was still wearing black to make a show of being in mourning, but it was hardly dour widow attire. Her dress was a barely-there affair constructed of velvet tied together with sheer lace and delicate golden chain ribbing. Glittering gold high heels combined with a sparkling birdcage veil completed the weird sexy widow fantasy look.

She deposited her vanilla-coconut-scented self into a chair, flipped her hair gently, crossed her lean legs, and fixed Quentin with a playful stare.

Quentin put what he hoped was a professional smile on his face and did unnecessary busywork at his desk: straightening an already straight pile of papers, shuffling a few pens here and there, and moving his computer mouse around the screen to no purpose whatsoever. At least she wasn't sitting on his side of the desk. Yet.

"I'm glad you've agreed to consider wealth management," Quentin said. Maybe he should ask her more about Shakespeare? Something to distract her from seducing him? Or to distract himself from *wanting* her to seduce him?

Why can't I tell her it's never going to happen? Because it still might. Damn it. He'd thought he could close the door to that possibility, but each time she showed up, he found he couldn't say no to her with any finality. She was like a fucking can of Pringles.[1]

Miami gave a little shrug and pouted. "It's my money. I should, like, be able to do what I want with it!"

"Yes, but we don't want a King Lear situation here." He was proud of himself for that one. He didn't know a lot of Shakespeare, but he at least remembered King Lear's division of assets caused a hell of a time for everyone. It still seemed like an odd thing for Miami to be interested in, but he'd take whatever he could to stall for time.

"It's King Charles. But, honestly, Prince William is, like, way hotter. I think the crown shoulda just gone to him, don't you?"

Quentin knew even less about the royals than Shakespeare, but he was aware of who the King of England was. "Um, yeah, I know. But I was talking about Shakespeare. You know, like Romeo and Juliet?"

Miami giggled in a rare display of her true personality instead of a put-on sultry laugh. "It's Leonardo DiCaprio. Not that Shakespeare guy."

Well, there went his one topic of discussion that might keep Miami from full-on straddling him in his office. If she did that, he'd be completely fucked. Literally.

Come on, he thought, looking at his watch. The meeting was supposed to start at eleven, and it was already 11:08. He didn't want to lose Miami in these moments with his floundering explanations. He felt sure she could be won over with the right pitch, one he hadn't thought he'd have to give.

"Sorry. I was delayed by a flat tire," said a clear, warm voice as Nina Crane entered the office in a breeze of soft but steady presence.

In her cream pantsuit with turquoise heels that matched the shade of her earrings perfectly, she looked like a model for a sexy business executive magazine. Quentin had never thought that kind of magazine would exist or interest him, but this tall, gorgeous Indigenous woman was making him rethink that.

"But of course, Ms. Cavallero, you'll retain the control and access to

1. Once you pop...well, you know.

every single penny of your own money." She rested a light hand on the girl's shoulder and smiled companionably before sitting down next to her.

Quentin was relieved he would no longer have to attempt to find topics of interest to keep Miami occupied. "Miami, this is Nina Crane, head manager at Wolf Wave."

Relief was only one of the reasons he was happy Nina was in his office again. The first time she'd come in so he could interview her before introducing her to Miami, he'd felt as if her entire essence had walked into the room and hit him squarely in the solar plexus. It wasn't love at first sight; Quentin didn't believe love happened that way. But it was as close as he'd ever come to understanding people who claimed to have experienced it.

Miami sized up the other woman in the manner of the head cheerleader wondering if the new recruit is going to usurp her at the top of the pyramid. "It's Ms. Lamar now." She uncrossed and recrossed her legs, flipping her hair, and fixed Nina with a petulant glare.

Nina didn't miss a beat, appearing to accept the glare not as a challenge but as a good omen that there might lie within the young woman's being some semblance of self-respect she could dig out and capitalize on. Along with the money, of course.

Keeping her expression and tone neutral, she went on. "Javier has left you a lot of money. *A lot.* You could leave here today and throw a party a night for several years, travel the globe, get haute couture designed exclusively for you, and be waited on hand and foot." She tucked a strand of long black hair behind her ear.

Miami perked up at this description.

"Yes, it sounds great, doesn't it?" Nina deftly laid a piece of paper on the desk between her and Miami before continuing. "That kind of lavish spending attracts attention, and not the good kind. You'll have 'friends' asking you for handouts. You'll have 'trusted' assistants stealing from you. You'll have criminals attempting to con their way into your life and hack their way into your accounts to bleed you dry. And you won't even notice. Until it's too late."

She flipped the piece of paper over. It was a heavy piece of cardstock, printed with deep black ink in clear characters and lines. "But if you choose to partner with Wolf Wave, this is what I think we can do for your money, even taking into account a very generous annual expenditure."

At the bottom of the neatly rendered form was a brightly colored line indicating eighty years in the future, showing a substantial growth of funds from the initial investment.

"We're a fully licensed, audited, and regulated company, interested in making you money, not taking it."

Miami's eyes were still on the bottom figure on the page. "I would really have all that when I'm, like, dead?"

"This is a conservative estimate, but yes, you could expect at least that amount."

Quentin felt something in the moment and said quietly, "No more worrying where the next soft place to land will be, Miami. Not now, not after ten years, never."

Miami looked up, and Quentin saw something human and vulnerable in her face. Gone were the practiced pout and sultry eyes.

Nina leaned back in her chair. "We take a monthly fee, based on a percentage of how well or poorly our investments are doing for you. So it's in our interests to make wise choices. We keep an eye on all of your accounts to make sure they're safe and that no one's swindling you. We set you up with a spending account and house the bulk of your money in a more secure place. There are a few extra steps for larger expenses, to ensure your safety and security, but you'll never need to ask permission to access any of your money."

"So, I could, like, buy a private jet?"

Nina smiled. "You could. Or, as a person who wants to think about their long-term wealth, you could fly first-class when you want to, or charter a private jet instead of owning one."

"But I'd still be flying on it? Like, just me and some friends?"

"Of course."

"Cool."

"It is pretty cool to fly on a private jet."

Quentin turned his head in interest, and Miami giggled. "You've been on one?"

Nina shifted her weight in her chair to face Miami. "A client once insisted we meet on his jet. At first I thought he was the type that was too busy to stop and was expecting a terse meeting in between his conference calls, but it turned out he had invited members of his personal staff to fly along with us, and we spent most of the time eating, drinking, and getting spa treatments."

"But you don't, like, think I should own one?"

"Well, if you want one, you should own one, of course. I was only giving you alternatives, but as I said, the decision on what to buy is yours."

"How do I, like, buy a jet, then?"

Quentin caught a twinkle in Nina's eye that made him think this was exactly the kind of question she'd been hoping Miami would ask. "That's an excellent question. And another question is, where would you keep it?"

"I thought if I had money, stuff like that would, like, just happen." Miami's pout returned.

"Oh, it can, but can you trust just anyone to do it and not tell you the jet cost three hundred million when it only cost two hundred million?" Nina cocked an eyebrow.

"I thought you said you'd, like, make sure that didn't happen!" Miami wailed.

"Yes, of course we would. But you'll need to hire us first."

Miami nodded enthusiastically. "Yes, I'll hire you."

"Wonderful!" Nina said, surprising both Miami and Quentin by pulling Miami into a hug. "I'll be thrilled to set you up with someone who will find out all about how to buy a jet, where to put it, and probably answer a dozen other questions we don't even know to ask about jet ownership."

"Not you?" Miami asked, uncertain.

"Sadly, no. I'll handle the bigger questions of your estate, but that will include overseeing your daily money manager, so you'll know I've got my eyes on it. I'll make sure you're taken care of." She passed over a small blue-and-red card with a QR code on it.

Miami scanned the code with her phone and received Nina's personal contact information.

"I do sleep, shower, and eat sometimes, but otherwise I'm always available should something come up." The warmth in Nina's smile radiated into the whole room.

Quentin marveled at her genuine care for such a clueless, vacant, and insipid person. But then again, $50 billion was a rather large account. He felt the devil on his shoulder using his hot little pitchfork to dig through his ear canal and into his brain. *You fucking idiot!* it screamed. *Miami wants to fuck you! She has $50 billion! Why did you invite that other chick in here? Sabotage it! It's not too late! Hop on that gravy train and ride it, cowboy!*

He shook his head, dislodging the devil but leaving the annoying little pitchfork dangling there. *Cowboy?* he thought. *He almost had me until he called me cowboy.*

The angel on his other shoulder didn't have much to say but wore a smug smile on his innocent, rosy-cheeked face. There went the devil again, undone by his own excitement. He could remove the pitchfork by lassoing it with his halo, but sometimes a reminder of a narrow escape was important.

Miami wiggled her bountiful bits out of Quentin's client chair and left without so much as an unnecessary toss of the hair or squeeze of her arms to accentuate her breasts.

Nina turned to face Quentin. "Well," she said, "thanks for the biggest account of my life. I think this calls for a drink."

"On you, right? I mean, the commission on this has got to be insane."

Nina stood. "Yes, yes, on me. You should have asked for a finder's fee."

Quentin started to stand, then stopped. "I should have."

Nina threw her purse over her shoulder. "Yes, you should have. But a drink will do just as well, won't it?"

Quentin thought for a moment and then grabbed his jacket from the coat hanger in the corner of the office. "It will do as a means to open negotiations."

"Negotiations? The deal is done! There's no such thing as a retroactive finder's fee."

"Ah!" said Quentin as they made their way to the door. "Not that you know of. But I don't have books and books and books full of case law for nothing."

"You think you're going to quote case law at me and prove that you can demand a retroactive finder's fee?"

"Not at all. But you'll pay anything to make the torture end after I finish the first volume, read aloud, in monotone."

"I won't have to pay. I'll just leave."

"And I'll just call Miami and tell her I've had second thoughts about you. She has quite the trust in me." The little devil perked up his ears and started climbing back up onto Quentin's shoulder.

Nina opened her mouth to retort, then closed it. "You'd do that?"

"I could always call her back again later and set her up with someone else for a generous finder's fee, of course."

Nina linked her arm in his. "How about we start with that drink, then?"

When she touched him, Quentin's stomach did a flip, sending the little devil for a dizzy spell down off his shoulder again. The exhilarating lift he'd felt in his loins with Miami was nothing to the feeling he had with Nina. Different. More. Better.

28

EGG COOKERS?

Calgary
Monday 12 p.m.

"No, I honestly think he's in love with her cat," Verona's new client said, as if she were discussing potting soil with her neighbor.

Mrs. Mary Barker had come in on short notice, desperate for a consultation. A white woman in her forties, she was short and stout with dark hair in a bob to match Uma Thurman's in *Pulp Fiction*. Her pale round face was decorated with long false lashes, deep red lipstick, a beauty mark above her lip, and bright blue-framed cat-eye glasses. She wore a vintage-inspired swing dress in a deep purple fabric, patterned with kittens frolicking with yarn.

She perched on the edge of her chair, white gloves covering her hands. Her cell phone lay on the desk in front of her, the only item proving she didn't travel through time from the 1950s. It was a bitter disappointment to Verona, who secretly hoped she'd received her first time-traveling client. But alas.

"We've got pussycats of our own, you see," Mary said, her voice high and girlish. "We're a proper family, you know, and the idea that he's out there with another cat...well, you can imagine it boils my blood."

Unbidden, Mary produced a picture worthy of 1980s Sears family photo-fame-and-shame. It featured mainly cats, but squeezed in with the cats was a painfully skinny man with a pallid complexion, a comb-over, glasses the size of his head, and a blue-and-gold argyle sweater. Mary, hair dyed platinum, her fuzzy white sweater melding with the cats around her, sat on a couch, as near to the man as possible with about five cats between them on a couch. She sported a wide smile, with crazy eyes.

Verona pretended to admire the photo while she collected her thoughts. It certainly was one of the stranger cases of infidelity she'd been asked to look into, and quite honestly, the novelty of it attracted her. If not time travel, a cat love affair could be an interesting diversion.

She handed the picture back. "So I'm assuming you're concerned with an emotional affair?"

"What other kind of affair could he have with a pussycat?"

"None, of course," Verona said. "Just being clear." Was Mary really that innocent, or just dafter than punk?[1]

"He used to come home and pet our little darlings"—Mary mimed holding and petting a cat in her lap—"and he'd speak to them, tell them about his day. The calls, the hang-ups, the times he'd accidentally say 'Have a dice nay' by accident." Mary gave a little chuckle. "The new and inventive names people called him, his successes. He'd pour his heart out. It was special." She swallowed hard as her voice became husky with emotion.

"He'd tell the *cats* about his day? Not you?"

Mary waved her hand dismissively. "Oh no, of course not me! Why should he talk to me?"

"But you were there?"

"Well, I try to give him his privacy, you know. It's a small apartment, so of course it's hard not to overhear."

"Of course."

"So that's how I know he's not talking to them anymore."

"Did you ask him about it?"

"Heavens, no! I wouldn't want him to know I'd been listening! No, but I got to thinking, if he isn't talking to *them*, who is he talking to? And that's

---

1. Daft Punk. Get it?

when I remembered that new woman he works with has a cat. And if he isn't talking to *our* cats, it must be hers!"

Verona's pen was poised over her notebook. "What's her name?"

"Mittens," Mary said with scorn.

"Mittens?" Verona asked. "Wait, the woman or the cat?"

"The cat, of course!"

"Right. Sorry, I meant what's the woman's name?"

"He's not interested in her, you know. He'd never be interested in her. It's the pussy." Mary punctuated the last three words by tapping her fingernail on the desk.

"I'm not suggesting it's the woman," Verona said. "It's just that the woman owns the cat, and it'll help me to know a bit about her."

"Well, I don't know much about her. She started about a month ago."

"What is it that Oswald does?" If Mary really didn't know about the woman, Verona would need to start by staking out Oswald.

"Works in a call center, doesn't he? Sells egg cookers."

"Egg cookers?"

"Egg cookers."

"What's an egg cooker?"

"Exactly what it sounds like, isn't it?"

No wonder poor Oswald talked to the cats. "Does he have a lot of success at that, then?"

Mary moved her head noncommittally, neither a nod nor a shake. "Sells a few every month, doesn't he?"

Not knowing whether this was good or bad, Verona let it pass.

Mary said, "Anyhow, he was happy until a month ago when this new woman showed up. She found out he likes pussycats, I don't know how, but she shoved this picture of her pussy in his face."

Verona had to bite her tongue to not react to Mary's phrasing.

Mary continued, unaware of her inadvertent double entendre. "Is that right, I ask you? Did he *ask* to see it? No. She just showed it to him, and right then and there started trying to steal him away from his own pussycats."

"How do you know that's what happened?"

"Gotta be, doesn't it? I mean, I remember Oswald telling our pussies about this new cat he heard about at work. Didn't think anything of it—why would I? Until now. Only explanation is this woman purposefully trying to get her cat in his life!"

You mean her pussy, Verona thought, fighting a smile.

Things had turned from interesting to borderline bonkers. Mary Barker was also one of the worst types of clients: she gave almost no usable facts, bristled at questions, and was most certainly deluded. It meant Verona would need to do all the legwork herself. But first she needed to ensure she covered her bases.

"Okay, Mary, before I agree to take your case, we just need to go over a few things."

"What else could there possibly be? He's in love with that damn cat!" Mary threw her hands up impatiently.

"Well, that may be, but it may not. This is what I'm talking about. I'll investigate until I find out if Oswald is in fact sneaking off to talk to this other cat. But if I find that he is not doing that, you're still required to pay me for my time and expenses as my fee schedule outlines."

"It won't matter. He is, isn't he?"

"And one last question that I ask all my clients. If I find out anything else while I'm trying to ascertain if Oswald is, uh, in love with Mittens, would you like to know?"

Mary's brow furrowed. "What else could there be?"

"Well, for instance, some clients hire me to specifically find out if their partner is cheating on them with a woman. And that's all they want to know. So, for instance, if I happen to find out that their partner is frequenting a gay nightclub, or doing drugs, or hiring a male prostitute, they don't want to know. Other people hire me to find out everything I can. So it may start with a suspicion that their partner is seeing another woman, but if I find out that they're actually stripping at a bar and using the extra money to travel for extreme plastic surgery, they want to know it all."

Mary looked revolted at the notion that anyone would engage in any of these activities, her eyes wide, her gag reflex waiting to be unleashed. "What does any of that have to do with my Oswald?" she asked, scandalized. "If you're implying Oswald would do anything like that"—she rose from her seat—"perhaps I've come to the wrong place."

Verona put on her most mollifying voice. "Oh, not at all, Mary. Of course Oswald isn't like that. I was just trying to illustrate that some clients want to know everything, while others want to know as little as possible."

"I think I've made it clear that I'm not one to eavesdrop, haven't I?"

"Crystal clear."

"Well, then, not that it matters—because Oswald is just in love with that pussycat, isn't he?—but I don't need to hear anything else about anything, do I?"

"Perfect." Verona smiled and extended her hand. "Then I'm happy to look into this matter for you."

Mary shook Verona's hand and smoothed her dress. "And once I know, then I'll be able to help him."

Verona had seen this response too often to argue. "What you do with the information is, of course, entirely up to you."

"Of course it is."

"If you'll just leave the name and address of Oswald's workplace, as well as your home address, I can get started as soon as tomorrow." Verona passed a notepad across the desk.

Mary wrote her address and the name of Oswald's office. "I don't have the address, do I? You'll look it up, of course."

"Of course." Verona smiled as Mary left the office, and once the woman's footsteps retreated, she allowed herself a heavy sigh.

Of course it is, isn't it? she thought over Mary's phrasing ruefully. What a thoroughly tiring woman. What else could Oswald be up to? Verona had a few ideas about that. She one hundred percent expected to find out old Oswald was having at least an emotional affair, not with a cat but with a woman. A woman who would listen to him. A woman who could have a conversation that didn't always end in "of course it is." But loneliness and horniness do strange things to people, as Verona well knew, so who knew what she'd find.

~

Monday 1 p.m.

“Hello there, old skunk,” Blair said bracingly over the phone.

“What?” Zane had too many things buzzing through his head to cope with an opener like that. He sat in a small room with a table, a phone, and blank white concrete walls around him. This felt a little more like the telly.

“It’s what Brits do, isn’t it? Call each other all manner of odd animal names in an attempt to bear each other up and keep that stiff upper lip—keep calm and carry on and all that? Also, the animal is always old, though I’m not sure why. Perhaps to convey a sense of wizened durability?”

“I don’t think I’ve ever heard anyone say ‘old skunk.’ We do say ‘old bean’ or ‘old thing.’”

“Okay, then, cheer up, old bean.” Blair’s smile was evident in her tone.

Zane appreciated her first phrases to him weren’t of pity or concern but of playfulness. It felt good to have someone act as if everything was okay, even though nothing was.

“You know I didn’t do it, right?” He didn’t realize how badly he needed to say it, needed to know Blair didn’t think him a murderer, until the words came tumbling out of his mouth.

“Of course I fucking know that!”

“So why the fancy solicitor, then?” He knew his voice sounded small and weak, and he hated himself for it. He’d always wanted to be strong for her. Like when he’d promised she’d be the one to need the gelato. Gelato felt like so long ago now. Everything did.

“I don’t want you going to jail because your lawyer’s incompetent. Plus, all the cheaper ones were creeps. She was the only one I didn’t want to punch in the baby bucket.”

He could imagine her actually doing that, and it made him smile, but like every other good feeling he’d managed to find since going to jail, it was short-lived. “Blair?”

“Yeah?”

“Twenty-five years is a long fucking time.” He didn’t know how to do this. He was used to breaking through her walls to find her vulnerabilities. Liked doing it, even, but stuck in here, he didn’t have the energy to do it. He was already raw and laid bare, and that was more than enough for him at the moment.

"You're not going to be in there for twenty-five years." She sounded so certain.

"What if I am?" The unspoken question, "Will you stay?" hung between them.

Of course, there was more than one way to break down her walls, and this rawness must be one of them, because instead of giving him a no-nonsense brush-off, she said, "I'll break down the very gates of hell for you if I have to." But because it was still Blair, she added, "And you know the devil is no match for me."

"I'm scared."

"I know. But I'm not."

"How can you not be scared?" A tiny bit of hope lit up inside him. Perhaps whatever she was holding onto would be big enough for him too.

"Because I know you didn't do it."

He was hoping for something more. Innocent people get convicted all the time, so that was hardly any insurance for his situation. "That's it?"

"That's it. Believe me, it's all that's going to matter in the end."

"But..."

"But what if we're separated for twenty-five years?"

"Yeah. That."

"Well, I don't know about you, but I plan to live longer than fifty-eight. So maybe the first twenty-five years of our marriage aren't ideal. We'll still have the next twenty-five. Hell, with life expectancies going up, I'd wager we'd have at least another forty."

That was it. She'd stay. He couldn't think through exactly what that would mean at the moment, couldn't imagine those intervening twenty-five years, but she'd stay. "That's some sweet bullshit," he said with a sad smile.

29

THE FRIEND BOX

Calgary
Tuesday 9 a.m.

With a breeze of jasmine and peppermint, Arden waltzed into the courtroom and threw down a hell of a case for Zane's release, leaving the prosecution scratching their asses for a reason the judge could decline it.

Zane sat silently, as he'd been instructed, and felt a little less doomed the more Arden spoke. She was confident but not arrogant, likeable and witty without being comical, firm and factual, and prudent at presenting emotional arguments with placidity, giving them weight and veracity.

"My client has just had his wedding interrupted by an arrest warrant. Not only was this unnecessary, it was cold and thoughtless. He could have been arrested quietly once the ceremony had concluded and saved him and his bride considerable embarrassment and hurt. Mr. Walker wants nothing more than to return home to the woman who by now should be his wife. Their honeymoon has, of course, been canceled.

"Mr. Walker is a British citizen who has been working in Canada for several months at a stable job, where he has been guaranteed a position for up to two years. He therefore has strong reasons to stay here—gainful employment and family. His flight risk today remains what it was when his wedding was so discourteously interrupted: zero.

"My client will suffer extra psychological harm being held in a cell, for a case that relies heavily on hearsay and circumstantial evidence. We will turn in the passports of both Mr. Walker and his fiancée, arrange to check in with local law enforcement, and agree to a stay-at-home mandate, and even GPS tracking, should the prosecution deem it necessary. Ms. Blair Grayson, Mr. Walker's fiancée, will be a surety, as will his parents and Ms. Tea Lindell, a close friend of Ms. Grayson's."

Yasmine Alami, an Indian woman in an expensive silk hijab, led the prosecution and did her bit, as she must. Her dark eyes flashed as she spoke. "While we can't deny that the timing of Mr. Walker's arrest was unfortunate, that is not what we are here to discuss today. We believe to ensure justice for Mr. Cavallero's family, Mr. Walker should remain in custody to ensure he will stand trial for this crime.

"As the defense stated, he is a British citizen, and the temptation to return home may become too great as the pressures of an upcoming trial begin to mount. And while the defense claims the case is weak, we point to the DNA evidence that ties Mr. Walker to Mr. Cavallero, and ask you to consider this as a strong reason to ensure nothing prevents him from standing trial."

The judge, the Honorable Martin Clough, a white man in his sixties with a long face, receding dark brown hair, and reading glasses, raised his eyes to Arden. "Counsel?"

"Your Honor, Canada is part of the Commonwealth, and the British government, along with the Greek authorities, has already gone through the bureaucratic process to allow Mr. Walker to stand trial in our country. Fleeing to England would provide no protection to him from the law. We are not talking about a man with gang connections that can make him disappear to Vietnam. We're talking about a man with no criminal record and steady employment. The woman he loves and hopes to marry resides in this country. As for justice for Mr. Cavallero's family, I see none of them here today."

This time Clough's eyebrows rose at the prosecutor, the light glinting off his bald spot. "Counsel, do you have any other reasons why Mr. Walker should not be released? I agree with the defense that flight to Britain seems unlikely, and they have given compelling reasons to presume Mr. Walker would do nothing more than go back home with his fiancée. Because he has no criminal record, I am finding it hard to see why he shouldn't do just that."

"Your Honor, the DNA evidence is a compelling reason to ensure that the accused is given no opportunity to miss his trial. While the defense attempts to make the case out to be circumstantial, we do have Mr. Walker's DNA." Silky-smooth delivery, no panic, no begging.

With a look from Clough, Arden jumped back in. "DNA evidence in a hotel room is hardly definitive proof," she said, stopping short of waving her hand dismissively. "How much DNA from other individuals might be in that room?" She squared her shoulders and faced the judge again. "DNA evidence alone, especially shaky DNA evidence, is not enough to withhold bail when no other risk factors are present."

Clough took a breath before addressing the prosecution. "Counsel, you mentioned Mr. Cavallero's family. Have any of them provided reasons or pleas for Mr. Walker to be kept from bail?"

"No, Your Honor. I would like to raise the possibility of Mr. Walker reoffending."

Clough considered this. "You think there is a high probability that he will engage in criminal activity, counsel?"

Yasmine allowed a beat to pass before answering. "Killing once makes it easier to do again."

Clough was unimpressed by this, but Arden jumped in nonetheless. "Mr. Walker is innocent until proven guilty. Beyond that, the crime he is accused of is not one likely to be repeated in the course of everyday living."

Clough gave a brief pause, considering each lawyer in turn before leaning forward. "I find that there is insufficient cause to withhold bail from Mr. Walker." He paused again, used to the reaction of defendants to his statement.

Zane did his best to remain composed but couldn't help taking in a breath. Arden and Yasmine gave no visible sign that this statement meant anything to them.

"He has strong ties to family, a stable job, and a home. He has no criminal record, and no known connections to criminal activity. There is little chance of Mr. Walker committing any offenses while released. However"—Clough continued in a measured tone—"the presence of DNA connecting the accused to the deceased gives greater gravity to these proceedings. Therefore I am setting bail at six hundred thousand dollars and will impose the following conditions of release: the passports of Mr. Walker and Ms. Grayson will be forfeited to the police; Mr. Walker will not leave his home other than to go to work, medical appointments, and meetings with counsel; and Mr. Walker will have scheduled check-ins with the police to ensure he is meeting these conditions."

There was no resounding bang of a gavel to dismiss everyone—quite the opposite. Arrangements had to be made, administrative details taken care of, and the little problem of putting up $600,000 had to be attended to.

~

Friday 4 p.m.

"Verona?" The voice, soft and even, made Verona's stomach do a flip, as it always did when she heard it.

She looked up from her desk, scattered with photos of an egg cooker salesman in a warm embrace—not of a cat but of a bona fide woman. *Told you so, Mary.*

It had been three days since she'd heard about Zane receiving bail, and although she'd been busy on her stakeout for most of that time, she'd not received any messages from Quentin about it. Which meant this visit was about something else.

"Quentin," she said, sending a silent thank-you to Oswald because she didn't have to shuffle pictures of him and a cat out of view. She didn't want Quentin to think she was stuck investigating shit cases now that the murder was tied up.

"Sorry to just drop by," he said sheepishly, the movement of his entering the office sending a waft of ginger and fresh tobacco right into her. It wasn't just a cologne he wore; it couldn't be. The way that smell made her feel like she'd been dealt a hefty box kick, it had to be his pheromones.

"No problem. I'm just glad you caught me. I've been on stakeout duty." She indicated the photos she was filing away.

Quentin settled himself in one of the chairs opposite her desk as if nothing was more comfortable than dropping by unannounced for a little friendly chitchat.

"What brings you by?" Verona asked when he let the silence linger. He should know that was a bad move, after the last time she derailed them into hostage discussions.

"What else? Our murder case."

But it couldn't be the case. He'd have texted her about that first. It had to be their failed date—it would be too awkward to call or text about that. This was the only way to revive their professional relationship without dealing with the mess. It was a "Hey, let's just forget it all happened and go back to being business buds, okay?" kind of dropping by. Unlike the first time she'd told him to "forget it" when they'd managed to revive things, she assumed this was going to be the real end. Last time she'd told him to forget it. If he did it this time, there was no going back. You can't go back after you both say "Forget it."

He had brought the friend box with him and was here tidying things up so he could wrap her in old newspapers and pack her away in it. Tape the box closed and put a reassuring label on it, one he could glance at anytime it caught his eye on his shelf: *Business Pal.*

She understood it, and in some ways was glad he'd done it and saved them both the embarrassment of talking about it. But those eyes, icy blue, that all-American-soldier jawline, those shoulders so broad, that effortlessly dressed-down clean wardrobe. She had to face the fact that no matter what happened, she was always going to want him on some primal level, with an ache that clawed its way from her loins into her very being.

"Our case?" she said, trying to sound composed—uninterested, even—as she busied herself rearranging office supplies on her desk to look like she was in the middle of a spring-cleaning frenzy.

She made herself stop, knowing how stupid and obvious it must look. She'd seen clients engage in the same kind of misdirection, the extra activity more telling than if they could manage to sit still. Quentin, doing what he did, would notice at once. She allowed herself a quick peek at him and was pissed off to see a little knowing smirk. He quickly checked it, but it had been there. He'd seen.

She crossed her arms and leaned back. "I thought this was in the hands of the courts now. It can't be our case anymore." She spoke as flippantly as she could, pretending she'd already forgotten the most interesting case she'd ever had and had moved on to bigger and better things. Just like Quentin had with her.

But he wasn't going to let her off easy, which was another thing she loved about him. He shifted his weight in the chair, a power move that, unlike her frenetic activity, made him seem more in control. He had the time to be comfortable. To let her wait.

"So you think he did it, then?" he asked.

If he wanted to draw this out, she had to be ready to play. "Not up to me, is it?"

"That's not an answer."

She sighed. "Truthfully, I don't know. I don't know much about the guy other than what we uncovered in our investigation and what they've been saying on TV. And his fiancée being adamant that he 'didn't fucking do it.' It does seem like there's something more behind her certainty than blind devotion, but I can't pinpoint what it is. I'm sure she'll come off good if she takes the stand."

She forced herself to make eye contact with Quentin. It was always a dangerous idea, because she'd either freeze up or start to have unhelpfully sexy thoughts. "But *could* he have done it? Absolutely. Did he? I don't know."

"And you're satisfied with that?"

Satisfied? I could be. With you.

She tore her eyes away, focusing on the Rothko print behind him. The oranges and yellows had always reminded her of summer and frozen treats. "Of course I'm not satisfied with that, but what else can I do? The police have the evidence and the suspect. There's nothing left to investigate."

"Just curious, I guess. I mean, he seems so...like a stand-up kinda guy, you know? Takes care of the dying. Picked a fight with an asshole because he was terrible to his sister. Maybe it's that accent."

Her eyes drifted to his forearms on display beneath his rolled-up shirtsleeves. "James Bond has that accent, and he's licensed to kill."

"Okay, yes. But this guy seems more Charlie Mortdecai than James Bond to me."

"Or Wooster,"[1] said Verona.

"The sauce?"

"Never mind." *Come on, Montero, this is your last chance to try to say something real to this guy. Maybe salvage something.* "So you don't think he did it."

"I think people surprise us all the time by what they're capable of, and like you, I think it's possible he did it. But no, I don't think he did it."

"And that bothers you?" She watched him closely for his response. *This.* This was why he had come. He was bothered by the idea that they may have put an innocent man on trial.

"It doesn't bother *you*?" he replied quickly, covering up the moment of letting her in. Going back to trying to pry *her* open.

"No." A lie. Let him dig. Of course it bothered her. She didn't want to see the wrong man have his life taken from him. Didn't want to tear apart two people who were obviously in love. But, most importantly, and selfishly, she did not want to let Javier win. That's the part Quentin couldn't know about, he'd think she was a terrible person. Maybe she was.

"No? That's it? It doesn't bother you that an innocent man's name is being dragged through the mud, and he'll probably stand trial and may even be convicted? Because of what we did?" He leaned forward, showing some of his passion.

His naive sense of justice and responsibility never failed to surprise her. She figured a divorce lawyer would be a bit more callous, more cynical by now. "Well, if he's innocent and is convicted, that's not down to us. That's down to the court system. And yes, I'm sorry he has to go through this if he's innocent, but again, I just did my job. I found some evidence, and I turned it over. What was I supposed to do? Hide it because he seemed like a nice guy?" The lack of control in this part of the case was maddening, but

---

1. That's Bertie Wooster, kids. P.G. Wodehouse, an old dead British dude, wrote some very funny things that are well worth your time to read. The sauce referenced would be "Rooster" sauce, a brand of hot chili sauce, also well worth your while.

Quentin had come here to try to unravel her, and she didn't want to unravel just yet. She'd rather push *him* to unravel.

"No." Quentin relaxed into his chair. "No, I suppose you're right. But if he didn't do it, who did?"

Verona drummed a finger on her desk. "I've been asking myself that same question since Blair told me he didn't do it. I mean, I assumed an arrest meant this was a pretty sure thing, but her certainty has left me... uncertain. But I don't have any more leads. This was the one guy who had a tie to Javier in Greece." Unless it really was a secret drug assassination, but she'd still not confessed any of that part of the case with Quentin, and now was not the time to admit it. Even Runi had only got the watered-down version, in order to keep her from insisting Verona drop the case.

"It doesn't bother you that a murderer will walk free?" His voice was soft, the way she imagined he might talk to her across a pillow. *Fuck me.*

It was surprising how much he cared about justice for a despicable human. She could never care that much, not about someone like Javier. "Murderers walk free every day, I'm sure. Just because I know about this one doesn't change a whole lot. The victim was a complete waste of space, Quentin."

She brought her eyes back to his blue ones and this time felt the strength in herself flowing through to him, instead of him flustering her. "Frankly, he wasn't worth what we've given him already. I don't care that he's dead." There, she'd said it.

"I know your feelings about him," Quentin said, "but take him out of the equation. Take the fact that there's nothing we can do out of it. You're okay knowing that a person who's killed someone is free to live their life? They might do it again, you know." He said it like it was another label he might be adding to her box, a subcategory to help him further shelve her.

She could lie. It would be easy. But no matter what she said, no matter where she ended up on that shelf, she'd be no closer to where she wanted to be: not on the shelf at all. There was nothing to lose now.

She held his gaze as she responded, letting him see she meant it. "In this case, yes, I'm okay with it. I feel confident that if this person does kill again, they'll choose a similarly awful human being. One less piece of shit for the rest of us to worry about stepping in."

Quentin softly exhaled through his nose and nodded once. Not a snort, but an affirmation.

Verona let the silence flow, felt within it that things were settling, like dust in the sunlight across her desk. She had let him see this tiny, real, and ugly part of her, and although he didn't agree with it, he accepted it. He knew where she belonged on that shelf, and while Verona had wondered if he was deciding between labels like *Virtuous* and *Morally Bankrupt*, it felt as if she was being shifted from the edge of the shelf, where things of little substance belonged, to a place closer to the hearth, with its warmth of familiarity, where she'd have the privilege of being taken down and visited often.

From that place, she broke the silence. "But that's not why you came."

Quentin smiled, and she was pleased to see the warmth cascade all the way through his eyes. "No, it's not."

30

CATMAN STRIKES AGAIN

Calgary
Friday 4 p.m.

Despite feeling like his head was the ball from Pong[1] pinging back and forth between all the people in the room, Zane was feeling good. Hopeful even. For the first time since he was marched back down the aisle by a stocky policewoman at his wedding, he felt things might go his way, and that scared him. Hope in the face of twenty-five-to-life somehow made everything feel more fragile, like hope itself might tip the fates in the wrong direction.

Arden nodded in silent introspection during the brief silence enveloping her conference room. The room was comfortably cool from the summer heat while avoiding the pitfall of overcompensating with AC. Natural light bathed the space through three tall windows, setting off the rich ginger color of the walls, throwing some translucency into the leaves of the plants hugging the edges of the windows and corners of the room. Sparse but calming art hung on the walls, the pieces featuring deep blue

---

1. A really old video game that used to amuse the primitive humanoids of the '70s. Nowadays it's mostly used to keep cats busy while their owners are away.

tones with vibrant gold swathes. The table was roughly oval, not geometrically perfect, with striking live edges. It housed a mishmash of files, papers, coffee mugs, and a plate full of macaroons. Around the table sat Zane, Blair, Tea, Arden, and her team of associates.

"Let's run it again." Arden took a green macaroon and leaned into her high-backed velvet chair. She closed her eyes to listen, and Zane's head started ponging around the room again.

Jules spoke first. "I've done a complete search of Mr. Walker's work history. No complaints, no wills changed at the last minute in his favor, no unexplained deaths associated with his patients. Families unequivocally adore him. It might look too good to be true, except I did find an old boss willing to admit that Mr. Walker once needed to sleep off a night at the pub in one of the vacant patient rooms when he got confused on his way home. That's it."

Arden nodded, and the woman sitting next to Jules spoke. Young but with a commanding presence, Bernadette was dressed in head-to-toe Burberry. Her voice was slightly husky, but her speech was clear and concise. "I received the cleaning schedule from the Mykonos Muse Hotel. The maids stick to specific sections but are rotated every quarter to prevent complacency. This means that a maid cleaning the budget-friendly suites wouldn't end up in the luxury suites within the same shift, throwing serious doubt on our theory that Mr. Walker's DNA could've gotten there via the maid."

She paused briefly, a habit, no doubt, used in the courtroom to build her narrative in the most effective way to convince the jury. "However, on this particular day, a change was recorded midway through the morning housekeeping rotation. The regular maid cleaning the luxury suites, Miss Lyra Xenakis, changed the second half of her scheduled rooms with Ms. Tasoula Kyrkos."

Another pause for dramatic effect. It didn't matter that the room was already captive; Bernadette seemed incapable of turning it off. She put down the piece of paper she was holding and took her glasses off, letting her deep brown eyes shine out unmasked. "On the morning that Mr. Cavallero's body was discovered by Ms. Kyrkos, she had been cleaning budget rooms, including Mr. Walker's. Mr. Walker's DNA could have been transferred to Mr. Cavallero's body through Ms. Kyrkos. Or, in the ensuing activity that follows the discovery of a dead body, the DNA may have been transferred from Ms. Kyrkos's cart, which was left right outside the room. Something as small as a hair falling off the maid's apron. Hardly proof that Mr. Walker was in the room, and definitely not proof that he murdered Mr. Cavallero." She looked to her left to another associate, who picked up the thread with no preamble.

Tall and thin, with dark skin, Kairo Jones's angular features were softened by kinky black hair pulled back into a thick ponytail and a neatly trimmed beard.

"In fact, Mr. Walker's DNA wasn't the only DNA found on Mr. Cavallero. We requested the list of all DNA evidence collected from the victim." He folded his hands on the table, not needing to refer to the piece of paper in front of him. "After brushing away the detritus of everyday life, it became clear that despite what the prosecution would like to believe, at least fifteen different individual transfers of DNA were collected from Mr. Cavallero, ranging from hairs, to touch DNA, to bodily fluids." He said this all calmly, but in his calmness there was gravity. Not the blasé calm of the disinterested but the steady calm of the expert.

"The lab, of course, hasn't been given a convenient match for the other samples as they have for Mr. Walker here. Nor was the maid tested to see how many DNA samples she had in common with Mr. Cavallero, and thus how much contamination she left at the scene."

He swallowed and continued. "The prosecution hasn't bothered to track down the other guests who stayed in the suites Ms. Kyrkos cleaned prior to entering Mr. Cavallero's room, to see if their DNA was transferred by Ms. Kyrkos as Mr. Walker's likely was. If they did, they might find that their murder suspect pool grows significantly. They haven't, in short, given any compelling reason why they think Mr. Walker's DNA was transferred only during a murder, while fourteen other people simply accidentally left their DNA behind. They choose to ignore the fact that Mr. Walker and Mr. Cavallero had contact earlier in the evening and that all touch DNA, as well as the single hair, undoubtedly transferred at that time. They base their entire case on a flimsy backstory cooked up by a small-time private investigator hired by the police's top suspect to clear her name. A PI with no experience investigating murder, preferring matters of petty infidelity.

"Well, I'm sure the prosecution has better things to do than pursue actual justice, but until we've fully investigated all fourteen individuals to ensure they have no ties to Mr. Cavallero, however small they might seem, I see no reason to permit Mr. Walker's DNA as evidence when all other samples are not only being excluded but also categorically ignored."

Arden opened her right eye to gaze at Kairo. "Might need to dial that back a wee bit, Kai," she said in a soft voice.

He nodded. "I threw the kitchen sink at it because I assumed you'll be delivering the main thrust of it."

She nodded slowly, opening the other eye. "We'll work that out later." A pause as she turned to Zane. "What do you think?"

"The defense is moving to dismiss all charges." Quentin let the remark sit there like the last piece of pizza. Nobody wants to take it, despite everyone wanting to take it.

Verona had no choice but to pick up the slice. "On what grounds?"

"Coffee," Quentin said.

"That's a terrible fucking joke. Are all lawyers as dad[2] as you?"

"Fine. They're disputing the inclusion of the DNA evidence. And without it, all the prosecution has is the fact that Zane didn't think too much of Javier. Something he has in common with the vast majority of the planet."

"Wait, how do you know this?"

"I've got friends in the courthouse."

"Well then, fuck yeah. Without DNA, they've got nothing. I mean, when I told the police what I found out, I knew there was no way they'd make an arrest on those grounds. But the fact that he matched some of their DNA evidence made me think maybe I'd stumbled upon something. So what's wrong with the DNA?"

2. As in dad jokes.

"The defense is keeping that close to their chest until they have the hearing with the judge. But I suspect, as will the prosecution, that they'll say the DNA could've gotten there from the fight."

"Which it could have."

"In which case—"

"He didn't fucking do it." This was getting worse and worse for Verona. Not only was her hunch about Zane turning out to be right, she was left with no avenues to investigate. Javier was going to win. *That motherfucker.*

"Exactly." Quentin rose to go.

"Wait," she said. "You knew all of this before you came in here."

"Of course. It's why I came."

"But you still made me have that existential bullshit conversation about murderers and justice and the inherent goodness of mankind?"

He leaned over her desk with a saucy grin. "Well, I figured you could use the diversion from Catman." He winked and whisked from her office, his perfectly shaped ass a beautiful reminder of his hateful unattainableness.

Catman: it was in the notebook she'd forgotten to close when he came in. Lying open on the desk with all her ridiculous nicknames for clients and her idiotic doodles and random thoughts. She had doodled Oswald fucking a very surprised-looking cat while his wife listened, her ear pressed to a glass on the other side of the wall. In big block letters at the top she had written *CATMAN STRIKES AGAIN!*

She should be horrified, but she wasn't. Not anymore. Would she have preferred he didn't know about Catman? Yes. Was it more fun to have him believe she worked cases with classy, sexy people conducting affairs out of posh penthouse suites? Of course. But then again, fuck it—Catman was who she really was, and she was starting to see that being herself around Quentin wasn't as terrifying as she'd imagined.

She should fucking frame it.

~

Friday 5 p.m.

"So you think there's a good chance the judge will dismiss it?" Zane's voice shook. He couldn't help it.

Arden didn't blink or even breathe. "He'd be an idiot not to."

After an impressive feat of silence for her, Tea spoke for the first time. "You're awfully confident, and that's wonderful. However, won't the prosecution have a story and reasoning that sounds just as compelling? I mean, they obviously felt they had a case."

Zane couldn't breathe. He was like a rabbit that had evaded a pack of coyotes, only to find himself in the jaws of a wolf, the dread so much worse after the elation of escape.

Far from dismissing Tea outright, Arden encouraged her. Perhaps it was a soft spot she liked to keep hidden, or the pluck in Tea, but Arden seemed to respect the young woman. Enough to let her in the room to begin with. Enough to not tell her to shut up because the grown-ups were talking.

"Of course they will. For every argument we've made, they'll have a counterargument. But the fact remains: the only piece of concrete evidence they have doesn't prove Zane murdered Javier. No one saw Zane anywhere near the room, there's no murder weapon to tie to him, and there isn't even a compelling motive. Unless they also want to bring in the myriad of men and women angry at Javier for his sexual promiscuity."

"Won't the fight look bad?" Blair rested her hand on Zane's knee. He reached out to hold her hand and gave it a squeeze.

Bernadette jumped in. "They'll try to make it sound bad, of course. Like he wanted to go back and finish the job. But based on the premeditated nature of the crime, the clinical, clean quality of it, it doesn't fit a man heading back in a rage to finish the fight. If his plan all along was a clean kill, why bother with a messy bar fight that draws attention?"

Nausea swept up from Zane's stomach in a rush of heat. He wanted to put his head between his knees, close his eyes, and breathe deeply. And this wasn't even the trial.

"Everyone, I'd like a minute with Zane alone," Arden said.

The legal team filed out first, with no complaints, no last-minute "I forgot to mention," nothing. Tea followed.

Blair turned to Zane. "Me too, I think." She gave him a kiss on the cheek.

"Thank you," Arden said as Blair left the room. She allowed the silence to fall before speaking again. "How are you?"

"I think I need to throw up," he said, feeling queasy and light-headed and almost nonexistent.

"I can see that," Arden said. "You may want to do that before we meet with the judge." She smiled.

"Cheers. I'll keep that in mind."

"There's no easy way to do this, but believe me when I say it's better to try this now than to wait for trial. Trial will be this, only more so."

"So there's something to look forward to, then?" Zane said, surprising himself by finding some cheek.

"I told you I don't take cases where I believe the person is guilty. I also don't try to get my cases dismissed unless I damn well think they *will be* dismissed."

"But if you believe all your clients are innocent, don't you think all their cases should be dismissed?"

"Of course I think that, but whether or not I believe we stand a chance of success is a different story. But they've rushed this. Probably because the press jumped all over it, attracted by the large sum of money and the pretty gold-digger wife. When the wife didn't pan out, they went hunting for something else to feed to the masses. It feels to me like they want to give everyone something to gnaw on until they get distracted by the next big thing."

"This is my life," Zane said. "I'm not a bloody chew toy."

"It's the press, Zane. They don't care about your life. They don't care about anyone."[3]

Zane took a steadying breath. "What are my chances?"

Arden answered with assurance, "Around forty-five to fifty percent of homicide cases in Alberta are stayed or withdrawn.[4] Even if the case isn't

---

3. My apologies if you work in the press and you are a warm, loving human. I didn't think you existed. Please give my book a good review!

4. This is a legit footnote, folks. Statistics Canada. Table 35-10-0027-01. Adult criminal courts, number of cases and charges by type of decision. 2017-2022.

dismissed outright, you have a good chance at some form of a stay in proceedings—and it would be good to consider them all to avoid a trial, but I'm not going to overwhelm you with that right now. One thing at a time. The prosecution must know their case is weak. We're prepared for the worst, of course, but I expect you to be spit out so they can move onto something meatier."

"Is it wrong to hope for another juicy murder of a different rich dude to come along to distract everyone?"

"Yes, of course it's wrong, but also perfectly human."

Zane shook his head and rose to leave the room. There was no precedent for this type of thing. Death? Death he could deal with. Dealt with all the time. Expected and natural. Painful and full of grief, yes, but part of everyone's life. But this? This teetering on a precipice between absolute freedom with the ability to live a life he was so looking forward to, and the absence of any form of freedom facing a life of separateness? It was like facing a living death. Watching the rest of life moving on without you in it. Forced to find an existence, carving out a life as a mere shadow.

It was no wonder he was reeling between horror and numbness. When he found Blair waiting for him outside, she embraced him, but he couldn't connect to it. He felt himself constructing protective barriers around every part of him. For all her talk of knowing they'd have more than twenty-five years left after he got out of prison, she'd skirted over the main issue. Those twenty-five intervening years wouldn't fly by as if they were nothing. They'd have to live them.

If he were dying, he'd melt right into her, savor every moment, let her live what life he had left with him, face it head-on. But faced with this pseudo-existence, he couldn't do that. Couldn't let himself love that hard, knowing there would be no real goodbye for them, just a gradual erosion of everything they were. Until one day she'd stop visiting and he'd surprise himself by not noticing.

31

SUPERPOWER

Calgary
Wednesday 10 a.m.

The newswoman wore a steel-blue pantsuit and a bright white blouse with a V-cut exposing just enough to be alluring without taking away from her professional vibe. She spoke quickly, with the ambition and confidence of someone who saw herself as the next Katie Couric.

"How does it feel to know you're marrying a man who might be a murderer?" Kassidy said, her tone implying that "might" meant "is."

"Oh, this oughta be good," Verona said to Runi. They sat together on Verona's balcony, watching the broadcast via Verona's phone.

Blair eyed the microphone that had been thrust into her face like a hooker wondering if the fiver was worth the blow job after all. "Pretty much the same as it did before."

In contrast to Kassidy's polished, wrinkle-free look, Blair was dressed down in a vibrant, flowy red blouse and denim shorts. Her hair was tied back in a loose bun, tendrils framing her tanned face. They stood outside the Scurlock law office, framed by green bushes and blue sky.

Surprised her accusatory style hadn't ruffled more feathers, Kassidy plowed on as best she could. "What do you mean by that?" She plastered on a false smile like Barbie's at Ken's wedding to Teresa[1] after things went south.

"What do I mean?" Blair said. "I mean he didn't fucking do it."

Kassidy gave her cameraman an eyebrow of "Shit, please tell me they aren't going to cut us" and said sternly, "This is live television, Ms. Grayson."

"Sorry," Blair said without a hint of remorse.

Kassidy squared her shoulders. "I'm sorry, but I'm sure our viewers at home are wondering how you can be so sure of his innocence. I mean, the police don't arrest people for nothing."

Blair's eyes narrowed like a sniper's focusing in on a target. "How can I be sure? How can any of us be sure of the person we marry? We all marry a stranger. The best any of us do is marry a stranger who loves us."

Kassidy gave an indulgent, patronizing laugh. "But we don't all marry someone accused of murder, do we?"

"Accused, yes, but not convicted. In fact, it'll be a surprise if he even stands trial. At least *my* fiancé has been investigated. I see you're wearing an engagement ring." She indicated the large glittering diamond on the newswoman's finger. "Can you say the same thing about *your* partner?"

"My partner has never been accused of murder." Kassidy grinned smugly.

"No, not accused. But perhaps they got away with it. I wonder how you feel knowing you might be marrying a murderer?" She emphasized the "might" this time just as Kassidy had attempted to understate it in her opening.

"But I *know* he's not a murderer."

"How can you be sure?"

As the cameraman swivelled back to Kassidy for her closing statement for the segment, Verona clicked her phone off. "You could tell Kassidy was fuming, couldn't you? I bet it's not every day she has interviews turned back on her like that."

Runi said, "You seem oddly on Blair's side."

"And why not? I can't help it. I like the woman. It isn't her fault if Zane

1. That's Barbie's best friend. Or at least she was in the '90s. Get off my lawn, I'm old!

killed Javier, is it?" *If he did it.* She couldn't commit to either side until she found out the result of the dismissal hearing. If the case went forward, that meant there was obviously enough evidence to support him being the murderer. She *might* be able to relax if that happened. But if the case got dismissed? She'd need a new plan, and right now she had no idea what that would be.

"No, of course not. But it is her fault for being so blindly devoted."

"I guess," said Verona. There it was again, the devotion, but it felt like something more to her, something she couldn't shake. It was part of the whole mess of ideas running through her brain. Why was Blair so sure?

Runi changed the subject, though not the way Verona had expected. Usually she pushed the conversation *away* from work, but it wasn't every day that Verona had a client accused of screwing cats. "What ever happened with your dorky egg cooker salesman? What did you call him? Catman?"

"Catman was indeed cheating on his wife. However, not emotionally, and not with a cat."

"No surprise there."

"Not to you or me, no, but to his wife it will be. If I tell her."

"*If?*"

"She said she only wants to know about the cat stuff. So I don't need to tell her that her husband is sleeping with another woman."

"That is some hefty denial right there, but also not surprising. You and I see a lot of extreme denial in our line of work."

"More than most therapists, I'd wager," Verona said, thinking of the amount of time she spent following Oswald before he actually made a move with his coworker. Those had been long, boring days. A man who sells egg cookers and returns home to a wife like Mary doesn't exactly have a thrilling life to watch. She'd longed for a way to make the case go faster. "This whole thing would've been so much easier if I could talk to cats."

Runi gave an exaggerated blink. "Excuse me?"

"The cats. His wife said he used to pour his heart out to them, but that he recently stopped. That's why she was afraid he was cheating."

"So if he wasn't talking to the cats anymore, what good would talking to cats do?"

"Because I bet he still *was* talking to them, just not when she was around. A guy so used to baring his soul to his pets isn't about to stop when he's got something juicy like an affair to share." She squinted as the sun peeked out from behind a cloud.

"Unless the need to talk to the cats evaporated when he met this new girl? Like he found he could actually talk to her?" Runi pulled her sunglasses down. They were red designer frames, in a shade identical to her lipstick.

"I assume that's a bit of what's happening, yes. For his sake, I hope so. But I still don't think that habit would break overnight. I bet you anything he told at least one of them his little secret. If I could speak cat, I'd have wrapped this up earlier."

"Knowing another language *is* like a superpower." She leaned back and crossed her legs.

Verona ran her fingers over the rough plastic grooves of her armrest. "How so?"

"Well, for instance, when Eomma is visiting, I often get stuck speaking Korean all the time and don't even realize I'm doing it. The other day, we went to buy her some new shoes, and everyone must've assumed we didn't know a lot of English, because I doubt the two women trying on shoes beside us would've been quite so open with their discussion of their boyfriends' penis size if they knew we were listening. Thankfully Eomma doesn't know enough English. I was quite happy to eavesdrop."

"Impressive or sad?"

Runi laughed. "I think one of them was about to admit disappointment, but when the first girl was bragging, she changed her mind. Didn't want to be the sad friend."

"Damn. Maybe I should learn a second language. It would make my job easier if I could play that trick. I'd have all these cheaters talking right in front of me without even knowing it."

"You could take on twice the number of cases." Runi rubbed her fingers and thumbs together, miming fanning bills.

"Yes..." Verona said hazily. Something was niggling at the back of her mind. People would say anything. Everything. They might even say something...

"Shit!" Verona bolted upright.

"What?" Runi asked softly, unruffled by the sudden outburst.

"This whole big Greek murder."[2]

"Yes?"

"Well, we've been assuming he was killed by someone directly affected by him. An affair, Zane attacking him. But what if it wasn't something that obvious at all? What if he was killed because of something *no one was supposed to hear*?"

Runi eased herself up in her chair. "You mean someone from the island killed him?"

"No." Verona felt wild in her sudden realization. "Not a Greek. Someone who speaks Greek but wouldn't be expected to. Someone who overheard something they weren't meant to."

"Well, of course it's possible. I don't get why you're all worked up about it, though."

"Because I know someone who speaks Greek. Who's very adamant that the man who's set to take the stand didn't fucking do it."

"You mean Blair?"

"I've asked myself over and over again why she's so sure. It's always bothered me, because it doesn't seem like some naive belief, not some Catman kind of denial. It's always been like she's known somehow that he was innocent. And how do you *know* something like that? You know who *did* do it. Because *you* did it."

Verona got up suddenly, went inside, came back out, and tossed a magazine on Runi's lap.

Runi picked it up. "*Tier1*?"

Verona flung herself back down in her chair and waved at the magazine. "I picked it up after I met Blair that first time outside the station. I was curious. Read her bio."

Runi read aloud from the back of the magazine. "'Blair Grayson has been a writer for *Tier1* for five years, after graduating with a Master of Journalism degree from Toronto Metropolitan University. Known for her lush descriptions and emphasis on the opportunity for human connectivity that

2. Perhaps even a big *fat* Greek murder, but I can't push my luck too much, can I?

travel provides, she creates space for readers to dream and explore. Blair's ability to quickly pick up new languages and provide local flavor and insights beyond the purview of any other travel writer has made her respected in the field.'"

Runi dropped the magazine in her lap. "It doesn't say she speaks Greek."

"Of course she does, that little minx."

"So what? So maybe she does. That doesn't mean she killed him. Over what? Some Greek conversation she overheard? It makes no sense."

"That depends on what she heard."

An image of a professional woman walking around the hallways of the Mykonos Muse filled her head. A manager who didn't exist. A young woman with dark hair, who could brush off any questions with her proficiency in the language.

Runi sat up and stretched. "So what are you going to do?"

"The only thing I *can* do. Talk to her."

Wednesday 5 p.m.

Zane's face was a mask of stiff jaw and dead eyes. His witty, self-deprecating, teasing self was replaced by a fortress of preoccupation, self-pity, and a thousand-mile stare. It was like living with a moody monk whose epiphany about the meaning of life was despondent apathy.

Blair had given him his space at first, knowing he would be nervous, anxious, and full of dread. But after two days of tiptoeing around while he stared at the walls with so much misery, it would make even the most hardcore emo kid sit up and take notice, she found herself wishing he was back in a holding cell instead of underfoot. She didn't want to feel that way about him, wasn't willing to allow herself to start despising his presence.

After a meal in which Zane ate little, said less, and heard nothing, Blair decided enough was enough. "Zane." She took his hand in hers.

He looked up from the wood grain of the table he'd been absently studying. "Hmm?"

"The point of being out on bail is so that you can live a little. You can refuse to eat, look at blank walls, and sit in silence in prison. You're home now. I'm not expecting you to act like this isn't a big deal, but I do think we should make the most of our time in whatever way we can. Nothing big, just, you know, be here. With me."

He clenched his jaw and shook his head. "I can't. I can't do that. Because living like it isn't all going to be taken away is so fucking terrifying right now." He pulled his hand away.

"This from the man who deals with death on a daily basis?" She wasn't going to let him get away with this. He'd been the one to break through her walls, to make her be real with him, to show her he was not only a safe place to be vulnerable, but where she could find relief in her vulnerability. After finding that place with him, she wasn't going to let it go without a fight.

"Death I can handle. This isn't death. This is worse." He stared at the wall.

"Except it isn't. Because it hasn't happened yet. Might not happen." She wasn't as good at this as he was.

"But it might. And if I...if I let myself believe it won't and it does—"

"That will hurt like hell."

"Understatement."

"So you live like I'm not here? Numb yourself to all the good in life now so that if it all gets taken away, you're prepared?"

"Preparation and training are key," he said ironically.

"Well, I'm glad to see some vestige of your sense of humor remains." She crossed her arms in anger. "But fuck, Zane, if you want to live like I'm already gone, then when this whole thing is over and you're a free man, you may find that to be true."

Zane looked up. "What are you saying?"

She stood up, letting her anger and fear burn off through the movement. "I'm saying I refuse to live like this. It's like living with a shitty carbon copy of you, all of your edges blurry, the details of you faint and, in some places, erased. Walking around our own damn house in silence because you're too busy thinking of your potential doom. If you choose to live like this, I won't fucking be here when it's done. I'd rather eat fire ants alive and let them gnaw their way back out."

"So you want me to pretend like nothing's wrong? Put on a big smile? Throw a party?"

"Fuck, no! I don't want you to *pretend* anything." Didn't he see? She'd never had to pretend with him, and she'd never want that from him. Was she so bad at expressing her love that he couldn't feel that from her?

She kneeled in front of him and retook his hand. Softness didn't come easy for her, but she'd do anything for Zane. "I just want you to be here with me. And face the horror of that getting taken away. I want you to be brave in your love. And know that if you are brave, I'll fight with everything I have for you." She didn't cry, but it was as close as she'd come. "I love you."

A smirk twitched the corners of his mouth, then a smile, then he slid onto the floor with her and engulfed her in his arms, inhaling fully for what felt like the first time in days. He let the smells that were tangled up in his memory of her rush in: nectarine, violet, almonds. Her skin was warm against his, her bare arms around his neck, his face on her shoulder.

How could he have ever thought it was better to keep her out? To cocoon himself against the pain of losing her? Whatever that pain might be, it was worth every drop of the feeling of being home in her arms now.

In that way, he realized, it was like facing death. The people who faced death, who held their loved one's hands as they passed, who didn't shy away from being present in their pain—those were the people who had that little something inside that nothing could crush.

He *was* facing death, he decided. Just a death that might have him living his afterlife on earth instead of wherever people go when they die. At least he was familiar with the kind of hell earth could dish out. Who knew what fucked-up nonsense the afterlife held?

32

THIS AIN'T POIROT, PEOPLE!

Calgary
Thursday 12 p.m.

Somewhere in the back of his mind, Quentin was aware that in a courtroom not far from where he sat, the fate of a man's life was being decided. It was no different from any other day in the churning cogs of the law but for one thing: Quentin had a hand in delivering this man into his present situation. It had been the right thing to do, but he wasn't convinced putting the man on trial was. He found himself hoping for a dismissal, something he had never hoped for in his life. He always favored hashing things out in court; don't let anyone get off that easy.

Thing was, it was really easy to feel that way when you read a name in the paper. It was a hell of a lot harder when that name was only there because you found it. He would normally have tortured himself about it, forced himself to examine the reasons he was thinking that way, but at that moment, he was too distracted to bother.

"Want the last one?" Nina pointed to the lone survivor on a platter of samosas with chutney on the table between them.

"I'll eat it if you're tapped out," Quentin said in playful challenge.

Nina raised her eyebrows in a "You did not just say that to me" and scooped the last samosa, dipping it generously before taking a huge bite, allowing the sauce to drip down her chin.

Sure, she was physically alluring. There was no doubt about that, judging by the male attention she'd garnered when she walked into the restaurant, but that alone wasn't enough to keep him from agonizing about the morality of putting the man on trial. It was her. The way she accepted the challenge of the samosa with a vicious, brazen attack instead of a meek offer to split it.[1]

"That was really good." She took a sip of chai. "Too bad you didn't take it when you had the chance."

The way she fucking threw it in his face. "I guess I've learned my lesson. Funny, though, because usually I don't need much convincing to finish eating with a woman." The innuendo was purposeful, he wasn't here to play games.

"I'll keep that in mind." She extended a delicate finger, dipped it into the chutney, and licked it off slowly.

Cascades of sensual energy ricocheted around the room before thudding right into Quentin. Lust, yearning, and affection clawed and bit each other to see who would win out.

The waiter, a young man with a slight build, beaming face, and deft agility when it came to hefting around copious amounts of food, placed bowls of steaming rice, aromatic curries, and fragrant naan bread on the table.

"Thanks, Moksh," Quentin said to the kid. He always made a point to use the names of the people who served him, because he remembered his first job bagging groceries at a local supermarket and the way those rich, entitled assholes had belittled him.

Nina smiled as Moksh disappeared, dished up some food, and took a bite, scooping up curry and rice in her naan.

Quentin didn't plan to have her eating with her hands, but now that he

---

1. Samosas are really hard to split anyhow. All the filling falls out, and it's just really, really sad. Don't do it. Eat the whole fucking thing, and don't spare the dipping sauce—that shit is good.

saw it, he wondered why man had ever invented utensils. There was something so damn sexy about finger food.

"I know a great dessert place around here, so make sure you leave room." They could easily linger in this restaurant, order the rose petal ice cream, and then leave, but he knew taking her to another place would extend their time together.

The curve of her collarbone and the hint of cleavage showing in her dress made him want to abandon dinner altogether, but there were ways of doing things with women like Nina. You didn't rush them. As much as he wanted to get to the part where he'd finally be running his hands over her beautiful skin that shone like desert sand, he wanted to show patience. Not the kind of frenetic energy that would have him rolling off her after five minutes, but the promise that he could take all the time in the world.

"You'll find my appetite is rather hard to satisfy fully." She held his gaze before taking a small sip of her tea.

Her challenge lit him up like the spices lighting up his mouth in combinations that melded and heightened each bite. His body buzzed in juxtaposition to the quiet, serene atmosphere of the restaurant with tapestries, fine silk, ornate lotus art, and a gentle sitar playing over speakers.

"Usually feeling unsatisfied just means you haven't found the *right* food." He leaned back to take her in. Gorgeous black hair, dark brown eyes, which were looking at him with desire.

"You want the last piece of naan?" she asked.

Quentin didn't hesitate. He took it as if it were a diamond about to sink into the depths of the ocean forever. He dipped it in the remaining sauce on his plate and made a show of taking a deliberate and satisfied bite.

There was no way in hell that watching him take a bite did the kinds of things to Nina that she did to him, but he could at least hope she found him impish in a charming way.

Nina placed her napkin on the table. "So about that dessert place?"

He was about to answer when his phone vibrated in his pocket. He had put all notifications on silent except for one from a colleague at the courthouse who had promised to notify him the moment the hearing was done.

"I'm sorry, Nina, but I have to check this." He pulled the phone out.

"Go ahead. If you're going to stick around, you're going to have to get used to me taking calls at all manner of unholy and holy hours."

The side of his mouth twitched up, and he tried to cover it. *If* he was going to stick around? She'd have to beat him with a hairy bull dick to scare him off. Even then, he'd be back.

He checked his message: *Case dismissed. They're heading out now. News is going to go mad.*

A surge of glee pulsed through his body like a rush of blood. The level of relief he felt at knowing Zane was a free man made him realize how much responsibility he had been carrying.

"Good news?" Nina ran a finger over the rim of her teacup.

Quentin watched her finger, distracted. Why was it that every little thing she did seemed so subtly alluring?

"Depends on who you ask, I guess," he said, attempting nonchalance.

"I'm asking *you*, you idiot."

So much for nonchalance. "Okay, okay. Yes, it's good news. I'll be able to sleep tonight." He was happy to be free of the whole thing. Happy he was with Nina when he got the news. He should tell Verona—

"Not if I have anything to say about it," Nina said softly.

After that, there was no room to contemplate anything, least of all Verona. Maybe he wouldn't need that dessert place after all.

Thursday 12 p.m.

"Oh, it's you. What the fuck do you want?" Blair said, giving Verona a hostile look before training her eyes on the courthouse across the street.

Blair stood in a sunbeam on the corner of the sidewalk, looking powerful and provocative in a dazzling slim-cut white pantsuit with a deep V in the blazer. Under the blazer, a plunging scarlet silk camisole and a long delicate gold chain drew the eye to the brazen sexiness of her exposed skin.

Verona paused to take her in, her effortless I-don't-give-a-fuck-nature. It was captivating, somehow giving her a charisma that made Verona want to stick around despite being told she wasn't wanted.

"That's certainly not the worst greeting I've ever gotten," Verona said, calm as a fart trapped in a closet.

In spite of herself, Blair said, "No? What was, then?"

"'Go home and fuck your mother with a plunger, you rusty slut hole full of smegma.'"

"Not bad," Blair said, but she seemed unimpressed by the colorful insult.

Verona thought, *Could this woman kill?* The answer came easily: *Yes, in a heartbeat, yes, she could. Confidence, resilience to stress, intelligence, charisma. Yes.*

"I mean, they both sort of mean the same thing," Verona said. "One just has a certain *je ne sais quoi* to it." She was used to being told to fuck off; when she caught someone with their dick out, they weren't too friendly about it.

"Yes, they do, but you're not taking the hint. I can be more creative if that will work."

"Nope, unlike a lot of folks, I'm completely comfortable being around people who don't like me."

"You might get uncomfortable if I tie your fucking smart tongue to my stilettos and start Riverdancing," Blair said. But for all her bravado, she was keeping a nervous eye on the doors of the courthouse.

"Nervous?" Verona gave a toss of her head toward the courthouse.

"Who fucking wouldn't be? Fuck, you itch like pubic lice."

"Even though you know he didn't fucking do it?"

Blair said with scorn, "That doesn't mean they'll do the right thing, and you know it."

"I'm surprised you're not in there with him."

"Better to leave him with his legal team. Besides, I need the fresh air. Too many reporters moaning and orgasming over the possibilities of what to write. Quoting what they want to write out loud. I mean, who do they think they're impressing? Fucktards."

"Say they don't dismiss the charges. What then?"

"I guess we're going to trial then, aren't we? Are you actually this dumb, or do you just like to fuck with people for fun?"

"You wouldn't...step in?" Verona asked. She was calm, but with vengeance underneath, like the surface of the water while a duck swims his fucking legs off for the last bread crumb.

Blair took a breath and looked away, the only indication that there was anything in Verona's words. "I'll do whatever it takes to get him out. He knows that. I'm not letting them put him away for something he—"

"Didn't fucking do," they said together.

Verona pushed on. "But say after everything, the jury comes back with a guilty verdict. You've got some time between then and sentencing. What would you do?"

Blair returned her gaze to the courthouse. "Hypotheticals are nothing but mind exercises to amuse those that have never faced anything real in their lives. If it comes to that, I'll do what I fucking do."

Verona smiled. It was the kind of answer she'd expect from someone like Blair. Someone who had answered the ultimate hypothetical question in the affirmative: If you had the chance to kill a person to stop them from doing something horrible, would you do it?

"You speak, what, eight languages?"

"Seven. Fluent in five," Blair said. "Conversational in two more." She pulled her phone out of her jacket and checked the time. "Look, it's real nice and fucked up of you to stop by to chitchat, but I'd rather be alone."

"I know you would, doll. That's why you greeted me so warmly. But as you can't leave and I don't want to leave, I guess you're stuck listening to me."

"You're worse than a fucking hemorrhoid. Popping up when I most want privacy."

"Perhaps I'll add that to my business card," Verona said offhandedly. She paused and added in Greek, "What did he do?" She'd looked the phrase up and practiced it enough to be comfortable using the non sequitur to catch Blair off guard.

Blair gave her a look of warning, the slightest twitch of her eyebrows the only giveaway that Verona had struck a nerve. "You recording this, little Miss Nancy-fucking-Drew?" she whispered with quiet menace.

"No," Verona said truthfully. She had considered recording the conversation on her phone, something she did regularly on cases, but decided against it. She knew Blair wouldn't be stupid enough to admit to anything openly.

Blair spat out a phrase in Greek.

Verona had no idea what Blair had said, but the meaning behind the words was clear. She stared at Blair, deep into her gorgeous blue eyes. Blair returned the stare with steely determination, but after a moment, the corner of her mouth turned up in the hint of a smile.

She could picture Blair in a toned-down business suit walking with purpose through the hallway to Javier's door. Coming up with some excuse to gain entry. Pressing the nail gun to his skull. Pulling the trigger. Then walking away like nothing ever happened.

Verona knew that was all she'd ever get out of Blair, but it was enough. She *knew*, and that was all she wanted. It meant Javier hadn't won at all. No, assuming Zane got off, it would mean they all won. Maybe she hadn't caught him with his pants down, but she damn well had caught a murderer.

"If it helps," Verona said, "I know he didn't fucking do it either now."

Blair let out a laugh through her nose. "Told you."

The front doors of the court opened, and a swarm of reporters spilled out onto the steps, Zane bringing up the rear, flanked by Arden and Tea. Flashes went off and questions sprang up like popcorn kernels from the crowd, but Zane was smiling.

Verona watched Blair's face change from hard and adversarial to relief. If it had been a movie, she probably would've run to him and smothered him with gratuitous tongue-kissing. Since it wasn't, she did the reasonable thing and stayed put.

The reporters formed a human wall, making progress from the courthouse to anywhere else nearly impossible. Arden was doing her best to repel them with her curt lawyer-speak. "We're delighted by the result and knew there could be no other outcome. Mr. Walker doesn't have anything to say at the moment, as he is understandably eager to get home and put this entire ordeal behind him. I would be happy to answer any further questions once my client is on his way."

Despite her cordiality and reasonableness, the parasitic press was unmoved. They demanded sound bites, wanted to catch some tears on tape, and hoped to raise fears the case might be reopened.

Resplendent in a sapphire jumpsuit of delicate lace, Tea stepped forward, her presence like a blazing lightning bolt thrown down by fucking Zeus himself. "My name is Tea Lindell," she said with quiet authority. It forced the throng to shut up for a few seconds lest anyone miss a precious quotable moment. "I have been granted exclusive rights to the story of Mr. Walker and his fiancée. So, if any of your employers would like to purchase that story from me, give them my card." She gave a wan smile and proceeded to make it rain business cards, like a baller with a fistful of ones at a titty bar.

As the cockroaches scurried around to pick up a card, Tea led Zane and the others through the gap in the chaos. Blair held Zane in her arms again. She did give him a kiss, but it was a quick one. Verona was near enough to hear her whisper in his ear, "Let's get the fuck out of here." She thought she saw a little nibble of the earlobe too, but it could've been her underworked sex life imagining things. When was the last time she'd had a little earlobe nibble? Too damn long ago, that's when.

Zane and Blair got into a car parked a few meters away, Arden and her team disappeared back into the courthouse, ostensibly headed for the parking garage, and the pesky little creepy-crawlies with microphones, notepads, cameras, and deadlines scuttled back into the dark holes they'd come from.[2]

After the flurry of activity, the ensuing quiet felt more pronounced, like closing the door against a violent gust of wind. Verona closed her eyes against the warm sun on her face and inhaled the sweet amber scent of the poplars. She thought about letting a murderer ride off into the metaphorical sunset with her fiancé to start a new life. If she could have done something to stop Blair, would she have?

---

2. Dear Press: If you give my book a good review, maybe I'll be nice to you in my next book! I'll find someone else to be hateful to. Deal?

She shook her head and smirked. *Unlike Poirot*, she thought, *in this case I* do *approve of murder.*[3]

Then she remembered Quentin was supposed to let her know the outcome of the hearing as soon as he found out. *That asshole.*

3. Poirot never did approve of murder, but there was that one case...

33

A RHINO WITH AN ITCHY HORN

Over the Labrador Sea
Three days later

After being arrested for murder on his wedding day, Zane no longer felt the need for a big wedding. Or a wedding at all. Or anything to do with courts and lawyers and justices of the peace. Or justice of the peaces. Or justices of the peaces. Or however you're supposed to fucking pluralize it.

Fuck the legal system, and fuck making their relationship legal. For now, they were happy to be sitting in a plane tens of thousands of kilometers above the world. Away from pesky press and any ideas about arresting anyone for anything. It was the first time in weeks Zane had felt relaxed, and he hoped that feeling followed him when they landed.

"Do many people go to Iceland for honeymoons, then?" Zane held Blair's hand on their shared armrest.

They had splurged on the plane tickets, not wanting to suffer in economy class for ten hours, especially with the risk that someone might recognize Zane. At least in business class they had separation from most of the passengers and a row to themselves.

"It's fairly popular. Not Bali, Paris, or Florida popular, but it's growing. This isn't a honeymoon, though, is it?" Blair teased.

"To me it is," Zane said. "I may never marry you, you know."

"You're a terrible fucking liar."

"Well, I don't care if it's a honeymoon or a vacation or an escape from a reality that's been a little bit of a wanker lately. I just hope nobody dies this time."

"Unless they really deserve it." Blair stroked Zane's chin.

"Well, you can get arrested this time, if you think it's worth all that." He placed his hand over hers.

"Oh, they'd never arrest me."

"Because you're so beautiful?" Zane leaned in for a kiss.

"There's that charming bullshit I've missed." She kissed him.

"Have you learned any Icelandic yet?" he asked as they pulled apart. He wasn't usually one for an airplane fuck, but after the stress and doom he'd suffered, he was considering it. No, better to wait for the hotel. Then they could order gelato after. Or whatever version they had in Iceland.

"Most Icelanders speak English." Blair picked up the in-flight magazine.

"But you have a thing for languages, right? So—"

"So yes, okay, I've been brushing up."

"And?"

"So far all I've got is '*Skildu okkur! Við viljum ríða eins og víkingar undir norðurljósum!*'[1] But I think that'll do nicely as a start."

"What does that mean?"

"'I'd like a pint, please.' I picked it just for you. You can start learning it now."

"Huh." Zane leaned back and enjoyed that his chair reclined past the ten degrees the sadistic airplane manufacturers gave to economy class. Those chairs were like having a one-inch penis—sure, it's there, but you can't do anything meaningful with it.

"I guess Icelandic is one of those languages that sounds intense no matter what you're saying." He gazed out the window at the sky.

"Definitely."

---

1. "Leave us! We wish to fuck like Vikings under the northern lights!"

Calgary
Sunday 10 a.m.

"Who is Verona, and why is she so pissed at you?" Nina's voice filtered to Quentin from his living room.

He worked some cheese into the omelettes he was preparing for them and looked up as she came into the kitchen with his phone. "Private investigator I work with from time to time," he said offhandedly. As offhandedly as he could, considering he'd woken up in bed with Nina and was now cooking her breakfast as she walked around his apartment wearing nothing but his bathrobe. It would be so easy to take it back off after breakfast. The idea sent a thrill of pleasure through his core.

"Well, what the fuck did you do to her?" Nina held up the phone to reveal the preview of the offending text message. A poop emoji was flaming, an expletive plastered across its mouth.

Quentin felt sheepish and did his best to hide it. "I sort of forgot to let her know the outcome of a case we were working on."

Nina caught his tone and narrowed her eyes. "You dick. You think that's funny?"

He slid the omelettes onto plates next to fresh fruit and croissants. "No. I know it was a dick move. But can you blame me?" He bounced his eyebrows at her in a cartoon-like expression of "hubba hubba."

"Oh, you will not blame being shitty to your friends on me." Nina stood up and grabbed the breakfast plates. "And you will also not pretend that she is just a colleague, because that flaming shit emoji isn't sent around any office I know."

She was terrifyingly and excitingly forthcoming. He wanted nothing more than to sit down and eat breakfast with her, even if the price was to attempt to unpack a relationship with Verona that he couldn't unravel himself. Especially if it meant that bathrobe would be coming back off.

Sunday 11 a.m.

"I swear the son of a bitch is fucking that pilot every fucking time they have an assignment together!"

Verona barely lifted an eyebrow as she took in her new prospective client, steaming and strutting on the other side of her desk. Mrs. Laura Holland was attractive in the way a respectable First Lady is attractive. She was dressed in a knee-length navy dress with three-quarter-length sleeves, her hair was tied up in a French roll, her makeup was precise but subtle, and she had the kind of creamy, wrinkle-free skin that meant she either wore SPF 50 every single day or stuck on the shady side of things.

The vehemence of her delivery was unexpected given her appearance, because women who liked French rolls and understated but flawless makeup liked the rest of their lives to match: controlled, precise, presentable, and polished. But a husband fucking around on you might ruffle even the most carefully preened feathers of any bird.

"What makes you think he's cheating on you?" Verona asked.

"Oh, I know the signs!" Laura placed a hand on the back of the client chair as if she was thinking of sitting down, but thought better of it and resumed her mad pacing. She was like a cat turning around and around until it finally decided it had degraded the blanket enough that it deserved to be sat on.

"His sex drive at home is almost zero. Then he goes away on a flight and voilà, he returns randier than a rhino with an itchy horn."

The simile was lost on Verona, but she let it go. "Could it be a case of absence makes the heart grow fonder?"

"Ha!" Laura slapped the idea out of the air with her hand. "He's not *fonder* of me. He's just working his post-new-sex euphoria out on me. Or he tries to, but I'm not having his soggy sloppy seconds!"

Soggy? Verona wondered, faintly disgusted. Laura certainly had a unique way of putting things.

"And is this the first time you think your husband has cheated on you?"

"As far as I know. There's never been anyone to worry about before. None of the other pilots or flight attendants ever held anything exceptionally alluring for him. They were all too much alike. But this damn pilot..."

"And has your husband shown an interest in other men before?" Verona asked. She found these kinds of delicate questions were best delivered directly, but without any judgement or emotion attached. It gave her clients a chance to get the hardest-to-say things out in the open, without their having to initiate it.

Laura stopped dead and stared at Verona as if she'd suggested they retire for a hearty bowl of steaming shit with corn lumps. "He never has before. Nor is he now. The pilot is a woman."

Well, that's it, Verona thought. *I am fucking sexist as hell.* "Of course. My mistake." She tried to sound casual, as if this was the kind of thing everyone screwed up now and then, like misgendering a pet dog.

"Skank!" Laura snapped, nearly spitting.

Verona had to assume Laura was speaking of the lady airline pilot and not her, though it was hard to be sure. Not that it mattered either way; it took more than that to disturb her composure. She let Laura pace and fume, and her attention wandered, as it so often had over the last few days, to Quentin.

That fucker hadn't notified her of the result of the dismissal hearing, and when she bugged him about it, he took a full day to respond with something so generic, it was insulting.

Verona: *You asshole! Why didn't you tell me how the hearing went?*

Quentin (one day later): *Oh yeah, sorry. I got tied up.*

And that was it. No further comment. No charming teasing to make up for it, no "I figured a prominent private detective like you would be able to figure it out for yourself" (to which she'd reply "Dick," of course). Nothing.

The temptation was there to bug him, see if she could make him bite. But he'd fucked up. The ball was in his court to make it up to her, and he hadn't bothered. After their small breakthrough in her office where she'd been real with him, she thought there might be something more between them. Apparently she'd gotten that dead wrong. Maybe they hadn't gotten closer like she assumed, maybe she really had repelled him.

Laura's voice filtered back into Verona's consciousness with "...and you just know she's the type who's good to go in all manner of positions."

Verona didn't know if she meant sexual positions or locations, like those tiny airline washrooms that are the subject of so many fantasies. Though why, Verona couldn't guess. Just trying to pee in them caused severe discomfort; she couldn't imagine trying to mount a man or being pummeled against the walls.

"So you believe this affair happens only when your husband is out of town?" It was easier to ignore everything Laura said and move on. Especially since she *had* ignored it.

"Yes, of course! She doesn't live here. Their only chance is when they get assigned to the same flights."

Free flights! She hoped he flew to Hawaii and not Atlanta or Pittsburgh. "The next time he's assigned a flight with Captain...?"

"Wood. Amy Wood."

"Right, Captain Wood." *Captain of the ship* The Wet Dreams, Verona thought. "The next time he's assigned a flight with Captain Wood, you let me know, and I'll take that flight."

"And you'll damn well catch them?"

"If there's anything to catch, I'll catch it."

The rest of the meeting was perfunctory, going over fees, expenses, and what was legally allowed and not allowed in terms of garnering proof. Verona did it all with the same part of her brain that allowed her to brush her teeth and pick her nose, while the rest of her mind wandered back to Quentin.

That dickwad. Whether he's a fucking ass or I'm dreaming of his fucking ass, I cannot stop thinking about him. And his ass.

Laura said, "Usually when he flies with Amy, they fly out to Detroit, so, you know, pack your bulletproof vest." There was a hint of a smile in her eyes. It was gone a moment later when she said, "Maybe that little slut will get murdered and save me the trouble."

"The only way it could be better is if he does the killing, right?" Verona leaned heavily into the dark humor.

The look on Laura's face told her she'd leaned a little too hard, but she'd already fucked the pooch by asking if Mr. Holland liked men, so what was there to lose? Just a free flight to Detroit. Perhaps she should've leaned a bit harder.

FUCKING LONG EPILOGUE

Mykonos
One day before Blair and Zane met

It was the golden hour. The lustrous glint of the Grecian sun illuminated everything perfectly, from the sparkle off the Aegean Sea to the grains of sand on the turd left on the beach by a stray dog. Like low lighting in a bar making a rough forty-five-year-old look like a sexy thirty-year-old, the golden hour rendered the world and everything in it flawless, photogenic, and full of promise.

The touristy thing to do would be to take a walk along the beach holding hands with a new lover. Or take a few selfies to post and make everyone back home jealous—adding *#nofilter*, of course, because the golden hour dominated any artificial filter like Hulk Hogan in the ring. Or sit at a waterfront restaurant with a travel journal and be introspective, hoping someone would take notice.

Blair steered clear of most of the obvious touristy things because the people reading her magazine could figure those out for themselves. She liked to give them something extra, something new, something they wouldn't find reading the *Lonely Planet* travel books (no offense).

What she didn't usually do was plan a murder.

Ten hours earlier

As she spoke, the maid was one step away from hyperventilating, and she buried her young face in her shaking hands. She sat on an upturned milk crate behind the hotel, an iPhone balanced on her knees.

She was a pretty girl, petite but curvy with wide dark eyes, a ski-jump nose, and full lips. She was likely taking her morning break from her housekeeping rounds and had found herself a quiet spot to call a friend. She wasn't expecting a guest to be hovering on this side of the hotel, least of all one who could understand most of the frantic Greek she was spewing.

Blair made a habit of thoroughly examining every hotel she stayed at, and that meant visiting areas that weren't necessarily off-limits but that most guests understood weren't meant for them. Places "the help" congregated. Where the trash was taken out. Where the chemicals for the laundry were unloaded. She could never expressly mention it in her articles for *Tier1*, but if she came across anything sketchy—from complaints about worker treatment to flagrant disregard for the environment—she'd drop a star from her hotel review.

The only way to hear the staff bitching about their work was to catch them when they thought no one was listening, so she found herself the ideal spot to lurk. She was perched on a low wall beside the building, hidden from the back exit, so it would appear she was pausing as she passed from the street, not spying. Blair wasn't in the maid's direct line of sight, but even if the girl had seen her, she likely wouldn't care, thinking her a tourist unable to understand Greek.

The poor girl was nearly in tears, speaking feverishly and quickly, but Blair picked up enough key phrases to parse out what was wrong. She spoke of "the man in room 345," a sexual assault, and the threat of losing her job if she said anything. Because of the man's standing, it seemed unlikely the hotel would do anything to help her. Especially since he'd threatened to tell the hotel management that he'd caught her stealing from him. Blair heard "...not the first time" and "...unable to take sick leave without a doctor's note." Eventually the girl calmed down as she formed a plan to switch routes with another, older maid. And Blair heard a name: Mr. Cavallero.

The maid did her best to compose herself: tucking loose hairs behind her ears, smoothing her uniform, shaking out her hands, and taking some deep breaths. Then she went back into the hotel, the back door banging shut behind her.

Blair had been motionless and calm as she listened to the maid's conversation. Her teeth set on edge, her jaw clenched, every muscle in her body tightened. But she remained still until the noise of the back door sent a shot ringing through her body. It was as if she'd been struck like a match, set ablaze with nothing to stop her from burning everything she came into contact with. And she knew exactly who needed to burn: the man in room 345.

Men like that didn't stop until they were stopped, and there was very little to stop most of them. Until now.

Blair never let bullshit pass. She shoved a girl down the hill in elementary school because the bitch had slapped her cousin across the face. She'd slipped acne meds that caused hair loss to an asshole in high school who slept with girls and sold their pictures to his pals. In college she'd recorded her professor offering her top grades for a few favors and called his wife and replayed the messages during the dinner hour. She'd filled her ex's gas tank with Coca-Cola and slashed his tires.

She'd step in where she could and stop injustice in its tracks, but it had always been with the threat of repercussions if she went too far. Even her revenge on her ex had been risky. But this time? There was no connection between her and Mr. 345. Nothing to hold her back.

Once she decided it was time to fucking Boondock[1] up, she didn't look back.

The plan came together with remarkable swiftness as she borrowed bits and bobs her mind had picked up while scouting around town and the hotel for her article. She moved from one part to the next without remorse, hesitation, or second thoughts.

---

1. Like the movie *The Boondock Saints*. Vigilante shit. Marvelous use of f-bombs. Watch it. Don't watch the second one; they really shit the bed on that.

Later that morning

Blair's travel wardrobe was perfectly picked, packed, and ready for any occasion she might find herself in, from a stroll along a beach, to an elegant dinner party, to wine tastings and invites to private homes. She never overpacked; after so many years on the job, she knew what she could live without and what was an absolute must.

One outfit she always packed was a simple but well-cut pantsuit and iceberg-blue blouse. It was appropriate for a brunch meeting with a magazine stakeholder, shaking hands with a government official, or, as she'd done on one occasion, attending a funeral. It was also the exact type of clothing she'd noticed the hotel management wearing, a fact she planned to exploit.

She took the suit and shirt out, bundled them in a cleaning bag, and walked it down to the front desk. Sofia, the day desk manager, was on duty. As much as time, etiquette, and cultural norms would allow, Blair liked to get to know the staff. It made her feel more at home, and she knew when she needed a little something extra, the bridge was already built.

"Sofia, how are you?" she said in Greek.

"Baby Christos was up at four again. I'm ready for bed," Sofia answered in fluent English. Blair knew she spoke English but enjoyed practicing her Greek anyhow.

"I'm sorry," Blair said. "The only thing that ever wakes me up that early is my bladder. Or jet lag. I imagine having a baby is like constant jet lag."

"He does seem to change time zones erratically. But what can I do for you this morning?"

Blair plopped her cleaning bag on the desk. "I believe you have rush service? I'm sorry to leave it so late, but I forgot I've got an early-morning engagement tomorrow, and this suit has been packed for about a year. I think a cleaning is in order before I wear it again."

Sofia said, "Oh yes, no trouble at all. We'll have it outside your room for you by six a.m. Will that do?"

"Perfect." If she hadn't already been so friendly with Sofia, she would wonder if the woman would perhaps forget to get it in for her. One of the many reasons it paid to treat the staff well. "And shoe cleaning? Is that overnight as well?"

"Yes. Put them in the bag and leave them outside your door. I'll make an extra note of it, just to be certain."

"You, Sofia, are an absolute lifesaver," Blair said. *Or an unwitting accomplice to a life-taker*, she thought. "Oh, and send up a bottle of red wine too, please."

She walked into town, planning to do some shopping and chatting up the locals about what they did when the cruise ships weren't in port. She liked to plan days like this on all of her trips—time to decompress and do whatever came up. Today what came up was the search for a murder weapon, but there would be plenty of time for that in between gelato, coffee, and buying handcrafted local goods.

After flirting with a shopkeeper and receiving an invitation to a private wine tasting the following evening, she bought a new beach bag, some leather sandals, and a small box of chocolates for Sofia. She ordered a pineapple gelato and walked toward the rural area of the island. The stone streets of the town gave way to simple dirt roads, with gentle rolling hills covered in grass and scraggy shrubs lining the sides. Properties were fenced with whatever was on hand, from old bicycle parts, to more traditional dry stone walls, to strategically grown cacti.

Cows milled and mooed, goats yelled, and chickens clucked and roamed. While the main part of the town featured houses connected to each other and the road by molded plaster, the countryside featured more fields than residences. A few churches sprang up on the hills as she walked, their iconic blue roofs brilliant in the sun. What she didn't see were any people, but it was hardly surprising for the time of day and something she had been counting on.

She finished her gelato and boldly stepped over a simple fence of intertwining metal garbage and onto a farm property. A small stone outbuilding stood a few meters in, and she made her way directly to it. It was the kind of unobserved trespass that was impossible in a city with cameras and alarms everywhere. The farmers here knew their neighbors and were accustomed to tourists spending their time on beaches, guided tours, or trips to Rhenia, not roaming their fields.

Blair didn't know exactly what weapon she preferred, mostly because she knew she couldn't be choosy. Doing something as idiotic as trying to buy a gun in a foreign country was out of the question. She'd need to take something at hand but was hoping to avoid too much mess or a chance for Mr. 345 to fight back. It was why she'd thought of farms—most farming implements were weapons masquerading as tools.

The stone building was dim, cool, and tidy. The floor was swept, the wooden workbench under the small window directly in front of her wiped clean, and it smelled earthy and fresh, not rotten. Tools were organized on a pegboard on the wall, and a large tool bench sat open beside a wooden table. A shelf ran alongside the wall to her right, housing power tools with various plug-ins and chargers. Right in the middle of the shelf, in Tonka-truck yellow, sat the perfect instrument of precision killing. It called her name, and she could almost hear angelic singing and see a spotlight from heaven shining down on it.

"Hello, my beautiful implement of motherfucking destruction."

The nail gun was cordless, lightweight in her hand, and equipped with a clip of three-and-a-half-inch nails. The battery showed a full charge, but for good measure, she fired a few nails into a piece of lumber lying in a bin by the door. It was responsive, quiet, and shot the nails deep, splintering the dry wood.

"Oh, hell yes." She stroked the top of the gun. "Easy to turn on, won't fire until I'm ready, and when you do, you always hit the spot and are ready to go for seconds? Unlike any man, and as trusty as my favorite vibrator.[2] Fuck yeah."

It would be quick, clean, and untraceable—everything she'd been hoping for. The gun fit easily in her new straw beach bag, and she tucked it in lovingly, wrapping her beach towel over the top. Then she peeled off a few hundred euros and placed them under the battery charger to make up

---

2. In case you wanted to know, Blair's name for her vibrator is "The Penis Eliminator." Because every good vibrator deserves a name. I think. I wouldn't know.

for her theft. She hoped the farmer would not report the crime if they were compensated.

She walked casually back to the dirt road and then into town and the hotel. She was sweaty and thirsty but happy with her day's work, both for the magazine and for mankind.

~

Six hours later

Blair sat sipping her pink lemonade with a feeling of contentment. There was the sun setting, the blue of the sky and sea, the drop of condensation on her glass for the English major to write a poem about, yes. But there was also her plan.

She'd been over it in her head from start to finish three times, and although life was full of unknowable, fucking annoying circumstances, she felt good about it. Not overly cocky, not even really proud of it, just a calm knowledge that she'd planned for all she could plan for. Only idiots thought their ideas were foolproof and believed in their invincibility. She wasn't an idiot. Things could, and most likely would, go wrong. But even if they did, this was the best plan possible—the one with the highest likelihood of a clean kill and a clean getaway.

The idea now was to not overthink it, not to ruminate too much, and try to have a good night's rest, all without the help of alcohol. She didn't want anything in her system to slow her down, dull her reflexes, or make her oversleep.

Which was why, when an unassuming man with a sexy British accent dropped by her table and asked to sit down, she didn't immediately tell him what she would usually say to an uninvited male guest: "Fuck off before I staple your balls to your ass and play a drum solo on them with the cutlery."

"Sorry," said the man, "but would you mind terribly if I joined you for, oh, say ten minutes or so? Or until you finish your drink? Whichever comes first?"

He was handsome and charming in the unobtrusive way only a Brit could be, and hell, she needed a distraction like a cheese-eater getting an enema. But she wasn't about to make it easy for him, because that would be no fun at all.

"Are you trying to do a speed dating thing here?" she fired back.

She liked the way he laughed it off, as if her mild hostility wasn't only expected but welcome. He wasn't afraid of a chase, and she was willing to run.

She allowed herself to dive fully into her time with Zane, to laugh, to remember the goodness in life, to fortify her resolve that these things were worth fighting for. Worth killing for. Everyone should be able to laugh and flirt in the sun instead of cry over what some fucking pervert did.

As the evening wore on, she knew she had to make a break and began searching for her opening. Any other night, she would stay and entangle herself mercilessly with Zane, perhaps even invite him up for a nightcap. Sleep in the next morning and linger over breakfast in bed. He was that kind of good. Almost good enough to make her abandon her whole murder plan. But not quite.

This was bigger than her desire to fuck an awkward and charming Brit.

The next morning

Blair expected sleep to be elusive, but she experienced none of the usual jitters she got before doing something brand new. Before her interview for her job at *Tier1*, she'd awoken every hour on the hour (actually one minute past the hour), thinking, *4:01 and all is not fucking well.*

Before she met her last boyfriend's parents, she'd dreamed that every time she spoke, all she could say was "You're all fucking cunts." But on the eve of her very first murder, she slept like a fat guy on a bed of cake covered in a blanket of frosting.

The alarm woke her before she was ready for it, but that was true of any morning she set the damn thing for before 6:00 a.m. She was used to feeling like a zombie before their first brain feast, thanks to the jet lag her profession constantly inflicted on her. She would shake off her grogginess with two cups of in-room coffee and a hot shower the way she always did.

The shower was for more than just clearing away the dregs of sleep; she also wanted to slough off as much loose DNA as possible before she stepped out of her hotel room. Anyone who has seen *CSI* knows that DNA is the smoking gun of the twenty-first century. She scrubbed her skin and her fingernails with a washcloth and washed her hair three times. She blow-dried it and tied it up in a severe ponytail, braid, and bun combo before using half a bottle of hairspray on it to glue everything in place. She also added the hairspray to her face to encourage her eyebrows and eyelashes to stay put whether they wanted to or not.

Donning the hotel robe, she walked out of the bathroom and eyed her Saint Laurent tote with a pang of regret. It was her favorite bag; it went with everything, was perfect for stowing her essentials, and she had bought it with her first bonus check. It hadn't been cheap. But walking around the hotel with a nail gun in hand wasn't an option, and a beach bag didn't fit the hotel management vibe she was going for.

Well, she'd already given up a night of sweet fucking with a Brit, so what was a bag that cost two grand? She grabbed it, divested it of everything, and put the gun inside. DNA or fingerprints on the nail gun didn't worry her—she didn't plan to keep the damn thing or have it found anytime soon.

She flung the bag over her left shoulder and practiced removing the gun with her right hand, making sure it didn't catch on anything on its way out. Her finger found the trigger easily, and the gun had a lovely balance to it. Adrenaline would be coursing through her body, so she needed to make sure there was nothing awkward about her draw and fire. She did it ten more times and was impressed at the ease of the motion. It was like the Saint Laurent was made for concealing and wielding murderous nail guns.[3]

She unpacked her travel first aid kit and took out the gloves. When she'd bought the kit at the insistence of her editor, Tory, she wondered when she'd ever have the need for it. It wasn't as though she was traveling

3. I'm not saying it *was* made for that. Just that it's an ideal bag for it. Maybe *that's* the next commercial: the bag for the beautiful vigilante. It's got a ring to it.

to war-torn nations for frontline reporting. She was rubbing elbows with the elite, staying at hotels with their own private doctors and rooms so clean you'd think they threw the sheets out every day and put on new ones instead of washing them. The idea that she, with her outdated first aid certificate, would need rubber gloves to patch up someone was laughable. The secondary use of clandestine activity hadn't occurred to her before today, but she was glad she had come prepared. She owed Tory a bottle of bourbon for that.

She opened her door and smiled; her suit and shirt, along with her shoes, were waiting for her, laundered, ironed, and buffed to perfection. She hadn't thought, even for a second, that they wouldn't be there—Sofia was too professional to let that happen. She whisked the items into the room, dropped her robe, and dressed, taking one item out of the bag at a time to minimize contamination from her room. She slipped on the shoes and tucked the gloves into her blazer pocket.

She swung the bag over her shoulder and surveyed herself in the mirror. With her severe hairdo, lack of makeup, and basic but professional outfit, she looked ready to start her shift as desk manager at the Mykonos Muse Hotel. The only thing missing was one of their shiny brass name tags, but she was betting a man like Mr. Cavallero would be more interested in her tits than her name tag or lack thereof.

It was time. She blew herself a kiss in the mirror and marched out the door, gaze ahead, shoulders set, a motherfucking destroying angel out to deliver heavenly wrath or some shit like that.

Room 345 was around the corner from her own, so her march of death didn't last long. She stood facing the door and took a deep breath before pulling her gloves on and rapping on the door with a light, authoritative knock.

She heard scuffles and footsteps, then the interior bolt sliding free. Mr. Cavallero opened the door. Salt-and-pepper hair coiffed away from his face, wearing a pristine white suit with a crisp, open-collar white shirt underneath. His heavy cologne wafted to Blair as she took in his dark eyes and imposing frame. He smelled like vetiver and myrrh, and his eyes held no warmth, only confidence and avarice.

"Mr. Cavallero?" she asked in the same tone she'd heard from hotel management a thousand times before. It wouldn't do to kill the wrong guy on her first murder attempt.

He nodded, leaning an arm on his doorframe, shooting off cavalier lady-killer vibes.

She put on her best Greek accent. "My name is Sapphira Papadakis, one of the assistant managers here." The name was complete bullshit, something she'd found using an online name generator. "I am so sorry to bother you, but we do have a complaint of some water leaking on the lower level, and although I am sure it has nothing to do with you, I do need to check your suite." She held up her gloved hands to demonstrate the dirty-job factor of her errand.

Mr. Cavallero gave her a salacious smile. "Of course, of course, it's no trouble," he said, running his eyes up and down her body before making a sweeping arm motion to draw her in, like he was Hugh Hefner inviting her into the sexy bounty of the Playboy mansion.

Usually she'd tell a man like that to go fuck himself before she pulled out his fingernails and used them to scoop his eyeballs out, but she couldn't detour her mission of death. Instead she felt grateful Mr. Cavallero was too distracted by his desire to fuck her to notice anything amiss.

With a friendly nod, she walked into the room and plunged her hand into her bag in readiness. Mr. Cavallero allowed himself a last, lingering leer before turning his back to secure the door.

She pulled the gun out of her bag, pressed it to the base of his skull, and pulled the trigger as the door clicked shut. He didn't even have time for a surprised gasp before a three-inch nail shot into his brain stem at a hundred miles per hour, dropping him instantly. Without wasting a breath, she stepped over his body and fired another nail directly through his temple, Jael[4] style, to make sure the son of a bitch stayed down. Keeping the gun aimed and ready, she found his pulse point on his neck and waited.

Her own blood pounded through her body, lighting up her temples, making her hands shaky, but his heart was still.

"Well, fuck." She straightened up and placed the gun back in her bag.

---

4. One of the most badass women in the Bible. For some stupid reason, they don't give out coloring pages of her in Sunday school, but you should look her up.

"That was smooth as hell. This bag is getting a five-star review. And fuck it—I don't care how much they cost, I'm buying another one. A girl can't put a price on vengeance."

She took a steadying breath. The adrenaline was coursing through her, wanting her to work it off, daring her to get sloppy, but she'd known that would happen. There would be time later to process whatever needed processing; in the meantime, Getting Away with Murder 101 stated once you executed a clean kill, it was prudent to GTFO.[5]

It was also prudent to ensure you didn't walk back to your hotel room with blood spatter on you, so she availed herself of Mr. Cavallero's bathroom to do a quick check. The gun had been an impressively tidy kill, with no spatter on her face or shirt. The suit was dark enough to hide a multitude of sins, and since her hand had been far back on the trigger behind the bulk of the gun, not even her gloves had blood on them.

"Why don't hit men use nail guns all the fucking time?" she said. "Fucking genius."

She dialed the AC up to max, hoping the cool air might delay the inevitable stench and decay of the body for a few days. The longer she could keep the murder from being discovered, the harder it would be for investigators to pick up the pieces, and the less likely it would be that they'd come knocking on her suite door, asking questions. She wanted to be less than a stranger on the same floor when this was discovered. She wanted to be back home, a random person with no possible connection to the man.

Mr. Cavallero's body was blocking the door, but it wasn't too difficult to roll him over enough to open the door and get back out; it beat trying to drag him across the room. She used the peephole to check for a clear path, slipped out the door, and hung the Do Not Disturb sign on the handle. She removed her gloves and stowed them in the bag with the gun.

A faint smile on her face, she walked back to her room. She'd expected she might start to feel something weird about what she'd done. Some pang of regret, some odd sensation of knowing she'd ended a life, but at that moment, she felt free.

---

5. Get the fuck out. Or at least it meant that when I was a hip youth, before I got all old and out of touch.

She let herself into her room, closing the door and leaning against it with relief and accomplishment. She'd nailed her first murder. Literally.

Compared with what she'd just undertaken, the rest of her plan would be a cakewalk, but it still needed doing. Now was not the time to get lazy and overconfident, letting little mistakes creep in, or assuming that since everything had gone well so far, it would continue to do so.

She hadn't seen any blood on herself, but that didn't mean the DNA wasn't there. If anyone in real life was as sneaky as those fuckers on *Bones*, she wasn't taking any chances.

She uncorked the bottle of red wine Sofia had sent up for her last night and brought it to the shower with her. She threw a bath towel in the tub and stepped in, fully clothed. She wanted to tip the bottle of wine right down her throat, because when else would she have the chance to do that with a bottle of red, damn the consequences? But instead she emptied the bottle's contents down the front of her suit, into her shoes, and onto the towel.

Sufficiently soaked, she removed her suit and shoes and threw them into a new laundry bag to be cleaned by the hotel again. If anyone working in housekeeping had a penchant for noticing things like a suit needing cleaning two days in a row, this would take care of that. No one could argue that a suit that had suffered an unfortunate wine incident needed cleaning, even if it had just been done. And they would clean away any trace of DNA she might have gotten from Mr. 345. Better yet, they might inform her they couldn't clean it, and she could tell them to throw it out.

She showered for the second time in as many hours. Her skin was tender as she scoured and scrubbed, and she shampooed three times again, more to wash out the excessive hairspray than for anything else. As the hot water ran over her body, some of the aftereffects of the adrenaline hit her, so she let herself linger and relax. Only one last part to her plan was left, and she couldn't rush that part anyhow.

How did she feel about killing a man? Well, not just any man. A predator. One who had and would continue to hurt women. She should feel sick, perhaps, or wonder at her moral stance, but all she felt was vindication. No one would miss the man. A lot of people would be glad he was gone, and a lot of people wouldn't even know they were glad, because they'd never become his victims. She felt at peace.

Noon

Blair felt like she was walking on a razor's edge. The slight panic of being caught with the murder weapon made her want to do rash things, like throw the gun into the nearest bin and hop on the first flight home. The logical part of her knew she had to see her plan through, even if it meant holding onto the weapon a little while longer. The instant relief of being rid of the damn thing would feel good for about ten minutes, until she realized how likely it was to be found.

She dressed for her lunch reservation and forced herself to walk leisurely out the front doors of the hotel for a relaxing stroll to the restaurant, just as she had planned days ago, before all this murder business came up.

The warm sun was soothing on her skin and her nervous system, and she closed her eyes to take a few deep breaths of the humid sea air. When she opened her eyes, she noticed with a thrill that Zane was standing not ten feet from her. She had enjoyed her little flirt with him the night before but never expected to see him again. Yet there he was, bookending her murder, perhaps even being something of an alibi, if not for the time of death, then for her demeanour before and after.

He stood in the bright sun, eyes down, hands in his pants pockets. He was worrying the earth with his right foot, drawing meaningless little circles and patterns. He looked like a schoolboy standing outside the principal's office after being caught in the act of writing rude things in the bathroom.

The sight of him looking so very English and out of place made her smile. She called out to him, and he looked up at her first in confusion, then in the kind of surprised happiness that showed her he was definitely interested. As if the invitation from the previous night hadn't been enough of a clue. Well, perhaps there would be time to take him up on that offer today.

He was handsome, not in-your-face-drop-dead handsome, but handsome. He had smile lines around his mouth and eyes, an open, sprightly face, and a wide, genuine smile. Looking into his hazel eyes, she decided in an instant to invite him to lunch. It was the first real deviation from her plan, but the small risk was worth it. He was clearly taken with her and would be too distracted to notice anything else. Hopefully. How many men paid attention to purses anyhow?

She was instantly glad she had invited him. His presence was like a salve to her frayed nerves, his easygoing manner made her feel like the heaviest of problems would float away on the clouds. He made her laugh. She wanted both to sit across from him on the boat to talk about nonsense and to take him roughly in the brig. She liked that.

Still, she had to keep one piece of her brain on business, and that meant finding, as Jack Sparrow would say, the opportune moment. That moment happened to be after Zane's third glass of wine, before dessert had been served. He stared dreamily at her, a peaceful smile on his face. A stripper spinning her nipple tassels while riding an elephant could have stampeded through the boat and he wouldn't have noticed because he was so caught up in her.

She excused herself to the washroom. "Hold that thought," she said in a sultry voice, leaning over and placing a hand on his for a moment. It was meant to keep him turned on, distracted, but she startled herself when her own face flushed with desire.

Just drop the damn gun, and you can do what you like with that lush piece of man, she scolded herself.

After a perfunctory trip to the washroom, she took a leisurely stroll along the edge of the boat opposite the kitchen, away from the eyes of the diners, and leaned over the side to admire the view. She hung her hands over the edge of the rail, Saint Laurent bag dangling. Before she left the hotel, she'd taken a smaller bag stuffed with her personal effects and housed it in the inside pocket of the Saint Laurent. She surreptitiously removed the smaller bag and let the larger bag fall, the splash barely noticeable above the sounds of the gentle waves rocking the boat, the seabirds calling, and the noises of the kitchen and diners.

She closed her eyes briefly and sighed with relief. *That's the first time I've been glad to see two grand go down the drain*, she thought.

Returning to Zane, she placed her smaller bag on the back of her chair and waited to see if he'd notice or say anything about her sudden change of accessory.

He grinned at her, his face showing no hint of anything but complete relaxation. "They keep bringing wine." He indicated his glass. "They can't give it away fast enough, it seems."

She reached for his hand, surprising herself by how badly she wanted to touch him again. "They'll keep doing that until you stop drinking it," she said, "or until they have to cut you off because you start pissing yourself."

"Oh, lovely! This is my kind of place!" Zane raised the glass to take another sip.

"Good thing we're walking back."

"The magazine wouldn't spring for a cab?"

"The magazine will spring for whatever I need, within reason. Getting myself so pissed drunk that I can't walk home isn't really a professional requirement. Strictly speaking. For my story. Maybe for a different type of magazine."

"Now that's a magazine I'd read!"

Blair gave a silent sigh of relief. It was done.

The gloves, even if they were found, would never be connected to her or the murder. They would just be another piece of trash. The gun and the bag had sunk to the bottom of the sea. If they ever were discovered, they would be so damaged by the salt water that there was no chance they could lift DNA, fingerprints, or anything else that could connect her to the murder. The bag did have a serial number that could be traced back to her, but there was no reason to do so since the gun would have fallen out of it. She dropped the bag unzipped for that reason—finding a nail gun in a fancy bag would be an oddity. Finding a nail gun or a bag on its own is just sea trash.

There was always the off chance something or someone could connect her with the murder, but if they did, it would be a very flimsy connection.

With no DNA, and no murder weapon, she was in the clear. She had stopped waiting for the gravity of what she had done to hit her—she knew by now it never would. She believed with her entire being she had done the right thing. It turned out she didn't feel guilty about things she didn't think were wrong, even when that thing was murder.

She returned her attention to the now slightly tipsy Zane and hoped he would ask for her number. She had thought he was a pleasant diversion, a holiday flirt, even a sort of alibi, but now she found herself wanting more of his charming bullshit.

If he ever found out what she'd done, he'd be as shocked and horrified as if someone accused the Virgin Mary of enjoying a good bean flick now and then. But that's what deathbed confessions were for. No need to ruin a perfectly good life together with an inconvenient murder.

AUTHOR'S NOTE

This book is set in real cities, however, extreme liberty has been taken on the businesses and hotels that are frequented to allow for some creative embellishments and atmospheric creation. As far as I know, Calgary does not have any secret sex clubs that operate like Fight Club, but I'd love to be proven wrong. If you know the password, you know where to send it. I took liberties when describing jail and courtroom scenes, as it is much more dramatic to have the defendant face-to-face with lawyers and judges instead of having a videoconference, which is how bail hearings are held in Calgary as of this writing. I have simplified the jurisdiction challenges and accelerated the trial process, too. Because art.

Hot Girls Die First
Verona Montero #2

The cocktails: strong.
The hookups: messy.
The corpse: a real buzzkill.

Private investigator Verona Montero hikes fifteen kilometers to a cliff-top lodge in the Canadian Badlands to dodge cheating dirtbags and a crush with better abs than boundaries. She expects R&R. Instead, a sex-bomb named Harper turns up planted in the front garden—daisies and all—and a storm turns the only road out into a mud smoothie. With the cops days away, Verona gets promoted to PI-in-residence with a complimentary bar tab and a house full of alibis that smell like last night's tequila.

The lodge is an adult summer camp for bad decisions: late-night room changes, motives with teeth, and alibis flimsier than a motel towel. When the body count starts flirting with plural, Verona's strategy is simple—ruin evenings, crack egos, and make the killer sweat through their resort wear. Otherwise her weekend getaway could turn into a permanent check-out.

ALSO BY KAYLEIGH SUGGETT

The Verona Montero Series

Alibi by Accident

Hot Girls Die First

Burn After Cheating

To find out more about Kayleigh Suggett and her books, visit

severnriverbooks.com

ACKNOWLEDGMENTS

I love reading acknowledgments, so I hope you do too, because I've got a lot of people to thank!

Thank you to my family and friends, who have constantly asked me if I'm still writing, what I'm writing, and when I'll have a book available for them to read. Although I'm generally terrible at discussing my works in progress, the fact that you all care enough to ask and genuinely want me to succeed means so much.

To some of my family (you know who you are): I'm really sorry for the vast amount of profanity and dirty jokes in this book, because I know many of you hate it. Still, your support and care got me here, so you really have no one to blame but yourselves.

Thanks, Mom and Dad, for being my biggest fans. Thank you to Mom for instilling a love of books and reading, especially mysteries. I'm fairly certain this book wouldn't be here without those late-night Nancy Drew readings, or without me pillaging your complete Agatha Christie works. And Dad—what can I say? I'm pretty sure a lot of these wacky antics and dirty jokes wouldn't exist without you.

To my extremely handsome, funny, and generally incomparable husband, Ben. He is my foil,[1] who thinks differently from most of the world and ended up with me; I'm not sure what that says about me, but I'll take it. Thank you for wanting me to become a *NYT* bestselling author so we can get out of this dump. Thanks for laughing at my writing. In a good way.

Thanks to my little one for so much laughter and wordplay already in

1. That's a literary term, kids, it means he contrasts me, but in a way that makes us both look awesome. Look it up.

your young life. For your silliness, your cleverness, and so many smiles. Thanks for the idea of using "vagina apples" in this book; you make your mom proud with those kinds of jokes. Thank you for learning how to put yourself to sleep so I could finish this book.

To the #WritingCommunity on Twitter, I would literally not have a book in the world without you. I found new resources, new publishers (*this* publisher!), and, most importantly, a community of writers and readers who encouraged me and gave me hope through their stories. I hated social media and loathed starting an account, but I'm so glad I found you. Thank you for shouting your lols at me and believing that my crass little mystery had a home. Special thanks to my fellow funny gal writers Tammy and Elizabeth.

A special shout-out to author K.T. Carlisle, who did the first full beta read of this novel. To have a writer whom I admired so highly give credence to my work gave me the extra boost in confidence I needed to believe my book belonged on shelves. I'm so glad Twitter brought us together, and I can't wait to continue to be thrilled by your plots and characters (go check out her books, k?).

To another amazing author and editor, Dustin Bilyk, for giving me the best free advice an author could get. For putting my well-being and success as an author before your own financial gain. For talking me through my initial publishing offer. For being an all-around decent human being. I owe you so much. People, stop right now and google Dustin so you can buy his books.

Thanks to Wes Cambron for introducing me to Becky, who designed my first cover when this thing was going indie. I've got a new cover now (obviously), but her collaborative spirit and excitement was infectious, and I could see the final product sitting on the shelves right next to a few of my favorite authors. It took a Floridian to bring us two Albertans together, and I'm glad we went the long way around to find each other in this small world. You should also definitely check out Wes's books. I had the privilege of beta reading them, and I can confirm they are highly entertaining.

Thank you to fellow SRP authors who took the time to answer my questions. Carolyn, LynDee, Shannon, and Mel, you made that contract the easiest thing in the world to sign.

Thank you to Andrew and Julia at SRP for taking a chance on me and Verona. Knowing how much SRP values marketing, it was especially gratifying to receive an offer, because it meant you knew my readers were out there. And all I've ever wanted was to find them.

Thanks to Rachel for reviewing my contract for me and making sense of the legalese. Sorry I bugged you so many times. I was excited or something.

Thanks to my first editor, Caroline, for your encouragement, for correcting my horrendous use of dialogue punctuation, and ensuring I stayed in the right character's head at the right moments.

Thank you to my amazing developmental editor, Randall. I had so many eyes on this book before it got to you that I couldn't imagine you'd have anything new to add. How wrong I was. Thank you for seeing the heart of this story, for challenging me to up the tension and pay attention to my character arcs, and most of all for making Verona shine as the main character she deserves to be. I never thought rewrites could be so invigorating.

Thank you to my copyeditor and proofreader, Kate, for catching all my mistakes and asking questions to improve the experience for the reader.

Thank you to my favorite authors: Douglas Adams, Jasper Fforde, and Christopher Moore. You inspired me to write stories that are funny but still have precision and heart and employ multiple literary devices. I wished more women writers were doing that kind of thing, so I decided to become one. A special shout-out to Mr. Fforde for the use of footnotes. I love those footnotes.[2] Thanks to Mr. Moore for his blatant use of profanity. I fucking love profanity. The late Mr. Adams got me started on this whole thing, and without him, I wouldn't know where my towel was.

And thank you, dear reader, for picking up my book and making it all the way to the end of these acknowledgments. There are millions of books out there to choose from, and I am so happy you chose to spend your time with my best gal, Verona. See you in book two.

2. Obviously.

ABOUT THE AUTHOR

Kayleigh Suggett's love of classic mysteries, British satire, and clever humor inspired *Alibi by Accident*, the first in her series of mysteries featuring private dick Verona Montero. She wishes that more female authors were writing in the irreverent style she enjoys, so she decided to become one herself. With a background in customer service and business administration, she draws on her experience of the oddities of human behavior to craft distinctly zany characters, fast-paced banter, and hilarious situations. When she's not coming up with a perfectly snide simile to add to her books she's a wedding singer, choir nerd, mountain-gazer, and NYT crossword frustrated solver. She lives in Calgary, AB with her husband and son.

Join the reader list at
severnriverbooks.com

Printed in the United States
by Baker & Taylor Publisher Services